TRYING TO BE RELIGIOUS IN THE BEST OF ALL POSSIBLE WORLDS

AN AMERICAN RELIGIOUS ODYSSEY

Charles J. Duey

iUniverse, Inc.
New York   Bloomington

Trying to Be Religious in the Best of All Possible Worlds
An American Religious Odyssey

The names of persons and places in this novel are fictitious. A few cities and institutions have been cited using their true names, where deemed necessary to the story, as Los Angeles, Boston, Miami and Princeton Theological Seminary.

iUniverse books may be ordered through booksellers or by contacting:

iUniverse
1663 Liberty Drive
Bloomington, IN 47403
www.iuniverse.com
1-800-Authors (1-800-288-4677)

ISBN: 978-1-4401-7024-9 (pbk)
ISBN: 978-1-4401-7025-6 (ebook)

Printed in the United States of America

iUniverse rev. date: 11/17/2009

Dedication

To a gracious and insightful teacher,
Iain Edgar Furnell, 1919 – 1967

Contents

— 1 —

Engaging a Guide

Reverend Gaines was a smiling entrepreneur. I would not have labeled him with that moniker on the Sunday I met him, not even knowing the word. I thought of him as a refreshing person doing a good job at preaching. Perhaps I should say he was a salesman for the Almighty, and I a potential customer, for he spoke to my need. I retain a clear impression of him, along with many details about that day and the months that followed. For I was like a freshly washed chalk board, seeking someone like him to write words of wisdom upon me.

Those were pivotal days in my spiritual formation, when I could not easily interpret what had come to me unbidden and yet wonderful. I learned that my experience is called an encounter, an enlightenment of a sort. I was dazed. So then, I needed the advice of a man of God, one who would become my big brother in the best meaning of the role.

He was not the first pulpiteer I sampled during a running tour of churches. He became my choice. For I had grown weary of listening to sermons on a number of dull and sometimes entirely inane subjects, like bridges and baseball, old college memories or an anecdote from *Reader's Digest*. And then there were the appeals for money. Some preachers are very appealing when it comes to that.

Gaines turned out to be a no-nonsense captain at the helm, who ran a tight ship. And we who were under his command felt we were on assignment for a very important mission. Our pastor often said "the plan of salvation" in the Bible was all we needed to arrive at Home Port. Gaines used God's Book as a trustworthy chart for defining the sea lanes while avoiding the shoals. All those aboard would be saved. The unreached would drift away, destined to sink into the depths.

The pastor had a talent for making those old biblical accounts and stories sound like messages to the twentieth century. But, I must make it clear, he did not use my nautical language in his church work. I am the one who knew such terms, having sailed upon Biscayne Bay and down into the Florida Keys during my youth. And then I served a hitch of six years in the navy. But I broke with all of that and returned to civilian life. I had enough of it. There were better things to do with life than I had imagined earlier on.

My newly discovered shepherd of the flock had his own jargon, sort of a sanctified patois, which he used to make ancient history sound like a lesson in current events. And we, his eager sheep, were alert each Sunday in anticipation of some new lesson drawn out of Scripture for our instruction. We worshiped in an orderly Presbyterian manner and did what most serious Bible people do, filling the offering plates with our tithes — literally ten percent — in gratitude for God's great salvation. The evening services were much more spontaneous. At the end of the day we sang our hearts afire while encouraging one another and mutually responding to the series of special speakers, mostly missionaries, who came to us from all around the world. Our church had become a designated stop for many independent missionary agencies that regularly covered the churches in search of funds. This was expensive, but our part was easy, for we did not have to go anywhere exotic or make any personal sacrifice. We simply gave money, and God had plenty of that, we were encouraged to believe. And God was using us as channels for funding those heralds of salvation. We, in turn, were endlessly informed, challenged and entertained.

Many fondly said that Gaines "fed us from the Word." His sermons were a barrage of old-fashioned words and phrases which dazzled the uninitiated. I did my best to get up to the level that was customary among my new friends. The Elizabethan English of Scripture was not hard to understand, and it sounded quite valid. The theology, however, was intricate, using concepts that were not common fare. Every sermon included a Greek word study here and an interpretation of the old English there. We loyal auditors took notes and made various marks in the margins of our personal Bibles, using red and blue pencils.

Not only was the minister a happy salesman for God, but also a natty dresser. For him, being a "man of the cloth" consisted of some wild haberdashery, and not a thread of it clerical. When I beheld the man that first Sunday, he was sporting a beige gabardine suit and accompanying yellow silk tie bearing the image of a hand-painted palm tree. And his dark red hair was striking, setting his appearance off as snappy. Yes, he was a snappy fellow tapping his white-and-brown wing-tipped shoes to the beat he heard from Heaven. One might recall a bygone ad for breakfast cereal — Snap, Crackle and Pop® — that said we could start the day with cheery good health. Well, why not, then? As the pastor said, "If God is for us, who can be against us?"

Richard Gere, in the blockbuster movie *Chicago*, struck me as a reincarnation of my former pastor. Oh, how wonderfully Gere, as a lawyer, soft-shoed his way through that court scene, moving so smoothly, putting his audience into a trance-like state. Yes, a great scene. But I had seen it years before.

I was surprised by Gaines' contrast to my usual idea of the clergy. I would learn that the informality in his style was his way of gaining a hearing, to lead a visitor from casual things to those that touch upon Eternity. And that's what I had in mind too, for myself. I would learn about God, Jesus and the Bible. These three, Father, Son and the Holy Scripture, were *the* Holy Trinity for our pastor. And I, open to his instruction, slipped into his way of thinking.

Most of Gaines' staid followers did not put much trust in the whimsical revelations and/or ecstasies of the Holy Spirit going on in other churches, especially among the Pentecostalists. They said that miracles, speaking in tongues, the laying on of hands and such, as depicted in the New Testament, had come to an end with the earliest Christian period, which ended with the death of the "eye-witnesses" to the ministry of Jesus. Walking on water or raising the dead and such miracles as Jesus did while on earth did not pertain to the present Church Age. We were bound to believe in those old miracles, for they were in the Bible. But there was only one Virgin Birth, one Resurrection, and only once did Someone successfully walk upon the water. We had the Bible, and that was our source of contact with God and His plan for the ages, laid out for any reader to perceive, with the help of a faithful instructor.

I submitted myself to the discipline. God helping me, I would learn the Bible from cover to cover. I therefore ceded my independence and even my intelligence to this mind-set for at least a while, at least long enough to be indoctrinated in some of the basics. But, I also read as I ran, and being so involved in scholarly pursuits, the system of dogma my pastor proffered did not penetrate as deeply as he intended. I thank the good Lord for all favors, great and small!

I learned soon enough that the members called their church *The Palms,* as in, "Where do you go to church?" "Why, we go to The Palms." To newcomers, a sign on the front lawn declared the location to be The Surfside Presbyterian Church. The building was a relatively recent addition to the northern section of old Miami Beach, perhaps erected in the years of recovery after the Great Depression, when Art Deco was so much in style. So, just like the minister, the building too stood out in its modern, with-it design. It had glass blocks of pastel tints for windows, arranged in high narrow rows, and decorative potted palms in glazed pots up on the platform.

Reflecting upon those comfortable, class-conscious days, I see now that they were very different in contrast to what developed in the decades of change after the War. Back then we had segregated toilets, segregated water fountains, restaurants and movies. Why, even our buses had a section for the "Negroes" in the back, where the motor fumes sometimes were bothersome. In not a few areas around Florida even brown-skinned Americans and a few others of suspicious origin were not welcomed among the Whites. Even Jews were made to feel unwelcome on some parts of Miami Beach.

It was not a problem to us back then to think that God loves all people and saves some from every nation, tribe and tongue. For we segregated our attitudes and went happily along, believing that somehow God would sift it out in the Great Blue Yonder, perhaps making us all of one color in Heaven. There would be one Faith, one Baptism, one God and Father of us all: red and yellow, black and white, we would be precious in his sight, all equally tan, perhaps. But that would be then.

Contrasts

I found the church's understated Art Deco architecture refreshing in comparison with my childhood exposure to church decor. We were Methodists back then, and worshiped in an older neighborhood setting on the mainland, one that was somber in contrast to The Palms. Our modest stucco and frame building incorporated various furnishings from Victorian England into a predictable setting of bench pews and varnished mahogany furniture around the altar.

A series of ministers dressed in either black or gray came to us at two year intervals, as so many beads on a string, each in turn exhorting us far too long from behind a high mahogany pulpit. Those sermons, punctuated with shouting here and crying there, were approved by a large stained glass Christ who was caught in the act of soaring to Heaven. This was a victorious flight, I was told, after I said it looked like Jesus was leaving us down here all alone.

Mother answered my question quite seriously. She said, "Jesus had to go up so the Holy Ghost could come down." When I asked why there was no stained glass window for the Holy Ghost I was told that one does not see him because he is everywhere. Mother then patiently explained that one *feels* God in one's heart. "And that is what Methodism is all about," she said, as though a child could understand such airy thought. Well, perhaps I did, in my way.

I eventually learned, while Mother was still with us — and I admit I'm fuzzy about this, so others might have taught me a few things — I eventually learned that getting a certain feeling makes a difference in religion. Then one's life takes on a love of both Jesus and neighbor. And that was why the preachers preached so hard and loudly, for they were our shepherds, leading us to Jesus, the Great Shepherd of all the flocks of the world. Yes, all. Jesus had Methodists high on the list, but there were also Baptists — God bless them — and Lutherans, even Anglicans. Oh, I almost forgot the Catholics. In spite of their errors, they too were children of God. Of all the emotions elicited in Methodism, I was made to understand, none was more prized than the feeling which produces a love of God and leads to good works on behalf of others.

Nothing of such a "certain feeling" seemed to have happened within my family during my childhood. I cannot recall being possessed by anything unusual in those years of my childhood and youth, never shook to the roots, or heard of anyone so moved in our extended family. In fact, my elders seemed to regard such shaking as more descriptive of Holy Rollers. We DuPeases were very reasonable and rational, though we surely loved each other. And we were sociable.

My family found a pleasant emotional outlet in music. We had a piano and several other musical instruments, which came in handy at evening dances on the porch. I remember my brother playing the clarinet with ease and rhythm. And some of that music came from thick records ponderously spinning on the old Victrola. Since I was the kid of the clan, my job was to keep the machine cranked just enough to give the music a natural beat. Tempo and rhythm were half the art of music.

But thinking about the Holy Ghost, I could easily imagine back then that a visitation of something of that power would shake a person something awful, perhaps like the Sunday morning train from New York shook us as it roared by a block behind our little church. That soot-belching behemoth moved the foundations so palpably that the windows rattled. For me, it was a welcome distraction, coming usually during the long Morning Prayer. *Boy!* They said that zephyr whirled by at eighty miles an hour on the final stretch to the city. I used to imagine its brakes failing and the whole shebang screaming on through the depot and into oblivion, people and baggage flying around in the air and the clamor of twisted steel and splintered glass falling back upon the streets.

My, how I loved to stand at the crossing next to the post office up in Little River and watch that iron beast roar by! Clackety, clackety, clackety — *and all those Yankees looking out the windows, their pasty faces a blur — the coaches zipping by so fast it was a challenge to count them. And it was easy enough to imagine them flying high in the wreckage.*

But I stray. There are so many memories tumbling around in my old brain. I must remain focused, for some day soon I shall board a train that goes non-stop to the City that has neither sun nor moon, for the Lord is the light thereof. I am sure of it. And before I board that Silver Meteor for points up in the sky, I have a story to leave behind.

The Foundations of True Religion

Our ministers in Methodism warned us and pleaded with us, through tears, about evil's dreadful consequences, with the dangers of cigarettes, alcohol and gambling high on the list. But none of these was as terrible as greed or hatred of one's neighbor, our neighbor being, we were to understand, each and every one a creature of the same heavenly Father. Those preachers urged us on to the altar rail for repentance and restoration to a simple life full of goodness. The lessons came through — even for children — that holiness is a thing to be earned through a serious religious life, that pleasure is a snare, but that self-denial pays a heavenly reward. And telling a lie was the worst possible sin in all of our no-nos. For God is Truth.

My family reinforced those principles, making sure I would behave as a good Christian is expected to behave. "We are *all* God's children and ought to be kind to one another," my elders reminded me at every opportunity. So then I took it as normal that everyone in Christ's world-wide Religion was of that same persuasion. Of course I was impressionable and destined to become an idealist. That meant I would attempt during many years to be a perfectionist. God forgive me for that. I was hard on myself and at times even harder on others. Dad always said I inherited my mother's inability to wait for things to develop, was forever fretting over how slowly the world turns. And it's true.

Those innocent and happy days of my early life were not destined to endure, so then I, following my brother and sister, drifted away from organized religion. I do not say we became reactionary or unethical, however. We slowly changed in our interests because our circumstances changed us, mostly due to mother's death, which was agonizing. She was a pious woman, and a good wife and mother too. Such virtues made her suffering seem terribly inappropriate. For the same womb that cradled me fell victim to a gnawing pain that I later learned was cancer, an unrelenting drain upon her diminishing strength.

Mother went into quietus while I was taking a spelling test at school. The office secretary came in, a hankie at her eyes. Miss Matthews whispered to our teacher, Miss Bullard, who in turn advised me that I should return home straight away.

As I walked into the living room Dad told me, in a shaky voice, that I should pray for Mother, for she had died. "She's gone to Heaven," he said. I could not take it in and ran to the bedroom door before anyone could stop me. I glimpsed her lying upon her bed, the doctor and a few others hovering around. They were pulling a sheet up over her naked body. I began to sob, gulping air between screaming laments, unable to make this fact fit into anything I knew to be true and fitting to the life we enjoyed, that I took for granted.

Something spiritual in our family withered on the day Mother died. I was particularly desolated, I, the child of her old age, who had no idea anything incurable possessed her until that moment. Oh, I must have been shielded from what had to be hard to ignore! But as much as I have tried across the years to recapitulate what went on in those weeks upon weeks leading up to my loss, I cannot discover the clues to how I was shielded, kept blithely dumb to what had to be obvious.

Across the years I pieced it together. It is probably best to shield the very young from an actual act of dying, but I wonder about shielding them as I was protected. For eventually the truth must be faced. Stretching bereavement across a week or two before the fact is not all bad. For we must grieve, one way or the other. Why dump the entire load upon the innocent after the fact?

Influence from a Biblical Tradition

Mother had prayed for me as I snuggled in her womb, much as old and barren Hannah had beseeched the priest Eli for his blessing, that she might have a child. And God gave Hannah a son, Samuel, whom she gave back to God as an understudy to Eli. Mother too had prayed that I would be born a boy, and she would give me back to God as a preacher. I was reminded of it a few times, when I was especially unruly or angry, and I typically reacted to those attempts to control me, did not care for such an imposition. It seemed to me that I ought to have a chance to make up my own mind about something so terribly serious.

Looking back on the years that followed Mother's death, I see now that I lived in deep grief and nurtured it as my only comfort. But then, I was no exception within the family, simply more inclined at such a tender age to express my sense of it than my two older siblings. We all, after her death, felt dismay and resentment upon hearing others — including our minister — talk of God's goodness and loving care for his children. God, they asserted, gives us first this life as a veil of tears, but beyond the suffering he takes us into Heaven to be with Him forever. Indeed. But what a price Mother paid to arrive at that Alabaster City! Nor were the church's happy hymns appropriate to our mood at that time of anguish and loss. It made sense to believe God made Heaven for the good and generous folk, but no sense came of such good people having to suffer corporal indignity to get there. And, had not God given her to us to nurture us? And did not Dad need her for support in his hard life? Yes, hard. The Great Depression was in full force.

It took a long while to recuperate from the loss, and by then each of us had found other things to do on Sunday morning than rise early and dress for church. I moved into my adolescence without much guidance, choosing my friends without asking my father's blessing, making important decisions by myself and earning my own spending money. I was content to go my own way, acting the hellion most of the time, just like all my peers. Dad, in his despair, had turned to bourbon as his solace, even before Mother died, and then slipped deeper into himself, drinking more, caring less about appearances. We siblings understood his pain. But family life was not what it had been, and apparently was never going to return to those happy times. And I, the youngest, felt especially abandoned, living with a father who had such great need. He leaned on me for support, and I felt inadequate, as indeed I was. Eventually my heart grew cold, and I rebelled.

Then, after the attack on Pearl Harbor, both my siblings joined the army and were soon carried away to exotic places. It followed quite naturally that when I was old enough, in the middle of that mess, I joined the navy.

Dad was left to manage or mismanage his affairs and himself as he chose. He died at the war's end, ironically, the victim of cancer. I was never sure if Dad died from rotgut whisky, or chain-smoking Chesterfields, or cancer or sorrow. It made little difference but was probably a combination of those plagues.

Developments

When I discovered Reverend Gaines more than a dozen years after Mother's death, and a few years after the war, I was finally reconciled to the mysterious ways of God and tired of the skin deep distractions of the world. It was time, I had concluded, to find my way back to the Christian Religion. *What had I forsaken in my confusion, what ignored?* I lived in a world full of religions without knowing much about any of them. With a maturing sense of heritage, I wanted to learn what it means to be a Christian. Not so much to be a church member as to know what a Christian is, where to find knowledge of my religion's history, how to read the Bible and what was necessary to believe. That is, I was not particularly interested in becoming a Methodist, for I had enough of regimentation in the navy. Besides, I could not bring myself to return to what was left of that little neighborhood church, so full of memories but by then bereft of the previous members. Times had changed and people moved away.

I was intrigued with the idea of an unseen God who nonetheless has a space all his own, perhaps somewhere out there beyond the planets. Indeed, *where* would God be found? What does he know about our situation? Indeed, does he really care, if "he" is a proper gender for God, who is a Spirit? Being a Spirit did not seem to require a gender. Why did Jesus have to go back where he came from rather than stay here to help get his Church underway? From the very little I knew about the various churches I had seen around the world — after observing a few before leaving home — it seemed the Lord could have helped out a lot more had he stuck around a lifetime, because his chosen disciples were not too bright. Perhaps then, when he grew feeble, the angels could have swooped down from Heaven at the last and borne him to Bliss. Well, I am not a very pious person even in my old age, which is apparent. But one cannot help thinking, and such thoughts do come to me at the most inconvenient moments, which I often blurt out, thinking they matter.

Back to the Palms

Gaines happened to be the minister who showed up in my sights when I turned in the direction of organized religion. Gaines, the sporty and smiling purveyor of dogma, and I, a mystic by both temperament and training. I wanted to know as much as possible about the Bible, and I decided he was the man to help me learn Scripture by chapter and verse, subject by subject, beginning to end. For I finally had come to the end of my wandering and encountered God waiting there, or better said, *God encountered me precisely when I had wearied of wandering*. Me, Tim, the incurably trusting soul who led a charmed life, escaping pitfalls and ruin as I danced through the years. It is ironic, however, that Gaines and I should end up confronting each other over an open Bible. Ironic. I would learn to love the term.

Somehow I had adopted a belief early on that if I learned enough out in the wide world I would become both mature and wise. And I suppose some of that did occur, but I ended up asking, *But for what?* At that moment something happened, just as I record in this account. I discovered that God is much more accepting than I thought, and mercy is of greater depth than I dared imagine. Indeed, I found my encounter with the Other overwhelming, so much so that the impact reverberates within me to this very day. That experience has reinforced me in times of doubt and fired a passion that has driven me to study, study, study. Oh yes, some say that too much study drives the reader mad, but madness contracted in pursuit of God is better than simply going crazy trying to adjust to a world full of violence and paranoia.

God help me that I may never give up my holy curiosity! I knew it then and I've learned it over and over: making sense of nonsense usually is more than our little brains can readily discern, but that is no reason to give up the struggle.

One must be careful, however, must doubt now and again, just to keep one's balance and to remain open to possibilities. I have never tired of questioning the mysteries of existence, concluding that there has to be an Intelligence behind the process, even if my little mind cannot fathom such a Holy Mystery. My Masonic father called God the Great Architect of the Universe, and that is not half bad. I have learned that I am not alone in my pursuit, for many another doubting believer has taken up the pilgrimage toward valid knowledge and left a testimony to the value of the search. I do not doubt that there is a blessed state where we shall gain the reward of wisdom, if we persist. *Non carborundum bastardi*, we used to say in the navy: "Don't let the bastards grind you down." It is ironic that the saying itself is bastard Latin, but that's okay. The sense of the thing comes through. Even Jesus and the Apostles said we should persevere. Denying, then, is a giving up, and giving up is a denial. Light, more light!

My goal then was to learn whatever is valid and wise that gives hints of truth, that reveals a way through the brush and orients a person in this overwhelming world of contradictions. Philip Wylie called his contemporaries a "generation of vipers." And even though he might have been self-righteous in his harangue, might have felt some of his preacher-father's disdain for fallen humanity, the man was not far off the mark. Had we not witnessed the untimely deaths of some twenty million persons during the Second World War? And did not Hitler and those who collaborated with him condemn about five million of that number, Jews for the most part but also others suspected of being Jews, to separation and then systematic debasement leading to the "final solution" of starvation and gassing?

I asked, *What lies beyond such nay-saying?* Where, how, indeed, does the oft mentioned Paradise break through our indifference to its allure? Where is the *Yes* to Life? This then is my story of how I found my way *to* the church, changed, moved on, changed some more and eventually found my place *in* the church.

A Serendipity

I had been a university student for nearly a year when I discovered Gaines and his happy congregation. Thanks to the G.I. Bill plus living in the old family home, I managed to eke by with only a part-time job. And that is how I managed to study as much as possible. I was grateful for all the "book-learning" I could get, as my high school years were pretty well wasted time as far as scholarship went. I majored in beer and drag racing. But I was alone in that big old house, alone with my memories and not satisfied finally to have most things going my way, so I had come to the end of my wandering and began wondering where I was going. And this led me, at the ripe old age of twenty-five, to seek instruction in my religion

There was a very attractive ad in the Saturday edition of *The Miami Herald* that offered me exactly what I wanted when I sought it: an introduction to Bible study. *Bingo!* I said aloud, as I read the announcement of Gaines' Bible program. The next morning I was there when the church doors opened, which would have surprised most of my friends and those of my close-knit clan, had they known.

God's plan — I quickly learned by attending The Palms — was to reap a harvest from among the nations, tongues and tribes of the earth. One by one individuals were being gathered, and one by one they brought others into this marvelous confraternity of the redeemed. And not only one by one, for anointed evangelists and missionaries were bringing them in by the scores, by the hundreds and even by the thousands. Indeed, we were told again and again, the fields were ripe unto harvesting and the day drawing nigh for the grand finale of human history as we know it. We were on the brink of Armageddon, Gaines insisted, very close to the Rapture, when some would be chosen but many more left behind. Some of this sounded vaguely familiar, but the details as well as the urgency of the topic were new to me.

Despite this literalistic definition of an end-times cataclysm, which my new minister proposed, I found him to be a calm gentleman. He never lost his temper or cried as he preached, and was predictably prepared for his sermons. This meant that he stopped preaching when he finished what he had laid out beforehand. God, he believed, would reinforce such a ministry from on high. And since God was all wise, Gaines did not have to fret over the details of success. Well, that was the impression. Success really meant very much to him, I would learn. Success and control. But for the moment, I simply heard that God has a plan worked out from the foundation of the world, even from the moment of Adam's fall into sin. And that was fine, for I imagined God to be capable of knowing what he was doing, and I could know it too, if only I would study and pray. Well, I had much theology to learn.

It was an interesting process: I would hear something that went counter to what I held as common sense. But what I thought foolish came from the Bible. It made no sense to trust God and also argue with God's Word. That was the reasoning. The Bible was God's true and infallible Word, right down to every word. I had to ask myself if I was indeed serious about learning the Bible, or would I remain with my old instincts and attitudes? It seemed I had to give up my horse sense for a higher knowledge. "There is a way that appeareth right unto a man, but the end thereof is death," was quoted to me by a few companions. It went on like that until I was pretty deep into believing in a Bible that was both mysterious and at the same time capable of being understood, especially if one would dare to believe in a God for whom nothing is impossible.

Many friends insisted that I had to trust God when things could not be explained adequately, saying that in time I would understand. I would have to surrender my intelligence to another human being, to many others, in fact, who professed to know more than I. Such superficial reasoning lost its luster before long; but not before I had done a job on myself or at least had consented to others doing a job on me.

Such wondering aside, Gaines was a punctual man, in part, I am sure, because he had served as a navy chaplain during the war. I liked that, being a navy veteran myself: six years of spit and polish, and therefore among the last of those shaken veterans to muster out.

Gaines and I shared the idea of running the church like a well ordered ship The membership made up the crew, with a team of seasoned petty officers to keep things shipshape at all times. *Full speed ahead,* our captain ordered from the bridge, as the officers scurried about tending to important things such as navigation and messaging. When I look back upon it, that analogy is appropriate, for there were very few tourists aboard the HMS Gregory Gaines. We were not sightseers on a pleasure cruise but able bodied seamen. We were Ship's Crew, the "salts of the earth" and numbered among those destined to eternal life at Home Port. We would deliver our cargo of souls directly onto Heaven's shores.

The Influence of a Good Woman

I have to confess a certain prejudice at that time for the Presbyterians but not much knowledge of exactly what they were or how they functioned. For I had not encountered them until late in my military service, while on duty at Bethesda Naval Air Station. I carried on a flirtation with a bonny lass of the Scottish Presbyterian tradition, and she persuaded me to take her into D.C. one Sunday to hear a preacher who had gained quite a reputation for his winning personality and poetic talent at preaching. He had been popular among the servicemen in the Capitol area during the war, I was told, as his church provided some wholesome diversion for lonely sailors and soldiers on weekends. The preacher himself would drop by and play the piano in the recreation room, singing along as the men and women in uniform harmonized on old-fashioned songs or hymns. The preacher's name was Peter Marshall, born in Scotland but come to America seeking work. Since he felt called into the preaching ministry he finally found his way into a theological seminary and was ordained to the Ministry of Word and Sacrament. The Scot took D.C. by storm, his church prospered, and eventually Doctor Marshall became the Chaplain of the United States Senate, an office he filled while still pastoring the New York Avenue Presbyterian Church.

I got this glowing report of the man from my girlfriend, who had attended his services occasionally. His fame was enduring, and she wanted me to take her there so we could share impressions. Moonstruck by her beauty, I felt her taking me to church was a step in the direction of a more serious relationship. Church became a very symbolic sign in my romantic zodiac, for I was smitten with my new girlfriend. In fact, she was the only woman I entertained in those years away from home who merited admiration, not only because of her beauty but for her character. And that says more about me than any confession of bad behavior could. Presbyterianism therefore appealed esthetically and emotionally to me and still does; so, my romance doubtless influenced my choice of The Palms as a place to learn religion.

But — it seems everything is conditional — Fifth Avenue Presbyterian Church and The Palms were at opposite ends of the denominational spectrum. This hard fact did not come to me immediately but across a stretch of many months. As I studied religion and looked around me in the church setting, I asked myself what sort of religious man I should become. Well, my decision came quickly that I would have to be my own man. And that seemed a good Scottish decision. I affirmed it as the best way in religion too. Surely, Jesus was his own man, and who better to emulate than that courageous carpenter from Nazareth, the subject of many of Marshall's sermons. In his words, Jesus was the Master, that is, the Teacher. It is interesting that after so many centuries scholars have finally come to recognize this identity as the best for Jesus, the Rabbi to the World, the pastor of the nations, bringing his sheep home to the fold. This Jesus, then, would be my model rather than one pastor or another. It was a good first step but not an easy way, it turned out.

Accommodations

Having Jesus as an ideal, I soon stumbled upon a fact of Reverend Gaines' snappy manner of dressing that threatened to undo my decision to trust him. For as I stood next to him and looked at his thick hair I saw that it was not his own. Something deep within me said that a man of God should not try to charm people by appearing as other than he is but accept what Providence has made of him. Are not bald men also children of God, and don't women find bald men interesting? Was my pastor rejecting some basic facts of life by puffing up like that, spreading feathers not his own, somewhat like a peacock? Had not St. Paul asked God to make things a little better for him, and God replied with something like, "Paul, be quiet. My grace is all you need." *And what a man that Paul was!*

Oh, God forgive me! I said to myself, repenting my stern attitude regarding the toupée. I recalled my Master saying, "Let him who is without sin cast the first stone," and also "Judge not that ye be not judged." Still, it was a struggle to accept a wigged preacher in modern times. But with a little help I adjusted, mostly because one of Reverend Gaines' best friends and a deacon of the church told me that he and a few others encouraged their minister's wearing a toupée. For, he said, they felt he could use some "spiffing up." He was slight of build and had a bad case of what was probably rosacea, so that his forehead and scalp were spotted, which was not the best billing for a preacher-man who dressed spiffily.

Now, we're all inclined to cover up our defects, as Saint Paul wrote, giving the most time to our least comely parts. So, ignoring my preacher's peruke at first, I then accepted it, finally agreeing that he looked much better with it, especially in the pulpit.

Alexander Pope wrote about such conditioning:

> *Vice is a monster of so frightful mien,*
> *As to be hated needs but to be seen;*
> *Yet seen too oft, familiar with her face,*
> *We first endure, then pity, then embrace.*

My adjustment to Gaines was not so much an *embracing* as an *accommodation*. After all, I reasoned, why should it matter to me? I have abundant hair and am three inches taller than he. But, on the other hand, it had not occurred to me that *I* might become a problem in any way for my pastor. For I lacked insight, so did not see myself as a young strutter in his chicken coop.

Aspirants to ministry have to be extremely careful about stepping into the pastoral office and charming church members, perhaps alienating them from their stated pastor. Because this happens occasionally, senior ministers are careful about selecting their assistants. But I dropped into that church as a raw and undefined enthusiast who was not at all bashful about taking part in things.

LEARNING THE ROPES

Being an understudy to the pastor reminded me just a little of navy boot camp, where recruits were not asked what they thought but told to say aye-aye sir! The pastor would not, of course, be so direct, but I knuckled under once again in order to learn the ropes as quickly as possible. As I look back upon it, I conformed to nearly everything expected of me in the early months, not so much for Jesus as for the Church. I really was an organizational man back then, and I was sure that the Institution was under divine orders.

At that point in my life I could still feel a certain something when I walked into a sanctuary and looked around at the orderliness of its pews, the special woodwork and high windows. I also liked the arrangement of the furniture: usually a pulpit on one side, lectern on the other, a nice altar against the wall and some figure in a stained glass window above it. This admiration for order and function loomed over me in much the same way I admired the clean lines of a ship and its placement of equipment. And, I supposed, the Church's earthly leaders were good and loyal officers of ascending rank, who stayed the course day-to-day to the glory of God. Accountability meant that the captain of a ship was accountable to those higher up in the structure.

I had in mind then that the Christian Church would be stable and dependable, an organization with standard operating procedures and promotions for steady service. I had advanced in the military from recruit to petty officer — radioman first class — and was sure of myself because I had been tried and proven able, had done the work step by step without fouling up. It is often said that the navy puts steel into a man's back. I surely value the discipline I received and am a better man for it. By that same rationale I assumed I would move up within the structure of the religious establishment by being obedient to orders and showing up for stated services. And as for going into ministry, I wanted to believe that as one ages one gains seniority, rises and takes on greater responsibility, authority and is respected.

In the navy we were *accountable*. There were no shortcuts, no lame excuses. A petty officer carries his credentials, a service record, with him from ship to ship, assignment to assignment, and begins his new duties as a qualified person. His superiors know who he is and what he can do before he arrives at his new station. They put him into his assignment because they need someone to replace the specialist who has just moved out. When I earned my first class petty officer rating I was first class anywhere I went in the United States Navy.

My initiation into the Church of Christ then took some things for granted. Adults would behave like adults. There would be an obvious pride in earning one's stripes as a volunteer in the Church. A volunteer, not a draftee. The real world of making it by doing one's job and doing it right, without complaint or excuse would be the rule. Well, that's what I assumed.

I was "learning the ropes" for a heavenly purpose. I still used a lot of nautical terms in those days, before I learned to talk like a Christian, especially like a minister. Oh, lordy lord, was I a raw recruit in the Church's service, one who could not tell an asp from its hole in the ground. Nor had I yet become aware of a pastor's need to coddle the members. We sang *Onward, Christian Soldiers*, but I think the import of the song was lost somewhere back in the arrival of modern democracy.

Greg, as I learned to call my new minister in the inner circle of his volunteers, had a quite formal demeanor. He remained the Reverend Doctor Gregory Willard Gaines at services and in public matters, but we closest to him addressed him familiarly, although with just a touch of awe. To be chummy with a doctor of the church was indeed a heady thing. Imagine, I thought, a man with a professor-level degree serving a local church!

Under Greg's instruction I learned that my personal Bible, given to me when I was a boy, was a cheap thing and inadequate for a serious student. But that "cheap" Bible impressed me because it had the very words of Christ printed in red. Even as a youngster I could find that section of the Bible and read the words of Jesus. They made a lot of sense. I had dug that faux leather edition out of the cedar chest at home, cleaned the green mold from the zipper and carried my prize to church. Dr. Gaines never said anything against my personal Bible, but I saw that he winced when I zipped the cover open in his presence. It did not occur to me that the early Protestants lacked zippers on their Bibles, nor did I know that no adequate witness to biblical authority would ever keep his or her Bible sealed.

The Scofield Version of the King James Version

Soon after that innocent moment in my orientation, Gaines sent me to the mainland to purchase a *Scofield Reference Bible*. Much later I would research Scofield's rocky career — he lived 1843 - 1921 — and wonder how he ever managed to gain the support of so many eminent Christian scholars and leaders. The more I learned of Scofield, the more I suspected that he was not a scholar himself but a compiler of the scholarship of others, some of them quite out-of-date. Not until I finally began seminary studies would I learn how radical a version Scofield had produced, but for the moment, that Bible was my prized possession.

My choice of a new Bible to carry around with me was limited to the ephemeral: a superior cloth spine and a genuine Morocco leather cover, the text printed on fine linen paper with India ink. But the very same footnotes and commentaries are embedded — scholars would say they are *glossed* — into Scripture itself, in every Scofield edition, no matter the price.

I had my name, Timothy J. DuPease, printed in gold leaf on my new Bible's front cover. That particular edition cost twenty-five dollars, but it was my choice, as it suited my idea of the sort of Bible a preacher in training would carry around with him. *Twenty-five dollars.* I was earning a dollar an hour as a part-time credit interviewer at the Sears store downtown, so the sum was considerable for one book. But, I had learned that "God deserves the best, and He gives back with an even more generous hand than we can ask or imagine." There was no need to worry about a few pitiful dollars. Oh, we were a happy and carefree bunch.

He owns the cattle on a thousand hills, we sang, *and I know he cares for me.*

Cruising for Souls

Among the features that never failed to impress those who wished to make the tour of our plant was the waterside dock behind the building. A forty foot cruiser, all mahogany and varnish, white sides and bright brass cleats, was berthed there, visible from the pastor's study as well as from the small parking lot just outside his office. That sleek power launch did what several Cadillacs out front do for most other churches. We did have Cadillacs parked in the lot on the other side that abutted a municipal playground. The neighbors down the street, enthusiastic church members, had agreed to dock their cruiser at church some Sundays so that the pastor could use it for evangelism. Visitors who showed interest in learning about the church would receive an invitation to join a few others for a brief cruise along the canals leading to Biscayne Bay. If the minister himself did not go along, an elder would be in charge. That outing became a continuation of the fellowship enjoyed at worship, with the singing of choruses and the addition of a few personal testimonies. This was accompanied by cucumber sandwiches and gallons of iced tea. It was all rummy good fun, without rum of course.

The yachting enthusiasts at The Palms, quite adept at Bible quotation, seemed to me to be more interested in converting people than in going into the Scripture in depth. "Wouldn't it be a tragedy," many said, "if someone not knowing the Gospel should come into the assembly only one time, and not hear the joyful message of salvation?" Anything other than evangelism was considered a waste of time.

I could not articulate exactly what I sensed was askew among my friends at that point in my church experience, but I began to suspect that I was being alienated from my American heritage in some subtle ways. However, I learned more about *religion* in those first months at The Palms than I had in previous years.

I was moved away step by step from such zealousness and certitude at least in part because of a hyper-active layman named Hal. His self-assurance was startling. He claimed leadership as a teacher without ever having paid the price of learning religion's long history, various customs or even the ancient languages.

It might help to get an idea of Hal's persona.

— 3 —

HAL, AND A HANDFUL OF OTHERS

Not long after my arrival at The Palms, Reverend Gaines put me in contact with Hal, about thirty-five years old, who taught a Bible doctrine class for new members. My new advisor was a handsome fellow, having a head of very dark and curly hair complemented by deep brown eyes that at times made him look like a forlorn little boy. His profile was made for Hollywood, and he would have done well there, had he been possessed of a bit of the playful spirit. But within the church he was successful enough as an unquestioned leader in the ongoing mission to gain souls. Perhaps the pastor had in mind that I needed a big brother to give me more time than he could manage. And, looking back on it, Gaines was not the chummy sort. But Hal would seek me out both at church and at home for serious conversations about my progress in Bible study. However, what he really wanted to do for me was not as much for my good as for his agenda. He would guide me toward a proper seminary.

As I came to know Hal better, I had to conclude that he wrestled with demons that would not give him rest. Had I known the Bible better, I would have equated his situation to the madman in the Gospel, who lived on a hillside of tombs and graves at Gadara. That poor fellow never was at ease, for the demons tormented him. I think the graveyard is especially symbolic. It is ironic that I can see it now but could not then. Perhaps I could have saved Hal from tormenting himself with such unruly behavior and irrational religion. For, it became apparent, Hal's experience during World War II left him shaken and in need of repair. He had killed the enemy, including civilians. And the killing was not in any one-on-one, front line encounter but by the most indiscriminate system: the high altitude bombing of cities. He was an active participant in those waves of American and British planes that had flown over Germany, dropping both large bombs and incendiaries, just as the Germans had done to the English earlier. The flames of the entire City of Dresden, I am sure, were quite akin to those of Hell in Hal's mind, so that he felt duty-bound to rescue as many of his contemporaries from eternal flames as possible. Motivated thus by guilt, he buttonholed the unwary, insisting they read salvation verses underlined in red in his large and very worn Bible.

Hal attempted to steer my course for me, all with the best of intentions, of course. He did have something to do with a few of my decisions, but not in a way that would please him. For he seemed to appear at just the wrong times and with his limited agenda of topics, so that I finally had to deal with his intrusions into my affairs — in the most delicate way possible of course. I had learned by then to use some tact. My military training was not in diplomacy, however, so I had to work at being discreet for fear of this very intense man. I had become convinced he could be vicious if provoked. Indeed, being under guilt, he behaved like a man beside himself. But enough for now. Hal will come back at some inconvenient time.

A parallel situation had developed in my relationship with Greg concerning my future. In his way, the pastor was also driven and could not see it clearly. He was determined to make me an extension of himself rather than encourage me to discover whatever gifts God had granted me. I began to feel just a bit uncomfortable with his nudging and rather rigid — I resist saying frigid — ways of mentoring me. But Greg was suave. As he had used Hal, he used others to get me into line with the program. As this turned out, it really worked rather well, for there were a few things I needed to learn.

A half dozen or more men in the church engaged in jail ministry, visiting the city's detainment center — not a prison — where they could present their message to erring men. My inclusion in this activity was arranged by Greg in an indirect manner. One of the laymen, who participated in the Sunday afternoon visits to those detainees, invited me to join the team. I knew it was the pastor who had worked this invitation into my training, as in a conversation not a week before he had said I should become involved in giving my personal witness to others. Perhaps I could speak at a mission for men in downtown Miami. I knew of such religious activity in our city from seeing the storefront sign at the Salvation Army rescue mission out on Flagler Street. I hastily declined his invitation, saying that I thought those giving witness to their faith were probably doing a good work, especially when they also housed and fed those poor lost souls. But as for me, I was not moved at all in that direction.

"Oh," I commented, quite disingenuously, "I think that is fine for them. If they want to reach out to the winos, okay. But I don't feel any special urging in that direction. No thank you." I thought that concluded the matter, though I really did sense my underlying cowardice in ducking the challenge, for it was a challenge rather than an invitation.

So then, on Sunday morning next, Will Braun, Esquire — who had been especially friendly from the first day we met — approached me. Smiling and asking how I was doing, he quickly got into a report on a jail mission he and a few others had undertaken as their personal ministry. All too soon he asked if I would like to join the group, who were going to visit the municipal jail that afternoon. I tried feebly to wiggle out of it, but

Will was a suave and very capable persuader. It did impress me that a professional man like Will would do this good deed, while I was loathe to participate. Inwardly ashamed in that moment I said I would join the group. It surely is hard to duck a job when they gang up on a guy like that.

At two o'clock Sunday afternoon I was picked up in the business center by a volunteer layman to ride along with two others to the missionary endeavor. I had my new brown Morocco leather bound Bible under my arm. It felt just then like a very large black pulpit Bible. I was sure that all who saw me, possibly some of them my personal acquaintances, would consider me to be some sort of fanatic and better avoided. At the same time, I knew we were doing an honorable thing, something not just anyone would be audacious enough to attempt. I knew difficult things eventually end, and I would soon be back home, where the Sunday paper waited my reading. We drove on, I mostly silent, listening to the chatter of my companions.

As we drove into the municipal parking lot, my insides rumbled so that I became alarmed. *Oh Lord*, I prayed, *help me get through this! I am truly ashamed of myself for being embarrassed, and I'll try to adapt to whatever my friends are doing. Amen?*

Four other members of the team were in another car. We parked and disembarked, a well scrubbed group of seven middle-class, middle-aged men full of camaraderie, and little me. I really was a pitiful person inside my adult body, but no one was paying attention, for the men had prepared themselves with prayer for this moment. A positive spirit and friendly chatter helped settle me somewhat, but not totally. My comrades, all experienced in this enterprise, made their way to the entrance and down a hall to the police desk, I trailing them by a few steps.

Play it cool, that's the way to go, I said to myself. *Don't stand out front and don't say anything. Just take it in and try to learn what you can. Period.* I was tempted to stay behind in the car and pray for them, as I recalled that one poet wrote, "They also serve who sit and wait."

The jailer led us down to the bull pen, where the Saturday night revelers and other petty offenders were billeted, surrounded by thick bars enclosing them into an area of tiered bunk beds and two toilets sans seats. The air was foul from vomiting and careless urinating. Stale alcohol breath and old tobacco smoke also mixed into this stench. Several narrow slits of windows high up on the walls did little to ventilate the room, though one exhaust fan whirred away as a symbol of relief. The small machine caused an irritating distraction, rattling along indifferently, so that it was difficult to ignore the blasted thing.

Our coterie of testifiers paid no attention to the inattention of the inmates but went into a practiced routine of friendly greetings and exchanges with those polite enough to respond. Before I gained a sense of order I was included in an octet singing good old Gospel hymns, as *Come Every Soul by Sin Oppressed*, and *Amazing Grace*. I hoped this mediocre harmony would make the men feel less set upon, for though we sang with zeal we were by no means a professional gospel team. In fact, given the way we murdered the music, we also should have been put behind bars.

Giving Witness to One's Faith when Nobody Cares

One by one my friends told the captive audience how they had passed from sin to sanctification, from guilt to joy and from death to life. Their sincerity won the attention of many, so that the meeting became focused. Then our emcee spoke in a more formal manner, mentioning that he was a lawyer over in the city across the bay, and had visited with prisoners and pled for them in court quite often. That got a hearing. He made a few comparisons of how they would appear before the judge that week and would at some time sooner or later appear before the Great Judge of all the Earth. His words struck home, as most were paying attention.

At that point, when the prisoners were quieted, he paused for dramatic effect, and then said, "Now we have with us today a student from the university, who is preparing for the ministry. He has had his own experience of conversion and is here today to tell us about it. Tim, come on out front and give us your message."

My message? Me? And a convert? Is that what they think I am; me, and here I am, a Christian boy from a Methodist family? I found myself disoriented at this introduction. It seemed a dirty trick at first, but then I realized how dumb I was. What had I imagined the afternoon would be, a picnic at seaside? And, what had I done to prepare myself other than passively join the group? The first lesson of getting out of my comfortable pew smacked me between my clueless eyes. My mouth went dry, my knees grew weak and I felt little quivering movements in my gut. But a man must be a man. I took the few steps forward without any idea of what I might say, glancing about with what I hoped was a confident demeanor. Lord, did I feel inadequate! And I could only blame the fool inside my skin.

Happily, there was complete quiet as I looked around, noting that most eyes were on me, though a few men flipped pages in a magazine or lay straight out staring at the ceiling. I concealed my inner storm with a calm exterior. Experience as a petty officer helped me stand tall, so I could assert myself just then. With a voice that came out of me as one in charge, which gave me a good beginning, I said that I was not really a preacher and that it was not my right to take any of their time, so I wanted to thank them for their attention.

One man shouted, "Oh, Reverend, don't worry about time, we got plenty a' that!" Everyone roared. With just this touch of humor we were off to a good start. I ignored being called Reverend, a title I did not possess, and began to speak as a friend to other men, not unlike a bull session among shipmates while underway with little to do.

"I want you to know first of all," I said, "that I am an ordinary man, surely not a preacher in any way. My life has been just like most others: raised in a regular family, and then six years of navy service, which is not unusual in our time. Any of you here veterans?" A few hands were raised. I nodded at the responders, took a breath, and continued.

"I guess you could say that I've had most of the common experiences of military men. I did a few things while away from home and family that offended my own conscience, for I knew that I was better reared than I was behaving. I found it to be a humbling fact that I was carrying on just like others whom I had judged previously as guilty of bad conduct. In short, I felt like repenting, but I did not know how to repent. I said inside myself, *If God in heaven is a judge at court, then I'm in big trouble, for I have sinned! How can I ever undo what is now done?* I did not understand that, in effect, I *was* repenting! All I needed to do then was change my ways.

"No, I did not see any way to go back and undo mistakes of the past. Whatever sinning I had done would forever remain in my life history, and much worse, would lie upon my conscience. To me that meant that my mistakes would haunt me for a lifetime.

"This thought hounded me. Oh, I don't mean that I broke down or anything like that, but I was ill at ease with myself. And then, just when I arrived at the conviction that there was nothing I could do to change the past, something wonderful occurred to me: I'd have to throw myself upon the mercy of God. Now that was not an original thought, just one I had heard about without giving it any importance, probably because I was not previously sorry for anything. Now isn't that a commentary? Probably the one benefit of sinning is that it humbles a man.

"I did not yet understand that *the nature of grace is that God forgives without our deserving it, much as some earthly fathers forgive their children, hoping that the future will provide new opportunities and some sort of growth, more mature behavior. And our response is and ought to be to accept this tender mercy.*

"I decided to pursue higher goals as a way of changing my behavior. Perhaps I could amount to something, make a difference in the world and help to solve problems rather than add to the pain of humankind. This thinking followed me into my first year at the university, where I hoped to learn how to become successful as a businessman. The world needs honest businessmen, I told myself. After all, we are all children of the Depression and have seen the damage dishonest money manipulators can do. It seems that some gluttons never have enough, even if it means we who have little must bear the pain of their greed. But even in this honorable pursuit of good business I found some doubt about myself. For it became clear to me that I was seeking success and fortune as a way of paying off a debt, but at the same time benefitting from it. And I was still not happy. For I had little idea of where I was going or what I might do with my life.

"Some wisdom from Jesus Christ came to me in those days. One of the first ideas I connected with was his question, 'What shall it profit a man, if he gain the whole world, and lose his own soul?' Also, I had heard the Savior's challenge posed many times: 'Whosoever will save his life shall lose it; but whosoever shall lose his life for my sake and the gospel's, the same shall save it.'

"It was during this state of mind that I had an overwhelming experience. While driving home at the end of a day's studies, a conviction came upon me that I should go into the ministry. It was not anything that I would call eerie but certainly intense.

"At first I wiggled around, looking for release from this idea of ministry, that is, actually becoming a professional. *God forbid!* I begged off, convinced that I was the least likely candidate for holy work, for I was worldly, and had little real knowledge of religion. Why, I argued, I knew a classmate or two who were very churchly and would welcome such an experience. *Why not pick on them?* I said to that Urging that prompted me, goaded me toward a decision. Now, can you imagine? I was actually talking back to God! And it was then that I realized that *somehow the Spirit was there directing me to act, and I was arguing against the greatest intelligence in the universe!* But then I sensed in some way not yet entirely clear to me that this was *my* call, and that when God calls, a man dares not turn a deaf ear toward Heaven. Everything became clear: Either I was to answer, *Aye-aye, Sir,* or *Not I, Sir!* For I had come to the end of myself. I said *Aye-aye* to the true Captain of my poor little boat, feeling that if I pulled at the oars, He would mind the tiller.

"The sense of an awesome Presence disappeared as quickly as it had come, and I was once more alone in my car. But I was changed, and thinking that things would never be the same again, I drove home shaken, confused but not afraid. In fact, I felt a great peace in my heart. Imagine that: my future had become overtaken in a matter of seconds, and my best plans tossed out the window. But I felt peace! Nevertheless, when I got inside the house I broke down and cried as I had not cried since I was a boy — but this time the tears were tears of joy. For I knew that I was reconciled to God, though not a word was said about my indiscretions, nothing of my past drawn up to embarrass me. *How gracious of God to do that!* God loves me, I said within, and that was enough! He revealed himself as my friend, my guide, and I needed no other confirmation."

And with these words I concluded, saying, "And that's it. I want to thank you for listening to me."

The complete silence of my audience came as my first impression, and I concluded that perhaps, just perhaps I had struck a chord of empathy. Then I realized that I had preached my first little homily. And I felt rewarded in doing it, for there was a distinct power in the delivery that was new to me. In fact, this was the first time I had shared my soul-shaking experience with anyone else. I sensed an aura hovering over those moments.

There, it's out! I murmured to myself, *and I am happy for it.*

This was a serendipity, for through this I discovered an inner talent previously unknown to me, and I was forever changed

Jesus said that once a person puts a "hand to the plow" there is no looking back. I had become a marked man, and I felt satisfied to bear the new identity.

The men looked as though they too recognized that something singular had taken place, and honored the moment with a respectful silence.

I stepped back and pulled my designing friend to the fore. William concluded the session with an invitation to make a decision for Christ right there, but it did not result in any commitment that I could see. Then the jailer came in and told us our time was up. He seemed a bit impatient, so we moved out.

As we eight evangelists entered the parking area, a few of the men commented how much they appreciated my testimony, while others remained strangely silent and removed. The contrast was palpable to me, and I wondered if it might also be evident to Will. If he sensed any reticence among those few teammates he did not indicate it. Rather, he was obviously happy at his little trick, smiling and shaking my hand, clapping me on the shoulder and saying I had to continue with their team in the weeks to come. But I took it all in with a feeling that something negative had begun in jail that afternoon and was in fact still going on among my companions. Whatever it was, it was not harmonious. This acceptance by some and withdrawal of others would follow my ministry from place to place and year to year in both my training and professional service. *What had I said, what done, that was incorrect or offensive? Why was I not still one with those who silently stepped away?*

Christians, I was to learn, can be unlovely, especially when it comes to territorial rights. Perhaps that does not cover it all. I would learn about "pecking order" in a sociology class. But time would show that I did not learn how to avoid the conflict in all situations.

A Convert?

The experience of being introduced to the detainees at jail as a "convert" also left me feeling uneasy. True, I had an experience that changed my course, but I was born into a Christian family and was baptized into the Faith as an infant. I attended Sunday school and at times during adolescence sometimes went to worship, singing the glad hymns of Christmas and Easter, which I loved. No one can sing those joyful hymns in the Methodist tradition, especially those by Charles and John Wesley, and not be affected for life. Surely I was a Christian, just like nearly everyone I knew growing up. Conversion, as I had previously understood the term, was for Pagans or atheists but not Christians moving from one denomination to another. We Methodists would receive a Catholic into the church without any ritual of conversion or rebaptism, so why was I a convert, having moved from one Protestant denomination to another? I tucked the question behind my ear for further reference.

What is worth saying is that for me this evangelistic church environment was a new and invigorating experience, despite my questions and doubts. We did not just sit there waiting for the preacher to finish his sermon. No, we expected God's Spirit, working through both the minister and our prayers, to speak to spiritually needy persons, as it did to each of us in our needs, and that some would feel the call to the deeper life.

In all, that was a great time and a valuable one in my training despite my endless questions. I still thank God for easing me into the profession by means of those gentle folk. Yes, gentle. They loved the Lord and loved each other. Above all, they held a heavenly hope, which they sincerely wished to share with others. And they were convinced that the days were short, that Heaven with its great compensation was near at hand. Most would insist the times were pointing to the expected fulfillment of all of God's purposes before the end of the twentieth century.

Reverend Gaines was preparing a sermon on the apocalyptic upheaval that is said to be necessary as a prelude to Christ's return, popularly called "The Rapture." It was pure Scofield from beginning to end. Gaines' sermon would change my attitude, and that precipitously, beyond anything the preacher intended by teaching such ideas.

— 4 —

"In the twinkling of an eye..."

Lo! He comes, with clouds descending, ...
God appears on earth to reign.

From the hymns of Charles Wesley, 1758

The congregation had been prepped for Gaines' evening lecture on biblical prophecy by a preparatory ritual of singing, which included *When the Role Is Called up Yonder, I'll be There*, and *We Wait for a Great and Glorious Day*. The Apostle Paul was cited where he states, "we shall all be changed, in a moment, in the twinkling of an eye," and "the day of the Lord ... cometh as a thief in the night." Then from John we heard, "We know that when he shall appear, we shall be [made] like him; for we shall see him as he is." Those early disciples obviously were convinced that the End Times were upon them, and the kingdom — the rule — of God over Israel was breaking out from an ages-long slumber.

The moment for speaking having arrived, Dr. Gaines rose to the usual height of tall men behind the pulpit, helped up by a four-inch slide-out platform he had designed. He looked intently out upon the congregation, and a hush fell over us, for we were fully expecting to learn things about prophecy.

He began simply enough, stating, "I stand here tonight to preach on a subject that receives far too little attention in the great majority of churches, and that is the matter of Christ's *Parousía*, or his Second Coming." Gaines raised his voice, although he never shouted, for he had cultivated a scholar's manner, *"The truth is, and you must be advised, Jesus Christ could return to Earth at any moment. The Second Coming of Christ is so near at hand – **so near at hand** – that it might occur while I am preaching this sermon!* Can you grasp it? Does it mean anything to *you*?"

That dramatic assertion created an electricity that sparked around the room. Some audible sighing rose from the congregation, and then many, although unaccustomed to their preacher baiting them for an *amen*, spontaneously shouted out, *Amen!*

He smiled and resumed, "Most preachers avoid this topic because they simply do not believe it. Their leaders do not believe it, nor do they include the sections of the Bible at Sunday morning readings that speak of Christ's return or select from their hymnals the wonderful songs that tell of our Savior's dramatic and victorious appearance upon the clouds of glory, when he shall descend to establish his thousand-year reign on Earth.

"Many people who join this church tell me that they belonged to one or more churches across the years, and that no one ever talked to them about the Return. But I tell you that it is a central truth of the Bible. It was the 'blessed hope' of those first believers who endured persecution and ridicule for their beliefs. They would rather die than deny this truth: *Christ was coming soon.* It is one of the testimonies of God's mercy that he has delayed the consummation of human history for so long specifically so that a great number from around the world — and I stress, so that you and I might be included — that we may all together be garnered into the Great Harvest of Saints. So, we must remember that in the sight of men a year is a long time, but 'a thousand years in the Lord's sight is as but yesterday, when it is past.'"

Gaines was so effective in his delivery that only at that point did I notice that he was speaking from the heart and not from a manuscript. It added power to his delivery, for he spoke without looking down at the pulpit. *Showmanship*, that's what it was. I wished to be able to speak like that. I did not know then it, but such preaching was so expected among his auditors that it was a proof of authenticity when a preacher "delivered the goods" as they were supposed to be preached. Nor did I know that these doctrines were so standardized and memorized that evangelists had them set and ready, could preach such a sermon on a moment's notice.

Gaines continued, "In the predetermined will of God, the times and events have proceeded to be interwoven into a master plan that is now being revealed for the saints of these latter days. For the Jews are even now returning to the Holy Land and building Israel again. It certifies to us that prophecy is being fulfilled. We must remember that Jesus cannot come back until the Jews return to Israel."

Gaines then spent several minutes citing passages from the Bible to establish proof of what he was saying. He spoke of Gog and Magog, the Revelation of John and cited several Old Testament prophecies. Then he launched into a detailed account of the interpretation of prophecy, of pre- and post-millennial tribulation and wars among nations. At that point the subject became clouded with ifs and buts, so that I had trouble following the details. Apparently there was a difference among interpreters about Christ's schedule for the final seven years of this "Dispensation of the Church," as it was called.

I had not heard before or somehow missed the detail that Christ would actually set up a kingdom in Jerusalem. What was the sense of it? The Temple had been destroyed, rebuilt and destroyed again. Then the Egyptians invaded it and carried away the sacred symbols from the Holy of Holies. And the Syrians, under Greek dominion, desecrated the Temple as well. Besides, it was destroyed by the Romans who also carried away all the golden articles of worship. A mosque was finally built atop the Dome of the Rock and occupies that locale to this very day. All this occurred without any angry intervention of God, who in more ancient times was recorded as strict about anyone entering the Sanctuary or touching the holy objects. I was momentarily distracted from the main thrust of his lecture at that point.

But, Gaines said, Christ would sit upon the throne of David and rule the world for *one thousand years*. It was not clear in my hearing whether the Return would include reactivating the old priesthood and animal sacrifice. That did not seem necessary. Christ indeed is the Lamb of God, who takes away the sin of the world. This restoration of Jerusalem, and its role as the center of the world was apparently something not discussed outside small circles of those who pondered and discussed the intricacies of ancient prophecy. Nor did Gaines elaborate on my silent questions. Nothing was said about how long we the redeemed were to live during that thousand years, if we would marry and have children, and our children have children as well. There simply was not time to learn everything within the space of one evening lecture. But he made his point that Christ would return quite soon.

As I drove home that evening, crossing the causeway that linked the beach to the mainland, I was more aware than ever before of the awesome wonder of God's creation and His careful plan for each detail of time itself. The full moon shone upon the windswept bay, where small phosphorescent whitecaps were visible, an eerie phenomenon that always impressed me, and even more that evening. But of what? I felt wonderfully hopefull that the answer had come via the evening sermon. Dark palms swayed in the breeze, their fronds moving gently back and forth, high-lighted by the evening glow, as though waving to the last hint of sunset or perhaps as a welcome to the returning Christ.

Were they saying in their very own manner that we should watch and not sleep? It all seemed so appropriate, as the calm before a storm: in one moment, peace, then in the next, fury. I shivered.

Fatigue set in, at last, as I prepared for sweet sleep. I had a schedule that would not let up, so welcomed a full night's rest and crashed into bed. I slept without tossing, slept deeply, even if my mind still had momentous matters to resolve.

After several hours of this deep, trance-like state, I had a singular dream, one beyond anything I had experienced in any previous dream. In it, some of the images of my preacher's sermon combined with those depicted in a novel I had read about a year earlier. That scenario was based upon the moment when American pilots in WW II flew over Japan and leveled Hiroshima with an atomic bomb. The novel depicted the end of the world coming via an atomic holocaust, which sent waves of thunder and huge black clouds rolling around the globe in a chain reaction. The idea of a chain reaction loomed quite large in the minds of most of us back then. But, although the book's imagery was horrifying, my dream was pure ecstasy. For in this reverie I was driving once again over the causeway, but this time the western sky was turning all shades of white and pink and blue. Thin clouds shimmered as though they were sprinkled with silver dust, and behind these airy strata came a rolling bank of great clouds, dark underneath but edged in gold. The sunset seemed to be reversed, coming as sunrise from west to east! History itself was being rolled up like a scroll, from end to beginning.

I knew, I just knew that *Jesus my Lord was right behind those golden edged clouds,* riding them as he would a surfboard, riding them back to the earth just as he had departed upon them. This time his outstretched arms were extended in a victorious greeting to us, a great smile of victory upon his handsome face.

Oh, how I loved Jesus! And I knew Jesus loved me with an even greater love. I had first learned this truth in my childhood: *Jesus loves me, this I know, for the Bible tells me so...* And now I would behold him, my Hero. Having overcome all inhibition, like a Holy Roller, I shouted, *"Hallelujah! Hallelujah! Hallelujah!"*

I awoke to my heart pounding against my sternum. Jumping out of bed before the dream had completely faded, I stood transfixed and tried to orient myself to the summer heat, for my skin was rife with goose bumps while I also sweated salty rivulets, which I could feel running down my chest and back.

Nothing arrived. *Nothing* lightened the sky. The silent night remained as still as a sealed tomb. A great indifference surrounded me, and I felt terribly disoriented. Then I became aware of the faintest glow from the street lamp half a block away and just a hint of moonlight added its charm to that moment. But I also heard crickets chirping, then the sound of a lone car racing along on the avenue nearby intruded into this confused moment and helped me return to the world of relentless facts. I reached for a pack of Lucky Strike cigarettes on the bedside table, fumbling a bit, and finally managed to light one. I inhaled deeply and blew the heavy smoke out, watching it disperse in the subdued light. I took another draw and exhaled again, noting how it made me think of flames and sulphur.

Coffee. That's what I need! I mumbled, stumbling into the kitchen. I fumbled with the percolator, aware that I was in a state that only strong coffee usually caused. Perhaps then coffee would have a reverse effect and calm me. I proceeded to brew a pot and sit and sip a steaming cupful. Black. Black and bitter. Only then did my metabolism abate to something I would term mildly agitated. I then decided to read the Bible for awhile, beginning with Matthew's Gospel, the last chapters. I turned to some of St. Paul's writings, ending up in John's *Apocalypse*. This time I was aware of just how terrifying some of that material can be, that there was a nether world within Scripture that I had not fully appreciated.

A deeper reading proved to be too mysterious for my poor non-theological mind. There was so much symbolism, as angels, beasts, wars, horsemen riding across the sky, and the Great Whore of Babylon (which was Imperial Rome, I had heard). In my mind I saw these figures as I had seen them in two large canvas paintings of Bible history that were stretched upon the walls at the bookstore where I bought my Scofield Bible.

Then I remembered how I felt when I first saw those graphic tableaux, how it all seemed rather quaint, as though produced by someone back in the nineteenth century. It made me think of Sunday school images I had seen in my childhood, sometimes as black and white engravings or at other times tinted drawings in Sunday school publications: Daniel sleeping with the lions resting all about him, human bones scattered about the den; bearded men walking along a forest trail next to a river; three men standing unharmed among the flames of a great furnace. My mind was ajumble with images that I knew only vaguely and had always considered artists' depictions of ancient fables.

By the time I poured my third cup of coffee, the eastern sky was becoming pale blue. I yawned, looked at the clock and began to think of the day's schedule. Monday was a major study day. I needed my allowed absences for something better than sleeping, so began to adjust to reality. In some way, my study schedule was not all that different from my navy routine under general quarters: stay alert and do not even think about sleeping.

There would be no Rapture, at least not for me. I doubted that my friends at church were up in heaven or on their way to Jerusalem with the returned Christ. So I drew a tub of cool water, and while it filled I brushed my teeth and tongue, as was my custom, in an attempt to get rid of the taste of smoke, to refresh my mouth. Then, while soaking in the water, my mind began to clear. I concluded I had fallen under the spell of my mentor, slipping slowly into enchantment due to my desire to learn the mysteries of religion.

Who would teach me anything beyond what I was receiving? To whom could I turn, if not to my very own pastor? This was a disturbing thought, one I could not answer just then.

SECOND THOUGHTS ABOUT LAST DAYS

The good, the true, the beautiful.

Plato; *Republic*; b. 7

Whatsoever things are true, ... are honest, ... are just, ... are pure, ... are lovely, ... are of good report; if there be any virtue, and if there be any praise, think on these things.

St. Paul, *Philippians*

The drive to school was ordinary. And that was fine, for the prospect of a simple day pleased me. People appeared glum to be into another week, poking along as though loathe to arrive at anything. At the university, students shuffled between classes. I needed no further proof that I had been wildly, imaginatively dreaming about the Rapture. Nonetheless, it brought me up short when I heard myself whistling a happy tune: "Jesus is Coming to Earth Some Day, What if It Were Today?" Well, not today, I reasoned. Later? I doubted it would happen either that day or the next or perhaps at any time. After all, one tires of waiting after the first thousand years. Two thousand is simply too much.

Such thoughts aside, I still believed in the eternal God, a Power who would nudge me to rise to better behavior and thought. Jesus the Teacher offers his relationship to the Father and the insights of the relationship as a key to liberation from the old traditions of the Pharisees. And then I remembered the ancient wisdom: What Jesus did he did at God's behest, and what he said he spoke as from his Father. We then, who believe in him and dare to follow him become his hands and feet, his eyes and ears. We are in a very real way his friends in succession of those first disciples. Dare I call this God-man my Brother? Yes, that is what he is! And we are collaborators with all the saints of the ages in carrying out the ministry of Christ. Here is a model of both divinity and humanity that we can understand. Jesus was a man of sorrows, humble and ready to give his all for the Father. And not for himself alone, for he gave his life for his friends too. He died for them and for anyone who cares to accept his heroic deed. There is no greater love. And, is not God love? *Yes*, I said, *Yes! I am not forsaken, for Jesus lives eternally in the hearts of his friends.*

By midday I was yawning. This year especially would demand all my energy, as I was doing extra credits each semester and had it figured to graduate in three years. From the practical side, by studying during the summer sessions I was able to keep the G.I. Bill subsidy coming in, and it was good money. As an aging student of twenty-six, I could not afford the luxury of free time or dilly-dallying, so my life was full of books and late night cramming. In effect, I had a purpose-driven life before the phrase was copyrighted.

I mused that it wasn't all bad to be older and serious but then, I confessed, it caused me to imagine I was clad in a cowl and bound with a knotted rope at my waist. And, just as a monk must struggle against the impulses of his "unruly member," I was terribly aware of my lack of intimacy and playfulness. My bones ached. Then too, on top of suffering a life too full of repetitious things, I was undergoing burnout. For others inspired and directed me to action but never thought to offer me a day off or a weekend away. I had never been more virtuous nor more responsible than just then, and the spiritual discipline was taking its toll upon both body and spirit.

What a deluge of emotions, demands, intellectual stirring and conflicting religious thoughts filled my days! The church activities intrigued me. But in spite of the novelty of this radical religion I had stumbled upon, it was apparently leading me into conflict with a normal life. And, it became apparent, I was associated with well-intentioned friends who willingly limited their exposure to the very things Paul encouraged the early Christians to seek, such as a cultural environment and an appreciation of refinement. It also occurred to me that according to tradition Paul was a university graduate himself, at the school in Tarsus. Surely he knew his philosophers and poets and the religious lore, the metaphysics and mysteries. In this, he would have been schooled in the subtleties of literary styles and techniques as well as poetry and public speaking. Ancient Hebrew and Greek traditions would have met in him and created an explosive and creative display. How else can one explain Paul's insights and eloquence? The Spirit of Jesus might have interrupted his persecution of the first Christians and illuminated his encyclopedic knowledge of ancient learning, but Paul learned all these things just like the rest of us. He earned an education by working for it. Why, to anyone today not trained in those ancient disciplines, Paul can come across as a wild man at times or as someone suddenly enlightened by God without having worked for understanding. The fact is, he was churning with ideas from Israel, Greece and Italy, and we must include the current religious fervor of the Mystery religions and the Essenes and their contemporary sects scattered among the hills of Palestine.

At that point in my training I was not one who could contradict Gaines' interpretation of Scripture. I had more questions than answers. For instance: the pastor talked about Jesus coming back, but I thought that Scripture said he was now with us and would not forsake us, "even to the close of the age." The Apostle Paul wrote that "Christ in us" is our hope of glory. And further, in the book of the *Acts of the Apostles,* Christ's presence was manifested in the gift of the Holy Spirit to the assembly of his followers on that first Pentecost.

Jesus went up, and the Spirit came down, just as my mother said. And the early writers of Scripture affirmed that the Spirit would look out for Jesus' concerns. Whereas Jesus was limited by his body, the Spirit could be everywhere at once. Or the Spirit could blow around, touching down here and there. It was all very mystical and full of sparks. The disciples were forever wondering when something new might occur, some new insight into religion be made manifest.

The possibilities were beyond counting. There were many such questions in which one could suppose there would be *a literal meaning or a spiritual meaning or both.* For instance, Christ at Pentecost was leading his Church into a new epoch. There would be henceforth a startling leading of the Spirit into new fields of thought and practice. And since the new had come, the old would pass away. In fact, Paul wrote that even if, at that time, some church members were actually original friends of Jesus "in the flesh," *they were no longer to think of him in that way.* Indeed, there are implications in such an assertion, and I think they have been mostly ignored. But such thinking is so charged with theological implications, that I am not surprised that it is usually — what shall I say? — put on the back burner. It simply is easier to ignore disturbing ideas that undermine an established system. And the Church did become an established system. Revelations ceased. Order was imposed. A system was put into place to make sense of the nonsense of so many people voicing so many opinions and theological mumbo-jumbo.

So, what's there to say? We need stability and order.

No one in my church, absolutely no one, spoke of Christ's return as a metaphorical concept. The Son sat next to his Father in Heaven, while the Spirit carried out their divine will upon earth, especially within the Church. No one argued that Jesus' *principles* might someday dominate the hearts of humankind — that is, the minds of humans to the point that *all the world* would think by the ethical standards of Heaven, living in peace, mutuality and equity. Meanwhile, through thick and thin, Christ's teaching that the kingdom of God was *within* us would be enough. It would play out so that all God's creation would resonate with the divine rhythm, I am encouraged to believe. So then, we are called to further the kingdom's coming to fruition by doing and teaching God's way, the only profitable way, in a needy world.

It would seem that this is what the old prophets foresaw: a time when the nations would "study war no more," and every family would have a garden and fruit trees. And no one would tell others about the Lord, for all would know him in the life they had. An old hymn puts it simply, "And he walks with me and he talks with me." It seems logical that the Savior has no need to sit on an actual golden throne in Jerusalem dispensing judgments, for he has his reign *in each of us*. As Jeremiah wrote, it will not be necessary to tell others to know the Lord, for all shall know him.

Pursuing what Paul studied in Tarsus

A survey of ancient Greek philosophers in a literature class brought other questions to mind. For it became clear that some principles of Christianity were similar to Plato's writings from hundreds of years before the Christian Era. Even earlier, in the person of Socrates, the teacher of Plato, we encounter a superb thinker, a master at exposing the essence of human thought, be it wise or foolish.

Socrates was a champion of truth, but his methods of teaching surely irritated many around him. Even the manner of execution, found in the *Phaedo*, dramatically portrayed the ideal hero's death as a moral victory over the vitriol of his foes, who were traditionalists and defenders of the established order. Only a skip of a few centuries brings us to the New Testament accounts of Jesus' problem with the traditionalist Scribes and Pharisees. In each case, the Status Quo — the Establishment — defends itself against any innovative interpretations. Actually, these two incidents show that the conflict is not about which are the best ideas but that leaders do not wish to be inconvenienced; they dislike any and all threats to their unquestioned authority to run things. The first requirement of an empire is obedience, be it secular or religious. There is only one orthodoxy, those in power assert, and it is well enough defined.

This crisis in Socrates' life seems to be what Christ also faced: either accept the consequences of what he taught and the way he lived or he would have to abandon his friends by running away from execution. And so, as Socrates, Jesus took the cup, not a cup of tragic death but of a love for his friends, and drank of it. Socrates did not tell his friends to follow him to death. But Jesus told his friends also to drink from his Passover cup, remembering him as the sacrificial lamb of God. So every disciple is called upon to drink and remember what happens to those who prize truth above pretense and who serve God rather than man. For life is full of lies and selfish posing for one or another form of profit. Vanity! These are the ways of death.

This is why Jesus is my hero. In the face of certain death he loved his friends as much as he loved God and his righteousness — spell that justice — and continued steadfast in his determination to champion love of neighbor while denouncing duplicity. To this day his is a religion that shuns the lie and the unlovely, the harmful thing, offering instead the good, the true, the beautiful. These are eternal, spiritual, redemptive. To identify with this is as close as we are going to get to Heaven in this life. In fact, this is the divine life, the light, that shimmers and flashes around the earth, ever pushing against darkness. And the darkness has not been able to extinguish it.

Such insights, being deductive, were not mentioned in my church. I do not say that my friends were lacking in generosity or compassion, only very limited in their scope, or perhaps their agenda. Employing one's imagination in that environment was considered dangerously close to heresy by the doctrinaire. Therefore my intention to attend theological seminary became increasingly attractive. In seminary I surely would be exposed to a variety of ideas and systems of thought. Perhaps then I would be better equipped to minister for good in the world, to spread hope and health where too often confusion and a sickness unto death have ruled.

— 6 —

THINGS WORKING TOGETHER

I felt extremely restive after undergoing that late-night dream about Jesus atop the clouds. My condition was not angst, not negative, for I did not feel I missed something or was deceived or anything like that. Rather, the world seemed a surprisingly beautiful place, in spite of the crime and grime. Ours is a planet full of wonder and grace, with the potential of becoming Paradise. I simply could not bring myself to believe that the Creator of such beauty was intent upon the destruction of both land and people. The grand and agonizing epic of the human race and the drift toward civilization should not end in cataclysm. Both the Creator and we of the Creation have put far too much into this effort to give up on it.

I reconciled myself to reality: conflicts leading to further light, *yes*; and with pain, *yes*; but pie in the sky, *no*. I had not lost my faith, only chosen an idealism that reached beyond my ability to describe it. But that ideal seemed possible. Christ the Lord might change the world for the better, through those who share his ideals. In fact, I had the impression that I was joining in his mission to change things for the better. It did not seem naïve to think of lighting a candle in the darkness and being fervent about it. Christ has his witnesses by the millions in many areas of the inhabited world, and each is a candle for goodness, mercy and hope. I simply joined them, expecting that others would be glad to have me in the common cause. What a wonderful army of volunteers!

The sky had never appeared so blue nor the birds' songs as bright as they seemed to me just then. Every morning dawned with the promise of better times.

> *He who binds to himself a joy*
> *Does the winged life destroy:*
> *But he who kisses the joy as it flies*
> *Lives in eternity's sunrise.*   William Blake

I beheld the possibilities for a redeemable world. In fact, I felt more strongly than ever the urge to gain a wife, and in due time we would have children. This bright attitude also led to a heightened awareness of the surprising number of really good-looking women of marriageable age on campus. No, I was not destined to become a monk. I would kiss the joy as it flies. And as for the monks, I would not intrude upon their solitude. Monks have a "singular" calling.

In the middle of summer — when hurricanes blow westerly, each in some frenzied path from Africa to Columbia's shining shores — I sat reading at the kitchen table, drinking iced tea and sweating, oblivious to all but my lessons. The phone's incessant jangle intruded upon that mute world. I sighed, then ambled into the living room and picked up the hand piece from its cradle.

"DuPease home," I said with no special inflection, a habit learned when there actually was a family within those walls.

There was a pause, and then a woman's voice asked lightly, almost apologetically, "*Johnny?*"

The use of that name snapped me away from my books and into the moment, for only one person had ever called me Johnny, and she was somewhere out there, in the amazing web of wiring strung from pole to pole, coming to me, whispering in my ear with that sweet voice of hers. *But where was her lovely body?*

All else forgotten, and not yet sure of myself, I too paused to gain my balance. And then I blurted out, *"Colleen! Colleen Hammelin! I can't believe this! Are you in town?"* For I remembered all too well and with some regret that she had become engaged right after high school graduation, soon after I joined the navy. "Yes, you have to be in town," I said, trying to control my excitement, "but where?"

She giggled like a teenager before answering. "Actually, I'm not very far away. I saw you the other day, and you really looked good, put on some muscle. Oh, you were so slim back when. No, skinny!" She laughed then, a woman's full throated laugh, and the sound brought me a pleasant thrill. Old memories of good times flooded my mind, so fresh that they could have been from a week ago. I sure liked her cuddling ways, her ample form and feel. Just to kiss her was to get in a little illicit rubbing. *Oh!* I tried to imagine her both as she was and as she might be, which was an interesting mental gymnastic. My metabolism kicked into high as I recalled those steamy teenage times.

"Okay now," I said, "don't play with me. Where did you see me? And why didn't you speak to me?" I was trying to compose myself, for I felt my pulse throbbing. But then I thought, *Can it, you goofus! For heaven's sake, she's married!*

"Oh, *you!*" she began in mock anger, "Aren't you even going to ask me how I am before you start off trying to find me out? I saw you, that's all. Would you've talked to me if I'd-a tapped you on the shoulder?" Colleen sounded like a hurt little girl, teasing, but there was also a hint of doubt in her voice.

I hesitated, groping for the right thing, and said, "You bet I'd-a talked to you! So now, tell me about yourself."

An image rose from memory of our high school prom, and my softly singing the piece the band was playing, *"I'm just a prisoner of love"*, as we snuggled on the crowded floor. I had crooned my warm breath into her ear, *What's the good of my caring, if someone is sharing those arms with me? Although she has another, I can't have another, for I'm not free! ... Alone from night to night, you'll find me, too weak to break the chains that bind me, I need no shackles to remind me, I'm just a prisoner of love.*[1]

We got into conversation as though eight years had not separated us, but only eight days, or at the most, eight months. "Why didn't you speak to me?" I asked. "Well," she said, "it just wasn't a good moment, that's all."

Women can be vague when they have a reason, and men are wise not to crowd them for clear answers. I moved on to another question. By the time we finished our prattling little dance, an hour had elapsed. We agreed to meet the next evening at a restaurant on the bay front, one we rarely visited as teenagers because of the refined menu and cost. But I had learned a few things about dating across the years, and I hoped she would be pleased with my choice. Yes, and I hoped she would be pleased with me.

During our hour's conversation Colleen told me she had married only weeks after graduation and moved away, but not very far. Her husband took her back to his family home, where he was dominated by his widowed mother. The marriage lasted a few weeks, which she said seemed more like years. She sued for divorce on grounds of incompatibility. Sherman did not contest the action.

I suggested that it sounded like his fault, not hers. Perhaps he married her in order to gain a draft deferment. Other than this one comment, I largely remained silent and let her vent.

Colleen returned home, her parents being sympathetic rather than judgmental. But before long she matriculated at the city university as a resident student and earned a teaching degree. She began her career at an elementary school a few miles north of our section of the city, renting rooms within walking distance of her work. Being so near the old haunts, she still returned to the old stores in our section of the city. Then one day she saw me just ahead of her at the new supermarket. Colleen admitted she stalked me for a few moments before rushing to get out of the store.

That was quite an hour's conversation, and it left me elated. I would mull it over in bits and pieces until we met for our date.

The next day I was feeling the tension. Not having slept well and unable to concentrate upon studies, I finally gave up and went home. I tried snoozing on the sofa but failed. I felt at a disadvantage, not having seen Colleen when she saw me. Was she still slightly plump? I imagined so. How about her hair? She had the brightest red hair of any girl in high school. But contrary to the stereotype of red hot hair equals red hot temper, she was the most easy-going girl in the class. Colleen wore her hair long, combed back and held with clips, hanging below the shoulders, a marvelous sight. In comparison, I was a blond, so blond that some accused me of bleaching my hair. The two of us used to cause remarks from strangers because of this contrast. In private, I would stroke her hair affectionately, which was a good way to get my arm around her shoulders. I sighed as I thought of it. *Careful,* I told myself, *you're building sand castles!*

I arrived at the restaurant a few minutes early and chose a table back in the corner, where a half wall jutted out with sansevieria planted in it. At least it would be just a little secluded, and those awkward first moments might not be noticed by others. I sat and watched the diners come in. No recognizable neighbors were there, and no one familiar entered.

And then suddenly Colleen was at the table.

I looked up at a familiar face, but not at the same girl I knew in high school. The woman I saw had shed her girlish pounds and become quite shapely. And she was clear of freckles. As I looked up at her I became aware of her décolletage, which could hardly be ignored. In my imagination she was aiming her gaze at me between the V of her bosom, which loomed before me.

hoped I was calm and of good complexion, but it did occur to me that she was not at all bashful about pushing up so closely.

Colleen was really quite stylish in a nice one piece dress, silky, in white with yellow and brown tones that complemented her hair. Noticing this, I realized I was sitting there while she stood smiling down at me. I rose, took her hands and looked down into her eyes, those bright blue eyes, only a few inches away. Oh, wasn't she a model, a beautiful woman! I wanted only to stand there and drink her in, but I knew something needed to be said, especially to break further thoughts I dared not entertain.

"Excuse me for failing to see you come in, Colleen. I don't know where my mind was. My, you are dressed so attractively! How are you?" Then I stopped, for my words sounded to me just a little unnatural, as though I were speaking into a bucket. I preferred to hear her voice.

She didn't answer immediately but continued looking at me, apparently without any of the disorientation I was experiencing. Her smile had not changed. Then she shook her head just a little, in an old familiar way, and her hair swung around gently. The tresses of high school were now cropped just above the shoulders and slightly curled throughout.

Some people improve with age, I thought.

"Johnny," she said softly, "don't worry about my slipping up on you. I seem to do that to people. My, that is a nice shirt." And then she reached out to her chair, so I moved to assist her. She sat smoothly as I slipped the chair under her. So far, so good. Her perfume was delicate, not like the orange blossom stuff the high school girls used to buy at the drugstore. I inhaled lightly, and my mind turned to mush. We must have ordered something to eat, for the waitress brought our plates all too soon.

After dinner we took a leisurely walk along the bayfront, then about nine thirty decided to end the evening, for the next day would be a busy one. I escorted my date back to the restaurant parking area. We kissed goodbye, and the fire of adolescence was in that kiss. It lasted too long to be only friendly, and yet it seemed not long enough.

Oh, Lord, she smells good! I said to myself and slipped my fingers up into her hair. I was surprised to feel myself trembling. Colleen remained silent, accepting my caress. For that was not the first time she had felt me tremble. Nothing needed to be said just then. I wanted that embrace; it was not enough, however. I moved my lips toward hers, and we kissed again.

We did not attempt to make an endurance game of the embrace, but it did last long enough to convey a message to us that we understood. I thought of it later and wondered if that very moment was when we made our future together a priority item.

Colleen sighed and touched the car door. "Johnny, this has been a wonderful evening. I look forward to seeing you again. But I must get some things done for tomorrow's classes. You understand?" I did, regrettably. We parted, agreeing that I would call the next afternoon.

I drove home in a daze, a frenzy, full of hope and afraid of what I was thinking. Suddenly my routine was stirred beyond anything that I anticipated as I plodded daily from class to class, to my piddling part-time job and back to my empty home. I was as spaced out as a daydreaming adolescent, wishing to be with Colleen more than reality would permit. But just then I needed sleep.

When I awoke refreshed, my first thought was of our parting embrace.

7

EYE OPENERS

I looked forward to my orientation times with Reverend Gaines. We had agreed upon a target of one session a week, but with the understanding that we would set it up weekly. At first we managed to keep on a regular schedule, but as time went on we found it more difficult to sustain our sessions. In part, our stretching out the time was due to his busy schedule, and in part it was his ability to assign the task to others. And that was fine with me, for I got to know the lay leaders better.

I was reticent about sharing my doubts, for my pastor was not the type to have any himself. I sensed it would not help to play the adversary. When I finally began questioning his ideas, I learned a few things that were eye openers. But we began well, and it was helpful to have him educate me about both the mechanics of religion and the intricacies of doctrine. Then I tried to pick up some history of Christianity, but he apparently was not interested in history, stressing more some of the mainline denominations' drift from old-time religion.

We met like this for thirty or more minutes of friendly conversation. However, we never became friends on a personal level, did not exchange bits of humor or share family items. I truly wanted to be his friend, but Greg did not encourage such closeness. As I look back upon those sessions I recall that I rarely addressed my pastor as Greg, even if we members did among ourselves, but simply engaged him in conversation in a neutral manner. Apparently I had picked up on his signals without understanding the dynamics, other than the need for formality. He could become engaged in a social way, laughing at the proper moments and asking about some detail of my past. But there was a certain reserve that was hard to define.

My first session at his office was delayed by something going on in another room, so the office secretary said I should go into the pastor's study and make myself comfortable. During the few minutes I had alone, I began reviewing his certificates and academic degrees, which were openly displayed behind his desk. Among them was a photo of a small church, a tongue-in-groove structure, set in a plot of yellow pines. Looking more carefully at the display, I noticed that Gaines was a graduate of a college in Tennessee. The name Bryan College on the certificate did not connect me just then to the politician of an earlier generation who was known as the great fundamentalist, for I was not aware of that piece of history. Nor did I notice that the diploma was only a certificate, not a degree. I would learn more of that custom later. Next to his certificate was his bachelor's degree in divinity granted by the Warfield Reformed Orthodox Seminary in some unknown town in Alabama, perhaps a satellite of Birmingham, nor did I recognize the hallowed name of that champion of Presbyterianism, Warfield, from an earlier generation. Lastly I examined his doctorate in sacred theology from the Pikesville Bible College and Seminary in Colorado. Three degrees. I thought of all those years spent in libraries and classrooms and I shuddered. And yet I was inclined to follow suit, God helping me, at least as far as the divinity degree. Neither my imagination nor ambition were fired for anything higher.

At this point in my survey of his office hangings, my mentor returned and invited me to sit down for a chat. I asked him rather soon about his education, especially mentioning his doctorate. How many years of study beyond the usual seminary regimen had that degree required? He replied in a nonchalant manner, saying he had taken the degree *in absentia* while a chaplain in the navy. I thought that was unusual though possible, seeing that many ministers had served as chaplains during the war, when ordinary routines were disrupted. Military life allowed time enough to do graduate study by correspondence, if a person would deny himself and really hit the books. It did not occur to me to ask where he got the books necessary for such study.

We moved on to talk about my studies at the university and a few other general subjects, which included sharing some family information, especially about my Methodist background. The visit was pleasant enough, but abruptly ended by an urgent call of some sort. He silently dismissed me while taking the call.

Our church, its schedule and the leaders were often in those conversations, as were the doctrinal correctness of various colleges and seminaries around the country. We also talked about foreign missions, how they were financed and administered, so that I learned quite a bit about a few Protestant churches in America, mainly those churches and schools that Gaines favored. I lacked either the guts or acuity to become a devil's advocate for some of the prickly problems I sensed could be pursued. Nor did I tell him that I doubted Jesus was really coming back on the clouds. Rather, I soaked up what I could of his theology, which was quite intricate as a doctrinal system but certainly not speculative. He helped me understand the Scofield Bible I carried around with me, of course, and I appreciated his explanations even if I began to have my doubts about dispensationalism.

Later I would learn that Scofield was befriended by a few influential persons in America who had contacts with Zionists in England. The Zionists were mostly Europeans and Americans who backed the return of Jews to Palestine, especially as proposed by Theodor Herzl, in the late nineteenth century. A few Zionists aided and abetted Scofield in promoting his annotated Bible.

That explained to me why fundamentalist Christians who study the Scofield Bible are so often enthusiastic about Jews returning to their historic geography. For they believe that Jews must once again take possession of the "Holy Land" and re-establish the Nation of Israel, which they have done, more or less. But they have not succeeded in occupying the entire City of Jerusalem.

Christians who embrace dispensational ideas believe that when modern Jews have retaken Jerusalem as their city, the stage will have been set for Christ to return as the Messiah. But at my point in religious education, when I was Gaines' understudy, many such arcane details were beyond my knowledge. I just sensed that something at the Palms seemed out of phase with what I knew of our Protestant American culture and history. For my family's attitude, and that of Protestantism in general, was to leave the Jews to themselves. In fact, we had heard that what they wanted was just that, to be left alone. Nevertheless my new friends were radical in their mission to convert Jews, but also to get them back to Jerusalem.

After the second session with Gaines, my mentor began lending me books from his shelves, and their subjects became our material for discussion. One of the first was a book on religious cults of modern times, some with ancient and arcane roots, as the Rosicrucian. The book included more religions and sects than I knew existed, and some of them were not that different from the behavior I was encountering at the beach church. But each group had some distinctive idea that set it apart, thereby disqualifying it as a legitimate church in the minds of my companions. Years later I would understand that my companions were greatly influenced by New England Puritanism, called Reformed Orthodoxy. In its Congregational form it spread from town to town, entering the frontier and spawning a series of religious revivals and a frontier form of individualism.

I discovered that I really did not care very much about those details and wondered why we had to distinguish such petty things in order to exclude others from ourselves, even if we continued to live in a diverse society that was held together by the Constitution of the United States. I was still thinking as a modern American, of course, where we often said, "Live and let live." Did we have exclusive title to the truth that permitted us to decide who was in, who out? I began to think of The Palms as "Greg's Little Acre." But, unlike Caldwell's character — Lester Jeeter, who kept moving God's dedicated acre to another spot — Greg had several "acres" going at the same time.

My pastor reached over to the mainland, where he had opened a collaborative Bible institute for "pre-ministerial" students. I learned very soon that there were various small churches being nurtured by these pre-ministerial students, but not as proto-Presbyterians. I also had the opinion that not one of his full-time students had attended college. Nevertheless, those very young adults were beginning "house churches" in various neighborhoods and organizing the attendees into quasi-congregations. The popular word at the time was cells. This was what the strict dispensationalists were doing, forming small independent churches that owed no loyalty to any outside authority.

The Bible institute also offered evening classes to adults each Tuesday. Gaines advised me to register and get on with my Bible education. We lay persons gathered at seven o'clock for singing and announcements, followed by two lectures. The institute was housed in a unique structure that was built by an evangelistic and missionary alliance of several churches in the northwest area of the city.

The building had the lines of a fortress much like those I saw in movies involving the French Foreign Legion in Algeria. However, the crenellated outer walls were misplaced in a residential neighborhood. I felt uncomfortable as I approached the whitewashed stucco building for the first time. For I had in mind the attractive church over on the beach. In contrast, there were no yachts around that fortress, nor Cadillacs, just aging apartment buildings and residences with rabble-scrabble lawns and gap-toothed hedges.

We non-credit Tuesday night attendees were lax about our reading assignments, mostly because we were already overloaded with daily duties. A night class for us became a time to learn about the Bible without having to read it very much. We sat back and listened to our teachers lecture at length about the marvels of Scripture as well as the rationale for the Bible being infallible and inerrant both in its parts and on the whole. In the process we also learned that non-Christians had crafted a *hypothesis* of evolution upon Earth, in which ape-men, "their" predecessors, foraged for a livelihood. The pseudo-scientists assumed that all this occurred long before Adam and Eve were created in the Garden of Eden. And worse, some of those liberals, who lacked the courage to leave the churches and declare themselves atheists, were wooing Christians away from true doctrine, turning the faithful into doubters. Liberals had in turn adopted "social gospel" programs to help the world save itself. I heard this with interest, for it was a new concept in my expanding awareness of the many conflicts within broad-based American religious thought.

One especially fervent teacher told us that liberals despised the references to blood sacrifice in the Bible. But blood was what our religion was all about. The ancient priests offered lambs and bullocks on the altar as a foreshadowing of Christ's self-sacrifice upon the Cross. In effect, the sacrifices of the Jewish Religion were a divinely ordered preparation for Jesus' eventual death on the cross. His blood flowed, in some mystical way, into a fountain and sinners plunged beneath that flood — baptized in it — are forgiven, their new robes of righteousness having been washed as white as snow in the Blood of the Lamb.

I took all this into my ever-widening repertoire of doctrine and trade words without knowing exactly what to do with it. My inclination was to run away from it, but I had nowhere to go just then. But it did seem strange that God, the Creator, and the giver of the Holy Spirit to his Church, could only get this amazing message of true religion out through a little sectarian institution on a back street. Meanwhile, the entire world seemed to know about Darwin's biological observations made after a long voyage around South America collecting fossils and new species.

Midway through my second semester that year Greg began easing me into a possible change of plans: a year or two off from college in which I could learn some hands-on ministry. Perhaps, he suggested, I might consider leading a small church, under his supervision. This should have flattered me. But somehow I felt he was far too ambitious by suggesting I become a preacher and a pastor overnight, no matter how humble the position. I said so, probably too frankly, and added that I thought it was customary for university students to go on to seminary in order to learn as much as possible about religion and theology, just as future lawyers continue their studies prior to actually practicing law.

Gaines let the matter drop for that visit, but he would bring it up again. For my part, I felt that he was not using good judgment, apparently seeking to use me rather than encourage my education. And I had recently turned twenty-six, so felt I needed to get on with the formalities of education. I held my ground about my need for further study. As for learning more of the man, I found him to be unusually silent about his own education and experience. I took this to be an act of self-effacement. Perhaps, I imagined, it was spiritual humility. It did not occur to me that he might have anything to hide, but he did, and it would eventually come to light.

I remain grateful for one big favor Greg did for me in his mentoring, and that was to counsel me in my struggle with cigarettes. I had either tried to quit smoking many times or actually quit smoking for brief periods of time across the years, and that included times before I felt any call to ministry. With my new religious influence I grew even more dissatisfied with smoking, for I knew I was being a bad influence on young people.

Greg suggested I ask the Lord to take away my taste fo cigarettes. *Taste.* That's the word he used, not habit or desire. No that was a novel approach. I had managed to keep my prayer rather formal, joining in at worship in confessing sins in genera and asking for a blanket forgiveness. And when I prayed in privat I usually prayed more through meditation than conversation. I di not think myself as so important that God would want to hear m peevish complaints or needed a lot of thanks. In fact, I though that too often our church members were rather egoistic in thei chumminess with God, as though He had little else to do tha attend their repetitious concerns. Someone had quoted a write of devotional books as saying that God won't do for us what w can do for ourselves, and I thought that wisdom included kickin the nicotine habit. Would the heavenly Father actually incline a ear to such a request and take away a taste? Well, I would try and see what happened. To my surprise it worked. After a wee of casual smoking I found myself disgusted with tobacco. It wa not only dirty and costly but also got in the way. I dropped th cigarette I had between my fingers and moved on without eve looking back. *The taste indeed was gone.* That was marvelous! felt better, smelled better and had a wonderful appetite. In fac I gained thirty pounds! It took perhaps sixty days to gain thos pounds and another six months to lose them again. But I did no ask God to take away my taste for food. I would not dare!

At a midweek prayer meeting, perhaps a month after quittin cigarettes, I gave my report, called a testimony among the faithful openly thanking God for doing for me what I could not seen to do for myself. After the meeting an elderly lady approache me and said that she was so pleased that I had finally become Christian, for she had been praying for me. I thanked her fo her prayers and then bit my tongue for fear I'd say somethin flippant and ruin the moment..

In spite of my tact and progress, Greg seemed mildl dissatisfied with me. I suppose I never managed to use th ordinary religious clichés as freely as others. I simply could not bring myself to say "Praise the Lord!" every few minutes or sprinkle Bible verses into my conversations. But the principal source of conflict between the pastor and me was my lack of enthusiasm for his dispensational system. He must have sensed my hesitation about the subject. I was suspicious of the division of world history into rather clear periods of God first trying one thing and then another in order to make his humans please him. The system involved a very simplistic, and, I thought incomplete, view of world history. For nothing was ever said about other races or religions as found in India or China, the pre-Columbian Incas or Aztecs, or the complicating fact of a quite ancient aboriginal race in Australia. Since I grew up reading a marvelous collection of *The National Geographic* — Dad was a regular subscriber across the years and saved every issue — I was aware of all manner of scientific achievement and discoveries. New facts were constantly coming to light that helped us appreciate our wide world.

And that was a clincher, really, in my suspicion that the dispensational system was remiss in its science. According to the official history I received at church, the human race consisted of three types: Shem, Ham and Japeth, the three sons of Noah. Shem was the father of the Semites, Ham of black Africans, and Japeth of the Europeans. One father, three separate races, and all in an instant, in the winking of an eye. How anyone could take this seriously was beyond me.

The clarification of my growing dis-ease happened quite abruptly. Greg persisted in his recommendation of a seminary in Texas that favored dispensationalism. But before the end of the first year in his church I knew quite a bit about that seminary through conversations and religious articles, so resisted accepting my pastor's advice. Then Greg's lay associate Hal moved in on me, and I suspect that he took up the task by assignment. One fine afternoon, when I had many odd jobs to complete, he parked his chrome and bright red Harley at the curb and rapped on my door, peering in through the screen. Once in my living room, and without niceties, he went to the matter at hand, counseling me about the dangers involved in going to a Presbyterian seminary There was only one seminary, he insisted, "the only one in America that teaches the one hundred percent truth." He admitted, under examination, that there could be a few good seminaries, though rarely denominational ones, and even the good ones were only "ninety-five percent or less" pure. "It is better to go to the masters of doctrine and learn right thinking," he declared.

Under that sort of pressure, I agreed to write to his chosen seminary for introductory material. So, when Reverend Gaines finally inquired about my research into the recommended seminary, I told him that I felt it did not have the curriculum I needed to become a minister. It was hard for me to defy Gaines so I tried to say less rather than more. He was visibly provoked his ruddy complexion displaying purple blotches. He suggested that I read the seminary's précis again and point out to him what was lacking. I then asked him if he had attended the seminary and he said no, but he agreed with their doctrine. I smiled and thanked him for his concern for me.

I then asked Greg why, in a country full of seminaries, this one seemed to be his choice. He surprised me by his energy as he replied that, early on in America, Christian schools began to modernize their theology and thus their interpretation of the Bible. At the same time a movement to socialize the Gospel had gotten underway. People were moving away from Trinitarian Religion to Unitarianism, re-writing the old theologies into modern terms and abandoning the old forms of worship. This was the basic cause of the Civil War in America, he said. The Yankees wanted to free the slaves because of their newly contrived ideas of social redemption. They used Scripture to justify their humanistic ideals, turning the Good News of Redemption from sacrifice for sins to good works and the reform of social structures They made the emancipation of slaves their prime objective But Scripture, he said, clearly endorses slavery, in both Old and

New Testaments. And that was permissible because some races are inferior to others. But the modernists were not satisfied with the Word of God as it is plainly understood, and continued to accommodate it to their interests.

The Yankees said the clear intent of the New Testament was to create a new egalitarian society, even if St. Paul told slaves to obey their masters. Therefore those modernist reformers had taken it upon themselves to kidnap the Bible and then use it for their own purposes. Not only that, but they were bent upon imposing their new ideas upon the Old South. "There is no one so rigid and unbending as a fervent liberal with a cause," Greg said. And so the Civil War was waged, killing hundreds of thousands of good Christian young men. Sherman destroyed Atlanta, and the carpetbaggers were foisted upon the Confederate States, ruining their economy. The newly freed slaves, who had not been killed off by the warfare in any appreciable numbers, continued to multiply. But they were worse off than before and created new social issues in the cities. Blacks were everywhere, emboldened to demand rights they did not deserve. And the Yankees were hell-bent upon allowing them the vote and the right to political office. Not only that, but the Yankees took away the states' right to govern themselves, so liberal ideas from up North were crammed down the South's gullet.

"And then," he said, "the liberals moved the churches into the political mainstream. The social gospel replaced the true Gospel as the agenda of the churches, and that was why most theological seminaries did not deserve endorsement in modern times. The rule had been and would continue to be among true churches that there remains a separation of church and state, and citizens ought not mix the two. Religion was a private matter, not something to be legislated by politicians, and much less by biased preachers. The Federal Government was under the sway of self-righteous reformers, liberals and modernists all, who would build the kingdom with human energy that lacked the direction of the Spirit.

Gaines was wound up beyond control and went on to say that far too many churches were involved in trying to cooperate with the Federal Government, leaving their "first love" for an infatuation with the world. I noticed in passing that not once did he blame Jesus for inspiring any of this liberation of slaves or social reform. He concluded, "This blending of church and politics has led to their compromise of our ancient principles, but we fundamentalists are not about to sell out to them."

At that point in his dissertation he had grown shrill, and his complexion was glowing. Beads of sweat were gathering on his forehead, all the way up to the paste that held his toupee in place. I realized that Greg had lost his showmanship, a rare occurrence, and I had caused it. So, I concluded, my persistence in asking questions was finally rewarded with a moment of unguarded truth.

I thanked him for his matter-of-fact presentation and asked his leave. Once out of the office I felt liberated from any further need to please him by being a good and loyal understudy. For I had come to the end of this particular episode in my search for religious enlightenment.

The days passed without any contact with anyone in the church, days when I had enough to do without attending the midweek prayer meeting. As I continued to reflect on the episode in the pastor's office, it occurred to me that I had not taken counsel from any other Presbyterian minister, nor did I really know any, for that matter. For Gaines had developed his own outreach in the metropolitan area apart from his colleagues. And I had not felt urgent about making a decision about my future, although I then saw that perhaps I ought to have been concerned. Choosing the most prominent Presbyterian church on the mainland, I called for an appointment with the minister. He got on the phone himself, as soon as the secretary explained what I was seeking, and asked a few questions. Reverend MacNea was very receptive, suggesting that we meet as soon as possible. We set a time for Tuesday of the next week.

8

REFORMED RELIGION REFORMING ITSELF

Having made the appointment with Reverend MacNeal, I became curious about the man and his manner, so was looking forward to our appointment. At the same time, it seemed convenient to avoid my own pastor for a few days, and thinking about this new development was a welcome distraction. I did not lack for interesting things to do, however, for Colleen was always happy to see me.

By Friday I had decided to attend the Sunday worship service at Eastminster Church. I arrived early enough to get a parking space near the church and then walk around the building, just to have a feel for the place before entering. Eastminster was a fine stone structure of neo-Gothic design. Being an older church, it was near the center of downtown and facing the boulevard. The trustees had managed to buy enough property to have landscaping and also park quite a few cars behind the building. Overflow parking on Sundays or evenings could use the city streets without difficulty, so the church had remained viable as the city grew around it.

An elderly gentleman, apparently a greeter, met me at the front door. He asked my name and immediately inquired if I belonged to the DuPease family in the Riverfront section. When I replied that I was indeed, he spoke fondly of my father, a brother Mason and a Shriner. He mentioned what a fine man he was and offered condolences, although they were years late. Mr. Wallace then walked me around the inside of the church, selecting several pamphlets for my reading as we passed a literature rack. Such personal attention from a friend of the family made me feel much more at ease.

By the time I was seated the church seemed a warm place indeed, although the sanctuary was much more stately than over at The Palms. It even seemed somber with its dark oak furnishings and light gray stone. The chandeliers provided light that compensated for the muted sunlight entering through stained glass windows. found the environment pleasing, especially since the church was air-conditioned, which was new. I had heard a few snide remarks back at the Palms about churches that had this new convenience "They'd air-condition Hell, if they could," some said. At The Palms everything was noisy and full of happy laughter before the service commenced. Here there was a meditative silence with an occasional cough, a bit of whispering and the sounds of book being taken from the pew racks or put back.

A Bach fugue, which I did not know but could identify in the bulletin, suddenly broke into our silence. It surely centered my attention. The stone walls reverberated with the bass notes, while the higher pipes sounded up into the pitched ceiling and came back mellowed by the wood.

The very first hymn set the spirit for the day, a composition recognized from childhood:

> *Faith of our fathers, living still, In spite of dungeon, fire and sword*
> *O how our hearts beat high with joy, When-e'er we hear that glorious word!*
> *Faith of our fathers, holy faith, We will be true to thee till death.*

All parts of the service were integrated into the theme of faith and faithfulness, so that there was a unity to the service. I was pleased by this calm and orderly march leading to the sermon.

The Reverend James Mathieu MacNeal, B.D., M.A., as he was listed on the back of the bulletin, was a tall man, rather thin and with a great shock of brown hair that was just a little unruly. He had a profile strikingly similar to that of Thomas Jefferson as we see him in our history books. And when he stood behind the pulpit he exuded an air of confidence that made me want to listen very carefully.

He began, "You have heard in the Gospel reading earlier in the service what John has to say about the Christ, the Word who was with God and was God, from the very beginning of time itself. I shall not take the time to read it again, for I trust your memory regarding this most beloved prologue to the Gospel of our Lord. John is setting the mood, if you will, of his sense of the Master's part in divine redemption.

"John wrote much later than the other three Evangelists, possibly in the last years of the first century, and had the opportunity to reflect upon not only who Jesus was as the Christ but also what this meant to philosophical thinkers of that era. John's comments are profound. They summarize the significance of Christ's saving work for our benefit. Every lesson that comes from the Savior in John's Gospel has a spiritual meaning that merits study and can be taken both religiously for believers at large and philosophically for those who delve into such thought.

"Hear again this opening statement from John's Gospel: 'In the beginning was the Word, and the Word was with God, and the Word was God.' This is one of the earliest confessions in the Church's history. It stands alongside that other primitive creed: 'Jesus is Lord.' The early Christians were exalting Christ over Caesar and the spiritual life over the carnal life. This simple confession is also the foundation for the Apostles' Creed, which had not yet been written. Much later, when the Church developed into an organization, those early Christian leaders adopted, a Emperor Constantine's behest, the now entrenched Nicene Creed. It too is found in our Book of Worship. But John really said it all. There is a beauty in simplicity. All church members, o whatever background, can confess that 'Jesus is Lord' to the glory of God. But theologians always want something more and got i in the creedal statements. And, you know, these creeds never end they just keep being redefined into longer statements, harder to understand. In fact, they are usually taught as confirmation material for our adolescents.

"First, John says, this Word is eternal. The Word was born into the world in a temporal form, as Jesus of Nazareth, who wa not simply another human but is God's *message* to the world. We could even say that Jesus is a word of wisdom to the world. This is a breakthrough in history. For the ancient world had run out of ideas and settled into formalities. Priests stood daily offering sacrifices for sin, but nothing changed. The Greeks sough wisdom, Romans hailed Caesar, and the Jews offered up thei bullocks and turtle doves. Jews and Gentiles alike went through rituals that had lost meaning. Here and there a zealot of some stripe appeared, but as quickly disappeared. The people had no vision. And then Jesus, the God-Man was born apart from all the pomp and circumstance. He came quietly, away from everything formal and predictable. He was a new beginning. But this time instead of being in an idyllic Garden, Jesus came into a world grown weary by sin and cynicism.

"Those first friends of the Master became convinced tha what Jesus said, God was saying for their benefit. What Jesus did God was doing in and through him; and this was done not only for a dozen or more friends but for us too. In the Nicene Creed we recite, *'being of one substance with the Father by whom all thing were made, who for us men and for our salvation came down from heaven, and was incarnate by the Holy Ghost.'* This is what John was saying quite clearly: God took on a human persona, and i is one we can understand. In Jesus He became one of us and declared the Good News to any and all, spreading it around as so many seeds to germinate and reproduce. ...

"Secondly, this Word of God made flesh has the power to infuse his followers with life, and not just ordinary life but life seasoned with a taste of eternity. And more, he gives understanding, a sense of the difference between right and wrong, and by his Spirit applies the Good News to our memory and our conviction. In this we are empowered to love our neighbor as ourselves and thus to live ethically as well as religiously. We may err from time to time, but we can live in hope of pardon for our errors, both because we are learning and because it is God who is at work within us to accomplish his own grand plan for Creation. ...

"Third, John says that Moses brought the Law, and the Law brought us down by the power of its condemnation. The law tells us what is necessary to be decent citizens in a world of indecent inclinations and how to remain clean amidst all the human filth that has piled up in the world. But, unfortunately, our failures create a bad conscience, which leads us to discouragement. No matter how many times we are forgiven, we fall once again into feelings of guilt."

At that negative point in his sermon, MacNeal paused and looked out upon his people. Then, smiling, he continued. "Wonder of wonders," he said, " in the fullness of time, he who is full of grace and truth came to bless and restore us, no matter how great our failure. Jesus insisted the heart of God — in both his teachings and his deeds — is the heart of a Father. A Father, I say, not one to condemn or to avenge his anger. Apparently the Creator saw something good in us, something he wished to preserve, and even more, to refine.

"I cannot help but insert a thought, that God, who seemed angry with his creation, relented and promised not to destroy the earth but to sustain it. Somehow, beyond human reason, God thought of a way to nurture his creatures into becoming something noble, perhaps a community that would reflect hi heavenly intent, that there be harmony in the world. After eon of time, the human race had come into being as something neare to the heart of God than anything before.

"But I am flying off into the mystical, and I have in mind a practical conclusion. Let us get back to the Bible.

"Jesus backed up his teachings by dying for them, and ir dying he certified his validity as the Son of his Father, a true hero and established his message as well: *Greater love hath no man thar this, that a man lay down his life for his friends.* You know, o course, that we are his friends if we follow him. And we learr elsewhere in Scripture that *God was in Christ reconciling the worl unto himself, not imputing their sins unto them.* Some people wil tell you that Jesus died because of our sins, in the sense of atonin; the wrath of God, and that has become a part of our cultura religion. But such an idea is not actually spelled out in the New Testament, as though we could find there the idea that God wa conflicted within himself. Rather, it is an idea that comes fron the Old Testament, where a lamb was sacrificed as atonement fo human sins. Jesus was called the Lamb of God, so it is easy enough to carry this imagery much further than necessary. But we can a least say this: Christ on the cross put an end to substitutionar atonement, put an end to the endless offering of sacrifice for sins which had already been forgiven within the heart of the Father Jesus acted out what the Father had already determined to do.

"The Lord was showing us, beyond our need for a clear conscience, how to live as children of the heavenly Father, hov to trust the Father, how to remain true to the Father *even if bein; true means dying for one's faith.* He is saying that God will justif; such sacrifice, and the dead shall not have died in vain. Greate love has no one, John reminds us, than one who will die fo his friends. And Jesus died for us that we might have a stron; confidence in him. And the testimony of the Church across th centuries is that we know the heart of God through the death o Jesus: that God is love. And we would die for this faith rather tha betray it or misrepresent it or sully it. Why, our greatest shame would be to disgrace the sacred name and sacrifice of Jesus. This is, on one level, hero worship, of course, but Jesus is the True Hero. Please remember that spiritual truth nearly always contains various levels of understanding. As one grows one comprehends more and more of the insights of sacred theology.

"This is the content of John's declaration of the Good News: What God demands of us God has provided in Jesus Christ. He is the Savior. Do you believe this? And I also ask, *If not, why not?* It is both what we need and want, which makes me conclude that God had our need in mind. Also, *there is nothing better to believe, but much that is poor in comparison that we might believe to our loss.* And, dear friends, unbelief is its own condemnation. Amen."

The organ swelled into a concluding and appropriately victorious paean:

> *God of grace and God of glory,*
> *On thy people pour thy power;*
> *Crown thine ancient church's story;*
> *Bring her bud to glorious flower.*
> *Grant us wisdom, Grant us courage,*
> *For the facing of this hour,*
> *For the facing of this hour.*

Both words and melody soared into the sublime, and I felt a great pride to be a part of such a wonderful thing as Christ's Church. Verse after verse wafted heavenward as a fervent prayer for ourselves, the Church and our world. My spirit was lifted, as though it were flying upward with the hymn, so that near the end I could not read the words and simply stood transfixed.

Reverend MacNeal took his place in the narthex and began greeting his flock as they filed by in traditional order. A genial buzz filled the area. I was able, by waiting, to have my time to shake hands and introduce myself. He picked up on my name immediately and said that he looked forward to seeing me on Tuesday. It seemed to me that this appointment might be a notch or two above the tenor of my recent sessions in my own pastor's office.

I left the church and quickly put all that away for reflection some other day. For Colleen was on my mind, as she was more and more my center of thought and passion. Our dating had become quite serious, *heated* is the better word. Oh, *boiling*! And we had a leisurely day to ourselves planned, probably with dinner out and some time alone that evening. We were in the middle of a long weekend, with Monday free, which meant we had time to burn, a luxury in those busy, busy days.

9

EDEN ALL OVER AGAIN

Behold, thou art fair, my love; behold, thou art fair; ... thy breasts like young roes that are twins [hopping] among the lilies.

Song of Solomon 4

The Apostle Paul wrote to the believers at Rome, "And we know that all things work together for good to them that love God, to them that are called according to his purpose." It is a challenge for one's common sense to accept that old belief as yet valid, but many have taken such ancient verses personally over the centuries, with satisfaction. I had the backing of the Christian tradition to quote from the Bible as though it were written for my instruction. In fact, I was encouraged by my pastor to believe that God was personally nudging events so that they would turn out to my favor. I have no idea what God had in mind for anyone else, but I would leave the conflict up to Heaven to resolve. I wanted to believe things were going my way, desperately wanted to believe, wished and had tired of waiting for that kind of leading. And I also had been reminded that with God nothing is impossible.

In my case I sometimes felt besieged. I was lonely, and my demanding life had become humdrum. That Colleen was

in the picture both helped and complicated matters. And ye
I would not wish her away, no, not away but nearer. We were
seeing each other every available evening during my expanding
mix of knowledge, religious wrestlings and casting about for a
professional life. At the same time she sympathized with me for
wrestling with my desire for her in a world that restrains love
with too many taboos. Oh, the ecstasy of being in love! After al
the loneliness of the years, what better medicine could there be
than intimacy?

Our affair tumbled along.

My old home was dark, but the moonlight so bright as to
give the rooms a magic glow, its light beaming in at a slant upon
the shellacked floors. Our voices in the unlit master bedroom
were so soft that, were someone to be listening at a window, the
whirr of the oscillating fan would have scattered those syllable
into nonsense. And that was appropriate, for love is a private
matter.

"There's something you need to know," Colleen said, her
voice almost a whisper.

"What?" I replied, not really interested in continuing the
conversation.

There was a long pause. "I think you better get a towel."

I wasn't in the mood just then to go to the bathroom and
retrieve one.

"A towel?"

"Oh, darn it! You *have* to know..."

"What?" I asked again, this time somewhat agitated.

In the lightest voice, only a whisper, she said it plainly. "I'm
still a virgin."

I had managed to clear the obstacle course my society's taboo
placed before me, and I truly felt I could consummate my par

of our mutual desire without any further hesitation. More than think so, I was aroused beyond recall, wishing only to hold her, caress her and enjoy her. And then she dropped "I'm still a virgin" into the fiery magic of the night.

Lying there, propped up on one elbow, and facing her, I could see that tears were glistening on her moonlit cheek. The savage in me was stimulated to cover her and take my pleasure, but my old-fashioned sense of chivalry said no. And, I must confess, I faltered.

"Virgin? Good heavens!" I more than whispered, "What sort of man could marry you and not make love to you?"

I asked the question in a shocked manner, blurted it out, and knew instantly it was clumsy. For her pain at the moment occurred to me, as I knew her story, even if not this one detail. I put my arm around her waist, and whispered, "Please, forgive me. I'm not really suave at this, you know. And I guess you aren't either!" She squeezed my arm with a strength that surprised me.

I kissed the tears on her cheek, savoring their saltiness. She cupped my head in her hand and tried to choke back her sobbing. I thanked Heaven for that moment free from further words, for I needed to recover my balance. I did not say it, but I silently swore, *Damn!* It was the first time I had even thought of cussing since my overwhelming spiritual encounter of more than a year ago. And why not say what I felt? For this was a night I had anticipated with dreams of an ideal love, one in which I would be suave, and she calm, trusting me; and we two would consummate our passion in a rapturous embrace, winging away into bliss. *Damn!* Indeed, *double damn!*

And so we lay in bed, lovers still separated, but by nothing more than a need to remove this final secret. The stalemate was overcome as quickly as it had arisen. For as we lay there, unconsummated, we had achieved a complete mutuality. But we needed to catch our breath, to begin again. I rolled to my left and sat up, swinging my legs over the edge of the bed. "I'll make some coffee," I muttered as I shuffled away, dragging my trouser with me.

While I watched the coffee bubble up into the globe of the percolator, Colleen came into the kitchen, wearing only her slip and sat across from me. "Want to talk about it?" she asked. How I envied her that maturity. Of course I wanted to talk, but nothing in my training helped me to broach just plain talk about intimate things of this nature. First one was supposed, I somehow had concluded, to make love and then might or might not deal with the consequences of such intimacy.

I smiled as I thought of the old joke about the rabbit on rampage: "Wham, bam! Thank you Ma'am." Well, I thought *This is no tryst, it is the real thing. We'll deal with it, and it'll be part of our life forevermore.*

We talked for the duration of one cup of coffee, moving our chairs together at the table. At first Colleen faltered in her story but grew confident as she finally found the words to define her years-long agitation. The words tumbled out in a story of how her beau had courted her at their church and then swept her away in marriage to his mother's house. Things immediately changed for his mother hovered over him and ignored her. At first Colleen gave Sherman the benefit of the doubt, imagining how he must have felt with mother never farther than a bedroom wall away. Then she thought that he had to be somewhat indifferent about sex because he was inexperienced, but nothing she did to entice him created a response in those first days, and then she gave up and became a woman spurned.

Sherman spent considerable time fulfilling his mother's demands, and even more time with his old buddies, out hunting and fishing mostly, he said. Colleen finally accepted that not only did he not want her but never would. She described all this quite calmly, finally able to unburden herself. The rest I already knew, she left him and all that rejection and sham. She left and did the only thing she could. She returned to her parental home, where there was a welcome unencumbered by any demand to explain herself.

We sat and looked at each other as only lovers can, seeing ourselves as keepers of a terrible secret, and that made us partners even more. She said she felt like she had taken a bath, it was so good to tell me everything. I said I understood and that for my part, I had always wanted her but never had the courage to make a move in that direction while in high school. Oh, I confessed, I had spent many lonely times those first months away at boot camp, wondering what might have been had I made decisions other than what I chose. But that was then, and this was now, I reminded her, and I slipped the strap of her slip off her shoulder, forgetting that I was in a lit kitchen.

I turned off the table lamp and took her hand, and by the light of the moon we moved back to the bedroom.

— 10 —

Afterglow and Undertow

The morn is up again, the dewy morn,
with breath all incense.

Lord Byron, *Childe Harold*

Sunday night, oh, Sunday, Sunday night! My life was wrenched from its demanding routine and filled with ecstasy. The earth shook, and the foundations of life shifted. But I, fatigued, fell into deep sleep as though drugged.

Colleen's gentle breathing was my Monday morning reminder of our night together. Our inhibitions had fallen away, much as cast off items of clothing around the bed, evidence of something wild and disorderly in our lives. Deliriously in love, we had embarked upon a new commitment. I shifted my weight and felt her shift too. We lay there silently, sensing each other's breathing, feeling the slightest movement but trying not to disturb the other. As I think back upon that moment, I consider it one of the most precious memories of my life. Later I would understand the magic:

And Isaac brought her into his mother Sarah's tent,
and took Rebecca, and she became his wife; and he

loved her: and Isaac was comforted after his mother's death.

Each of us felt, we discovered later, that we had been born again in our embrace. How many rebirths can one person experience, we asked? Or is it better to say that we are refreshed? Who knows? It made no difference to us just then, for we were not analytical nor did we ever again try to parse that evening.

Monday was a holiday, a delightful pause in an otherwise frenzied schedule. Like any other couple in love and exhausted, we lazed, went out for brunch and then enjoyed the beach. The late afternoon hours were spent back at my home. Colleen's red hair did not include a red hot temper, but I found her possessed of a passion so uninhibited as to be daunting. Somewhere during this second day of our new beginning, I thought that I should be feeling some sort of guilt, at least a twinge, but I was happily distracted from formalities for the moment. Nevertheless, in the back of my mind I caught a glimpse of Reverend Gaines clicking his tongue against his upper teeth. But he could not compete with Colleen. I ignored him, and he faded away as so much smoke.

Not until mid-evening did we began to think of Tuesday and its schedules. There were things to do for the next day's classes, so Colleen dragged herself away by eight o'clock. I had to admit to myself that I was relieved, for exhaustion had set in. By ten I checked my clock to be sure the alarm was not on, smiled at my defiance of all things common, and slept to eight. And like many another man, I kept this little secret to myself. Women like that: keeping a secret, that is, not male defiance.

The holiday weekend was a new beginning but also a daunting challenge. We had broken the inhibition that kept us apart, and now freed, were destined to struggle for a new way of life, to pay whatever price, that we might find ourselves not only free but open in our commitment.

Tuesday I awoke thinking not of Colleen but of Pastor MacNeal. If I had been soaring aloft the day before, thinking the next day about facing a man of God, right after such stolen joy, brought me back to earth. *Do ministers have an insight, a sense of one's misbehavior? Might he detect an afterglow?* And thus I bothered myself.

As I drove into town for the interview I whistled a happy tune. But, I had to admit, I was also smitten. *Let's see*, I said to myself, *what are my priorities now?* I began to rehearse my agenda. By the grace of God I arrived at my destination without running into any other cars.

Reverend MacNeal was ensconced in a spacious office done in the conservative manner of old money. I looked about at dark oak furniture and paneled walls and a large and polished desk with papers upon it in neat stacks. As soon as I walked in, the minister shut the door and turned to me. "Please sit, Timothy," he said. "Feel free to relax, and we'll talk awhile." He smiled and sat down, swiveling around in his handsome leather chair, the brass tacks shining as though to distract me. But MacNeal continued saying, "I suppose you wish to talk about your professional education, as you mentioned last week. Is that it?"

I hardly heard the question, for his office with its brass tacks and oak paneling had distracted me from my agenda. It occurred to me that while Gaines was intent upon diverting me to a fledgling house church in an indistinct neighborhood, my denomination was simultaneously looking for seminary graduates to work with ministers in churches like this. It was only a flash of recognition and not my primary concern. I snapped back to the present and rallied to his query. The conversation moved along as I had hoped.

MacNeal was personable, easing in a question about my family life from time to time, asking about my experience at The Palms, interweaving his own thoughts about college and seminary education as we continued. In all, he was quite disarming. I felt much more at ease than I had thought possible, my private life apparently of no concern to him just then.

Yes, he said, he was a Princeton Seminary graduate, although his pastor had recommended the "other" seminary a bit farther south, at Richmond. He had gone to Princeton University for one year and then decided that if he was going to attend the seminary too, it would be better to transfer somewhere else for a few years, to get a change of scenery. He switched to Yale, serving as a part-time youth director at a Congregational church just up the Connecticut River from Old Saybrook. It was a good decision, he said.

We then talked about the Texas seminary recommended by Dr. Gaines and my questions concerning the curriculum. This, I said, led to my dawning awareness that I had not met any other Presbyterian pastors during my many months at the beach church nor met others from nearby Presbyterian churches.

MacNeal replied, "Tim, I think we should talk about that, although it is not why you came here. Not directly anyhow. You ought to know that your pastor is not in the good graces of the presbytery and does not associate with his fellow ministers in the metropolitan area." He looked at me with a solemnity that was new to our conversation. He continued, "Mister Gaines does not support our common objectives, is loathe to have our missionaries speak at his church and has not supplied any lay leaders for our boards and committees for two years. In other words, he is an utter maverick. He sends his college-bound young people to independent colleges, and any candidates for the ministry attend the Texas school you mentioned. Only one member of his church has gone to a denominational seminary, my very own Princeton. And that young man is now a persona non grata at The Palms. He was accused of losing his faith while at seminary. It would be better to say the young man changed his opinion about some items of faith."

Then he said, looking directly at me, "You must understand that it is entirely possible to lose one's faith while in seminary for there is much to learn that is never taught in Sunday school and then there are matters like religious foolishness and duplicity in the ministry. But those who lose their faith do not go into pastoral ministry. No, they normally just get out of institutional religion."

This information required some discussion, so I countered, "But how did Reverend Gaines become so non-supportive? I know for a fact that he went to a Presbyterian seminary up in Alabama and that he also has a doctoral diploma. He is a professional man who has high standards — and an ethical man?" I ended the statement as a question, an indication of my confusion.

"Ah! His credentials. You may as well hear it from me. His seminary is not recognized by our denomination. It's a reactionary school that holds nearly all things Presbyterian suspect. And as for that doctorate, you need to know that it came from a degree mill, a quick in, quick out correspondence course; probably cost him three or four hundred dollars. We did a little research on him because of that diploma. He has a nominal education: two years of bible college, two or perhaps three years at a seminary and that's it. When he came to us he withheld the fact that he possessed such a certificate, but very soon people were referring to him as 'Doctor Gaines.' We inquired about it, and since he could not produce an adequate diploma, that became the breaking point. He must have given the elders at his church a song and dance routine, as they have remained loyal to him. In fact, they have become distanced from the rest of us."

This disclosure left me speechless. My mind raced over the past year's experiences under Greg's tutelage, recalling various incidents that suddenly made sense. My face felt as though it were afire. At the moment I was inhibited from expressing the anger building within me, and that was probably for the best. For considering that I was not being entirely open about my own conduct just then — and no one was asking — I needed to be discreet about Gaines' deceit.

The intercom buzzed, breaking our exchange. Reverend MacNeal turned to answer it and then said, "Oh, he's here early is he? Please tell him to come in." Turning to me, the pastor said that a colleague had arrived, and that before I departed it would be good to meet him.

There was a rap on the door before the caller entered, not waiting for a reply. A middle-aged man, smiling as he gently shut the door, provided a break from the intensity of our conversation. He was slightly pudgy and with thinning brown curly hair, dressed in summer clothes, a beige jacket over his arm "Hey y'all" he said cheerfully and looked in my direction. I immediately liked his disarming style and stood to greet him.

Pastor MacNeal answered his colleague with, "Ralph, I'm glad you're here. Now you can meet a new man on his way to ministry, Timothy DuPease. Timothy, Reverend Ralph Hatfield."

The new minister made a quick read of me and, as he extended his hand, said, "So, Timothy DuPease. A descendant of the Huguenots no doubt. We Hatfields have some DuPuis in our ancestry. Glad to meet you."

It all came out so fast that I didn't know how to answer, especially because I did not know the details of our family history. "Thanks," I said, fumbling for what to say next. I had not yet recovered from the astounding revelation of Gaines' duplicity, and I felt dizzy.

Reverend MacNeal answered for me. "Ralph, we've been deeply serious these last few minutes. I doubt Timothy is in the mood for small talk just now. You need to know that he's in tow to Gregory Gaines, and I've told him about that mess."

"Uh." That's all the response Reverend Hatfield gave. He looked at me and then back at his colleague.

We then sat down and chatted a bit. As I talked about my military service, including that I was last in Bethesda, near Washington, D.C., MacNeal leaned forward and said,

"Washington! Why what a coincidence. Did you ever attend the New York Avenue Presbyterian Church?"

I affirmed that I had, without giving details.

"Well then, you must have heard my good friend Pete Marshall preach." MacNeal was beaming. He asked for an account of my experience.

I could not recall the sermon, for I was not an experienced listener, but I was impressed by the building and the interior, the choir, and by Marshall's charismatic personality. He held the congregation in the palm of his hand and made them laugh a few times. My response seemed to satisfy the question.

Reverend Hatfield interrupted this interchange in what I was to learn was his spontaneous style, saying, "By George! I can't believe you've been there. Talk about coincidence, I have just finished reading *A Man Called Peter*, written by his widow only recently. Catherine. In fact, there it is." He pointed to a book next to his jacket on the sofa. He went on to inform me that Marshall died of a heart attack soon after I had visited the church, and that his wife wrote a biography of his unusual and captivating life. Then Hatfield pressed the volume into my hands, insisting I read it as a model for ministry. I thanked him as I took the book, not knowing what a treasure I held in my hands.

Our visit lasted only a few minutes longer, as I had been advised. I expressed my gratitude at having the interview and departed. I felt both good about having passed the initial test and dismayed about Gaines' fake doctorate.

The drive to work was only a matter of minutes, just enough time for me to understand that I had more on my plate than asked for. I would put some items on the back burner for the moment. As for the loaner, I put the book aside but resolved to read it as soon as possible.

That week I wrote to Princeton Seminary, asking the registrar for any material they usually send to student inquirers.

Colleen and I had a date arranged for dinner and perhaps a movie on Friday, and I had in mind that we would probably spend the night at my place. I picked her up at six o'clock and we went directly to a restaurant. We tried very hard to behave ourselves at dinner, remaining on opposite sides of the table and only playing footsies most of the time. But Colleen was not herself. She tried to pay attention but she seemed distracted, frowning whenever she was not engaged in talk. I asked her about it after dinner. She dabbed her eyes and said she just didn't feel well, and it wasn't a good time to be out, that's all. I was nonplused and suggested that perhaps we should call off the movie. She agreed. The drive back to her place was made in silence, and when we got there she began to sniffle again.

I wondered what I had done or what could be bothering her. She acted irritated that I would even ask. Oh, she said, it was just "that time," and there was nothing we could do about it.

Ah! Me, the bachelor. I agreed to just let her out of the car and wait for her call. Tomorrow, perhaps?

When I got home the phone was ringing. Colleen, composed but cool, said we needed to talk, but it could wait until Sunday afternoon. I agreed but suggested that we might go to church Sunday morning.

"Where?" she asked.

"Perhaps a neutral church," I said. Or did she prefer her family church? She said that group did not respect divorced persons and that she was not really welcome there, especially by the women. I agreed that we should wait and talk on Sunday afternoon. With that we ended our interchange.

I was strongly tempted to attend worship at Reverend Hatfield's church, but opted to stay home and catch up on various tasks. *Backslider*, my conscience said, and I replied, *Oh, shut up!*

The Sunday afternoon appointment to talk ("just talk") resulted in some mature decision making. We agreed that our love was too precious to endanger by sleeping under the same roof in unavoidable view of friends and neighbors. Beyond this, our religious training informed us that we were being irresponsible, and we did not wish to be trapped into a double life, for we fully intended to remain within the Church.

Our agreement to discipline ourselves opened the conversation to Colleen's status as a divorced woman, and my intention to study theology. We decided that we would have to do some church visiting and give ourselves time to sort out our feelings. She was more than willing to cooperate. Interestingly, we covered all this without ever openly considering marriage.

Pastor MacNeal agreed with me that it would be a good idea to worship at some of the Presbyterian churches in the area and get to know both the leaders and members. Colleen agreed to go with me on Sunday mornings but not the evenings. Her school duties were consuming more time as the semester got underway. For my part, I needed my evenings for study. This compromise was becoming a less than spontaneous affair.

And there was the matter of my membership in The Palm Church. Although my decision was to remain distant, after two weeks away from all activities I was feeling uneasy. Predictably, Gaines chose to call at that moment of anxiety. But of course. He was a shepherd to his flock, and I a stray, one who had been at church as often as there was a gathering. It did not occur to me at the moment, but he must have felt uneasy about our last encounter in his office, for he really stepped out from behind his persona. But he did call, and I had to deal with it. He wasted no time getting to his concern about my absence, asking if I was well.

I said, "Well, Greg, I have felt uncomfortable lately, as you probably suspect. And this feeling led me to think that I needed a little space for reflection. So, I should tell you that very soon then I made an appointment with Reverend MacNeal at Eastminster Church, to hear what he knows about Presbyterian seminaries. You recall, I'm sure, that I said I would continue to look into the subject. And then I thought it would be helpful to attend a service, to hear him preach. And he was helpful."

After a slight pause, Gaines said, "Well! I must tell you I did not think you would do that, and I am provoked with you. I told you those institutional men are so fixed upon their procedures that they've forgotten their 'first love,' the Lord Jesus. I must stress, Timothy, that you are straying into dangerous territory. Why would you take his advice, a man you have only just met, and reject mine?" He sounded properly miffed.

I thought, *My! I didn't know he cared so much.* But I said, "Well, the fact is, I feel I'm entitled to more than one opinion. It does seem I should be able to talk to someone else without provoking resentment." I was amazed that I had said this.

"Just be warned," he said, sounding miffed in his response, "that most denominational seminaries teach higher criticism and vain philosophy. One of our young men went up to Princeton Seminary a few years back, and he immediately began to lose his faith, to preach a form of religion but not the power thereof."

I could stand no more, for we were playing a game, not of cat-and-mouse but of two tomcats making low growling sounds. And I was beginning to feel the need for saying something direct, so I blurted out, "Well, at least your young man studied with well educated professors in a certified seminary rather than resorting to a mail-order degree mill." At that, I stopped, thinking, *Oh my God! What have I done?*

Gaines did not respond. After a long silence, in which we said nothing, I heard the telephone at the other end click, and the disconnect tone began. I sat listening to the hum for a moment, then put the phone on its cradle.

That I had made such a belligerent comment, even if it had merit, shocked me. I paid him no respect, in spite of his many hours given to my training. But my cutting remark laid bare a deeply hidden secret. He had pretended, and I failed to play his game. Yes, I struck home, proving MacNeal was right. Gaines flipped his lid, I thought, and smiled at the image of his toupée popping off his bean. I basked in a rare moment of truth but then recalled that I too was in need of repair.

But before that moment's sad conclusion, I truly had wanted to trust him and consider him my good friend and advisor. Yes, that was it. He had misled me. He was not a real friend, I concluded. Behind his persona of running things for Jesus he was a tyrant, and that explained his calm control of every occasion. It also explained why I did not fear I might betray his friendship when I moved so deliberately into my affair with Colleen, for I sensed that I did not owe him the unwavering obedience most gave him. The modern concept of brainwashing had emerged by that time in our American history of conflict with Russia and China, and many younger Americans were quick to see the subtle implications at work in our own political machinery and, yes, in some of our religious sects.

Aside from that after-the-fact observation, our mentoring relationship had taken a twist similar to what shipmates undergo in the navy. We would pair up, share experiences and go out on beer drinking sprees together, and in general become really good friends, sharing family secrets and personal experiences. We would help each other in tough times and lend each other money, usually without keeping track of exactly what the balance might be. Then we would be reassigned, one to shore duty and the other to a new ship. A meaningful friendship was broken, one man at sea, one ashore. *Adieu!* We used to say. *A turn of the screws erases all debts.*

I did owe Gaines a debt of gratitude, in part for what he and his leaders taught me, even if some of it was questionable, and in part for what he allowed me to learn as his assistant and Man Friday around the church. That debt would go unpaid. But I would struggle with his indoctrination for years to come. Indeed, I eventually concluded, I had paid dearly, and more than once, and something was due me in turn. In fact, simply recounting this denouement is a confession of my uneasy feeling after all these years. Why, why oh why, must Christians insist upon being right and oh, so very righteous all the time? Why do we not more readily trust each other with our doubts and temptations? Why, when we disagree, must we insist on justifying ourselves at the expense of others? Why do we imagine that God has favored us above those we dislike?

My connection with The Palms Church ended. No elder or fellow member called. No newsletters arrived in the mail. I had become a shunned person, I concluded, cut off but probably prayed for a few times before being allowed to sink with the sun, never more to rise. The Palms was, I had to accept, a church that brooked no variation in doctrine or loyalty.

This shunning accomplished at least one part of its purpose, for I did feel the sting, and my helplessness in it all, but I also felt resentment. For heaven's sake, I had been an unpaid volunteer in the church, who also tithed. *Tithed.* Ten percent up front to the Lord's work at The Palms, just as the pastor expected. Of course I had heard the pastor and leaders express their disapproval of liberals and the denominational leaders, who were "blind leaders of the blind." Such judgment was rather impersonal, leaving names unnamed, so it never occurred to me that a pastor such as Reverend MacNeal might be thought of as spiritually blind.

I sailed away from phase one of my apprenticeship. But I did not see clearly that people of faith are seafarers in every generation. Well, I use nautical terms where the Bible calls its wanderers pilgrims. Where, I asked myself, was the stability, where my compass and my chart? When I left the navy behind and returned home I thought I was opting for a steady life.

It took a while to think through, to *feel* this new situation and embrace it. The answer began to form in my mind as I talked with Will, my attorney friend from church who engineered my first sermonette at the municipal jail. He was a free spirit, quite suave and sometimes droll, never saying a word of criticism or judgment about anyone. Typically, he used to quote, "Beware when all men speak well of thee."I would not have been surprised had he said it just then, when we met casually on the street downtown. Talking frankly about my disappearance from church, I told Will of both the pastor's and Hal's warnings about liberal seminaries and how that disappointed me, but I said nothing about the pastor's bogus degree.

"Tim," Will said, in his wry manner, "you should know that some people are sure of what they believe, and others are cocksure."

I thanked him for his wisdom and moved on, sending my best wishes to his wife. They were a lovely and hospitable couple, given to a ministry of friendship among a variety of acquaintances.

Things were to work out for good much more quickly than I was inclined to expect in my confused state of mind. During that interval I read the book Reverend Hatfield lent me about Peter Marshall's life and ministry. What a refreshing inspiration it was! Without being fully aware of the dynamic, I discovered in Marshall my role model. His sermons became my guides, his prayers models to be repeated. My new standard for ministry included a form of spirituality that I could comprehend, a mixture of piety and mysticism in alliance with established religion.

But most of all, Marshall was a man of personal conviction and integrity. I would buy a copy of the book for myself and read it again, keeping it in my small collection of books as a favorite to be opened from time to time. And this discovery was easier because Jesus was also Marshall's Hero.

The Christ Marshall preached was a man among men, a rough-handed carpenter, who knew life at a common level and championed the common people. *That* Jesus did not put up with pompous fops nor religious poseurs. *No sir!* "The Master," as Marshall called him, was a kind and fearless teacher who enjoyed sitting at table with the common folk and teaching them by telling stories they could understand. God's unconditional love was often his theme.

The Master is still making his way along the paths of the centuries, walking into our times with his wisdom and compassion. We may encounter him, or he encounter us, in our daily tasks. For he is our friend, a man without guile, fearless, generous and one it is very good to know. He spoke for God and still clearly speaks for God, so anyone who has ears to hear may yet learn a thing or two. I like to think of this truth as, *The Bos'n is still pipin'*.

I identified with that experience. Surely then the silent Nudge that moved me to the ministry was no less than the Son of God, the Lord of the Church and the Savior of the world. At times while reading Marshall's biography I felt that same conviction for myself, that same love, that gratitude.

WISE COUNSEL

The Reverend Ralph Hatfield pastored a church in Salem Gables, a planned residential village near the university. His church, the Inverness Presbyterian, was situated on the boulevard within the De Leon Center, a sedate hub of stylish retail shops and restaurants. The church's architecture was of Mexican Colonial style, with free standing bell tower. One might think it an ancient building, but in fact it was fairly new. The entire community had sprung up within a few decades, as investors rushed into Miami, especially after the Great War to End All Wars. Much of the money came in from the Northeast and New York, Cleveland and Chicago.

Colleen and I arrived well before the service, as Reverend Hatfield suggested it would be good to meet, if only for a few minutes, and to walk around the plant as we chatted. When we arrived there were already many cars in the parking lot as well as along the streets around the church. Along with those who prepared for the morning worship service, there were Sunday school classes for all ages, including a large men's class that met in the balcony.

"Ah, there you are!" Pastor Hatfield fairly shouted as he came toward us. "I've just now cleared a few minutes for our little tour around the building." He bustled about like the genteel dean of a cathedral, greeting the volunteers as we scurried along. Colleen was pleased to be received with such enthusiasm. We saw what was essential of the layout very quickly and then went to his office, where he checked the calendar and wrote my name in for an interview. With that, we parted company, as he was a busy person. The sanctuary was full of chatter, in contrast to my previous experience at the Eastminster Church. The usher had been alerted to our visit and gently led us nearly all the way up front.

During the morning announcements the minister welcomed visitors especially, naming us as his guests that morning, adding that I was a pre-ministerial student at the university. We stood, so people could see us, and noticed that there were several other visitors who also stood. We had all taken care to wear our Sunday best and looked like we enjoyed being seen. After the service I was impressed by how many members took the time to speak to us.

Afterwards, we compared notes and agreed we could fit into the congregation. But much would depend upon the next few weeks, as we got to know the pastor better. My session in his office was to take place the next week. However, I received a call from him on Tuesday saying that a cancellation made it possible for us to meet on Thursday, and would I be able to make it? Yes, I could and would.

"You're right on time, Timothy, and welcome!" the pastor said as I arrived.

We shook hands, then Mister Hatfield launched into a series of questions. Was my lady friend a serious item? How long had I known her? Was she Presbyterian? What did she do? I began to think the pastor was more interested in Colleen than in me, and I smiled slightly as he continued poking around my private life. He picked up my uneasiness and moved directly in on my intentions to be a minister. How had I found my way to the beach church? Was I serious about studying theology? What impression did I have of Eastminster Church and Reverend MacNeal? This must have gone on for ten minutes before we wore off our initial energy. To this point he was still asking and I answering. But then he took a new tack and invited questions. He practically challenged me to ask anything I had in mind.

I liked his way, really. I decided to ask about his ministry beginning with how long he had been at this church. I soon knew that he was married and had twin adolescent sons and a ten-year old daughter. His wife, Lois, was from New Hampshire. They met at Rollins College, up in Winter Park, his home town. He and Lois married after his first year of seminary in Kentucky. This was not the accepted practice in those years prior to the war. He said the two of them plus a few others blazed the trail for the changes that came in the forties. Increasingly, seminarians especially veterans, began studies as married men. Lois majored in science and worked as a lab technician, which enabled him to study more and work part-time at a church near the seminary. She was presently doing clinical work at the university hospital, mostly because their children were getting closer to college age. He said the church was generous enough, but he would never be able to put two boys through school at the same time.

"So you and your wife have married religion and science," said, hoping for a laugh.

He chuckled at the suggestion. "Oh, did we used to have rowdy debates!" he said, raising his eyebrows and smiling broadly. "Seminary was quite an experience for some of the students, those who came from conservative homes and churches, often from small towns and orthodox backgrounds. We had a heavy course on the relationship of science to religion, or was it the other way around? Anyhow, we read much of the material coming out of both religion and science on the subject of evolution. The subject was really hot back then, and it had split Princeton Seminary not very long before. Most of old-time orthodoxy would not concede an inch to science. 'The new science,' they called it. But most of us conceded the legitimacy of scientific findings. All too many feared that engaging in debate with scientists was like letting the camel get its nose into the tent. Once inside, the tent has all hell to pay!" He laughed loudly, then continued, "Lois was very helpful to me in those studies, for she not only had a logical mind but plenty of science tucked away in that ample brain of hers. But eventually one must admit that the two subjects demand exclusive spaces. So, it is not so much a case of denying things as trying to affirm them while not losing sight of the benefits of our ancient wisdom."

"Oops!" he said, "I see we've been at this overtime. I have some items that need my attention, so I must move on. As they say, 'Do the next thing.' I hope we can continue these sessions, for there are some things I think you must decide rather soon."

I agreed, and at his suggestion stopped by the secretary's desk to arrange our next meeting. It would be the following week. And since I had been frank about Colleen, but not entirely frank, we agreed that she should come along.

When I initiated talks with Colleen about simplifying our life, she grew cool. She was a divorcée, I was to recall, and would have to produce the papers of divorce in order to get a license to marry anew, short of lying through her teeth, so her status was bound to become public. I was going into the ministry, she also reminded me, and would probably find such a marriage inconvenient when seeking a church. Nor could we sneak away to a justice of the peace, not if I was going to work for the church. We played ping pong in this way with our relationship and my calling. I was not sure if she was simply expressing her inner thoughts or nudging me toward a major decision. I suspected we were not entirely rational about the matter back then, knowing it was tough and at the same time wanting to resolve it amicably.

By then we had agreed that it was time to consult with someone, most logically a minister. Hatfield gave the appearance of being broad-minded, so perhaps we could gain a counselor We looked forward, therefore, to the appointment.

We entered his office with great hope but no experience a such counseling. He turned out to be a go-getter, moving directly to the task. His first item was to ask us to call him Pastor Ralph a name he preferred over Reverend except in formal situations And, if we felt like it, just Ralph would do. From there he stormed into our privacy, gathering facts together as he sped along.

He summed up what he thought was our concern. "So then you two are at the point of making some major decisions but fea what deciding might do to you." He drummed his fingertips on his desk.

We nodded and said a weak yes in reply. I assumed that he could read between the lines and therefore intuited more than we had said.

"So...," he said, again, "I must ask you: Are you willing to continue with me, if I take over and give some opinions and advice that you'll need to weigh carefully?"

The pastor had not moved from behind his desk to a spo nearer us. We were so inexperienced in such counseling as not to expect anything more than what we got. We then agreed to hi proposition to give us direct advice.

"You two are not unusual in any way I can see, and you situation is repeated more often than you would expect, especiall in the senior year, when our ministerial students prepare to mov into career studies at one seminary or another. As likely as no there is a woman in the picture, and graduation from colleg often implies a marriage quite soon. You can see the recipe fo precipitous decisions and feelings of anxiety, I believe. But yo two are older and for that reason I think we could be just a ta lenient here." He then smiled for the first time since our initia greetings and said, "Now, let's get to this divorce of yours."

Hatfield drew in a big breath, as though he had somethin very serious in mind. He did, in fact, and began, "There are a fev New Testament references that take a severe stance about divorc and remarriage among Christians. If we were to take these words literally we'd be right back with the Medieval Church, demanding a chastity that is hardly ever achieved. And that means feeling guilty for having very natural appetites. You know what I mean? Good! That sort of rigidity is the rule of the monks, and there is evidence that they did not always obey it either. But I want you to consider that nowhere in the Christian Scriptures do we find a codex of marriage and divorce laws for the faithful." He paused, and seeing a hint of questioning in our expressions, continued.

"If one takes the words of Christ literally regarding divorce and adultery, then you two should not marry, and especially as far as being leaders in the church is concerned. But that old rule was written back when everyone expected the end of days to come at any time, and marriage was a long-term matter. It hardly made sense to marry and perhaps also get pregnant, when the End was near. The End, you know, was to include weeping and gnashing of teeth. There would be wars and earthquakes, armies against armies. The citizens of Jerusalem would have to flee to the hills, and all of that. Also, the old rules were given in context. Our Lord was talking to his fellow Jews, who permitted bigamy and more, perhaps four. And the old rules allowed a divorce procedure that favored the husband and not the wife. You know, don't you, that women were chattel back then? Because of this context, and because the Apostle Paul also had a few things to say about the subject, the Church at large has usually had some sort of working codex at hand to resolve marital complexities." He paused and looked for reaction.

"Ah! Do I sense you wondering what a codex is?" We nodded, so he continued. "It's a formalization of the various rules and practices, which then also permits dealing with exceptions. We call it church law. The Roman Church has had canon law to guide it beyond the literal words of Scripture, and we Protestants have developed similar rules. Of course, we modern Protestants, being so independent, often choose to ignore other persons' ideas and do what we feel is right, or at least what is best. We are moderns, you know. And I don't mean that we are modernist but that we are a democratic people. We have no kings or bishop telling us how to lead our lives. We say, 'Let your conscienc be your guide.' But there are norms, even in the Presbyteriar Church." He laughed.

Hatfield paused, looked serious once more, and said. "I thinl you two should quit playing games and get married."

Colleen spoke out immediately. "But no church would accep me as a preacher's wife!" She said it with such certainty that I wa stunned, and then she began to cry, which upset me. But I saic nothing for fear of losing my own control.

"My dear, please don't be so hard on yourself," he said. "Ther are conditions we have not yet considered." The pastor did no seem at all disoriented by a woman's tears. He passed a box o tissues to me to hand to her and continued waiting while sh blew her nose and settled down.

Then he said, "There are reasons for divorce, beginning witl the New Testament, so that just the fact of divorce carries n stigma at all. Perhaps there are extenuating circumstances fo your separation. The churches within Christendom have ofte declared a marriage null and void, or to put it in formal terms they have 'annulled' marriages. Do you think there is anythin like that in your situation?"

Back on track! I practically jumped up. "Of course!" exclaimed, "Why didn't I think of that?" And then I felt foolisl for I was, in effect, answering for Colleen. It was a clums moment, but she let me off the hook, saying that yes, she ha heard of annulment for marriages not consummated, but that he church did not consider such legal action scriptural. And beside she had not demanded a civil divorce on that basis because i was far too embarrassing to divulge her personal situation, so sh opted for the more common reason of incompatibility. State lav was very lax regarding divorce based on such claims.

I was pleased by her maturity in making such a revealin statement to Pastor Ralph. And he must have understood wha she was saying, for he did not ask anything further of her. So, at last, our dilemma was now defined. The discussion went rapidly for the next few minutes. And then he offered to marry us post haste and so put an end to our agony.

Our wedding was simple, celebrated in the church chapel on the Saturday morning before Thanksgiving break from studies. The ceremony was attended by a few friends and close family plus church members who assisted the minister. We were soon away and headed on a honeymoon that lasted for the week, a time of joy and release. We returned to a schedule that left us breathless most of the time.

Pastor Ralph took me into his ministry practically immediately. I was given part-time employment at the church as their youth director, supervised by the minister of Christian education. I then "moved on up" from a part-time credit interviewer at Sears Roebuck to part-time servant of a servant of God. For me, this role of assistant to the pastor proved a godsend, for he taught me the basics of the church calendar and its liturgy, the use of various colored paraments and assigned readings for Sundays. He did much to sweep away some simplistic ideas from my previous indoctrination and replaced them with a sensible approach to religion.

— 12 —

UPGRADING THEOLOGY

As being is to becoming, so is truth to belief. If then,
Socrates, amid the many opinions about the gods
and the generation of the universe, we are not able
to give notions which are altogether and in every
respect exact and consistent with one another, do not
be surprised. Enough if we adduce probabilities as
likely as any others; for we must remember that I
who am the speaker and you who are the judges are
only mortal men.

Timaeus

The Collected Dialogues of Plato
Quoted from *The Whole Shebang*,
by Timothy Ferris

Reverend Gaines did not inveigle me to join his church, neve
tempted me with false promises, nor did he attempt to teac
me anything that I did not consent to study. After all this time
am still convinced that our relationship was a mutual agreemen
But, once I had yielded to his influence and volunteered to wor
with him to promote his ministry, he slowly and deliberatel

attempted to use me for his own purposes. And that meant he tried to lure me away from what I believed was my calling. Our separation was written in the stars, I suppose, and it left us both disappointed.

In spite of our unhappy ending, I felt grateful for his personal times with me, the guidance he gave, his explanations of how denominations and missionary agencies function and his way of putting up with a very uninformed enthusiast. It has even occurred to me to wonder if I was an irritation to him because of my rather simple enthusiasm. As for his personal idiosyncrasies, I prefer to leave them for Heaven to resolve.

Farewell then, to my first mentor; and, thank you but no thank you too.

Pastor Ralph was something else, though not inferior to my previous pastor. Far from it! While Gaines was reserved and taken with a system of inerrant Scripture and the immanent return of Messiah, Hatfield was fully immersed in the life of his community and in the dynamics of contemporary theology. This included a passion for social action. He obviously enjoyed being the pastor of so many cultured church members and those times when he was legitimately in the center of things. He also enjoyed stealing the limelight at times when he would have done better to play it cool and give others a chance to shine. But in all, he was moderate and full of good-natured fun, never foolish nor resentful, so he swept along from day to day free of inhibitions and rarely in need of repentance. And I, I was very pleased to have found a passage back to the real world into which I was born and the one I wished to understand, where I would be free to probe for insights. Once again I could say Yes to life. It seemed enough to me to have some things to learn, to risk, to feel the tingle of discovery and rejoice in growth.

When I sat down to my first professional training session with Reverend Hatfield, I expected to learn about Presbyterianism.

But much more than that, I learned about contemporary religious thought. However, we began with the implications of the Enlightenment in the eighteenth century, then the onslaught of science in the nineteenth. Hatfield was doing for me what most scholars do with their subjects: he introduced a topic by first reviewing its background. He also commented that the church is usually a century behind the world around it, only cautiously admitting new ideas into its theology. It was not easy to make general statements about church history even within a single denomination. But we would try to sort out some of the major themes.

Prior to this mentoring I had learned scattered items about nineteenth century religious reaction to scientific theories. But I did not put these things together in any systematic way. Nor was the university faculty concerned about theology. Rather, the period of the Enlightenment was presented in most classrooms as a dynamic breakthrough in European thought that led to corrections of ages-old superstition and ignorance. We were told there was a type of chain reaction across several centuries: first the Protestant revolution came, freeing at least some Europeans from Catholic dogma and interference in politics. Then, after the religious wars that decimated Europe, the Enlightenment came, freeing nearly everyone from superstitions and ignorance as well as debunking some of the old shibboleths of Protestantism. The secular age had begun, although it was not called that in the earlier years.

Over a period of about five hundred years the Christian nations have slowly emerged from the Dark Ages, when thinking was local and quite simple. Relics such as the bones of saints from earlier times had become items of particular adoration, regarded as having spiritual power. Parish priests often were as ignorant as those to whom they ministered, but few knew this for the priest could appeal to the authority of the Church. It is said that in earlier times so many splinters from the True Cross from Golgotha were sold to local churches that if collected into a pile there would be enough wood to build a ship. Numerous churches had foreskins from the circumcision of Christ. And most shocking: concern with fertility had also invaded the churches, so that in some of them a statue of a "Saint Foutin" with a wooden penis attached was on display. Barren women could scrape off a few shavings and ingest them in water or wine in order to become fertile. Statues of the saint were especially popular around France. In earlier Protestant writings this abomination was occasionally cited to justify some of the more destructive acts of Protestants, as burning statues of saints in the public square or defacing sanctuaries and tearing down monasteries. That history is easily ignored and hidden from general discussions today, when we are more concerned with ecumenical healing. And this is not all bad, for all of us, from every denomination, have learned many things since the Reformation tore us apart.

The implications of a swing from religion to science was not a major item among the humanist lecturers at the university. Looking back on this from a later date, I believe they felt little need to attack religion in a world rushing toward a secular and scientific orientation.

John Dewey's philosophy of education reigned supreme in my field of study. He believed we could and should change ourselves for the better by our education but also by experiencing modern theories through hands-on experience. This is not as simple as it may appear, for he was actually proposing that we could trust our educational process, as we had learned quite a bit in the past several centuries. And he was at the same time insisting that we no longer could depend upon rote learning from the doctrinaire masters of the past. Scientists had their laboratories and future teachers would have to actually teach a semester and write a critique of the experience before graduating. Such thinking eventually produced technical schools as well, where students would learn the new sciences in both classroom and laboratory or even supervised on-the-job training.

This was a liberating philosophy. It would be my responsibility to decide many things for myself, but I would be accountable to both myself and society for my actions. This has come to be called the meritocracy. Such a philosophy was intended to develop a better social psychology and a better citizenry. This approach to public education was not termed ethics but was in fact the base for an new *ethos*, not a completely new one but one that built upon the ideas of a democracy of the people, by the people and for the people. This was a major shift over the past two centuries and more. Democracy was in its ascendancy, separating itself from both kings and bishops. The people would rule, sharing both the financing and benefits of a freely dispensed public education. All manner of new ideas of equality and secularity were being expressed. The most disturbing change, for the churches, was that outright atheism was more readily tolerated. It was not a new concept but had a fresh appeal to the secular mind.

But I stray, as old men often do. We cannot resist sharing our wisdom, which we have gathered across the decades by much study and sacrifice. It is common among us to fear that all progress might fail as we fade into history.

Reverend Hatfield said he was neo-orthodox. The term did not provoke me, for it seemed that everyone was "neo" something. New is not a bad word. For me it meant that he was probably a person who accepted the modern world.

An Excursus - The Move away from State Religion

As for orthodoxy, I hadn't the least idea what Hatfield was talking about. I had heard of Greek Orthodoxy and Jewish Orthodoxy but was not curious about them. At that time Roman Catholicism was simply known as Catholicism, no one bothering to mention that Catholics were orthodox. I thought of such religions as being led by bearded old men dressed in black. Supposedly they believed in stoning sinners and heretics — by permission of their theocratic leanings as well as the support of the king's government — while our civil law prohibits such brutality. Now, that's an irony.

Thinking about this, I had learned earlier that the Protestant men in black, the New England Puritans, had drowned or hung quite a few so-called witches along the way to establishing their "City set upon a Hill." That they too were orthodox had not occurred to me, and I was surprised to learn that the original Congregational Religion of New England was under state support until early in the 1800s, when the new Republic got around to voting on the disestablishment of religion. Connecticut was the last to go secular, in A.D. 1818.

That the founders of our American Republic were not loyal supporters of the established churches came as a surprise the first time I read of it.

Back to Pastor Ralph and His Mentoring

Pastor Ralph was insistent that I understand that neo-orthodox Christians also believe in the fundamental tenets of their religion. He would have me know that "We attempt to interpret the old ways in modern terms understandable to educated people. We accept that religion is about sin and salvation, for instance. But we have studied the changes in thinking since the Enlightenment and have produced a system of theology that takes factual knowledge into account. This new theology is more existential, dynamic, than the older creedal systems," he said. "We have moved away from absolutist thinking to more practical action in an attempt to define a dynamic religion in a democratic society. We believe that Christianity still has very much to contribute to civilization both at home and abroad."

Then he said, practically as a throw-away comment, that *theology is faith seeking understanding*. I had not heard this before and commented on it. It is from Anselm, I was told. Such an approach to religion was what I had sought from the beginning and I expected that making sense out of the intangible would prove to be a daunting task. He said that modern theology is no foremost a discipline of propositions. The need to give spiritua knowledge a viable place in society has resulted in contemporar theology. God is still honored, but not to the neglect of the poo among us, the disenfranchised and the marginal. In a moderr democracy there are no privileges for religion. Religion mus compete for time and space just like all other entities. Therefor it must make its cause known by participation in the due proces of law and order.

Some critics of modern theological efforts might say tha humans had shifted the emphasis from satisfying God to satisfyin, themselves. But that is simplistic. According to the Gospel, Go in Christ abandoned Heaven for Earth, coming in human form to do for us what we could not do for ourselves. That is no only theology but sociology. Jesus was not so much concerne about Temple sacrifices and the nitty-gritty of interpreting th laws of purity as he was in our behaving in some believable socia manner, being good neighbors and practicing an ethic of love.

An Educated Approach to the Bible

Switching then from theology to understanding how to read th Bible, Hatfield went on to define two literary terms: simile an metaphor. "I want you to understand that the Bible is literature Tim, and not just religious prophecy or doctrine. From boo to book and cover to cover the Bible contains many forms o composition, reflecting the cultures of each epoch. Moses gav the Law, but the prophets exhorted the people to do justice an love mercy. Then, jumping 'way up to the Gospels, Jesus taugh by way of parables. We understand, as did the original disciple that most of the parables he used were not factually true, onl *metaphorically* true. For instance, he would say, 'The kingdor of God is like unto...,' and give an example. That is a *simile*. H was making a comparison, so that we might catch the *essence* of spiritual concepts. So, the parables probably never actually happened *but could have.* Parables are still recognizable today as stories that ring true. We must also remember that Jesus taught in a society that was largely illiterate. So stories were a means of teaching people who had never read books."

Hatfield continued teaching me such simple truths, which I could see were true according to the dictates of common sense and world literature. No longer would I be tempted to pick and choose Bible verses from here and there in order to make a case for one belief or another. Rather, in order to allow the Bible to speak to me, I would have to read each work in context. It was all so wonderfully clear.

We moved on in these conversations to the ancient idea of a millennium, as an actual Kingdom of God on earth that lasts one thousand years. I learned that by the 1700s, a system of Bible doctrine was in place among Protestants that included the details of the return of Christ and the defeat of Roman Catholicism. Jonathan Edwards (1703 - 1758), along with many others among New England's Congregational ministers, believed that the end times were coming very soon. They promoted evangelism as a means of preparing a people for Christ's kingdom on Earth, and that is why church membership became very important, for true Christians would rule along with Christ. But there was a proviso to church membership: one needed to be born again — *regenerated* in the doctrinal language of the day — in order to qualify as a true Christian. This movement to purity eventually split the churches, for being baptized was insufficient by such thought. The rites and ceremonies of the Church meant little in comparison to one's personal experience, and testimony of it.

Some of these ideas came about because many ministers of the time considered the New Testament to be written in such a manner that they could read it like one long letter from God, who had their instruction in mind, especially about the end time taking place in their time. And not only could the ministers read the Bible in this personal way, but individual church members would also read it in this manner. Ironically, democracy encouraged this lay attitude. Before long the Protestants were disagreeing with their "priests" in matters of theology. A born again believer with a Bible in hand could brand an ordained theologian as unregenerate and therefore an inadequate pastor. He was as dead as a wooden pew! It is obvious that such reading failed to take ancient history into account.

Verses were taken out of context — what we call proof-texting — in order to build a system that pointed to the conclusion of human history and that right soon. They also interpreted the secular wars between Catholic and Protestant nations as having significance to the end times. Many serious students among the prominent leaders of both religion and the society of that era studied the Bible to determine when Christ would return. Some put the latest possible date as in the early twentieth century. They were certain that Catholicism would be defeated and Protestantism exalted. Such theology and speculative prophecy were developed before modern democracy had become a fact when both Protestant and Catholic kings vied for land and influence.

This latter-day Protestant expectation of a thousand-year reign of Christ on earth has been repeatedly declared among some Protestants since the 1600s, giving origin to a long series of cults that occasionally established communities in preparation for Christ's return. And what was taught in Europe was repeated in the colonies. As one enthusiasm died out, another rose up to gather believers from among the churches, to gather them "out of" the churches in many cases. One of the more recent is the Watchtower Society, or Jehovah's Witnesses. They believed that Christ would set up headquarters in America's West, probably San Diego, by the end of the second decade of the twentieth century. Originally, they thought that only about 144,000 souls would be saved. That idea and the date of consummation were later changed and now the predictions have largely been abandoned. The Witnesses are making adjustments.

Another group that had similar ideas, The Seventh Day Adventists, began in the nineteenth century, in Pennsylvania, with the expectation that there would be a literal resurrection of the dead. The first Millerites, as they were then called, actually met in a cemetery on the determined date for The Resurrection, and then met again the next year. By that time they had become distinct from their Christian neighbors.

The belief that Christ will return has taken on a new life in the most recent "Left Behind" fervor that was sparked by Hal Lindsey in his book, *The Late Great Planet Earth*. Such present-day writers are well read in dispensational doctrine, *usually as Scofield presented it in his version of the King James Bible*. Many of these same people believe that humanity appeared fully formed only six thousand years ago.

I was happy to be on this new track, for what I learned appealed to my common sense while agreeing with modern scientific discoveries. I said to myself, *This is reasonable and respectable*. For better or for worse, I embraced this knowledge as best I could, hoping now more than before to make sense of things from a religious point of view.

The Summary

Hatfield concluded his sessions with a little homily, saying that "following Jesus is far better than living in a suspended state of never knowing nor committing oneself to something noble." He said that having worked through much of the learning the world has to offer and after weighing the evidence, he still had to settle down somewhere. "Settle down," he stressed, "or live insecurely by dint of my own craft and power, which are sure to wane." Then he quoted Voltaire, to the effect that *if God did not exist it would be necessary to invent him.* "For," my pastor said, "we are not sufficient unto ourselves. Creation demands a higher power a mysterious force, far beyond our comprehension, beyond our own invention, a power that can span the Universe and is not limited by time. This power that creates and sustains us is what I call God, and this God is proclaimed in the teaching and faith of Jesus, who calls God his *heavenly Father* and encourages us to regard him as our Father. Believing this takes faith, but it is a good faith, a personal faith, that ennobles those who catch the vision of it."

I understood his common sense and appreciated that he was a committed Christian, but as he spoke these last ideas of faith, thought of my experience of a call to ministry. I asked where he would place a personal experience such as I had. *Am I just a needy neurotic?* I asked him.

Hatfield immediately replied "Yes!" I failed to catch the humor of it and must have looked shocked, for he laughed loudly before going on to say we're all neurotic and needy, so I shouldn't feel special about it. God did not make any of us perfect but is still working on us. In fact, he said, the professional clergy is an odd assortment of imperfect creatures who spend too much time worrying about their sins and mistakes. "The call to ministry isn't about them, it's about Good News. The Apostle Paul said it well when he wrote that he had the heavenly treasure in an earthen vessel, and his call was to preach Christ, and him crucified."

I felt better then, for I had begun to think that my pastor was only a rationalist, who simply played a game of leaping into faith when he chose.

He said quite solemnly, "The Christian Religion has a long history and many traditions, even conflicting opinions on many subjects. But we have always taken our faith seriously, for it is a matter of life and death here and now. I don't mean heaven or hell hereafter, I mean real life right here, right now. Jesus is indeed the Way, the Truth and the Life. By him we come to the Father. So please don't get caught up in nitpicking or in trying to decide who is right and who is wrong. It would be better to remember that the Lord requires of us to love mercy, to do justice and to walk humbly with him."

We both became silent, as though the moment was a gift of the Spirit. I surely felt so, and believe Ralph did too. My teacher finally invited me to pray with him. I bowed my head, which caused the tears forming in my eyes to fall onto my folded hands.

13

ALL THINGS DECENTLY AND IN ORDER

Very quickly after our whirlwind marriage, Colleen moved her worldly possessions into my house and began to make it her own. She was happy to park her car in the driveway and leave it there overnight, thus healing the old place of its melancholy. The neighbors added to our joy by organizing a potluck supper at large house down the street. This reminded me of the old days and our dances, but no one had a phonograph in place, so we just milled around and chatted. I was quietly grateful for their lack of meddling in the previous months of whirlwind romance and appreciated how warmly they included Colleen in the circle.

Only the young can summon those supernatural reserves of energy to cope with the complexities of life while spending hours in rapturous intimacy. We did rather well all the way through the December holidays, but then after New Year's Day I came down with a terrible dose of the flu. My strength went out to sea, leaving me face down upon the shore. My reserves had flushed out of my system during a three-day siege of hots and trots. I felt I was at the threshold of death but no longer cared. This gave Colleen her first trial at nursing a sick man. She did well, and we were thankful for her teaching contract, that allowed her sick time for the task. And the school must have been happy to keep her away from all those children during the danger of contagion.

The church members were telephonically supportive, but we lived so far away from their part of the city that no one came to visit, except the pastor, and that only after any danger of infection had passed. By then I was ready to get back to studies. The semester exams were soon upon me, and I managed to scrape through. I had sailed along in fair seas, navigating around the shoals so that I assumed I could handle anything that came over the horizon. I felt invincible, especially while on board God's great Ark, the Church. The flu was just one of those blips on the radar that soon fade away.

Things were about to get worse.

Pastor Ralph said that I probably wouldn't hear anything from Princeton before mid-February and that I would have little trouble getting in, so not to fret. However, they might write and ask for a mid-year update, just as a matter of form. "Remember," he said as a good pastor should, "'God works all things together for good to those who love him.' Have faith and be patient."

When a letter from the seminary arrived the middle of January I supposed I would be asked for my most recent grades. I opened the envelope with real anticipation of good news. It would have been better to feel some tension, for the registrar informed me that I was not scheduled to enter studies that year. Due to the number of early applications from very qualified students, plus a few who had already waited a year for entry, my application failed to receive approval for the entering class. I was therefore being placed on the list for the following year, with one condition. I was instructed to take two semesters of Greek, as New Testament studies were done in that language.

Pastor Ralph read the letter, turning red as he finished the page. For a moment he stood behind his desk in silence, then looked over at me. He said, "Tim, I am disturbed and embarrassed

by this news. I don't think it is bad news but certainly not wha
we expected. First, please forgive me for not thinking of thi
detail about Greek. Many seminaries have dropped languag
requirements, and others provide Greek classes during the firs
year of studies. I'm going to call Reverend MacNeal and see i
his experience might provide some sort of solution to this." H
suggested that I go on about my duties at church and he'd ge
back to me.

I wandered around the buildings without direction, endin
my stroll in the nave. The atmosphere was gloomy and full o
shadows in our usually bright and cheerful house of worship
for a rainstorm was threatening from the west, and I felt tha
this ambiance suited the moment. I sat down near the chance
and looked up at the rose window, still slightly colorful from th
eastern glow. Spiritual virtues in symbolic form surrounded me
virtues I knew should be within me: calm, beauty, consciousnes
of God's presence, prayer.

Prayer. I had not prayed. Bowing my head, I tried to forn
some appropriate words but failed to come up with what migh
have fit the moment. Just then I was thinking of some of th
Psalms that express impatience with God. "Why standest tho
afar off, O Lord? Why hidest thou thyself in times of trouble?
"My God, my God, why hast thou forsaken me? Why art tho
so far from helping me, and from the words of my roaring?
And then I thought of the crucified Jesus, who had used thes
very words as he bore pain and humiliation. This put things int
perspective, and I felt just a little ashamed of my self-pity.

I tried anew to pray, and this time at least I could understan
that I was not alone in my pain. Of course! We never are,
mused. And then it occurred to me that I was praying even if
had not begun in some formal way. In fact, I was sitting back wit
my hands unfolded, my eyes open. But now my thoughts wer
centered in upon truth rather than my misery. I took comfort i
the insight, trying to stay on track, to see the issue through. Bu

all that came to me was the reply Jesus gave to his own prayer for deliverance, *nevertheless not as I will, but as thou wilt.*

These words were a corrective for my confusion. Now the decisions that were made by others regarding my future seemed more like an opportunity rather than a delay. It was up to me to find the possibilities yet dormant within my situation. That matter defined, I rose and walked back into the day, to discover that the dark clouds had been driven to the south and were gloriously backlit, displaying silver linings. *Indeed*, I murmured, *it is a sign from Heaven.*

Pastor Ralph called me back to his office and said that some students without a knowledge of Greek took an intensive summer course prior to entry into the freshman year of seminary. But, he added, since I would not be going to Princeton that year, why not consider choosing a seminary that would both accept me for the fall semester and also provide instruction in New Testament Greek? He seemed very positive about the idea, suggesting that I could then transfer my credits to Princeton in the following year and be up to speed rather than a year behind in my agenda.

Talk about an answer to prayer. This one came so rapidly that I was left reeling with an elation nearly as strong as my previous agony. I asked my pastor for suggestions. If one seminary was overly subscribed, perhaps others would present the same situation. He agreed, offering me his study phone and a list of recommended schools.

The pastor's own seminary in Louisville had a waiting list for the autumn. So did McCormick. And Austin and Richmond. We were told by the registrars that Presbyterian schools were indeed popular, for apparently the churches' pastors were doing a good job of influencing their young men, many of them veterans. Quite a number of those who had been overseas and seen the great needs of Third World countries as well as the ruin of the Old World, felt the ministry was where they could help repair a broken civilization.

After the telephone call to Richmond I was out of resources. Pastor Ralph nodded when I told him of this and looked out the window for awhile. I looked around the room for a few moment and then said that I thought I needed a break. Thanking him and suggesting we give the task a rest, I went home.

Home. Before this setback I had thought it was nearly time to sell the old house. It felt strange to think of selling out my family home, especially since Colleen had brought me such comfort there. But I did not wish to become an absentee landlord. Colleen and I had talked it over and agreed I should contact Attorney Will Braun for assistance, just in case we two did have to move out as we previously planned. I called him for an appointment, and within days we met at his office. We chatted for a few minutes about my progress in studies and our plans for moving somewhere but nowhere we could name. My legal paper would be simple enough to prepare, so Will gave me a slot in his appointment calendar for the following week and assured me he would pray for us "without ceasing," as the Bible recommends.

When I arrived at his office, he had some literature in hand. "I want you to have this information and I hope you find what you are seeking." He then handed me an airmail packet marked as coming from the Office of the Registrar, Chaderton Theological Seminary, San Retiro, California. I looked up at Will and beheld a smiling man, one who knew he had accomplished something for my benefit. We then got down to the matter of the forms he had ordered. I settled with him and made my exit.

After reading the literature from Chaderton Seminary I felt it deserved serious investigation, so asked Pastor Ralph about it. He checked with Reverend MacNeal and then reported back to me. It was a fairly new school, non-denominational and conservative. MacNeal recognized the names of a few of the professors as being Presbyterian. He said a year spent in studies there would be a good exposure to both theology and the evangelical environment.

Go, if you can get in, I was advised, but keep an open mind.

Before the middle of the semester I received a letter of admission. The idea of moving to California for a year became increasingly attractive the more Colleen and I discussed it, so we began making the practical adjustments for the big move.

14

THE STRAIGHT AND NARROW WAY
AND
THE SONG OF THE OPEN ROAD

Colleen's parents, faithful to their church and its strict ways, wer
nonetheless happy that their daughter found a good husband th
second time around. And although they would miss her, the
were content that she was leaving for a good cause. They wer
also pleased to have a minister in the family, but would never ca
me reverend. That title was reserved for God alone, they saic
True to my promise, I would not provoke them to discussion
about their views, since Colleen had threatened to leave me :
I riled her Daddy over religion. With that choice before me,
opted to mind my own business, and since he did not pressur
me, we got along very well. If anything, I was awed by his grea
store of memorized Scripture. There was no doubt in my min
that he could tie me in knots, were we to argue.

One evening, not too long before our departure, the elde
Hammelins invited us to attend a service with them. It would b
a nice way for them to introduce their daughter's new husban
to old friends. They were really enthusiastic about this proposa

The church, they said, was having a week-long rally with a guest speaker from Tennessee. Friday evening seemed best for the visit, so Colleen and I joined her parents that evening. We felt just slightly uneasy about going to a rally, but we did love her folks and wanted to give them something, like a family activity, to remember.

The Second Avenue Church of Christ was built by the members, block by block, so the architecture was predictable. Ancient style buildings were not a part of their religion, nor, for that matter, of their culture. And there was a doctrinal justification for such simplicity. Inner beauty was more important than outer appearances, they said. As was the custom, volunteers maintained and added to their physical plant as a part of their church tithe. In a Southern tradition practiced among country churches, no parking lot was provided or sidewalks poured. The sandy soil was covered by strong grasses, and paths worn into the lawn by constant use. Cars were parked in the old style, circling the church in rows, as the pioneers had circled their horses and wagons in earlier times. I would learn later in my education that these folk were direct heirs of the older Puritan tradition of Colonial times and sought to strip away all pretense and churchly pomp. No candles were used in worship, which was called a meeting, and Christmas was not observed at church, since Yule customs were from Europe and not Palestine. They insisted that Jesus was most probably born in the spring, not the winter. Rome observed a year-end festival in which they recognized Janus, not Jesus.

Excitement was in the air that final night of the rally. We arrived early enough to get good seats, as the Hammelins suggested. People waved to each other as they got out of their cars, exchanged greetings, calling out to friends farther away as they headed for the church house. The people were the church, they said, and the building housed them. Church in the New Testament means a called out group of chosen people. Therefore the building was not the church, only the meeting house for Christ's church of living saints.

While we were walking toward the auditorium, the guest speaker and the church's regular evangelist joined us from another path. Mister Hammelin took the opportunity to introduce me as his son-in-law. During the week's meetings, the Hammelins and the guest preacher had become friendly enough, though I guessed that this outsider knew nothing about Colleen's divorce.

Colleen's father beamed with pride as he spoke. "Hello there Preacher! I want you to meet our daughter's husband. Tim, meet Evangelist Tomkins, from the Great Smokies, where religion is taken straight from the Bible!"

Mr. Tomkins extended his hand, which proved to be large and powerful, and gave me a firm shake, saying, "Nice to meet you, Son. I don't think I've seen you here this week. You Christian?" He did not acknowledge Colleen's presence in his rush to interrogate me.

I was surprised, probably a little confused, at such a question. "Are you a Christian?" *What was the man thinking?* I said, "Yes, go to the Presbyterian Church over in Salem Gables."

Tomkins beamed, for this was what he wanted to hear from me. He replied in a loud voice, sounding somewhat quizzical, "*A Presbyterian?* Why, a man would hardly know they were Christian with a name like that! And the Methodists and Episcopals, they must be ashamed to call themselves after Christ! Why can't these folks just be Christians like it says in the New Testament?"

I was caught by surprise. I knew we do not find the Methodist or Presbyterian churches named in the Bible, but did not expect to be set straight right then. The evangelist was making a point for the faithful standing around as we conversed, I supposed. But surely we were all Christians. Why then this correction?

In innocence I interjected, "How about John the Baptist? I thought the Baptists named themselves after him, and that certainly comes from the Bible."

"Baptists? Yes, that's exactly what they are, followers of John the Baptist, who came *before* Christ as an announcer! Why, they don't even baptize a Christian baptism like the Apostle Peter said to do. They baptize like John, a baptism of repentance, but not of the washing away of sins! Why, we have regular debates with the Baptists about this. Yes, we do, and we win every time! They don't even know the Bible they carry around tucked under their arms."

A group of men had gathered around us, perhaps ten. I looked around at the smiling faces nodding their agreement to the preacher' every word and felt like a minority of one. Well, make that two, for Colleen stood next to me, not just holding my hand but squeezing so hard it hurt. The elder Hammelins said not a word but were smiling in apparent agreement.

Mr. Tomkins broke the spell with, "Well, now, it's time to start the meeting, so let's all just mosey along to the auditorium." He smiled at me and added, "I hope the meeting helps you to learn a little more about the Bible and what it means, so listen careful, now, y'hear?"

I felt so beset I could not reply. Surely my face was red, for I could feel my ears burning. For a moment I wondered how a doctrinal debate between this warrior and Gaines would fare.

No musical prelude of any sort greeted us in the auditorium, as the believers were thoroughly convinced there were no musical instruments in Christ's church, there being no mention of them in the entire New Testament. They sang unaccompanied except for a finger-size pitch pipe that a young man pulled from his pocket and blew as loudly as possible before each hymn was sung. A low humming resulted, on pitch. The congregation did a wonderful job of singing a capella and in harmony. The auditorium, built of cement blocks and stucco, was bereft of carpeting, so that voices carried clearly, and without echo when there was a full house. There was no public address system at the pulpit, nor was it desired. Ministers simply spoke up and could be heard in all quarters of the large room. I would soon see that this orating lent an authority to preaching, and that it kept things more interesting for the auditors.

The pulpit was obvious by its absence, but then I noticed i
pushed over into the corner near the drape that concealed the
large baptistery. I asked Mr. Hammelin about it and was informed
that this evangelist did not like such "trappings," so had ordered
it removed. He wished to roam across the platform without an
pretense of appearing to need a pulpit to hide behind. I had to
admit that he was attraction enough, with his great shock of white
hair and large belly, seeming more like an Old Testament prophe
than a suave minister. But he did at least wear a dark business sui
rather than some jazzy ensemble that so many evangelists chose

People sang joyfully, anticipating what they considered th
most important part of the evening. As they sang, the visitin
evangelist moved to the platform and began to pace back an
forth, looking out over the assembly. Then he knelt on one kne
and cupped his forehead in his right hand, putting his Bibl
down on the floor and resting his left hand upon it. This act c
piety was accomplished with some effort, for he was an old man
I was amused to see him casually shift his large stomach to on
side as he knelt. But he was a saint at prayer nonetheless, his pur
white hair resembling a halo.

As the congregation continued to sing, he rose, with effor
dusted off his trouser knee and stood impatiently looking ou
over the crowd. He had become a man of God ready to do th
work of an evangelist, and there was no need wasting time whe
the moment for action arrived. He paced back and forth as th
people finished the last stanza, joining the singing from memor
As they sat down, he opened his Bible, peering down into th
mass of upturned faces for only a moment.

He began in a strong voice, "The Word of God says man
things, and all of them are true, from the first to the last. That
right! The Word of God cannot fail, nor can it be broken, *Joh*
10:35. I want to remind you that a man with a knowledge of th
Bible who has not a college education is far better off than a ma
with a college education who knows not the Bible." He stoppe

speaking and waited for the customary response. A distinct masculine chorus echoed back to him a hearty *Amen!*

"I am here to proclaim to you this evening what the Bible says about the last days. Oh, it will be a blessed time for the saints, but horrible for the cursed of the earth, for the sinners and unrepentant. Then there shall be weeping and wailing and gnashing of teeth, *Matthew* 25:30, and those who have not washed their robes in the blood of the Lamb, *Revelation* 7:14, shall not see the Glory. Amen?"

"Amen!" the assembly responded as one.

"Now, a lot of sinners think that if they can get away with their sinning through a lifetime and die without getting caught, then they're off scot-free. Their idea is that if they are not caught while living, then when they 'shuffle off this mortal coil' there's no judgment." He paused, staring out over the audience, a look of shock on his face. "Oh! I didn't mean to use that phrase because it's from Shakespeare. I don't read that worldly man's works, so full of lust and violence. Why I wouldn't be caught reading him on a dark night in an alley with my eyes pierced out. No sir! We don't need worldly literature. In fact, Scripture tells us, 'There is a way that seemeth right unto a man, but the end thereof are the ways of death,' *Proverbs* 16:25, and 'narrow is the way that leadeth unto life,' *Matthew* 7:14.

"I tell you this, that in the Great and Terrible Day of the Lord, there will be a resurrection of the unjust and there will be a final judgment of them, as Peter wrote in his second letter, chapter two and verse nine, 'The Lord knoweth how to deliver the godly out of temptation, and to reserve the unjust unto the day of judgment to be punished.' Amen?"

"Amen!" echoed back to him from a multitude of mouths.

"Now the first thing you have to know is that true believers need have no fear of the devil, that old deceiver, who walketh about as a roaring lion, seeking whom he may devour. Right here in the Bible it says that the devil is going to be bound and thrown into the bottomless pit before he can conquer the saints."

The evangelist struck a dramatic pose, his large, leather bound and worn Bible open and thrust forward in his left hand. AIt says right here in *Revelations*, chapter 20 and the first three verses..."

Many people already had their Bibles open to the reference from the moment he mentioned the bottomless pit. Some were still fingering the pages, however, and a riffling of paper could be heard throughout the auditorium in that moment.

He read: "And I saw an angel come down from heaven having the key of the bottomless pit and a great chain in his hand, and he laid hold on the dragon, that old serpent, which is the devil and Satan, and bound him a thousand years. And cast him into the bottomless pit, and shut him up, and et cetera and et cetera."

I could hardly believe my ears; the man was actually substituting "et cetera" for words from Holy Scripture. It is the only time I had heard that usage and have not heard it again anywhere.

Mr. Hammelin was enjoying this preacher. He nodded at each of the endless quotations, finding them with feverish paging. But I found myself wandering in thought to other places, especially thinking of our journey west, the things remaining to be done, our finances, one thing leading to another until my mind was completely distracted from the sermon.

Then mercifully, as quickly as it had begun, it was over. That was a Friday night, I reasoned, and no one would mind if the preacher sent them home on time. With only a few comments and announcements, the service was concluded.

People moved out, some hurrying to their cars, others standing around in groups conversing. I was pleased at the last to learn we would have no call to come forward and be saved that night, for I feared he might start in on me again. The evangelist had made his way down the aisle, obviously in a hurry, but a man stopped him as he walked by near us and began complimenting him. "Preacher, that was a real good sermon. I followed every reference you gave, and I want to say that nothin' was wrong with it!"

The man from the Great Smokies apparently was accustomed to this type of compliment and managed to edge his way to the rear of the room while commenting on the other man's knowledge of Scripture. He said, "Keep it up, you'll become an evangelist yourself someday."

It had been announced that he was to depart early the following morning for Jacksonville, where he would preach on Sunday. Many continued to wish him well as he moved along toward his auto and drove away, his faithful wife beside him. Taking a wife along on evangelistic tours was biblical, everyone knew, as Peter and others did it in New Testament times.

◆

I too would soon drive north, my faithful wife beside me. But we would head for Florida's Panhandle — across the state from Jacksonville — where the road would lead us into the Gulf states and then northwesterly for a good poke, until we connected with that famous wagon trail, Route 66. Colleen and I would pull up stakes like the westering pioneers, but not before doing some last-minute visiting in various homes and attending a church service of appreciation and farewell. My wonderful wife proved her love, tearfully embracing her parents, walking away from her colleagues and students, and fearlessly sitting beside me as I careened along those terribly narrow tarmac highways. She remained optimistic and cooperative every mile of the way. She also had checked out the teacher situation in school districts near our destination and arranged an interview for time soon after our planned arrival.

I had bought a like-new Dodge Fluid Drive sedan with some of the deposit from the sale of the house. It was a beaut: light gray on the body, shiny black on the top, with whitewall tires and large chrome hubcaps. There was a green sun shade added to the top of the windshield, rather like the bill of a baseball cap, that gave the auto an added touch of class. Those were hectic days but also energizing, as papers were signed and filed away, things dumped or given to friends. Saying goodbye included supper on many occasions, with talk of old times and promises to keep contact. At the last, clothes and linens were fitted into the trunk and back seat of our modern version of a covered wagon, and when there remained no excuse to tarry, we pulled up stakes. With luck, Los Angeles could be reached in seven days, but perhaps more depending on weather and tires.

With nothing further to say or do, and burdened by weary minds and hearts, we drove away toward a heavenly calling, leaving family and friends to their worldly cares. I cited by memory, as we drove out of town, those memorable words of St. Paul in his Epistle to the Philippians: "Brothers, I do not consider myself yet to have taken hold of it. But one thing I do: Forgetting what is behind and straining forward to what is ahead, I press on toward the goal to win the prize for which God has called me heavenward in Christ Jesus."

I mentally marked the six years in the navy and then three more back home — action-packed and full of change — as a time of transition from callow youth to manhood. I was truly ready for whatever the future might lay down before me. It was novel to imagine that I had just turned twenty-eight. Life was so hectic. I had often thought that, after the loneliness and sometimes bleak surroundings of military duty, I would return home for good. I would marry and raise a family in the old familiar surroundings and among my clan and companions. But I discovered in the three years back home that no place in this world is my home. As a chorus says it succinctly, "I'm just a-passin' through." Nonetheless, I harbored the idea that after seminary I might return to my lovely land of palms and golden beaches, where it did not snow, and cloudy skies were blown away within a day

I harbored the thought and kept it warm, cuddled next to my heart, for many years.

A few miles sped by without a word. I broke the quiet because I could not stand my own churning thoughts. Colleen was happy enough to talk out all the feelings she had stored up for the past few days, especially about leaving her aging parents behind, her father even then at retirement age. And then we settled into silence once more.

I had chosen the long, lonely highway up the middle of the state, a road built through the dairy land and cane fields of the everglades, as straight as an arrow, aimed north to Lake Okeechobee and then westerly around it. That first day took me on my own memory lane. My mother was born and raised in Middle Florida, a vast land filling with orange groves even then, with great expanses of natural beauty. But we would not reach that area until the next day. First we would traverse the glades immediately outside Miami and bid them farewell.

Beyond the highway, across the rain darkened ditches and out upon the sea of saw grass, hammocks of earth grew scrubby brush in meager defiance of the surrounding swamp. This flat landscape offered its own type of austere beauty, a sameness of line and limitation of color that supported the light blue heavens, an overpowering dome. If the earth was expansive in its scope, the heavens dwarfed it by a vastness not easily captured. The Florida sky would be full of fantastic cotton- ball clouds at one time then clear within a few hours. Settled clouds farther away painted the horizon into images of great mountain ranges, purple and gray.

A motorist could speed on for hours and never reach those fantasized hills. Again, occasional thunder-heads of dark, threatening gray clouds blended into black centers, thrusting themselves for miles into the sky and heralding a rain storm here or there along the way. When the skies first filled and then sloshed over in such fury, drivers had to stop alongside the highway and patiently wait, for the roadway would disappear within the deluge.

Usually, when there was a bright and warming sun, narrow deep canals along the sides of the highway provided a contrast to the tarmac. Between the road and before the water there was a buffer of sandy soil leading down to tall reeds with their sausage-like seed pods. Next came the still surface of rain-dark water that abounded with lily pads displaying their blue petals. Beneath them, garfish, some as long as a yardstick, lurked in wait for prey in competition with alligators, those hulking denizens of the primeval wilderness. Catfish, bass and bream swam there, an attraction for the occasional fisherman, bamboo pole in hand and bucket at foot, having in mind a pan of crisply fried filets.

Experienced motorists set out from Miami with a deep respect for those ribbons of crushed coral rock and sticky tar that traversed the watery land. The respect had nothing to do with admiration. For the highways, and we used to call them that, were built so stingily that one would think the engineers intended to punish both car and driver. And it was even more dangerous than imagined, for broken glass and scrap metal embedded themselves in the asphalt and lay there waiting the hapless worn tires of the less fortunate.

We two were romantics, thinking of ourselves as pilgrims in the biblical sense. God was leading us, we knew, and all things would work out for good. I, oblivious to the dangers, hurtled on thinking only of the destination. Aside from some nostalgia for home and family, this pulling up roots like the Hebrews of old was pure adventure. I was thrilled by the hum of the tires and the rush of wind through the car. A New Testament author wrote that the Hebrews were looking for "a city which had foundations whose builder and maker is God." And we two? Had we not prayed and searched, following the portents and signs that came before us? Had not God led us in our seeking? Yes! We knew God was with us on the road. We could feel it and rejoiced in being with such a Presence.

It was amazing how quickly I had moved from nostalgia to anticipation. As the car sped along we sang hymns and choruses, but on the long stretches between towns there were times of holy silence. Jesus our Friend was the subject of most of those compositions. He was the Gentle Savior, the Coming King, the Suffering Servant, the Way to Bliss. And when we would finally see him, "we'd ask the questions, and He'd tell us why, when we talked it over, in the bye-and-bye." Oh, how joyful the feeling of the open road that was taking us to a marvelous future!

I could not possibly have imagined then as well as I would finally come to experience it, that the road was to become very long with occasional stops to prepare for the next leg of the journey. But just then the drive was a means to an end, not a way of life, and we drank in the sensations of nature while listening to the humming tires. The summer air rushed in, swirling about as it blew our hair first one way and then another.

Goodbye, I finally said within myself, *goodbye dear land of my birth, goodbye family and friends. Farewell to the old and familiar. Hello to the West of our great Nation, to the Plains and the Rockies.* There loomed before me three challenging years of study and learning and fellowship. I would discover new friends and beckoning doors of opportunity.

A half day in New Orleans provided a tour of the old city and lunch at Antoine's. The French Quarter has an old-fashioned, even a musty appeal, and the cuisine at Antoine's — may it endure forever — lived up to its fame. Imagine, I had to dig a jacket out of the car trunk in order to get in. And that in August!

While speeding across Texas I detoured a few miles for a glance at that touted seminary which Greg and Hal insisted was the Lord's chosen institution for right doctrine. I had no desire to tour the place, just wanted to see it from my moving car, so

drove on by. My curiosity was superficial, perhaps a soothing o
any bad conscience I might have had because of my prejudice
a way of justifying myself. And like most half-hearted efforts, i
did not satisfy. I departed the city thinking that I had wasted m
time and that I could be better occupied burning up the asphal
leading to Amarillo. Colleen had no interest in my side trip. Sh
read magazines and distracted me with tidbits of conversatio
not at all religious.

From Fort Worth the road led across the plains, sma
grasshoppers in abundance smashing against the grill an
windshield, some invading our space. That highway was anothe
typical blacktop of the time, mostly straight and forever narro
for hours on end, following the roll of the land. The prairie grasse
had become parched to golden, and the dry air reduced huma
perspiration to salt that felt grainy to the touch. I was drivin
eleven hours a day most days, plus necessary stops. Sleep cam
quickly those evenings, and mornings dawned as we tucked i
a hearty breakfast. Going out to California we had ample cas
for hearty diner meals. It would be different driving east three o
more years later.

Fort Worth claimed to be the gateway to the West, bu
Albuquerque proved to be a truer one for me, with its pastel hil
and grandiose views of the sparsely treed mountains. From the
the trip led to the famous Route 66, straight as an arrow acro
the desert lands.

That highway finally takes one to Needles, port of entr
to California. The drive took us into a new land far away fro
everything we knew, into the Mojave Desert, famous as the buri
ground for many inexperienced pioneers. And it was still a dese
known for its cruelty to motorists, whose cars often broke dow
in the middle of nowhere. I planned the crossing so as to do th
hottest stretch late at night, though it remained a blast furnac
in the dark. Our headlights picked up nothing but wastelan
populated with giant cacti, their hairy branches outstretched

arms waiting for our car to break down. I felt they just might rush out to roadside and devour us. Colleen remained eerily silent during those threatening hours.

The no-man's-land along the sides of the highway was strewn with the shells of junked cars, some of them there so long they were covered with red rust. Old mattresses and piles of trash were heaped into smoldering mounds sending putrid smoke into our car. We imagined ourselves making a trek through the biblical Wilderness of Sinai — did the ancient Hebrews discard old mattresses along the highways? — or perhaps we were on the approach to Hell itself, not the biblical one but that of Dante's depiction. But, to put things into perspective, we spent only a day and a night in that trajectory from an old world unto the new. It was hardly a trek.

For the first time in those many days we two experienced the shock of an ugly America, rather like the urban slums along railroad tracks leading into so many cities, and began to wonder at our choice of moving to California. But the next day, after spending the night in Needles, we easily reached the pass in the San Bernardino Mountains that provides descent into a captivating world, a green one, replete with orange groves, green fields, clean towns and cities on the plateaus among the rolling hills.

The last lap of this week-long drive would carry us all the way to San Retiro, taking us northeast of the tangled city that is Los Angeles. We passed through the centers of Glendora, Arcadia and San Gabriel. Along the way we missed a view of the mountains to our east because the smog, a gray haze, eliminated a view of anything beyond perhaps a mile. We were utterly overcome by the traffic but so excited that we drove on to our destination, not far to the east of Simi Valley. This, at last, was to become our portion of the Promised Land — in America — where we would sojourn a few years rather than forty.

– 15 –

ORIENTATION: PART 1

OVERVIEW OF A NEW WEST

A winding road leads into the seminary grounds, giving the locatio
an aura of seclusion. For a relatively new institution, it seems to b
old, as in old money. It occupies an old location with an old buildin
nearest the gates. My first impression is that I have stumbled upo
something a little off the beaten path. But that's okay. It's nice to fe
cloistered, especially after three years on a large campus surrounde
by asphalt parking lots. I learn, however, that in California, "W
never did it that way before" does not apply even to religion, for th
is a land of the grand, the terrific and the bountiful. If we think
will work we'll try it.

Fillmore Chaderton, the founder of the seminary, was sti
very much alive and on campus quite often, especially for chap
services. The Chadertons, it was whispered but never flaunted
had a distinguished   lineage back to a gentle Puritan divin
Laurence Chaderton. He was the first master of Emmanu
College and a Translator of King James's Version of the Bibl
This ancient Chaderton was a Presbyterian but remained withi

the Anglican Church, as did many of his descendants, but not all. Some dissidents sailed for America early on, where they could practice their Puritan faith without harassment from the king. Word was out among the students that, in the succeeding fourteen generations that had finally produced Fillmore Chaderton, there were many Presbyterians, some of them ordained ministers, and at least one in each generation. Fillmore chose to serve God within the Baptist tradition, mainly because the Presbyterians were too organized and "restrictive" to his free style of Bible teaching and red-hot evangelism. His flair was to gather converts into the Faith by way of his gifts as a leader and speaker, one of which was a voice that could crack with deep emotion when mentioning inner spiritual experience. He would simply say "God" with such reverence that he would choke up. It was not unusual then to hear light sobs among his auditors. His gifts included gaining converts from among some of the most miserable of humans. Occasionally one would write to him and tell of contemplating suicide but hearing his message just in time and turning to God. These letters were sometimes shared with his radio audience. Across the many years of his ministry converts came to him from all walks of life, from many denominations, from near and far, and they all lived their faith in the here-and-now.

The faculty also held him in high esteem, not so much for his theology, which was not deep, but for his intelligence and business acumen. He was a self-made millionaire and generous with those nearest him in his various endeavors.

Brother Fillmore had "caught a vision," as it was said, in his later years for founding a seminary that would be both academic and mission-minded. He had the money to carry out the dream, and knew a great many evangelical scholars. In short order he gathered a board of trustees and a remarkable faculty. The word went out, and the students came, a few at first and then more, scores of them. These in turn encouraged others to seek admission, so that within a few years property was bought and buildings erected. It was all so very California.

As a newcomer to such piety and vigor, I would find my challenge in separating fact from fantasy in this wonderful land of America's far West. For this was not only Chaderton Country but also Walt Disney's Domain, a land into which Hollywood's visionaries pumped unlimited energy and wealth. Disneyland was destined to grow, running neck-to-neck with the burgeoning churches. Amusement à la Hollywood had become an amazing industry before Disney, a phenomenon that filled a need previously served by the traveling carnivals and medicine men. But Disney was something new, a land of fun and scary rides. In this realm of glitter, glamour, sex symbols and stupendous stomach retching plunges, all under the watchful and benevolent eye of Mickey, wholesome entertainment could morph into new form of religious expression.

New churches would emerge in such a land, churches built differently and managed by very businesslike pastors who were also chief executive officers. In fact, a few such independent institutions were previously established and thriving, as the Angeles Temple, under the guidance of Aimee Semple McPherson. Nearby Garden Grove became the locale, some decades later, of drive-in church with a television station, a spectacular choir and celebrity appearances from around the world. That work grew and spread outward and upward into a cathedral of glass, which was a daring concept. At first the humorists made jokes about so many panes, keeping them clean and so forth. But eventually this phenomenon of bigness was duplicated by dozens of natural born promoters and visionaries in the suburban sites around burgeoning America.

The Era of the Super Church was born in California and driven by a theology of positive thinking not much different from that of the Reverend Norman Vincent Peale, another entrepreneur in New York. He had built a nationwide outreach through his publications and devotional material and then became the nation's leading motivational speaker. His book, *The Power of Positive*

Thinking, achieved national popularity and was a direct influence upon the super-church movement. The Reverend Robert Schuller openly admitted his admiration of Peale and had him as a guest speaker at his own drive-in church east of Los Angeles. However, to my knowledge, Peale never appealed to the faculty of Chaderton seminary and was never invited to speak there. Some critics used to say that they found Peale appalling but Paul appealing. St. Paul, that is. Later I learned that Peale lived in Pawling, New York, and that made me wonder if he was appealing in Pawling. Jesus said that a prophet is not appealing in his home town. When I finally met Peale, in Pawling, and heard him preach, he was indeed appealing. I liked the man and eventually used several of his stories and illustrations in my own sermons.

My Florida never had it quite like California, although given time, Walt Disney's Mickey Mouse would do some mission work in Orlando. Super entertainment parks and super churches would attract super crowds, both using similar techniques of advertising and accommodation to the expectations of modern America. Pews were replaced by cushioned theater seats; wrap-around audio systems would reach the auditors in distant corners and even into the parking lots. Television would reach into all the classrooms. So, it turned out, blessings for religion resulted from the profit-driven research of our modern entertainment industry. Amazing! And perhaps that is why the conservative churches slowly stopped condemning Hollywood and its "moving pictures." That, and television. The new generation of electronic devices and professional entertainers replaced what volunteers used to do in the churches weekends and Wednesday nights.

Where else than where I was could I find such an environment, such stimulation, such enthusiastic congregations of generous folk? Truly, though Colleen and I had left much behind, the horizon was broad, and a rosy-fingered dawn was rising, amply spreading its rays around California, the Golden State.

– 16 –

ORIENTATION: PART 2

FACING HARD FACTS

First year seminary students — officially called juniors — face
schedule of courses loaded with little-known details of religion
Some of those facts are shocking, challenging the ignorance c
sometimes smug attitudes of those students who previously hav
not faced controversy. Seminary becomes the place to have one
faith challenged in a friendly manner. Added to this is the genera
environment of such a school, for a professional school is not a
extension of college. We were to learn about these differences an
also be informed that our professors were on our side, but not a
nursemaids.

The faculty members of Chaderton Seminary were aware c
our various dreams and weaknesses. For they had gone throug
similar studies. It was obvious that they had survived the rigors an
discipline of theology. Each of them, I am sure, hoped to preven
the dreamers from shipwreck and the doubters from losing faith
Therefore a mixture of preventive medicine was prepared an
administered to each entering class before studies began.

Our class retreat was offered at a campground far up Mount Wilson, famous as the site, at the very top, of a premier observatory, but long visited by a variety of enthusiastic happy campers from Greater Los Angeles. Questions would be entertained, friendships begun and a variety of subjects presented by a few chosen seniors plus three professors. We would worship together, the whole bunch of us, as a gathering of individuals from the wider Christian community. This was important to stress, for some entering students would have their doubts about others.

Attendance was mandatory at what was formally designated "orientation." I suppose it would have been too daunting to have termed it a "*dis*-orientation." There is something about the evangelical mind-set that is rather direct, that needs to get to the point because knowing the truth is extremely important, while wandering in the Wilderness is hardly an exercise for such true believers.

We initiates were a typical assembly of idealists. Most of us came from church-saturated America. A few more came from Latin America, Europe and the Middle East, India, Formosa, Japan and Korea. Our common denominator was that we were mostly old-line Protestants, but even at that, we included Anabaptists and Brethren of various origins along with some newer expressions of exuberance, as Pentecostalists. There was at least one Jew among us, from a Jewish/Christian church in some Midwest city.

I learned very soon that many were also largely innocent concerning worldly ways, especially those from Wheaton College or Bob Jones' Bible college. Our fundamentalist colleagues had been sheltered and hemmed in by rules of behavior designed to keep them from sinning. Students from such institutions typically signed pledges not to attend movies, drink alcohol, smoke, dance or gamble. These students were admonished to avoid subjects such as sex and atheism, not even to talk about them. At Bob Jones — it later become a university — the coeds had to have permission to date, which meant to walk around the campus together. If they dared to hold hands they could be censured. Interestingly, few ever mentioned at seminary that they had broken any of these strictures. But many marriages resulted from such innocent relationships, and quite a few went into ministry. Couples coming out of such rigid mores usually laughed about their entry into adulthood, however, and openly admitted that they would not subject their children to that sort of discipline. In fact, I found the students in general to have a keen insight to what I would term a lusty humor and capable of surprising tolerance.

One daring evangelistic young man from a strict background had carved out a niche for himself by frequenting bars and having a beer, then striking up a conversation with someone that would soon turn to matters of faith. No one among the students seemed to be bothered by this, but among a few he became known as Brandy Rummer, a play on his real name that was similar to this little joke.

Ah! I have digressed, as was the custom of the Apostle Paul, so that makes it okay.

Modest four door sedans, each packed with newcomers and driven by the few who could afford them, joined the file of professors' cars and a few vehicles carrying wait staff. All those old-fashioned cars groaned and shifted gears going up the tortuous and forever ascending route that ends at the observatory. That center of science was one of the world's premiere research institutions, where famous and dedicated astronomers peered out into deep space seeking discoveries among the myriads of blinking suns. We, however, were not headed for that geographical and intellectual summit, nor destined to the top of the mount as was Moses. No, we would simply settle in at our church camp and get down to earth about the looming theological process back at San Retiro.

Our Chaderton caravan symbolically turned off onto canyon road short of the observatory, leading downhill to shaded campground. There, amid rustic accommodations, we would be encouraged to take a good look within ourselves and evaluate our desire to serve the cause of Excellence. That was a daunting idea. However, despite the challenge to excel, we were to understand that as candidates for the most honored profession in all of Christendom we were to be humble; and if not, then someone sooner or later would do their best to goad us in that direction. As heirs of the martyrs and saints of a glorious past, we were being prepared to carry the Good News of Redemption and the Hope of Glory to our contemporaries.

Theology, we were to learn, was the "Queen of the Sciences," but a queen in dire straits because her formerly loyal subjects had become captivated by various modern allurements. And for the moment, we were a bright bunch of ignoramuses, an uninitiated assembly of untried saints who, in our foolish youth, thought that a passing knowledge of God's grace was sufficient to our needs. What we needed even more, our mentors advised, was a good dose of humility coupled to an irresistible challenge to learn, learn, learn the many disciplines of academia until we had it right. Now, that is a complex statement, but it is good grammar. We would, by hard work and a measure of God's grace, become capable of justifying the ways of theology to the minds of men.

Down to the Nitty-Gritty

Professor Iain Edgar Furnell, a rising star among the faculty luminaries, was the featured speaker at that retreat in the shaded canyon. Furnell specialized in what was a new subject to many of us, officially called apologetics. I discovered quickly enough that apologetics had nothing to do with making excuses for one's religion but very much to do with presenting a reasonable explanation of the Faith to those who were seeking, if ever so hesitantly. Some of the early Church Fathers, as TertullIan (A.D. 160-230), were apologists in disputations with Pagan philosophers, so the field has a long and distinguished history.

Well, back then apologists did a lot of disputing, sometimes energetically, with adversaries. Furnell was irenic, I was to learn, which means peaceable.

Furnell was accompanied on this retreat by a much older professor, Wilmer Lessor Beane, a popular preacher, and Rodney Clarence Morrison, a professor of practical theology and homiletics. This latter dignitary was a widely educated man, who had served large Baptist churches back East. He had a great store of wisdom to share and was fondly regarded as a no-nonsense and startlingly frank person.

I lacked such details about those men, hearing only that these professors had several books each to his credit. It was a heady draught indeed to have such bigger-than-life-heroes of the Faith to ourselves for a bit more than two days.

The first evening was reserved for worship with an emphasis on music and a few personal testimonies from seasoned students. I was impressed by the hearty singing of all those young men with strong voices and sufficient musical training to be able to harmonize. Many could ably sing a solo, no doubt, and surely knew the hymns, for the assembly room grew sweet with their resonance, reflecting a palpable happiness and a vibrant attitude.

O Zion, Haste! was a favorite from day one. I had not heard it before, and its message seemed to me to summarize the evangelical *esprit*:

> O Zion, haste, thy mission high fulfilling,
> To tell to all the world that God is Light;
> That He who made all nations is not willing
> One soul should perish, lost in shades of night.
>
> Publish glad tidings, Tidings of peace;
> Tidings of Jee-sus, Redemption and release.

I was struck by the third stanza especially:

> Proclaim to every people, tongue and nation
> That God in whom they live and move is love;
> Tell how He stooped to save His lost creation,
> And died on earth that man might live above.

This was a positive theology I embraced immediately. I still feel it is a hymn written in time for all times. Even later in life I still find hints of knowledge I could not have captured then. *And died on earth that man might live above* has a distinctly existential sense to it. Indeed, I do feel today that I have been permitted to "live above." And that is enough, though, God help me, I shall not refuse any added benefit Heaven may hold.

I mentioned the medicine that was mixed for us. This inoculation, in the form of a lecture, was adeptly injected on the second evening of the retreat. We hardly suspected it was coming, for the speaker first entertained us, then massaged us and at the last slipped the needle in before we could react. It was not Morrison, the wise and frank old debunker of clichés, but the much younger Furnell, the sparkling scholar, the darling of students and young pastors, who delivered the sting. I believe he was challenging us, but it sounded just a tad menacing that evening. The truth has its way of disorienting and then reassembling a person. Truth can hurt in some circumstances, and this was one of them. But I remember the admonition, if I may call his speech that, so he must have chosen his words wisely and spoken them clearly. They were dramatically reinforced for me by my experience across the following months.

He began innocently enough, smiling and looking just a bit impish. We were all eyes and ears.

"Well, hello, you mélange of erstwhile sophomores, that is, *wise fools*. Welcome to Chaderton Seminary!" There was a momentary silence while this greeting sank in, and then came a wild hooting and clapping of hands. The speaker resumed his address, "Well, you are no longer sophomores, in the college sense, but are now juniors, and a step above that sophomore stage of learning. We shall move you along as the year progresses from hard to harder, and again we shall move you into the 'middler' category the following year, into further knowledge, until, God willing, you finally become "seniors" and then graduates. Please be assured that our desire is that you continue in the seminary as our successors in ministry, so we designate you with this appellation of sophomore not in order to embarrass you but to challenge you. As I continue, I hope you arrive at this comprehension.

"You have no doubt by now found yourselves better informed and feeling at home among your peers. We leaders have commented among ourselves that you seem a promising assembly. You will no doubt do honor to the tradition we are building at Chaderton. I wish you well, success in your studies and a fruitful ministry. And believe me, this is no idle desire. You will need every ounce of your reserves in order to excel here. This is an advisory statement: In spite of the fact that we are your friends and advocates before the Throne of Grace, and although you shall invoke the mercies of God on many occasions, no one will succeed who does not study seriously and continuously — without ceasing, as the Bible puts it.

"You have come from around the country, and a few of you from other lands, in order to become ministers of the Gospel under our supervision. No doubt some of your family and friends, your churches included, have sent you away to theological seminary with the hope that we would make saints of you in three years maximum."

Chuckles and a few hoots rose from the audience. I was new to this insider sort of humor but liked it from the very first. There was nothing comparable to it in my experience either at church or school. I would learn that the "Wheaton Boys" were at the forefront of such camaraderie.

"But, you must either know or quickly learn that a seminary is not an angel factory. It is a professional school, where God will not give you a good grade if you do not deserve it, so study assiduously. Prayer availeth many things, but has no direct influence on your grade-point average. Nor will you become renowned unless you work at it prayerfully, humbly. Given a sufficiently long life in service to God, you might become aware, eventually, of your shortcomings and pride, repent of your many failings, and attain unto holiness. But that is too far away to deal with tonight, so let's get down to business in the here and now. I wish to deal with your status as juniors, newcomers to our academic discipline."

Furnell then commented on the Apostle Paul's admonition to his disciple Timothy, which had been read earlier. Furnell chose one verse for consideration just then: *Study to shew thyself approved unto God, a workman that needeth not to be ashamed, rightly dividing the word of truth.* He said that the verse was usually applied by most quoters only to Bible study. But the actual wording in Greek, *spoúdason*, means to be diligent rather than to study, and, he said, it means to be alert to please in all things. So, book study is only a part of the apostle's admonition, while pleasing God is the emphasis. Therefore to excel only in Bible study would be to miss the mark. One needs to be ethical, compassionate, humble, quick to praise and slow to criticize. And then he added, as an aside, that Timothy's name is Greek and means "honored of God." God had honored him with ministry and expected a good return.

I liked that. It was a great honor indeed to be named Timothy, and to be among such sterling new friends. I resolved to try hard to be a good student as well as a genuine person, honoring God as he had honored me.

He continued, "More than a few of you come to us from sheltered homes and churches of evangelical traditions, where you were coddled and spoon-fed the articles of the creed. You will find that in this academic community your pet doctrina opinions will be challenged, and some debunked, not only by the secular scholars, whom you will study, but often by your fellow believers. In fact, we your faculty are committed to making you think outside comfortable religion and to lay bare your prejudice and ignorance. *Yes, I said you are burdened with prejudice and ignorance, which is the heritage of us humans.* A religious background does not automatically immunize you against jaundiced attitude and comfortable platitudes. If anything, it causes smugness, so we must revamp your religion.

"We shall all be gentlemen, of course, gentlemen who hold that Truth is one, even as God is one. We shall struggle for a firmer grasp upon understanding than we have yet attained. Then he suddenly changed in temperament and shouted, "**To pursue and serve the truth is the first duty of a Christian scholar. Our Lord said that he was Truth, and that in truth we would be set free.** If you have not discovered it for yourselve you soon shall: *religious people do not like to learn anything that challenges their previous convictions. They by far prefer platitudes to paradox, and you are included in this rule of thumb, because I know through experience that we are all disinclined to admit we just might be wrong.*"

Paradox. The word struck me, for though it was familiar, had not heard it in some time, not from anyone religious, and it seemed strange to hear it from a theologian. But the speaker was moving too fast to allow reflection. I would have opportunit soon enough to appreciate the idea.

"Whatever your background and experience, you are now going to have some common tasks that will try you, will caus moments of doubt. You may wonder about yourselves or even your faith. Now, doubt is not all bad, of course, for it can b a step to greater faith. We hope to teach you how to deal wit doubt, but nonetheless you must learn how to struggle with it o your own terms. I am saying, my young friends, that growth is a process not only of learning new things but of *unlearning* too.

"A room can only contain so much furniture, and you must decide which old pieces to put out at the curb and which new pieces to install. And when your room is full of what you deem worth keeping, why, build another room! God's rich store of things both old and new, of treasures waiting to be discovered and ideas that never as yet occurred to you, await your purchase for your coming ministry. For, as has been quoted many times, there is more in the wider world than your little systems have imagined. Or to put it in the words of an ancient scholar, if you achieve a viewpoint beyond the horizon of your fathers, it is because you have stood upon the shoulders of giants. Stand tall then and lean into the winds. You can finish the race if you do not lose heart."

He paused again, smiling, and looked at his colleagues sitting in the front seats. "Okay," he said quietly, "I've mixed my metaphors here, but I think you understand my intent." Morrison, our designated professor of homiletics, guffawed at this. And the speaker turned a rosy pink. We students burst out in applause, laughing for the first time in his delivery.

Then Furnell stopped completely, shifting to his right and gazing up as though looking at something beyond the rustic rafters. He next looked down at the floor, until all sound had ended. His gaze returned to us, and he seemed slightly sad as he resumed his lecture.

"The final subject I must deal with tonight is that of your survival, no matter who you are or how you are situated. You need to acknowledge that we are an accredited institution. Therefore, no exceptions will be allowed in grading, for there are both state laws and accreditation standards that we must respect. You will be graded on the curve, so the pressure is on. You should, ideally, maintain a minimum grade average of B-minus. It may seem unjust that you had to have an acceptable college record and now be faced with such competition. But this is a professional school, and some will discover that they were not meant to graduate from this seminary. This possibility should not be taken as a judgment of anyone's worth. God's love is not earned by scholarship. But this is the fulcrum among professional schools: a graduate may expect to be considered for advanced study, should he wish to continue in any area of research.

"There are one hundred and two of you. That is a large class, the largest we have admitted in our brief existence as an accredited institution. But by the time we come to graduation three years hence, your number will be cut in half. I can predict this with some certainty, for it is what has happened to each entering class."

Furnell was not smiling, nor was he frowning. He stood tall, calm and open faced, letting this last bit of information sink in.

No one moved, not a sound was uttered, no feet shuffled on the hard floor. Finally someone cleared his throat, and then a ripple of sighs ran across the audience. This sighing was more like a collective letting out of breath, practically a hissing. And then again, silence.

I wondered who would become the first sacrifice upon this fearfully strange altar and hoped I could survive. For I had reason to wonder, coming from such a secular milieu and apparently not "prepped" sufficiently in the more competitive realms of academia. In fact, I felt a bit like a barefoot Florida Cracker at Harvard just then. But my anxiety was distracted by our speaker.

"So then," he said in a very ordinary manner, "we begin. Doubtless there are some questions among you, and perhaps we can address some of them tomorrow at the final session, when we shall evaluate this retreat. But for now, let us enter into a time of prayer before dispersing for the night." He sat down.

A prayer hymn was sung: *Have Thine Own Way, Lord! Have Thine Own Way!* that goes on to say, *Thou art the potter, I am the clay. Mould me and make me, after thy will, while I am waiting, yielded and still.*

We filed out into the moonless night in silence. The air was dry and clear. Nonetheless, most of our assembly probably did not notice the extraordinary sky that the astronomers atop Mt. Wilson were scrutinizing, for many among us found it preferable to tend their feet. Nor was there a prolonged gab session at the dorm that night. We retired but did not sleep at first, I knew, for there was sighing and there was shifting. But I, oh, so weary, dropped into the arms of Morpheus.

The next morning's sessions were subdued in contrast to the previous meetings. But by lunchtime our spirits were revived, and the noise level in the dining hall rose to a din typical of religious folk sitting together at table. We finished up the loose ends of the retreat quickly and piled into our cars and vans for the race back down the winding road to civilization and full schedules.

17

Brain Fever

Paul, thou art beside thyself; much learning doth make thee mad.

> (Words of Festus, upon hearing St. Paul's defense before Agrippa.)

Beginning studies turned out to be full of challenges just a
Furnell told us they would be. The hardest course was taught b
a big man with a very capable intellect, who felt we numbskull
needed a jolt, an awakening, into the world of labyrinthin
thought and philosophical disputation. And he was right, for w
were old enough to stand on our own, though few of us ha
been challenged before by his manner of teaching. The man wa
determined to turn back the bothersome incursions of Liberalisn
into established scholarship, and along the way he was preparin
a cadre of select students to join him in the battle for a Reforme
Orthodoxy.

Professor Carolus H. F. Oldham was a much-sought lecture
on biblical theology, and he therefore had the opportunity t
recruit among the young and disciplined students around th
country. He was brilliant, a "double doctor," in both philosoph
and theology, with a best-seller in religion to his credit. His écl

dazzled most of his students, which in turn dazzled him. He was a happy fellow in those days, full of brio as he gave his lectures to eager students.

Oldham taught epistemology, which, we learned, has nothing to do with the epistles of the Apostles. Such ignorance among us was blown away during the first lecture. To this day I cannot reconstruct what Oldham might have said in that introductory soliloquy. As he rambled on he looked out the window, at other times stared at the ceiling or floor, and occasionally at the students for a smile or a nod of agreement, which he did not bother to acknowledge. All the while, his mind was churning out multi-syllabic zingers for us to decipher, as *hermeneutics* and *teleological*, with an occasional bit of Latin lingo that had to come from philosophical concepts learned at high altitude. The more oriented students, who knew very much about Oldham and his books, said the initials H. F. between his other names had been interpreted to mean "High Frequency."

Some classmates were taking notes, but I had no way of knowing one thing from another. As the lecture ran on, my fingers became numb, as did my feet, and even the tip of my nose. I felt an urge to walk outside and jump up and down to restore my circulation.

I did learn — after the session — that epistemology is a discipline that has its origin in the Greek word for knowledge, *epistʻmʻ*. In practical terms, it means to seek understanding from whatever facts we have gathered or from the ideas of others we consider worthy of consideration. But, at best, the argument goes, this is a world of contradictions where what appears is often not what it seems to be.

We students were going to seek out the *validity* of our knowledge. Validation became an important concept to us in those classes. *How can you be sure that what you believe is really true?* In other words, we would have to examine and seek to validate our assumptions.[2]

When Caesar asked Jesus if he was a king, he ignored the accusation that he aspired to kingship and replied that he came into the world to bear witness to the truth. Apparently Pilate was satisfied that the accused was no threat to the emperor, but he found Jesus' quest novel. Pilate countered with, "What is truth?" For educated men in that ancient cosmopolitan society were convinced that truth was tainted with uncertainty. I imagine Pilate did not really expect an answer but was brushing off this naïve Jewish rabbi from the farmlands to the north.

Pilate represents much more in John's Gospel than his position as a procurator of a small nation would immediately indicate. For Pilate becomes the the soldier, the politician, the pursuer of the possible, the ladder climber and the cold-blooded sustainer of the laws and punishments of the Roman Empire. In a minuscule way but nonetheless effectively, he *is* Rome, cynical, militant Rome. To him might is right, and power decides which way things shall go, for Pilate has taken an oath: Caesar is Lord.

Oldham believed that nothing short of divine revelation would provide certainty, and the Bible served that need. Specialist in Reformed theology, adeptly using the Bible, had defined the dogma that comes out of infallible Scripture. *Well*, I wondered, *why am I in seminary?* My friends at The Palms had already put such iron-bound ideas into practice and could quote the Bible to counter any and all liberal, humanist and atheist ideas.

I had observed that reading the Bible creates all manner of questions in the mind of the serious student. For beyond reading that ancient compilation of documents called The Word of God the modern student has to deal with scientific findings. They may not be truth with a capital T, but it is difficult to ignore them.

It is no help then to learn that there are hundreds of denominations within Protestantism around the world — hundreds — and within each one there are Bible-believing folk who fear joining with others who might corrupt their faith or lead them into error. Apparently, having an inspired Bible is no assurance of reaching accord within the churches.

Aha! That is why Gaines had me read that strange book on the chaos of cults in the modern world. Each sect failed at some point to measure up to the interpretation of an orthodox theologian. In Gaines' thought, Scofield was the right choice even if he was not exactly a classical scholar. I felt a sudden chill run up my spine as I grasped my first comprehension of epistemology.

We Protestants had cast off from the traditional authority of the ancient Church and taken upon ourselves a revised Church that had to define anew what authority is. At first we were Lutheran or Reformed or from a small minority of Anabaptist sects. In place of a pope and his cardinals, our first Protestants agreed that the Bible would provide us with correct doctrine both to reform the Church and provide clergy to teach what to believe and how to behave. From there we went downhill. For divine revelation is a high-class ideal that tends to get sloppy. Had not Lutherans and the Swiss Reformed split early on regarding the meaning of Holy Communion? Luther said the bread of Holy Communion was the Body of Christ, for he was in, around, above and below the element itself. The Swiss said the bread was a memorial of his sacrifice. And this one point was enough to keep the two churches apart.

Such a confusion of ideas and practices was my main reason for attending seminary. Oldham was taking me back to the mentality at The Palms that I had found lacking. At least that is the way I saw it then. Was I missing something?

The final exam for Oldham's course in epistemology was simply one question, a humdinger, long since forgotten — a Freudian lapse, perhaps? That question required an essay that left most of us grasping for words. It was no help that several students knew the solution and quickly handed in their papers. They got the best grades, of course. Most of the rest of us managed a poor C.

With this shock, added to a few others during that first trimester and throughout the year, a few students folded their tents and stole away to points unknown. The attrition mentioned by Furnell was taking form in an alarming fashion, and that much earlier than we would have imagined.

Escaping the Cloister

In contrast to such high-level thought, first-year students were also expected to take up "practical work" in some church of our own selection. The supervisor of this activity had a few requests for student volunteers to serve in local churches, but not nearly enough. I was not assigned to anyone and quickly discovered that most Presbyterian churches in the area already had more than enough talent on hand, as California was a magnet for retired clergy. Every pastor, it seemed, had both an associate on the payroll as well as volunteers and often could call on a pensioned pastor to help out wherever they were needed. This dilemma influenced my decisions about what I might do for my ministry. I had arrived in California without a letter of recommendation to any Presbyterian church, which I had not asked of my pastor and he had failed to provide. I was left to seek out a church that would accept my talents and get to work. That simple. And then there was my choice of Spanish as a major study, which would have led me, reasonably, into teaching Spanish. These factors inclined my thought to doing something among the Mexican population in the area.

The Lord works in wondrous ways, his marvels to perform.

I located a Presbyterian church far from San Retiro, in a Mexican neighborhood near the University of Southern California. I had heard that the pastor also taught in a small college in Lo

Angeles, so I felt he could use some help. The Reverend José de Gallegos was quite open to my inquiry. We conducted our interview entirely in Spanish. I knew the grammar, even if my Cuban inflection was less than desirable in Los Angeles. Gallegos was receptive to having me join him in ministry, as he was already busy and had no paid staff. I would come aboard as the youth minister, teaching in English but knowing the language the teenagers heard at home. Within a short time I also helped in the morning worship, which amazed the members, who had never known a *gringo* in their denomination who spoke their language so well.

A group of young married couples who were Presbyterian but did not know the why nor the what of their affiliation asked me to meet with them one evening a week. They said no one ever explained their Protestant religion to them, and they did not know how to pursue the subject. I asked around at the seminary bookstore and came up with a pamphlet on Presbyterianism and another on the Westminster Confession of Faith. I was also offered a short catechism for training adolescents in the essentials of doctrine. Equipped with those pieces of helpful information, and without admitting my ignorance to my new friends, I taught them as I learned. Each point in the creed was explained by an elementary system of Question and Answer. Every answer in the catechism had a proof text from the Bible to back it up. We learned that the chief end of man is to glorify God and enjoy him forever. And so forth, for over one hundred questions.

There is more to this tale within a tale, and I shall return to it.

Arcane Facts and Miscellanea

Among the new discoveries at seminary were many eye-openers never discussed in church Bible classes: Hammurabi, king of Babylon, ca. 1750 B.C.E., received a code of laws from the gods long before Moses received the Decalogue — commonly called The Ten Commandments — on Mount Sinai. There were a few other parallel stories in the ancient world, as the story of Gilgamesh, a Sumerian king, who was commanded to build an ark in preparation for a flood. This story is part of a collection of epic poetry. He too made sacrifice to the gods when he disembarked on dry land, much as Noah was reputed to have done. Such discoveries caused scholars to conclude that the Hebrew Scriptures were not entirely unique, and even if the Hebrew Religion was more esthetically attractive, it seemed also to be later in composition. Therefore, the *idea* of the Bible stories as literally the original stories from eyewitnesses — beginning with Adam and Eve's progeny — became doubtful. This doubt caused a more careful reading of the ancient texts, and the result was the discovery of other contradictions and evidence of accretions to the text across the years. Scholars, having a growing catalog of ancient literature and having developed some sophisticated dating techniques, began to read the biblical texts with new insights. This led them to make comparisons with Jewish scholars, and they discovered that the rabbis also had some observations and questions to contribute to the growing knowledge of ancient Scripture.

This more detached and critical approach to the Bible was only part of a new way of reading all ancient literature. Christians were being forced to acknowledge that the Bible made sense mostly as a collection of ancient lore — at times including wisdom — but in many cases was not historic fact.

Those ancient Mid-easterners, the Hebrews among them, were keepers of tribal lore, which served their purposes very well. They were superb at hyperbole but they understood little of physics. Their world was crowded with gods and spirits moving between heaven and earth. Sacrifices were made, the pungent odor ascended into the sky, and the gods were appeased.

Higher Criticism: The Scholar's Tool and a Labyrinth

Our course in higher criticism of biblical literature was conducted by an old gentleman so unassuming in his public persona as to make one think that his class was a Bible study in a basement of some country church. But when Dr. Haraldssohn began talking about ancient literature and its analytical study, comparing the various works of the Old Testament with other ancient literature of those times, I learned that this was not only an issue of Scripture versus other ancient literature but also a class in philology, that is, knowing what other books were out there from ancient times. This has an implication for theologians. We would be expected to know as much as possible about the classic literature of the world, especially about other religions. Most of us would never find the time to keep up the reading across our busy years as pastors and missionaries.

Our professor proved to be a sterling scholar in the field of biblical criticism. His approach was to know the published material thoroughly and then show how the more fervent of the critics missed one point or another somewhere or failed to take in some salient biblical or historical truth or spiritual insight.

This way of defending religion seemed to me to be nit-picky in the extreme. The idea of literary criticism was not entirely new to me, since in college I had learned of old arguments that Plato could have created the myth of Socrates, whom he claimed as his mentor. Then there were conjectures, in later centuries, about who might have been the genius behind Shakespeare. For surely, a village poet could not have written those masterworks. Therefore, viewing the Bible as literature instead of revelation was not completely out of the question. But the process was tedious and endless, for every solution brought a counter-proposition.

Charles J. Duey

Observations about Ancient Times

The early history of the Church and the compilation of its Apostolic writings — really, its Scriptures — is a story that stretches over three centuries. In order to appreciate a modern, printed and bound New Testament, one needs to know how the pieces came together and were edited. Some texts were emended to fit the doctrinal ideas of influential bishops, or worse, to support political preferences. Holy men were implicit in such deception because they believed they were doing it to God's glory. And this fervor impelled them into excluding and persecuting other Christians who disagreed. But eventually those three centuries resulted in a widely accepted collection of writings that we today call the New Testament. It really is a marvel to behold, for we all seem to have agreed upon the twenty-seven Gospels, Epistles, history and Revelation that survived all the rigors of scrutiny and debate.

Not everyone agreed, and not everyone went along with the new Roman Catholic and Apostolic Church. But this is not the place to pursue the details of such history, other than to note that Church history recognizes an end to one era and the beginning of another: the Ante-Nicene Fathers before Constantine and the Post-Nicene following the emperor's recognition of Christianity. There are also writings covering the time of the Council at Nicea. In all, there are many volumes of history, debate, affirmation and declamations waiting the scholar's perusal.

Beginning with Emperor Constantine's courtship with the Christian Religion, Rome was able to intrude itself politically into the church's theology and practice, so that conflicts would be resolved in favor of the emperor's preference for one Roman Church with one set of Scripture and one creedal statement to be used throughout the empire. The irony is that there were so many priests anxious to have such support for unanimity. Their purposes were not so much spiritual as theological, and I suppose, managerial.

Constantine the Great melded aspects of his Pagan sun worship — Mithraism — into this official Christianity and declared such doctrine to be definitive and uniform among all churches. Not all believers went along with this, and for the first time in Christian history some were in, some out. There had been disagreements about a definition of Christian belief before Constantine but nothing comparable to this with such far-reaching implications.

Whatever innocence I had managed to save was then dashed upon the rocky shore of hard facts not taught in most churches. *Humans* had written about God, sometimes quoting him as though he had spoken in their hearing. So then, God was not the author of any specific book. In fact, the words of Jesus in the Gospels were written down decades after his ministry, which explained why there were so many differences in the details of the four Gospels, some items in one Gospel but not in another, and with an occasional conflict of wording or circumstance. And there is the stark difference between Matthew, the literalist, for instance, and John, the philosopher. One wonders how two such different views of the life and work of Jesus could have come from two eye-witnesses.

I could see it: *No wonder it was necessary to have critical scholars in both textual and historical studies, who would spend their lives reading ancient documents of all sorts, in order to make sense out of the residue of antiquity*. Change then was part of our Christian heritage; change and growth. The more we know, the more we have to deal with. But there is no road back. One freezes in time and becomes a fundamentalist about ideas prevalent in a historic period, or one moves on with history, dealing with the issues as they arise. The painful part about such activity is that one must have faith in something — or Someone. I was not quite sure how to pursue this idea just then, but I was getting close.

A Crisis Moment

Dealing for the moment solely with the cascading effect of new information, and having learned more than I ever imagined was out there to be learned, my previous assumptions and certainties were in tatters, and I was in need of first aid. For although Pastor Ralph Hatfield helped me considerably, there simply was not enough time for me to work my way through the logic of what was becoming clearer and therefore challenging. So, for the interim I was operating on good faith within the "system," whatever the system was. *Perhaps, I began to think, there is no system. There are various attempts to devise systems, but none has achieved perfection. My head spun like a top. Where is God if not immediately present in all this confusion? Is not God a God of order? Why has God not made order out of this chaos we call the Church?* I wanted answers but found little assurance.

Tumbling over my confusion, capitulating to this mass of evidence and contradiction, I faltered. For it seemed God had withdrawn from the human scene of action, was unknowable, perhaps only a pious theory. I could not bear this alone, so confessed my loss of faith to a few friends with whom I prayed in private several mornings a week. As I confided in them I was overcome by a deep sorrow, a loneliness I first experienced when my mother died. We were already on our knees, in the privacy of a student's apartment, so the others prayed for me one-by-one as I tried to gain control of my heartbreak. More than one of those who prayed aloud confessed that he lacked the courage to say what I had said. *Aha! There were others who also struggled with doubt.* By the time my companions finished this form of support, I was at least able to rejoin the group with an appearance of composure. Apparently I was still among friends, for I had been affirmed. I felt thankful for this hint of grace.

The eerie thing about the experience is that none of us ever referred to it after that, and I resumed going to classes as though nothing had happened. This is a classic example of what the psychologists call denial. I discovered that there was a lot of it going around. In fact, reflecting upon my experience, it occurred to me that the entire religious system was in denial, and sometimes dangerously unaware of the unhealthy practice. But, sad to say, denial sometimes is all we have protecting us from calamity. We fail to understand our faith as a tool to deal with doubt.

I gained another insight. Could Professor Oldham also undergo such personal agony? Was he bereft of friends with whom he could express an honest doubt? After all, he had been converted to an evangelistic viewpoint and moved on, thanks to his great intellect, to a hide-bound theology forged out of the heat of early Protestant debate. Surely his mind interacted with modern science and some of the valid theology taking place all around him. I had heard that it is lonely at the top, and I felt sympathy for him.

Denial may not always be bad, but neither is it curative. I became numb, as one dead yet walking, and went through a period of depression in which I felt as if someone else occupied my body. A mummy took my notes and read my books. My marital love life froze, our time together sterile in every way. The episode dragged on and was as horrible as it sounds. Bless Colleen's compassionate nature, she did not pressure me, only watched helplessly as I withdrew into myself and away from her warmth.

And then, when I had fully come to accept myself as an agnostic — I could not bring myself to admit to worse than that — without plan or purpose, wondering why I was still in seminary and pondering what I should do, just then a new attitude began to develop within me. I remembered that Furnell said that seminary studies would bring doubts, and that each of us would have to learn to deal with them. He also said that the faculty would help us cope, and stressed that it was our duty to learn the truth, for in truth we would be set free. I was prepared by then to recognize that Jesus had said something very similar to that, and I was ready to apply it to myself in the here and now.

Words of wisdom from various instructors and chapel speakers began to return to comfort and advise me. One speaker at a worship service said that it was natural for a student to be broken down, as layers of old and inadequate thought were peeled away by the sharp sword of truth, and that new and better understanding would eventually fill the void in our hearts. "Behold, I make all things new," he quoted.

I slowly learned that one work of the Holy Spirit is to destroy an individual's internal idols, be they doctrinal assumptions or intellectual concepts, perhaps something even as trite as speech patterns, and then to go after the external distractions, societal or professional, until nothing of human invention remains between oneself and the Spirit. One's consciousness must finally be laid bare and open to the truth of matchless grace. This is what it means to be overwhelmed by Love.

God the Father is enough, the only Certitude, and that a matter of the heart. So, since the Scripture reminds us that the heart can be deceitful, we are left with a paradox. Yes, a paradox! Here is the word that lays it all out in the open: God is not either/or but both/and, unknowable yet available, distant but felt in the present, demanding and gracious, provoked to anger but abundant in steadfast love. We, however, wish Deity to be simpler, easily defined.

Indeed, I did feel empty, completely empty, aware of it and not happy with it. But I was not entirely empty of faith, for I really *did still believe in God, only not the God others presented to me but the One who could speak a hidden word, who could provide a personal assurance, who spoke to my doubt.*

I recalled hearing a quote from Saint Augustine at a chapel service: "Too late I loved you, O Beauty so ancient yet ever new! Too late I loved you! And, behold, you were within me, and I out of myself, and there I searched for you." Ah, the old saint knew the value of paradox!

If there was ever a time when I was converted — I am not entirely sure that is the proper term for what I experienced — it was in this process of finding the deeper meaning of our Christian religion. Enlightened? Too dramatic. Liberated? Yes! I could then say with other Christians, "I know whom I have believed and am persuaded that he is able to keep that which I have committed unto him against that day" (2nd Timothy; 1:12).

Finally, I learned to doubt fearlessly, *for my opinions do not really matter, except for my own spiritual pilgrimage.* God will remain God: immortal, invisible, wise. And I, poor ignoramus, will continue to learn and change. As Dr. Furnell said, "Doubt is the path to greater faith."

The weeks rushed by during my recovery, weeks filled with mounting joy, until, without any awareness on my part, April in full splendor displayed itself to me. Such beauty! But it was also time to prepare for final exams.

Southern California was exceedingly appealing to me that May. As I stood in the sunlight before class, it dawned upon me that I had not corresponded with Princeton Seminary about transferring there in the autumn. While Colleen and I were preparing supper I mentioned this oversight to her and my blasé attitude about it. She replied that she had been waiting for me to say something, anything, but that she saw such a happy intensity in me in the previous weeks and an absorption in my studies and work that she decided to leave me to my own devices. I looked at her for a moment, awed at her wisdom, and then thanked her for such patience. Only then did I think to ask her what she felt about our future.

Colleen told me that she was very pleased with her year in the public school system. Her voice trailed off as she looked up from setting the table. We stood for a brief moment looking at each other with clear eyes, and then we hugged. Our present resolved

and our future settled, we went into the bedroom and made love.
Meanwhile, the food simmered, unattended, to its ruin.

❧

God within me, God without.
How shall I ever be in doubt?
There is no place where I may go
and not there see God's face, not know
I am God's vision and God's ears.
So, through the harvest of my years,
I am the sower and the sown,
God's self-unfolding and God's own.

Anonymous

18

ALMOST CALIFORNIANS

The glory of God is a human being fully alive.

St. Irenaeus, Second Century A.D.

Summer brought heat, and heat increased the smog. There were better places than Los Angeles just begging to be visited. But first, just to get into the swing of things, we began with some local attractions. As soon as Colleen was free from her teaching schedule we began with day drives to famous tourist attractions, as the La Brea Tar Pits and the Hollywood movie tours, the Huntington Museum, a drive to Redondo Beach, Riverside and Disneyland in Anaheim. Then, emboldened, we pointed the Dodge north, sampling a buffet of nature's sights and lovely nights which we heaped upon our tourist trays.

The entire state seemed to have been freshly fashioned but yet smacked of yesteryear. An abundant land opened before us, full of vineyards and orange groves, date palms, fields of grain, stately horse farms and rolling hills. The people moved along at a breathtaking pace, especially on their highways.

Vigorous! Refreshing! We were energized as we drove through the San Joaquin Valley and into Sequoia National Park, and again in Fresno and Merced. Contrasts, contrasts! Wooded highlands and irrigated valleys, winding roads with something new around each bend. We even came upon a bit of desert, but far cleaner than the one we encountered on our way to California a year earlier. This land was ours to enjoy, a land we gladly embraced.

Photos only touch on the beauty at every turn in Yosemite National Park. One needs to drive through that wonder, hike its trails and take the high road to vistas so vast that there are no words to describe them. We held hands often, in silence, and felt we were being nationalized as eager immigrants into a new world, a world so far different from Florida that we expected to be asked for our passports at any moment.

And then, after the long drive in what seemed an endless forest that finally gave way to crowded Modesto, we once more entered the highway system. There was only one place to go then, so I pointed the car toward the metropolis that George Sterling poetically dubbed "the cool grey city of love." San Francisco was every bit as beautiful as advertised. We greedily took in each new marvel, of wooded hills and views of the bay, houses with flower boxes at the windows and cool breezes blowing in from the sea.

That evening we ascended Nob Hill and dined high up in the hotel, which provided us a view of the city sparkling below us. It was such a contrast to our usual life of abnegation that we felt just a bit decadent. We discovered, too late, that tourists were advised to bring along some heavier, darker clothes, for San Francisco even in the summer, has a dress code much more conservative than Los Angeles. Our conspicuous ignorance did not keep us from enjoying the decadence, to us, of dining in such sumptuous surroundings. Imagine, we commented — as we attacked our dinners, ending with cheese cake topped with strawberries and whipped cream — imagine, some people do this every weekend.

The Big Sur is a must-see, so we chose it for the return drive to the reality of our daily life. At the end of the trip we drove through a crowded Santa Barbara and soon were in San Retiro. The summer would go on for another two months. By August end we were rested and ready for another active year in southern California. Oh, such promising days!

Even the smog seemed less invasive.

Events then happened in rapid succession, arriving uninvited, that would change my plans. The first item was the arrival of a letter from Pastor Ralph informing me that the General Assembly of the denomination had met in late June and, among many decisions, voted down a motion to designate Chaderton an acceptable institution for training Presbyterians. Some of the delegates, mostly ministers, felt that the institution was divisive, "schismatic," he wrote, a term reserved for the worst sort of school. Ralph advised me to rethink my decision to remain in place for another year. Perhaps it would not be too late to reapply to Princeton, or should that fail, to seek out a western school, as San Anselmo Seminary, north of San Francisco. For, he said, the assembly's decision included a resolution that any Presbyterian students at Chaderton transfer to denominational schools. *So much for ecumenism*, I thought, and sighed a great sigh.

Pastor Ralph also mentioned that Reverend Gaines had split The Palms church, moving his followers over to the mainland to begin an independent "fellowship assembly" named, rather predictably, Calvary Bible Church. I've never seen a census of church names, but that one must rank high among fundamentalists. Well, since "Bible" churches are known for being anti-denominational, Gaines had become — at least and at last — honest about his personal agenda. But he left the remnant of members at The Palms badly demoralized and financially strapped.

Hatfield advised that although it was to my advantage to have gotten out of that situation prior to the schism, nevertheless, should I remain at Chaderton, I would probably have trouble finding a church upon graduating. Guilt by association has always been a terrible stereotype to overcome, and Christians are as prone to succumb to its power as are politicians.

Trouble comes in bunches.

Hatfield's letter arrived the same week that the Presbyterian church in which I was serving had its own crisis. The pastor Reverend Fernando José de Gallegos y Alcorcón, a rather high class Spaniard, and a professor of Spanish literature, was being pressured to move on and make room for someone else which meant someone who would reflect the preferences of the congregation. This is an interesting phenomenon, that the taught become the dictators of what shall be taught. I know that democracy allows this, but I had the impression that the people of God were more pliable, humble, anxious to find ways to please the Lord, no matter the inconvenience.

The pastor was not embroiled in any moral or financial trouble connected to his work. He simply did not suit the religious taste of the membership. For one thing, he spoke Castillian Spanish lisping his cees and dees as most do in parts of Spain, as Madrid. But Mexicans avoid the sound. And he used a vocabulary that was not as familiar to his church members as they would prefer. He also made frequent references to Spanish classical poets and philosophers, such as Miguel de Unamuno and the mystics Sant Teresa de Jesús and San Juan de la Cruz.

My pastor introduced me to the lovely spiritual insight of Saint Teresa's *Sonnet to the Crucified*. The poem is exceptionally well-crafted in Spanish, using the subjunctive mood, moving rhythmically to a touching conclusion.

Sonnet to the Crucified[3]

> I am not moved, my God,
> to love you for heaven's hope,
> given by promise from above,
> not moved by fearful fires
> to leave off my offenses.

> You move me, Lord,
> seeing you nailed to a cross and bloody.
> Moved am I to see such wounded flesh,
> such offenses, and your death.
>
> I am moved even more by your love for me.
> And, in such a way that,
> were there no heaven, yet would I love you.
> Yea, were there no hell, yet would I quake!
>
> Such love leaves no doubt:
> Were I not to hope that which I hope,
> even then, as I love you, thus would I love.

In spite of his trouble with the membership, Don Fernando remained an ecumenist, living in hope of bringing Christians together. He was well versed in the modern Presbyterian emphasis on the world Church. And he was from the liberal edge in Spain, where the Protestant Church and Spanish mysticism had met in the persons of Miguel de Unamuno and his understudy John Alexander Mackay. The Scot had gone to Spain to study with Unamuno, who was one of the early enthusiasts for the writings of Søren Kierkegaard. Mentor and student were different in both culture and religious experience, but they converged in an existentialist interpretation of the living Christ. And my Spanish pastor at the Mexican church was a product of that vision. In Christ, he believed, following the assertion of St. Paul, "There is neither Jew nor Greek, there is neither bond nor free, there is neither male nor female: for ye are all one in Christ Jesus."

This sounds so wonderfully perfect. I only wish some of the purists among us could bend a bit and let us together find a more excellent way.

Pastor Gallegos took this view of the existential Christ with him in his ministry. Along with tutoring me in the Spanish mystics, he taught me much about these modern leaders, about existentialism and the ecumenical vision for the healing of the divided Body of Christ. There was a great work yet to be done in Latin America, and not only in the Americas but everywhere again and again, for that matter. For, as we say, *God has no grandchildren.* Each person must decide at some point, whether to commit oneself to a life of faith or to passively remain in a crisis that leads to desperation. Or, if baptized, whether to accept one's baptism into Christ and the Faith or settle for something less stimulating, less promising.

I was quite taken by my Spanish mentor's acceptance of abuse and rejection from within his parish. The membership did not deserve him but at the same time were not equipped to appreciate him, so they wished him out of there.

It had not occurred to me that I was part of the problem. My heart was pure, I felt, for I worked as a volunteer. But I was a *gringo* nonetheless, and although I spoke passable Spanish I was obviously a *yanqui.* The Yankees had taken California and much more land clear over to Texas away from Mexico, and no one was inclined to forgive and forget. It was no help that my red headed wife knew little Spanish, nor did we live in the neighborhood just as their pastor lived in another area. The locals felt uneasy with this, as though outsiders were taking over their church. Should the institution begin to sink, they feared we might abandon ship. And so, ironically, they threw us overboard, which is a form of abandonment while also a self-fulfilling prophecy. Talk about ecumenism and the failure to grasp the concept, we faced it foursquare.

There were some tears shed as we two ministers parted, going our separate ways. I do not know if his wife had undergone anything like that before, but for Colleen it was a second rejection. However, people recover in one way or another from such pettiness.

The congregation would find another minister to wrestle with their local issues, and he would take some young assistant under his wing. But for me, it was more complex, for that church was the third Presbyterian congregation I had served in a period of three years. It would be proper to say the third fellowship from which I had departed, and each time I left friends behind. "Here we have no abiding place" was becoming as true for me as for the Wandering Jew.

These unexpected reversals left me reeling. How could I reconcile my previous optimism and exuberant faith to these complications? It would not be easy. But I knew that being committed to Christ was no bed of roses. That cliché went around the seminary. It was up to me then to find God's will for the next interval of my training.

We former juniors, numbering just over one hundred, began the second year as seventy hardy middlers, who were beginning to feel like survivors. Within three months that number would be reduced to only three score, due to Presbyterians urged by their pastors to leave Chaderton A.S.A.P. By the end of spring exams a few others would opt to bleed away.

I was deficient in a knowledge of Presbyterian administrative policy, and having no close relatives in any of the denomination's churches back home, felt quite alone. But I knew that going to a new seminary would cause me to feel even lonelier, as I would have to reorient myself completely and overcome a reputation as a stray. At least at Chaderton I knew the routine and was familiar with the professors. And everyone said that the courses became more enjoyable as time moved along. I looked forward to the year. In effect, I opted to remain outside my denomination's oversight, which was a natural consequence of never having been fully under it.

Colleen and I talked about our dilemma several times and finally decided to sample the field from among congregations other students had found interesting. No longer driving to Los Angeles in heavy traffic was a happy thing, really, and less costly.

No one would be taking attendance, so we could enjoy a Sunday evening at home.

One church that appealed to us, that was also in contact with the seminary, was conveniently close, within the downtown area of El Retiro. The Bethany Community Church was still slightly ethnic in origin, being founded by Dutch immigrants of an earlier generation. They had gained a mixed fellowship of pious and enthusiastic supporters from the community, and also sponsored several missionaries working in various countries. We took up regular attendance with the intention of joining them before long.

Classes were going well, and with learning came self-assurance. Studies were more rewarding and often complementary, so that one subject enlightened another. I also had begun to read the secular press, seeking to inform myself of the world beyond the seminary. There was a *Time Magazine* feature article on William F. Buckley, Jr., a devout Catholic, who took the nation by storm with his book *God and Man at Yale*. He quickly became an icon among political conservatives, and some among us read him and quoted him as though he were an old acquaintance. But he was in favor of Senator McCarthy's anti-communist crusade, and I was not sure that the crusade was going in the right direction. Some of us students even bought pink shirts at the local department store and wore them as a protest against McCarthy's "pinko" campaign. Nevertheless, my exposure to a regular dose of politics and the economy was a godsend, and I began to see the dynamic implications of a personal ethic in the political field as well as in religion. It was all quite heady. One professor warned us about becoming drunk on such a mixture, akin to sitting on two bar stools at the same time. He would have us decide if we were going to preach Christ or politics. "They are separate," he advised. Well maybe.

I believed that Jesus was crucified because he was critical of the political practices of his countrymen, as the prophets of earlier times had been of their generations. He did not stumble into politics unknowingly but deliberately strode forward, acting out a lesson for his disciples. There is reason to believe that Jesus knew he was headed for trouble with the authorities from the beginning of his ministry and decided not to run away from it but to confront it. Taking up one's cross is to dare to challenge those leaders who say one thing and do another. After all, he was the heir of the prophets of old, and they spoke to unjust and unfaithful kings, who abused their subjects and failed to do justice in the land.

Jesus has inspired countless followers in these succeeding years to take their cross and follow him. And here's the hook: taking up a cross does not mean that one is going to be killed, only be willing to make a sacrifice. A cross can mean years of self-denial, or persecution. Yet it is true that many have died. Some theologians point out that Christ lived a saving life, as demonstrated in his deeds and teachings, and that he was obedient in every way. Moreover, God did not need a death in order to love us. Indeed, Jesus himself portrayed his heavenly Father as a lover of the wayward. I know that many have seen much more in his sacrifice and have applied it to the blood sacrifice of the Temple rituals. I will not deny them their interpretation. The New Testament writings include the idea of atonement, and this has usually been taken as blood shed for the remission of sins. But God did not require the death of his Son in order to forgive sins. Some say God had to satisfy his own laws and need for vengeance, but I say that with God nothing is impossible. God is not obligated to think as we think or do as we do.

As I struggled through this drama of the cross, often called the crisis of the Christ, I saw something wonderful: although Christ died, love did not die. No one can kill love, for God is Love. Brutes can nail Love to a cross — and I capitalize the L — and poke spears into its heart, can bury it and roll a stone over the grave, but they cannot kill Love. Love comes back and keeps on loving. Love is so strong it overcomes the grave. It rises from the ashes of human failure and opens its arms to all without distinction. Roman soldiers, thieves, the lusty, the prim and proper, the self-righteous, along with the humble, the leprous, the tax cheater and the collaborator in oppression: all are accepted and can find a new life if they will but kneel at the foot of that cross where love was put to the test. And since with God time is limitless, God is allowing time to justify that Love, not for his sake but for ours. We are the ones who need to turn around and take a long look at the cross. For only then can we look forward with confidence.

Such new thinking, for me at least, was reinforced by an Anglican priest, J. B. Phillips, who had done a thoroughly modern translation of the New Testament, which became the rage among young evangelical students. He then followed that up with a small book with a large impact, *Your God Is too Small*, that challenged us to think outside the box. We had to admit that we were accustomed to thinking only in terms of our own religious indoctrination, so he gave us an excuse to break away. In my case, having done some of my breaking away, he needed only to reinforce me.

From the Sublime to the Conceptual

Colleen had grown increasingly quiet coming into the spring of that second year. Perhaps I had not noticed her changing as Easter approached, did not catch her loss of appetite, especially at breakfast. But with the cessation of extra services at church, we both let out a big sigh and kicked off our shoes. Colleen did not recover her former sparkle but became even more withdrawn. Something was askew, I knew, and in my very direct way I broached the subject. The old psychological trick of blaming oneself when things don't go right took over, and I asked her what I had done to offend.

The good news was that *I* had not done anything all by myself, but that *we* had done something spectacular. We started a baby, that's what! If anything, Colleen was blaming herself, because, she said, she had neglected to keep her supply of contraceptive cream in stock, and one weekend, when we had managed a mini-vacation, we were at risk. She said, sniffling only slightly, she thought it would be okay, because she had counted the days and knew it was a safe time. She was now late for her second month, having tried to believe when she skipped the first month that it was just a fluke. But now she could "feel" her pregnancy. She had an appointment later in the week with a gynecologist recommended by a teacher friend.

I smiled. I beamed. I stood up and shouted a war whoop! Then I marched around the living room like a macho man. When this little exhibition ended, I looked at Colleen and saw that she was smiling. Relieved would be a better word. For we had made an agreement that we would not begin a family until I finished my studies, and then, I said, she could have a dozen kids if she wished. But now I was not thinking about that agreement. It didn't matter any longer, for all doubts about our ability to have children were removed. Only later would it occur to me that Colleen was pushing up to thirty, and the urge to begin a family was bound to become a more serious matter to her, possibly allowing her to become negligent about family planning. But, what do we men know about such things?

The middler year studies came to an end, and the following month Colleen took leave from her career and turned to her grand adventure full time. She said the obstetrician set a date no later than early November. Dr. Carver was a gentle medic, one of three in a joint practice: Carver, Hurter and Burns. Their juxtaposition of surnames on their office sign did not slip by pregnant patients, even if we future fathers were a bit obtuse.

There were also some adjustments necessary over on father's side of the bed. I had no idea just how often such self-denial

would be required. As I've said before about myself, ignorance i
bliss. Had not Jesus himself said that we should take no though
for tomorrow but become as little children? Just for a fleetin;
moment I thought of my former classmate, who had droppe(
out of school because of his wife's fecundity and his own lacl
of restraint. I was somewhat impatient with him for doing wha
came naturally, and so complicating things. Had I not been mor(
prudent than he? Well...

As someone said, *Time wounds all heels*.

19

DOWN TO BRASS TACKS

Pursuing a call to ministry was not working out as I had imagined. I do not mean that I had some clear plan for my future. However, it seemed reasonable to enjoy stability and mutuality within the religious community, but to that point I had found conflict, mobility and some contradiction. To add to this, little Charlotte or William was kicking Colleen from within, more by night than by day. What would I do for this child God was giving into our care? The reality of impermanence and vulnerability began to dawn upon me as I meandered among the churches and compared notes with other students. The thought was dawning that I might never own another home or remain in any one location for more than a few years. So then, what might I do for my children? Colleen and I had not dared talk about this openly, but it seemed time to deal with it.

I had heard this idea quoted from *Proverbs* many times: "Trust in the Lord with all thine heart; and lean not unto thine own understanding. In all thy ways acknowledge Him, and He shall direct thy paths." I did not know it at that time, but later would comprehend that now is the only time there is, so it is wise to "go with the flow and use a light oar." I think I read that

in a book by Robert Raines. It helped to know that for the mos
part we were rafting upon the River of God. Our free will wa
limited, I began to discover, by many factors, as the river and the
direction of its flow. But I had an oar named decision, so it fel
like I was in charge. I might have chosen to get off the raft, bu
I wanted to believe I was in a divine current. Where else would
choose to navigate? This see-sawing went on for some time.

Colleen hoped to return to teaching, but only after spendin;
those first several months at home with our baby. I was thinkin;
that we should plan for longer. I could quit studies for a year and
find a full-time job, perhaps as an associate minister in trainin;
or as a Spanish teacher. I was teaching an evening course in basi
Spanish at the city college and could hope for a recommendatio;
from the dean.

At that point in my seeking answers one came to me withou
even trying. Several of the seminary students had positions at th
Los Angeles Juvenile Detention Center, and as one prepared t
move on, he usually passed the job on to another student. I wa
told of the coming vacancy by a graduating senior, who was als
from Florida. With just minimal orientation to the situation,
grasped the moment, jumped through the administrative hoop
and got the job.

Five nights a week, from ten o'clock to six, I served as a jaile;
counselor to adolescent boys. My job was to finish the day's pape
work, then sit in watch at a central desk with a telephone t
the main office. I was to stay awake, first of all, and tend to th
occasional emergency. It was possible most nights to manag
several hours of reading assignments. The job also provided conta
with several graduate students in social work and psychology, ;
well as one studying law. Our bull sessions provided me with
good source of second opinions and a chance to try out my ide;
on well educated and usually skeptical young men. I lost son
disputes, but to my credit, a few of the doubters eventually tol
me they had begun attending religious services. Many of ther

had very real domestic problems and were growing desperate for some way to hold married life and sanity together.

Charlotte Marie arrived on schedule. Colleen apologized for giving me a daughter as my first child, for, she said, she knew I wanted a son to continue the family name. That I had made such an impression upon her was a surprise to me. I couldn't be happier than I was with our daughter. She was a bright and healthy infant, so what was there to complain about? I probably coddled the new baby even more in order to convince her mother that I was not disappointed.

The other men at work asked a few questions along the way, so I proudly carried the newborn's ID photo to work with me. One of the bachelors took a quick look and said, "She looks like a peeled orange." But I could take a joke. Then, looking at the photo with that devastating comment in mind, little Charlotte did appear to be much like all other newborns with squinty eyes, fat cheeks, no hair and little red spots on her face. Sort of orangish, peeled orangish. Oh well.

A Question of the Ages

One day Oldham said in class that it was not necessary to believe that Adam and Eve were created by fiat in Eden only six thousand years ago. This was novel, for a person so traditional in his creed, so I sat up and listened. He proposed that humans were somewhat older than that, perhaps by another ten or at the most twenty thousand years, and the biblical account was telling us about the human race coming into a *social consciousness* as they began to cultivate the earth as gardeners. This would remove them from the hunter-gatherer class of wanderers to the civilized level and the need for accountability. The domestication of Adam and Eve took place, he estimated, perhaps as recently as ten thousand years ago. From the way I heard the proposition, Oldham was still saying Adam and Eve were actual persons in a garden, and the "given" of this proposition was that they were the "first" gardeners and also the representatives of the entire human race. To that point, I had heard only of two arguments about our human origin: either/or. Either God created via an evolutionary process, which the scientists taught in public education, or by fiat, as orthodox theology asserted. Apparently Oldham was proposing a compromise solution, that God created Adam and Eve, supposedly by fiat, but much earlier than supposed from a literal reading of the Bible. This gave the educated Christian a few extra thousand years in which to account for the upheaval of the continents and the burial of the dinosaurs under flooded plains.

Such ideas, I was to discover, had been entertained ever since the advent of modern science, when thoughtful persons suggested that the earth had to be much older than six thousand years. Rather quickly scientists began to speak of possibly allowing for a million years, and then even more time was allowed. But Christians continued to insist that however old the world was, the appearance of humankind went back to one couple, Adam and Eve. Perhaps some said, the seven days of creation were epochs, but in the sixth epoch, God made man. For there was a basic theological premise that had to be preserved: *It all began with Adam and Eve,* who in fact tainted us with the sin of disobedience.

The old idea that we humans were "born in sin," and alienated from fellowship with God would be maintained. Further, such sin is why a savior is needed, and why Jesus died in humanity's place, upon a cross that he sanctified as an altar in order to satisfy the immutable laws as well as appease the wrath of God.

The ancient problem of sin and salvation is forever with us, and taking it literally or figuratively ought to be allowed, since none of us has a perfect system worked out. But I thought I heard Oldham defending the fundamentalist idea that Adam and Eve were real and actually lived in a garden not very long ago, finally implicating all humans in the stain of what is termed "original sin." That sounded definite and therefore beyond question.

So then, returning to the classroom lecture: What was my professor really teaching? What I heard smacked of *implications*, and that moves one away from certitude. Oldham was not always a literalist, apparently, even though he seemed very sure of himself. Now it appeared that interpretation was permissible as long as he had control over it. *Yes!* **Control**, *that magic word of those who must be sure. So then, was he going to allow only his interpretation?*

Oldham did not like Emil Brunner especially and had his doubts about Brunner's compatriot Karl Barth, a Swiss theologian (1886-1968), who took the Christian world by storm during his lifetime, not only because of his great intellect and insight, but because he risked his life by protesting Hitler and his Nazis in their attempts to enslave the Church in Germany. No, Oldham believed, better to remain back with Hodge and Warfield and the old creeds, bypassing modern debate entirely. This conclusion was not much different from what I heard from Hal, who also felt cocksure of his doctrine. The difference was that Hal cited Scofield as his authority, while Oldham cited the orthodox schoolmen.

It is obvious that I have delivered myself of a diatribe, and I feel slightly guilty for having wandered so far from my story. But... this too is my story.

I was so troubled by Oldham's remarks that I stood and begged the question regarding Adam and Eve. This was the first time I recall taking exception to one of my mentors in a classroom, and I rarely did it after that, although I have had a few frank moments with teachers in private since then. They tend to be more patient in private than they are in public.

"Dr. Oldham," I said, "you have often taken the side of the older ideas in matters of refuting modern scientific theories, but now you are trying to push the age of Adam and Eve back perhaps twenty thousand years, instead of only six thousand, and making them the sole representatives of a world population. It seems to me that we are being drawn into an untenable position where we make only the concessions we must make but refuse to accept any scientific conclusions which complicate our creedal suppositions." At this point my voice was beginning to quaver, for not only was I challenging an eminent conservative scholar, but I also wrestled with such an interpretation, not being sure just how far I should go. But I took a deep breath and continued, "Must we evangelicals always live somewhat removed from the mainstream, somewhere back in time, as before the advent of modern science? Aren't we in danger of being pushed farther away from reality?"

There was absolute silence in the classroom. Oldham stood motionless at the dais and looked at me with his piercing dark eyes. He was a large man, and right then he seemed even larger, for he was looking right at me in apparent disbelief that I was doing this, or perhaps because he regarded me as cheeky and naïve. I could not tell if he was angry with me or sorry for me. And his slightly hooked nose seemed to me to have become a raptor beak just then. I expected him to swoop down upon me to tear out my eyes. But rather than attack, he turned from me and resumed his lecture as though I had never said a word! Nor did he ever call me into his study to deal with my challenge or straighten out my confusion.

I do not remember anything else he said that hour, and somehow I managed to survive the incident, mainly because I did not pose any further questions. Things returned to what some must have thought to be normalcy, and I, tight-lipped to the end, managed to pass the course, although I felt he did not pass my examination.

Soon enough, over coffee, I would learn from others that Oldham espoused the creationist ideas I mentioned above. This in itself was an admission of *interpretation* of the Scripture. But Oldham would not go all the way from old orthodoxy to neo-orthodoxy. He compromised, saying that God created the whole shebang in epochs that ended some twenty thousand years ago with Adam, the crowning glory of creation. Such thinking would rule out the conclusions of paleontologists and anthropologists, of course, which would leave him free from conceding anything to modernists, while not quite offending fundamentalists.

Furnell, the Apologist, or, Thank God for more than one opinion

My chosen mentor during those formative years became Dr. Furnell, our retreat speaker at the campground far up Mount Wilson. He proved to be fearless in matters of faith, though well known for shyness when in public. Furnell was the sort who introduced the contemporary thought of such theologians as Karl Barth and Emil Brunner as having both spiritual insight and intellectual value. They appealed to me especially because Furnell described these scholars as theologians of hope. To me, this meant that they were future-oriented more than guardians of the past. Granted, they knew Reformation tradition, but they were much more concerned with orienting young students to the task of engaging themselves in the present.

Furnell devoted some time to the idea Jesus argued, that in effect, God has no grandchildren, nor do God's children worship a grandfather. "I am the God of Abraham, of Isaac, and of Jacob" was taken to mean that generations come and go, but God is still working. Jesus added that he too was still working. God is the Living Presence who is also the Alpha and Omega, the beginning and the end. Therefore, we study for knowledge but also need a personal experience, for God is not dead.

I also have some memory of Furnell quoting Luther as saying God is playful. God hides from us and makes it a game for us to find him. Each generation therefore has the task of discovering its own knowledge about the Father, much as we come to a new appreciation of our parents when we ourselves mature. And, must add, only a God who is still with us and still is gracious could play with us in this fashion. Perhaps, then, God has the good of all his creatures in mind and does not destine anyone to punishment for being playful or curious.

Interestingly, to dwell a bit longer on this idea of God having no grandchildren, I learned more than one spiritual truth in the halls of Chaderton, and sometimes heard it explained over coffee in the refectory. In these discoveries I finally came to understand what my mentors, from the early days with Hatfield to the senior year with Furnell, were talking about when they used the term existentialist. They had baptized the secular philosophy of the existentialists — who did not necessarily embrace religion — with their own theological twist, that came from Christian experience. For us Christians, existentialism is more of a mystical knowledge of God, not that we capture God's Essence, but that we have come to participate in the mystery of Spirit. Jesus comes alive to us in a dynamic way, and we come alive, having made contact. And then we become "living letters" to the world, that God is love and in him is no shadow of variation.

John's Gospel is sometimes referred to as the deep Gospel, the Gospel of levels of understanding, in which a reader learns more and more as the years go on. An existential reader returns to John for guidance. Paramount in John we begin to capture the idea of experiencing God in a life-changing manner. Jesus teaches, "I am the door: by me if any man enter in, he shall be saved and shall go in and out, and find pasture. The thief cometh not, but for to steal and to kill, and to destroy: I am come that they might have life, and that they might have it more abundantly. I am the good shepherd: the good shepherd giveth his life for the sheep" (John 10:9-11).

Jesus said he would become a seed sown, and would spring back to life and produce a hundredfold. And those seeds would produce yet more, spreading out around the world as new fields are prepared for sowing. This means he had in mind something greater than the world's people coming to the Temple and making endless sacrifices, with blood and bile running down upon the stones and the smoke ascending into the clouds. My mind boggles as I imagine all that activity and the scraps and ashes, the heat of a great fire and the activity of keeping it stoked, endless lines of worshipers waiting to give their animals to those who would prepare and then slaughter them, then cart the fat, the kidneys and such to the great fire.

However, contrary to what one might imagine — all this bleating and confusion at the very center of worship, the lines and pens of livestock — contrary to this and because of it, Christ's image of God's good news of forgiveness being spread around as seed has a great appeal. Instead of killing animals to feed the fire, the seed is sown among the living and in short order is turned into bread to feed the world. Ah! Jesus said something about being that bread.

To experience Christ, who is life, is to live indeed. I pass from death into life abundant before actually dying. I could therefore imagine us humans as existing along the delicate green fringe of divine pulsation, as God's power makes its way across the eons of time. Shimmering and flashing, God speaks and life abounds, animating creation upon this unique planet, this Garden of Eden.

Furnell was a firm believer in the Protestant emphasis on justification by faith. He agreed with St. Paul, who hammered home the truth that God requires a deep conviction that what he has done for us is enough. No religious ritual we perform has power to sway the Almighty God. Nor do our doctrinal certainties save us. We may entertain doctrinal certainties, but what we really need is to embrace Christ. Trust in God, who

can bring things together for a good end, is therefore a righteou
work. For trusting God is doing what is just and merciful out of a
grateful heart for what has already been done for us by the Savior
This surely is what is meant by existential faith. For we canno
know things with certainty, only sense what is good and true and
beautiful, and share our insights with those near us.

Considering all this, the ancient idea that truth is slippery
and therefore our judgments will always be compromised by ou
limited intelligence is apparently as close as we are going to com
to factual truth. But this truth is a small **t** truth. Jesus is a capita
T Truth, for he himself is that Truth.

That is, we testify that there is no one else like Jesus. For w
know him. He has appeared to us and won our allegiance. W
are so sure of this that we would die for him. But we will not ki
to defend him, since he, in love, refused to kill to defend himsel
He had that greater love, such a love that he would die for h:
friends. It is seldom in a lifetime that we find anything wort
dying for, but we find it in the totality of the life of Jesus, wh
became the Son of God by proving it.

Although Furnell never said these things as clearly as I hav
written here, I think he had them in mind, for I picked them up.
also know that they are not my original ideas. Surely not! Becau
he understood Kierkegaard so well, he was willing to challeng
our assumptions. He stimulated a class discussion about wheth
an idea was valid and then supplied some possible alternative
He also recognized some of the paradoxes of Christian thougl
and the snares of biblical interpretation, but then at the end
the hour he would say, something like, "Well, it's as good as v
have. If you find anything better, go ahead and pursue it." F
obviously felt there was none as winning as Jesus nor anythir
better than New Testament insights. We students agreed wit
him, usually enthusiastically.

He also challenged our inflated opinions of our own religious beliefs by concluding, "All right, now, go out and live it." If any reader wonders what that means, it is this: A religious belief that does not result in benefit to others is useless.

This admonition usually came at the end of the hour. I found it the best ethic offered at the seminary, Oldham the ethicist included. I would, with time, come to understand that not everyone who talks theology is capable of applying a classroom lesson to daily relationships. Yes, ethics as a subject is apart from ethics as a practice. Now, who might have first said that?

Furnell, as much a "double-doctor" as Oldham, developed one doctoral dissertation around the theology of Reinhold Niebuhr and another on the philosophy of Søren Kierkegaard. This made his thinking much more contemporary and open to nuance. I liked the way he remained within the Christian Religion without feeling a need to either deny anything or defend anything. But, ironically, this practice served us better than it served him. For he tried to teach his fundamentalist friends, his brethren, how to bridge the gap between the then and the now. He wrote a book. They rose in fury against him. And he died. But that came later, and by then I was far away and into my own ministry.

Back to the Future

Colleen and I settled into our new family mode quite readily. We had already decided to stop shopping around the churches and had taken up membership at the Bethany Church. Pastor Cornelius Hendrikson was attentive to us from the beginning of our visits and saw to our finding a place there. We learned quite quickly that he had been instrumental in guiding several seminary students into his denomination, some as pastors and some as missionaries. We liked the people and felt his program was aggressive and positive, so we joined and found our place among new friends.

The community church did not have a set creed, which pleased me. Bethany belonged to a "free church" movement with roots in northern Europe, that was born of the Pietistic enthusiasm of an earlier century. Those free Christians did not have or want bishops, nor did they look to any government for oversight or reinforcement. They sought financial help from within their circle, asking each member to decide what they could give. And although they did not disdain theologians, they were convinced that Christ with them was creed enough and their Bible in hand offered advice right out of the heart of God. In this manner they quoted the Psalmist, who wrote, "I am a companion of all those who fear thee, of those who keep thy precepts." That sounded good, but it is daunting to practice with any consistency. Just to be safe, they kept a *cautious respect* for the creeds of the Church. For the creeds provide an outline for doctrine and an anchor in history.

We had crossed over the line of hesitation and made the plunge into a new form of Protestantism. Essentially, it seemed very much to me like my childhood religion, but I had learned enough to know that it was different. However, we had reached a crisis point in our search for service and found the Bethany Church.

The wisdom of the saints says that when God shuts one door another is opened.

20

LOOKING WITHIN, LOOKING AROUND

Graduation was held in the seminary's chapel, that gray mass of reinforced concrete, its pinnacle pointing heavenward, but its footings sunk into the earth. The flying buttresses added a dash of a somewhat imaginative architecture, a symbol of what the board of trustees hoped for their new school: reaching up to Heaven's gates, digging into the traditions, upheld by generous supporters. The chapel would seat perhaps eight hundred people, were every seat taken.

Scholars robed in academic garb of black and blue and crimson with a rainbow display of colored hoods added a festive air to the hubbub. Mortar boards and some floppy tams added to the pageantry, each tam or mortar board with a tassel, in gold, black or red for the religious, and a few other colors for secular specialties. The space was full of sound also: from the booming organ; from a sixteen piece orchestra tuning up; and from people chatting and laughing. This busy-ness was reminiscent of what we were told the old cathedrals of Europe were like as centers for the community.

That evening I was nearly overcome with the pageantry and fuss, feeling both tired and stimulated. But as St. Paul exulted

about himself, I had "finished the course." And now I would
receive my crown: a piece of sheepskin, a title without prebend.
We always joked that a minister's pay is small but the retirement
plan is "out of this world."

We graduates lined up in class order, the dean checking
us out one last time. We turned and scrutinized one another,
exchanging puerile insults about being surprised to see the other
there. "My don't you look *good*, for a change," one said, and heard
in reply, "You look good too, but looks are deceiving." We were
forty-eight giddy survivors: forty-eight out of one hundred and
two. Furnell had been on the button with his prediction. No one
said anything about this in my hearing, and I suspected that, as
I, others were thinking how bittersweet it is to make it through
when some had fallen to the side of the road. *Adieu, mes amis...*

Pomp and Circumstance swelled from the organ. We grads
commenced our procession, now each a Bachelor of Divinity. Just
like the lawyers' Bachelor of Law, we had a professional degree that
left us short of being named either masters or doctors. Later in
the century our degree would be upgraded to Master of Divinity
and the lawyers would receive a Doctor of Jurisprudence. But that
evening we were unconcerned about such vanity, for we were the
honorees in a grand festival and looking forward to ordination at
some near occasion.

The Reverend Dr. Daniel Boone Armstrong was the featured
speaker. He had aided Brother Chaderton in getting the seminary
underway, but preferred to remain the pastor of a very influential
and mission-minded church: Connecticut's historic Powder
Keg Church in New Haven. Old Powder Keg was of colonial
Congregational tradition, famous for its part in the American
Revolution as well as its tradition of sending volunteers to
missionary endeavors.

Armstrong was obviously enjoying the festivities, beaming a
smile that would sell Ipana Toothpaste, and chatting in *sotto voce*
with his companions on the platform. His brio plus dark black
hair belied his age. Springing to his feet, he walked briskly to the

podium, changing to a grave solemnity as he arrived. Looking out over the audience, much as an emperor might have reviewed the forum before speaking, he stood patiently until quiet reigned.

His first words were exuberant, even grandiose, but so was the occasion.

"In the name of Jesus Christ, the Lord of the Church and the Savior of the World, I greet you on this most solemn and holy occasion. We are here to award forty-eight graduates their earned and honored degree of Bachelor of Divinity. There are also two graduates from previous years, who have attained the degree of Master of Theology. These men have worked diligently during these years, denying themselves much leisure or other personal interests in order to master the knowledge of the ages, so that they might serve our Lord Jesus Christ in his churches in many lands. Along with these graduates, we include seventeen young ladies who have distinguished themselves in religious studies. Tonight they receive the degree of Master of Religious Education.

"We are now commissioning these our graduates to go forth, as the Lord said, unto the ends of the earth, to preach and teach the Truth, bringing all nations into obedience to the precepts of Almighty God."

He continued in this stately genre for a few minutes before shifting to his real agenda, which was made clear quite soon.

"We who live in this post-war morass have seen the drift of Western civilization away from its birthright, to the point that I must say we were formerly a Christian civilization. Russia, our undesired and unworthy ally in the recent war, has extended its tentacles into the Free World, cynically ensnaring one nation after another, and disseminating a doctrine of godlessness into nations that once were a part of Christendom, that were meant to carry the Gospel into all the world. Indeed, only a remnant remains, as the prophets foresaw, but this remnant holds firmly to the Word of God.

"Denomination after denomination has been enticed into the National Council of Churches, in collaboration with the World

Council of Churches, to promote a world-wide ecumenical affiliation of religion, that will eventually be taken over by the sinister powers of godless political philosophy. And that is, in plain words, Marxist-Leninism. I have no doubt that a future dictatorship will arise and seek to take control of the entire world. Even now many churches have betrayed the Gospel to a false doctrine of worldly politics, which they expect will save the lost from their despair. But such worldly aspiration is manipulated by the Devil himself, and the end of all this grouping of ever larger ecclesiastical and political associations is designed to accomplish nothing less than the enslavement of humankind to the sinister designs of Hell!"

I sat back in my chair and looked around at my fellow. Some were nodding enthusiastically, more than I would have expected, while a few of us were looking at each other with our eyebrows arched. This was not what I expected at our evening of celebration.

The speaker continued, "If they could, they would destroy the churches, but they cannot! For our Lord Christ is the Ruler of Heaven and Earth. Before these hypocritical denominational leaders can derail the purposes of God, we faithful witnesses to the Truth shall overcome them. And the weapon we have that is invincible is The Sword of The Spirit, which is the written Word of God!"

Ah, there it was, in all its glorious simplicity! We were being trained to beat back Communism by undermining the liberal and ecumenical endeavors, and that within the churches. I was startled at this revelation, for one of the expressed aims of the faculty was to prepare graduates who could return to their denominations and work within them as reasonable witnesses to evangelical scholarship or else go on to graduate study in legitimate universities and seminaries. Were we to present ourselves cloaked as something other than truly well-meaning ministers and scholars? Ought we employ subterfuge? Say yes when we mean no? And was the larger world beyond our hallowed halls so easily divided between good and evil? I looked up at the professors sitting on the platform and could see that most were not smiling or nodding in agreement; only keeping a grim silence. Once again I felt that deep disturbance in the pit of my stomach. Why do good and honorable men remain silent in the presence of such bullying and posturing? Well, I've lived some decades beyond that evening, and I too have remained discreetly silent on a few occasions, so I must not condemn, just ask the question.

What was even more disconcerting that evening was that I knew these same hyper-active types were pro-military, expecting the armed forces to beat back socialism. Dwight Eisenhower was then president of the country, and conservative Christians were rallying behind a military answer to a political problem. Intolerance and witch hunts were undertaken by a national agency, the House Committee on Un-American Activities, which sought to stifle the free exchange of political debate. Later, in 1959, Harry S. Truman said that the House Committee was the most un-American agency in America. But I stray from my subject.

Armstrong, looking down upon us honorees, assumed an awful scowl, that turned slowly into a warm smile. He did have a certain charisma, and a strength of conviction, which he exuded when he felt comfortable, that is, powerful, in charge and appearing the fearless leader. Tonight was his opportunity to make such a show, and he was not in the mood to cloak anything in subtlety. He smiled then, and most seniors relaxed just a little. But I felt slightly dizzy. My psyche was not prepared for this harangue in the midst of such pageantry and camaraderie.

"You graduates of Chaderton Theological Seminary," he said, "I charge you in the name of God to keep the faith. As the Apostle Paul wrote to his disciple Timothy long ago, 'Now the Spirit speaketh expressly, that in the latter times some shall depart from the faith, giving heed to seductive spirits, and doctrine of devils; speaking lies in hypocrisy; having their conscience seared with a hot iron,' I too exhort you to beware of the subtle traps of this present age, for Scripture admonishes us, 'be constan in season and out of season. Do not submit again to a yoke o slavery. Exhort the brethren, encourage faith and good works speak the Word of God to all people without exception. Remai steadfast in purpose, always rightly handling the Word of Truth.' And thus he finally concluded, much to the relief of many, an certainly me.

Our degrees were awarded with dispatch, each of us walkin across the chancel to receive the diploma and a handshake from various dignitaries. I wished finally that there had been someon from my family present to witness my honor. But I had Colleen i the audience, my love, my steady support and happy companior She had been awarded a degree of her own at the previous night gala: a P.H.T., for "Putting Hubby Through."

The program concluded with a martial hymn. Then the crow spilled out into the fresh air, rushing for the parking lots, whi some of us briefly tarried with friends. But we too drove away o diverse paths, in reverse of our gathering three years earlier from around the world.

Night had gained a firm hold upon the land by the time th last cars drove away. Bright stars winked down from their distar places in the heavens, spheres now shining almost as brightly i our sky as they would appear high up Mount Wilson. Up ther at the observatory, finely trained astrophysicists were even the peering out into the Milky Way, so full of mystery and enigm and making history by revising the Hubble Constant downwar from 500 to 50. These quiet men, working through the night were seeking answers to age-old questions of theological origi For had not the ancients attributed divinity to the heavenly hos And did not Luna demonstrate her powers over the tides of a the Earth and even a woman's twenty-eight day cycle? Those go held great power over the ancient peoples of Earth. But now o contemporaries, just a little higher up the mount, were strippir the starry panoply of its divinity. The gods faded, but I stress that the wonder increased. May the Creator help us, that we never fail to marvel at the splendid display of those myriads of heavenly lights telling us of galaxies beyond galaxies.

Meanwhile, we students of "the heavenly vision" had learned to look for answers within. Doubtless those stargazers up there on the Mount were discovering facts that would answer some very old questions, for the heavens declare the glory of God. But no one has yet found a god among the stars, only evidence of overwhelming power, and not a little chaos, which inspires awe. God in human knowledge dwells at the core of our existence, that we might "seek Him, if haply we might feel after him, and find him, ... for in him we live and move and have our being" (*Acts* 17:27, 28a). Well, that has to be a no-no proof-texting sort of lapse on my part, but I stand by it.

If seminary studies taught me anything certain it was that my search for God had only begun, just as I was only then beginning to understand myself as one called to a mysterious and even at times a terrifying undertaking. Yes, terrifying. It was expedient then to know the truth and to avoid error; to teach wisdom and not platitudes; to aspire to a morality better fit for angels. Who could persist under such standards? Indeed, who would not fail in one way or another? At the Last Supper, the disciples learned that one of them would betray their Master, and learning this, each asked, "Lord, is it I?" A good question, then and always.

Addendum

I had several discussions with Reverend Hendrikson during the previous months and was happily drawn back to my learning sessions with Ralph Hatfield. But this time we talked mostly about my interest in becoming a teacher, probably in some missionary work. For, I told him, I felt that I could not dare go into pastoral work had I not at least considered the challenge of becoming a missionary. It was simply one of those ideas that lodges in one's heart and won't go away. To me that seemed a basic spiritual principle in my formation, for how would I challenge others to take up a cross and follow Jesus, had I not done so myself? Hank was in agreement with my thought, and was even animated. He explained in the most positive terms that his church was involved in overseas educational work as an important part of the denomination's program of outreach. This brought to mind the example of John Mackay, who began as a missionary, working with the YMCA in Mexico and then as a professor at a university in Peru.

Hank suggested I make application to the mission board for assignment to South America. He would recommend me, which meant his church would contribute to my support. In fact the denomination also called and commissioned missionary couples, so Colleen also would become a bonafide missionary. We should be able to make the cut, he stated, adding that it would include a year's residence for me at the seminary in Boston.

I hesitated. Another year of study? My excitement subsided as I heard this detail, for I was justified in feeling tired of books and exams -- and in Boston, that city of long winters? I expressed my feelings to my pastor, and he countered by offering to take me on as his assistant for a year, as a time of learning hands-on ministry and becoming in turn better known. This would help us to raise local support for the work overseas.

After a *tête-à-tête* with Colleen I opted to continue in the church for another year, and she would return to teaching. That was a great time of recovery from the previous stint at self-denial. For an entire year we two were fully employed without unusual expenses, so were able to build a cushion against the future. We moved into a roomy apartment, nicely furnished, and began to feel like professional people. I still cherish my memories of California and the way things worked out for good.

It was a rare privilege to be the understudy of such a vibrant preacher. He allowed me to occupy the pulpit twice a month.

once in the morning and once in the evening. Along with my many preaching and teaching duties, visiting the area hospitals added considerably to both my experience and self-confidence. I was actually doing ministry. That is, *I was a pastor.* The bonds of friendships formed in such ministry can last a lifetime.

We had enjoyed living in California and felt it a privilege to work among church members who were a happy lot and generous in their affirmation. I had, at last, a social life that was not limited by the rigors of study. The longer I labored in ministry the more I appreciated these benefits. Actually, I was beginning to have second thoughts about a commitment to overseas missions. But I had made the attempt to discover divine direction, and it led to foreign work. I would continue, Colleen agreeing, to offer my services to that endeavor. There's a saying that sticks in my mind, that speaks exactly to such a situation:

> *When your ship, long moored in harbor,*
> *gives the illusion of being a home, put out to sea.*

By the end of that fourth year in California the arrangements with the mission board were to proceed to Boston for orientation in the denomination, at my expense. I would take a few classes at the seminary in order to become acquainted with the faculty and administrators at the home office, and they to observe me. There was the added incentive that I might find a church in which to serve for the year, a small church, possibly one between pastors. If not that, then I might work as an assistant in some larger church. There seemed to be ample opportunity to earn my keep within the system.

Colleen had little Charlotte to mother, and I thought that was enough for her. She admitted that it sounded desirable to be a wife at home and a full-time mother for the year.

As we pulled away from our friends, who were there to help us tie up loose ends, I looked back in the side mirror and could see a few well-wishers waving to us, much as we had experienced in our departure from Miami. They receded much too rapidly, diminishing in size, and then were blocked from view.

Again, the Dodge Fluid Drive, older but still strong, carried us across the country, this time from west to east, and considerably much farther north than Miami. I drove more responsibly then, our little girl set up in the back seat, and a small U-Haul trailer in tow. Much of our extra baggage consisted of books I treasured and used in preparing studies and sermons. Pastor Ralph's example of a personal library was on its way to becoming my reality.

21

Boston's South Side

A comfortable apartment in the suburbs satisfied Colleen's tastes. We paid the first and last month's rent and soon had our few possessions in place. It was near a famous old seminary, Andover Newton Theological School, in Newton Centre, which was just fine with me. This would make occasional research easier, as I could use their library. The seminary was established well over a century before and had developed a nice arrangement of buildings on the top of a small hill. ANTS, as it is called, was the first seminary in America to stand free from a mother institution, in this case Harvard. They pulled away from that colonial institution in 1807 because of rampant Unitarianism among the faculty.

The denomination accepted my year with Pastor Hendrikson as my internship in hands-on church work and licensed me to serve as a pastor, with the understanding that I would submit a qualifying paper of my theology and practice by February for ordination in April. With a license in hand and a target for ordination, I was approved to do supervised pastoral work.

My only reservation about ordination was that although I belonged to a non-creedal denomination, I would be expected to affirm the Apostles' Creed. I personally liked the Creed but feared being locked into some sort of orthodoxy again. But other students assured me that the tradition was just that, a tradition, and no one, neither professor nor executive, was going to make me qualify my confession to some standard concocted by other persons. I could accept the creed on my own terms, and would be accepted in good faith. I was to understand however, it was added, that confessing the Apostles' Creed proclaimed to the leaders that I was a Trinitarian, and to this I subscribed. This understanding left me reassured, for I felt then and still do that we all change as we live and learn, but slight changes are no reason to keep changing churches or to seek to change the basic construct of the Christian Church. As for affirming the basic tenets of the Protestant Religion, I still feel it is best to keep the ancient Scriptures and practices in place but to let both minister and members deal with their preference of interpretation. Well it's an ideal...

A small church in Quincy agreed to take me on as an interim minister for the school year, while they made a careful search for their new pastor. My first pastoral task caught me entirely by surprise, for an elderly lady in the church died about the same time I walked into the office. I had not conducted a funeral before, but with the help of the small gathering of family and friends, I glided through the service book's ritual of "Witness to the Resurrection," which I heard Pastor Hendrikson recite several times. And then the people did their part, giving vignettes from Hattie's life and singing a favorite hymn.

The year allowed me to continue honing my skills as a pastor and preacher. Colleen was a helper in that ministry, doing what a pastor's wife usually does, that is, volunteer her services. In this case the congregation was supportive of her piano playing, which allowed her to gain valuable experience. And the ladies' society, The Phoebes, took her in as one of their own.

As I look back on that year, after four decades of ministry, I think the Lord was telling me something about the rewards of pastoring. But I was not practical, or perhaps attentive, so missed the message and continued thinking of an assignment to teach in South America. I therefore persisted in the idea of becoming a missionary or at least trying to become one before I would challenge anyone else to go overseas. That is not necessary, I now understand. Why had it not occurred to me that God is in charge of such matters? I am only one of religion's sales reps, while God is the Manager.

Just before Easter, when new converts are usually baptized, I was ordained. The charge was "to administer the Sacraments, to preach the Word of God and to bear rule in the Church." I wasn't sure how I'd "bear rule" in a church without a defined set of rules and regulations — other than Roberts Rules — and where the laity usually made all the important decisions, including the size and conditions of my stipend. But the term "bear rule" sounded impressive. I was thirty-three years old, so it was about time to feel in charge of something.

The ordination took place in the church late on a Sunday afternoon, with the district minister and the missions executive officiating, and with four other pastors from our churches in attendance. The congregation was extremely honored to sponsor this important event and had prepared a wonderful reception with finger foods and a large flat cake, accompanied by urns of strong coffee and a spot of tea poured from a silver service. It was nice to be so affirmed and loved.

All ordained ministers present, including two pastors from town churches, gathered around me as I knelt at the chancel steps, facing the cross, and all laid their hands upon my head or shoulders as the presiding official read the prayer for God's approval and guidance to accompany me in my ministry.

The weight of all those hands increased as the rite proceeded, so that I physically sensed the symbolism of the bearing a cross.

The ordaining minister pronounced the charge to be faithful and steadfast to my vows and confession. It seemed so sudden. One moment I was a student on assignment and the next an ordained clergyman, a "reverend." I recalled that a prisoner at the jail on Miami Beach had called me Reverend many years before, and felt unworthy of the title. This time I accepted the title but knew it was not yet one I deserved. Perhaps in a year, I thought. I have to admit that the solemnity of this struck me, along with having all those clergymen passing on a solemn charge from ancient times, their hands upon me being one of the most honored traditions of our Religion. By the time I stood to receive their congratulation my eyes were damp. Someone put a few tissues into my hand, no doubt some older pastor, and I was soon recovered. But I could hear some sniffling going on among the witnesses in the pews. A simple and unadorned rite has a power all its own.

The official from the Central Office presented me with my papers, properly signed by the church's president and sealed with the impression of the cross and the dove. And then we turned to a lively hymn after which I gave the benediction. The church chairman announced that we would recess to the hall for both greetings and refreshments.

I had become a man of the cloth, but not a man with a clerical collar. No, we were a free church administered by laymen, not an establishment church where ordination put a man into a social class apart. And some laymen were all too ready to let me know that I was not a priest!

But there was no denial: I had become The Reverend Mister Timothy J. DuPease, interim pastor and candidate for missionary work in South America. It sounded good to me, and it must have sounded good to Colleen too, as she simply beamed. I took her hand, and we proceeded to the reception.

Spring brought not only honor but humiliation as well. I was to discover the vagaries of a system that is fueled by voluntary contributions. For a surprise fell from on high, that is, from the missions office, plopping down before me as a tablet of stone with only two bold words engraved upon it: NOT NOW.

The Reverend Rolf Hanbury, executive in charge of missions, called me into his office one day in May and informed me that his departmental plans were in crisis. There was no money available for more personnel in Andezuela, for a budgetary crunch had developed. There would often be such crises in missionary work, he said. In this case I would have to wait another year. Hanbury was quite matter-of-fact about this, as though volunteers pulled up roots and drove across the country all the time only to be told that plans had changed. He went on to assure me that something would work out, and that Colleen and I should be "much in prayer" about what the Lord would have us do. With my education and background, and Colleen's, he added, we were surely of great value to the missionary effort, and he would keep us in mind as a priority matter. Then he gently led me back to the building's main lobby. He would keep in contact, he assured me once more, then walked away.

I was nonplused, of course, by this confrontation with what I was to learn was a missionary way of doing things. At that time I was not a commissioned missionary and not on the pay list, so really was still an applicant. No, I was an orphan, and so was my wife!

Was God trying even harder to tell me something? I think of that experience at times and wonder. But "What might have been" is no way to second guess God. In fact, it is a poor way to reflect upon life.

Colleen had come along and was waiting in our car with Charlotte. I rehearsed the event until we had exhausted all possibilities of its meaning. But still we sat there like lost children. We did not wish to sit over coffee in some diner, where others would see us as we imagined we appeared. Rather, we settled for our car as sanctuary, not for long, but long enough to recover our balance. We hugged too, as best we could, in the front seat and tried to comfort each other.

Eventually I drove back to our apartment and Colleen brewed some coffee. Oh, blessed coffee! Next to prayer, coffee was our solace of choice. I had to admit to myself about then that a good jolt of whisky would help, had we kept a bottle in reserve. Just then we could not or would not pray. Coffee had been with us at our highest moments and at our lowest, so it would continue to be the sanctified substitute for praying when no prayers came to mind worth mouthing.

The next day we took Charlotte along on a drive to the south shore, not to church but to a cemetery, in Marshfield, where we walked around, hand in hand in silence for a bit and enjoyed the early spring. Many of the Pilgrims who settled the town in the early 1600s were buried under the church floor, so that the indigenous folk would not know how few remained of that little immigrant community. Some died of disease, some of exposure and want. And they died in the faith that impelled them to sail to another land, very far from England, their beloved home. It was sobering to review the pioneer hardships of our country's first settlers. Their sacrifices were far beyond anything we had encountered in our pilgrimage. However, we really were not in search of morality lessons just then, so did not dwell on the Pilgrims for long.

A small bayside seafood restaurant provided us a simple lunch before we drove back to the apartment. While Charlotte slept, we also climbed back into bed and slept until our child's prattling brought us back to reality.

The next day we returned to our routines.

Professor Elmo Van Dell, my missions teacher, and a former missionary himself, called me to his office for a consultation mid-morning. In short order, without ever mentioning whether he knew about the mission director's decision, Van Dell advised me that an emergency had arisen in northwestern Alaska, at a

Eskimo mission school on a large peninsula to the north of the Yukon River Delta. The principal had to return to the States for family health reasons and would be out of the loop for a year, so was bringing his family with him. Would I be interested in going up there to manage the school in his place, he asked. Colleen could also teach, and the classes were co-ed. We could take over the apartment in the school, furnished.

Wham! For the second time that week the mission leaders were loading up my life with changes beyond belief. *Would I be interested in going to Alaska for one year?* Just like that. The only inducement was that I would gain some professional experience and standing by being the principal of the school. It just might help me in my projected work in South America to have this in my dossier.

Would I? The truth be told, I had my doubts, not because of the work but the geography. What did I know about the Territory of Alaska beyond a cursory acquaintance with our American history after the Civil War, or a few geography lessons and photos across the years? Walruses and Eskimos were up there, to begin with. Also, it was called Seward's Folly back when our Secretary of State bought it from Russia, in 1867. But then gold was discovered in Nome, and that changed America's interest in the new territory. In fact, one of our first missionaries to Alaska had made a stake during the gold rush and became rich. I learned that detail in a church history class, learning also that one missionary was sued by the denomination for mixing church work and business. And since he had become independently wealthy, it was thought just that he compensate the denomination. That produced some stir for quite a while, and the stir produced some scandal of its own.

As these few facts buzzed around my throbbing head, I stalled for time. I managed to ask a few questions. Then I added that I'd have to talk with Colleen. We would pray about it. That's always a dangerous thing to do, for once a person prays about it, he/she in effect has given up control. Prayer doesn't have to be that way, but it's what takes place anyhow, mostly because we want to

believe that if we pray God will send an answer, and that righ
soon; and an obvious answer at that. How, then, does one say no
to any proposal that comes from an unexpected angle? Angle
not angel.

If I had felt numb two days previously when our assignmen
to South America was pulled out from under us, I was equall
stunned just then. I skipped the next class and went to the librar
in search of an encyclopedia. Then, prepared with a few facts,
drove back to our apartment. No one could ever imagine suc
a story. We were still destined for service at the earth's equato
but were being sent there via the Arctic Circle! I was becomin
a reincarnation of Wrong Way Corrigan, the pilot who filed
flight plan from New York to California but landed in Ireland.

Alaska was still a territory and a foreign mission field, eve
if it was part of our nation, even if English was the offici:
language. Alaska was also cold, colder, I imagined, than nearl
everywhere except for the North Pole itself, or probably Siberi:
which was not that far away. They say up in Nome that they ar
as close as you can get to tomorrow and still be in today, for th
International Dateline runs a jagged course from north to sout
just west of Alaska.

I hated cold weather with a passion. After spending a fe
winters in northern latitudes during my navy service, includir
one winter at sea, I had hoped never to live in snow and ice agai
But here I was in Boston, against my better judgment, whic
should have taught me something. Colleen and I, Miamian
survived that awful winter of northeasters, the piles of snow ov
the sidewalks, the slush and soot, hacking endlessly and blowir
snotty noses. Then on top of our disgust with the severe weath
we never had in either Florida or California, we were being aske
to go where forty below zero was common, with blizzards rushir
in from the northeast, again. And we would live in an Eskin
village. My mind was awhirl.

The mission school was located in an Eskimo village, Muktuk, technically a reservation set aside by the U. S. Government. There was a small air strip for irregular mail deliveries, and in the few months when the village was not iced in, an occasional steamer would anchor far out from the shallow delta area and send barges in with supplies. The cutoff for such deliveries was October first, so nothing would arrive by sea again until after June first or even later. We learned this much from our mission executive, who himself had served in Alaska for a few years. He was quite enthusiastic about our proposed assignment, so animated in fact that he made it sound like an offer we dared not refuse.

Arrangements were made for us to fly to Alaska. We began reading the details of what we would need and how to order canned food for the nine months we would be iced in without resource to a grocery store. Someone did mention in passing that the school had a root cellar, so we could order oranges, cabbages and carrots, but not to over do it. These orders would entail an indebtedness — to be paid off from our monthly allotment. That sounded a bit like being in debt to the company store. As had others before us, we worked out the arrangements with the finance office.

22

SEWARD'S FOLLY

The old Dodge went to a new owner, who was happy to get it for five hundred dollars. They say women come to love their cars, sort of give them a personality. Well, I felt a bond with my good friend, a symbol of freedom and the open road, and I was not ashamed to say so. It seemed heartless then to hand it over to someone I did not know, so at the last I felt a piece of my life went with that car. The cash it brought in was quickly spent for winter supplies.

Then there were goodbyes to say and final telephone calls, as we had done before. But this time we divested ourselves of nearly everything we did not plan to carry along. A crib and end table were passed on to returning missionaries. My books were stored in a damp basement at the missionary house. Others said they would do okay for a year or so.

Unto the Uttermost Parts of the Earth

Boston to northwestern Alaska became an odyssey by distance but relatively nothing in terms of flying. The old sagas of classical times actually covered much less geography but involved adventures of great conflict, love and bloody battles across many years. The Alaska story would be picayune in comparison with Jason's for example, but would involve challenging the fates and battling for justice and many things of spiritual importance. Oh, and Jason left his wife at home.

A four-prop commercial flight was taken in several stages over a period of more than thirty hours: Boston to Chicago, Chicago to Seattle and a few hours layover. The next morning we flew to Anchorage, changed planes and proceeded northwest over Mt. McKinley and a touchdown in a nondescript village tucked into the fir forest, then flew on for a few hours to our transfer point at the FAA airport on Norton Sound. That was the end of large planes and scheduled flights for our little family. From there it would be by bush plane, by appointment.

All those boring hours were spent aboard a DC-6. Large prop planes could not possibly shield the passengers from the numbing noise of such powerful engines. We felt like zombies when we stepped down the portable ramp provided by the no frills airport in Selawikki. The facility was so simple as not to have an auxiliary starter for such a large airplane, so while we deplaned from the port side, the pilot kept the outboard engine on the starboard side running, to provide electricity to restart the other three engines. As soon as we were on terra firma, the ramp was pulled back, and the pilot revved up the other engines, creating a terrible storm of sand and pebbles as the plane moved out to the runway. I stood on the hard packed earth in a state of exhaustion, my wife and daughter no better off for wear and huddled against me for protection from the wind. A local employee and I held onto the baggage while the plane taxied away. And then all was quiet.

My impression, once the plane was out of hearing, was of the utter silence of the land. It offered a primitive tranquility, however, which would prove to be medicine for anyone feeling overworked or crowded by others. A weary soul could walk away from town quickly and just soak up silence. But just then we were still at the airstrip. We stood within a hundred yards of Norton

Sound and could feel the wind in our faces, even taste the salt in the air. To the east the tundra spread itself out for countless miles Nature's barrier to the incursions of civilization.

In the northeastern sky I could see the outline of low windswept mountains, for there were no trees nearby to obstruc the view. The sun was still lying low in the sky at seven o'clock sliding at a shallow angle for those mountains on the norther horizon. To the south, where the village was to be found, wil grass whipped about in the breeze, while the makeshift cabin beyond were so low as to be hidden by this sparse vegetation tha helped hold small sand dunes in place. Many of these house cabins really, each unique according to the whim and skill of it builder, was roofed by whatever was handy. Some had salvaged ti sheets as coverings with logs or building blocks atop to keep th tin in place, while others had packed sod atop their cabins, whic was green in mid-summer. Others had combinations of variou boards, tar paper and sheet metal as improvisations against th merciless winter winds. No matter what was used, it had to b anchored or nailed or strapped into place.

Culture shock is too polite a term to describe what w experienced upon deplaning in Selawikki. The FAA strip wa situated a mile outside town, by the sea, but we flew in over th village, a helter-skelter variety of cabins oddly placed, most : some proximity to the dirt road that led out to the air strip. had a rapid glimpse of a way of life that appeared daunting for i simplicity as well as its lack of order. I could glimpse that fronti setting even as we zoomed overhead in descent to the landir strip. The flat land surrounding the airport and its lone buildir seemed immense, far different from anything Stateside, that i "Outside."

There were perhaps a hundred cabins oddly spotted arour a slightly more populated center that included a few two sto buildings. One was the elementary school, another the tradi post. At the airport there was a power plant purring in t background, but in the village there were no electric poles, and the only diesel generators were owned by "outsiders," the primary school, operated by the U. S. Government, and the mission. Those two power plants operated on an as-needed schedule.

A Protestant agency managed an orphanage in the village; and by means of contacts within the wider missions community, an overnight stay had been arranged for us at the missionary compound. The word compound may connote the idea of a fortress of some sort, or at least a fenced-in area. In that village it only denoted a parcel of land that the mission used however it wished. The buildings were impressive because they were frame structures with pitched roofs, but no better nor larger than the few public buildings. All were in need of a good paint job, and laid out not so much for style as function, as getting from one to another quickly.

The director of the orphanage had come out to meet us, along with two of his children and a few Eskimos. A few villagers had tagged along out of curiosity and huddled behind the lee side of the building, the women dressed in long brightly colored corduroy smock-like dresses that would serve as covers for their fur parkas. These outer coverings, like house coats, were adorned with rick-rack in bright colors sewn along the hem and wrists. When the women smiled, their teeth appeared to be missing but in fact were worn to the gums, we were told, from chewing hides to soften them for sewing. The women were accompanied by O'Ryan, the taxi driver, a short, wiry man, half Irish, half Eskimo, who worked as the village postmaster, clerk and janitor. His vehicle was the only sedan in the village, a veritable status symbol, which he used as a source of cash, hauling stuff and passengers. The village was just a span away, but with a child and baggage to manage, I chose the taxi. The five minute lift on a gravel road cost ten dollars. Everything was expensive. Even baby-sitters got five dollars an hour from the few outsiders living among them. It seemed nothing was cheap that far north, where most everything was delivered by air. A loaf of twenty-cent bread went for a dollar. The orphanage baked its own.

At the mission house a snack and coffee were waiting, and before very long we three were shown to our bedroom and left to prepare for the night. The mission station itself fit into the simple frontier style: a few clapboard buildings and a long work shed that housed the generator. Bags of coal were scattered along one side of the shed. Just outside the large kitchen an old wooden bin held empty tin cans, which had been flattened to save space. Some cans had spilled over and were scattered about.

By the time we got to bed it was nearly eleven, but some teenage boys were still outside playing basketball at a makeshift court just beneath our window. We learned that during the summer, Eskimos sleep whenever they feel like it, often taking catnaps, saving regular sleep for the darkest months of winter. Also, when the sun goes south, one experiences a depressing lack of ultra violet rays at that latitude. Our summer sun, however, had just dipped beneath those distant mountains, but its glow was still sufficient for outdoor activities. We could hear the ball bouncing and the boys shouting. The game broke up about midnight.

All around the village were sled dogs staked and chained, each before a small shed. They barked endlessly from the openings of the sheds, which were mostly made of old fifty-five gallon oil barrels. But without snow, the dogs were seldom needed, so remained chained to their barrels and forever yapping.

All this confronted us in those first hours of our overnight stay. We had been told that Muktuk would be quite similar to Selawikki, but that was sterile information before we undertook our first flight. Having arrived, I stood in shock, struck by the thought that I was in, indeed I had to be in, *Siberia*, that dreaded land of political exiles. Never in my wildest reveries had I ever played with the idea of going to such a desolate place as Siberia, but here I was, and I had brought along my wife and daughter. *God help me*, I thought, *I am a reckless and irresponsible husband*

and father. Why didn't I ask for some photos of the mission work before giving my assent to this assignment?

The next morning our hosts helped carry the luggage down to the river's edge, where a large pontoon plane was docked. It was painted a bright red, so bright as to be defiant, and looked like it could handle just about anything. The pilot, I was told, was half Eskimo, half *Gussick* — a corruption of Cossack, the name for the original Russian settlers. The pilot, married to a local woman, had been flying supplies and mail around the area for nine years. That, the missionary said, was a pretty good safety record for a bush pilot, especially, he added, "up here where most clouds have rocks in them, and there's no shortage of clouds." Work was scarce, and flying paid the bills with something left over. These men risked their lives every day in service to others.

This pilot seldom used the small runway outside Muktuk, our destination, as he preferred the river and a dock convenient to the general store. We had no knowledge at arrival of just how dangerous this form of travel was. The casual conversation of others later on would inform us how pilots occasionally flipped their planes and died in the water. It was just as well that our ignorance shielded us from such facts. However, there was little choice in transportation, really.

Once aboard the plane and buckled into the narrow seats, a cranking sound and a whirling propeller announced that the flight really was going to happen, and that right soon. The plane would deliver us to a settlement along a river, soon to be frozen into the landscape for the duration of our stay. There was no time to think about it, for the engine leapt to raging life. The plane moved out into the river and headed for open water, picking up speed as it moved with the tide. That takeoff seemed to go on far too long, but then the red monster freed itself of the water's drag and roared up into the air, climbing rapidly. The village disappeared into the hazy shoreline as the plane banked and headed north.

Muktuk became a replay of Selawikki, without a long airstrip. We were greeted by a missionary and his children, a few smiling women of the village, and an assortment of people at the dock. This time the trading post was nearby, a large rambling wooden structure that had never felt a paintbrush. At its center it had a second story, with a few glass windows. We learned that this was the hotel. Below, in addition to the trading post and grocery store, there was a large room that doubled as a village assembly hall and movie theater.

The missionaries never went to the movies and took a dim view of their students sneaking in for a peek. Such worldly entertainment, the resident missionary said, was tainted by women painted up like harlots, lots of smoking, drinking and shooting each other. Movie stars drank, all of them, he informed me, and alcohol was of the devil. He went on to say that liquor was a blight among the locals. Many of them could not control themselves, so once they began drinking they went wild and then collapsed into a helpless stupor. In the old days many of them drank until they were physical wrecks. This was especially disastrous during the good months, when hunting and fishing were pursued as a means of preparing for the cruel winters, so the villagers often lacked provisions at the worst time of year. Whisky was the curse of the white explorers and prospectors, who often were heavy drinkers themselves, but who also traded whisky for pelts and foodstuffs. The natives died from malnutrition and tuberculosis. Complete families could be laid out at the cemetery across a span of three or four years. The missionaries therefore battled the whisky trade persistently, warning their flocks weekly about the need to live holy and sober lives.

My new colleague added that the first missionaries were also commissioned as sheriffs by the Federal Government, and as such dragged the unruly into the local lockup. Then on Sundays the missionaries switched roles and preached to them. These tidbits came as a revelation to me. There was nothing of this nature the literature I read in preparation for the year, nothing said by my superiors at the home office.

Learning that painting her lips made a woman appear to be a harlot came as another surprise. For Colleen had stepped onto the dock still wearing her usual cosmetics, and perhaps that was what caused our slightly cool reception. Within a day I was informed that cosmetics, and especially lipstick, were regarded as worldly, so our female students were discouraged from using them. In all innocense I asked what was wrong with a little lipstick, and one of the women on staff informed me that if a girl wore lipstick she'd probably smoke, and if she smoked, well, *heavens only knows what she might do!*

I replied, thinking of Colleen, that we two had not been advised about such a restriction. I also mentioned that our sending church had no such ban on cosmetics. Even the pastor's wife used lipstick. Why then were we not advised about this beforehand, since it was so important?

The senior missionary replied, as coolly as an old Boston Brahman might silence an immigrant brick layer, "Well, you know, we never had your type here before." He must have meant it as a declaration of fact rather than an insult, but being a veteran of many winters in the village had toughened him, I suppose.

Colleen removed her lipstick and managed to remain both beautiful and refined without it. Oh, those gentle missionary folk were "the salt of the earth," regarding personal integrity and dedication to Christ and religion. But they hurt me deeply by this inability to welcome us without reservation, and this resentment was deepened by such shallow religious practices being imported to the natives of the land. Liquor was one thing, but cosmetics was another, altogether another. Such shallow "holiness" smacked of the worst that Christianity had come up with in the States across the years to blight the church-members' conscience. And I had read somewhere about the early mistakes of missionaries who insisted that their converts wear European clothes and take up western customs. But considering that I had just arrived,

I restrained myself, saying nothing that I would regret, so we slowly adjusted to each other. It took far too long and was not complete at the end of the school year.

Muktuk was a replica of Selawikki in its layout and general scenery, with only minor differences. The short landing strip built at Government expense was seldom used but maintained as weather permitted. Weeks would go by in winter without suitable conditions for air traffic, weeks without mail or beef or eggs or fresh vegetables. And when we did get them, they cost a dollar a pound extra, beyond the already inflated prices in cities like Anchorage and Nome. During the really long frigid siege incoming planes equipped with large aluminum skis landed on the thick ice and taxied near enough for dogsleds to go out to them for supplies and passengers. The trading post was large and served several smaller villages upriver, so there was some variety in foodstuffs, as incoming dog teams brought fresh frozen salmon trout or venison. Travel was by plane for those who could afford it or by outboard motorboat or dog sled, depending on the season. One blizzard lasted three days and completely covered the smaller cabins, while forming snow drifts across the area that were as tall as the larger buildings, up to twenty feet at their origin, that tapered down and tailed out a few hundred feet away.

Villagers fished upstream for salmon in the summer and trout in the winter. There were sparse pine forests upriver, where the men did some trapping, and that was about it for work and entertainment. After the river froze, but not evenly, some brave soul would drive the mission's Caterpillar tractor upriver to the scraggly forest and drag back a load of logs, the sole heating fuel for the small church. A storage area for fresh logs and stacked firewood had overrun the church's side lot years earlier, so many a guilty conscience was assuaged by the labor of cutting and splitting the logs in the winter months.

School was not scheduled to begin until September, so we had a month in which to do some very heavy work There w the matter of an old army dormitory that lay in unassembled sections in the lot next to the school. It was to be put together for the boys. Such heavy work fell to me and a volunteer carpenter, Virgil, who came up from Kansas for a year's service. We enlisted the school boys as soon as they arrived in town, and they worked hard, for it was apparent they were going to have a nice insulated dorm for the winter. Virgil worked twelve hour days on the dorm while I diverted my strength to some of the other heavy work, as getting the large bags of sugar and flour from ground floor to the attic, a climb of three levels. The senior missionary excused himself because of a bad back. On more than one occasion when I would enter his office I would find him reading a magazine or writing a letter. He had taken over the principal's office, I noted, away from his wife and out of sight from the rest of us.

I finally concluded that I was green and he a veteran of some fifteen winters. He knew what mattered and how to delegate work, while I attacked all tasks as though they demanded my immediate attention. And, I had to admit, he knew the school well, while I had not found time to learn the schedule nor draw up lesson plans. The picture was coming clear, and I had to admit that it was no great honor to be the principal of such a small school. We all did everything as it needed doing. But I wondered why the executive in Boston had not advised me in a detailed manner about all this.

Just before September was upon us, I was made to understand that I would by no means be the principal of the school, no matter what the home office told me. I was a new arrival and would teach English, Bible, social studies and woodworking for the boys. There was some justification for this decision, for the staff knew from many years of such assignments that new missionaries seldom lasted long enough to merit starting off at the top. But this pre-emptive demotion was only one part of my initiation into the work. I was appointed to tend the furnace, since my apartment was on the second floor, and I was the only male missionary in that building. Me, a Florida Cracker, who had never tended such a cast iron horror. It was the largest I had ever seen and had all manner of doors, vents, flues, pipes and gauges. I possessed some rudimentary knowledge of mechanics and carpentry, and I was mechanically inclined. But no new arrival of my poor experience could be expected to tend such a furnace. That would become apparent by the end of September.

Colleen was assigned to the home ec class for the girls and also taught piano and played for morning chapel. She worked in tandem with a single woman on staff who was a tremendous help that year. The two became dear friends. She was the resident mother for the dorm girls, advising and counseling them in many situations she herself had not faced, as she was single and from a strict family that frowned upon dating in high school, prom dances and many other social activities.

The dorm girls, in turn, cooked for the boys. Eskimos preferred sun dried salmon with rendered seal oil, which was staple for the locals. The young women also knew how to bake white-flour bread in a wood-fired stove, which Colleen had never done. And so it went, from one initiation to the next. But the girls esteemed my wife and adored Charlotte, so our apartment became a gathering spot for ten giggling teenage girls in their free hours and evenings. And these girls were often joined by the local students, who should have been busy at home.

Caring for and feeding these teenagers was not our only concern, as faculty, for we knew that idle hands are the devil's workshop, so the busier and more tired the girls were kept, the less they would succumb to invitations to sneak out to see the boys.

And then there was the matter of preaching. I was to take my share of the three weekly services, as my senior missionary informed me that he had run out of things to say, and no one was listening to him anyhow. Also, I would be in charge of the photo club as a social service to the students — and the confirmation class for the ninth graders. I was the frosh on campus so would accept all this because I was supposed to. There would be no need for Reformation history in the confirmation lessons, but a lot of memorization would be in order. I passed out copies of Luther's basic catechism — that had somehow become the standard — and had them memorize the approved answers and Bible verses to back them up. The kids' great ability to regurgitate such stuff on demand made the public meeting a success. I looked good even if they did all the work.

On another level entirely, my initiation as a greenhorn began with a humbling that would rival a Jesuit novice's acts of humiliation, which they do to improve the spiritual half of their existence. Since I was the only man in the school building at night, I emptied not only our private bathroom's "honey bucket" — there was no sewage system in the entire village — but also emptied a weighty five gallon receptacle from upstairs that was used by the girls. This meant carrying a really full can of viscera down the stairs and dragging it by sled about fifty yards to the sound, where I would dump it either into a sump, as weather permitted, or leave it out on the ice a few yards from shore. The spring thaw would mercifully carry this sludge out to sea. Meanwhile, it remained there in small frozen mounds, a testimony to the physical half of our existence.

I asked why one of the strong young men didn't perform this chore, and was told that the girls dropped their sanitary napkins into the bucket. The boys were embarrassed beyond measure to be seen carrying "that"; and besides, men didn't do such things. Men, no. Greenhorn missionaries, yes.

All that parsing of Greek sentences, the little flash cards for Hebrew vocabulary, and many taxing and arcane vagaries of theology never prepared me for dealing with these basics of life. The Bible says we are dust. We came from it and return to it; but I think "dust" should be spelled "muck."

One especially icy night I stomped upstairs calling out as I ascended, "Honey bucket, honey bucket." This was the signal for the girls to vacate the bathroom while I hauled their offering downstairs and away to the sea. The trip accomplished, I returned and put the bucket back under the toilet seat, turned and stepped over to the stairway. The girls, not being as pious as my colleagues, stood at the dorm door giggling and saying, "Hello, honey... bucket!" I turned to them, smiling, gave a broad wave as I took the first step, and lost my footing. My heavy winter boots were wet, and the stairs were worn oak. Suddenly everything blurred and I felt a terrible vertigo as I sailed down the steps bumping and thumping and somehow turning around, so that when, in a matter of seconds, I arrived at the first floor I was head down and my legs up the wall. I ached in the rear and was numb in my left arm but very much awake.

The clatter disrupted a private meeting of the visiting field director, who had just flown in, and the senior missionary. They ran out in time to witness my embarrassing upside-down pose. Of all the people to have as witnesses, no one was less desired than the director, for he had something against me from day one. The first time he flew in for a visit we got into a conversation in which he let me know that he had a master's degree in education. I gave an approving nod and asked him where he took it. "Down in Seattle," he said, and turned the question back to me. "Where you study?" I answered the University of Miami. "Oh," he said, "Playboy U. I heard they offer a course or two in sail-boating down there." I tried to ignore his little jab to the kidneys but picked up his challenge and replied that it was possible, for they had a top-notch marine biology department. He grunted and changed the subject, but not for long. We simply did not match. And then when I fell down the stairs, who would be in town, in the same building, but this Type A Male.

"Are you okay?" the director asked, his lips tight against his teeth, betraying the smile he really didn't care to suppress.

think so," I said in a weak voice. The mission nurse examined me and asked a few questions, helped straighten me out, then said I could try to sit up. I looked at her with a silly grin on my face and said that it seemed just a bit hard to move in that confined space. The two men helped me get out the door and to an upright position, and with great care I examined my limbs. By then it was apparent that I was not broken or bleeding, so the snickering began, quickly turning to laughter. I stood there completely ruined. Pride would serve no purpose, so I began to laugh also, for I felt silly. And that was all there was to what could have been a crisis. The men went back to their meeting, to which I had not been invited, the girls to their silly visiting, and I to my apartment, in search of a few aspirins.

The redeeming feature of the school year in Muktuk was to encounter the charm of the Eskimos. They were, in spite of all their poverty and hardship, a basically happy and congenial population, the students especially ready to laugh at nearly anything. This is not to imply that they were simple, for only intelligent and determined people could survive in that environment. They were also cooperative to a fault, never expecting any sort of deference, although we were guests in their village. They behaved themselves and did their homework. They also spoiled Charlotte Marie and insisted on having her eat with them in the student kitchen/dining room, feeding her seal blubber and dried salmon. She would return from those meals reeking of strange and fishy aromas while freely mixing Eskimo words into her limited vocabulary. "Mommy, I want *agootuk* like the girls downstairs" she would say, as though we were deprived. *Agootuk* was blubber whipped into a froth and dubbed Eskimo ice-cream.

Since many students lived in the village, Colleen and I were invited into their homes, where the elders eagerly cooked up coffee to go with whatever they had on hand, often home baked pastry. It was truly amazing to witness their generosity in an environment of great need. I could not help but admire them, for they were the children of God in some very practical ways.

At one point early on I nearly ruined the furnace. I threw some waste oil atop a pile of scrap cardboard and wood pieces inside the furnace one chilly morning and then went back to the bench for a match. Just as I turned around, the oil fumes were ignited by some live embers, and I saw the iron doors of that cast iron monster boom open and flames shoot out at me. Fortunately, the explosion was only a weak one, so the furnace survived. But I was sooty from top to toe; and the rooms on that level were covered in coal dust. Upstairs, nothing should have been affected, but the kitchen pipes blew out, and the soot in our apartment was unbelievably thick. We all shared a furiously silent and very long day of cleaning up after that disaster. Whatever hubris I had brought with me from Outside that had survived until then was properly and finally dumped. My companions were quite gracious, in all, for the moment never came up in conversation.

Only after this fiasco did the senior missionary relent from the hazing he had foisted upon me. Apparently he was satisfied that Colleen and I were not going to dissolve in self pity, so the initiation came to an end. He took me into the furnace room and demonstrated how to bank a furnace and keep it burning for hours at a moderate heat. I professed a measure of gratitude for his helpfulness, wondering why things had to begin this way and why they went on for so long.

As winter set in my questioning the ambiance around the mission began to be answered. The fact was, northwest Alaska was starkly harsh, especially because of weather. And there definitely was a psychological factor, which was complicated by the lack of ultra violet light in midwinter. It was dark most of the time, dark and stark. There were winter storms that sucked the heat right up the chimney. To endure an Alaska winter in company of others is to bond with them in mutual misery. Some fail at their orientation and scramble back Stateside. There is a factor called "cabin fever," in which a victim will do even crazy things in an effort to get out of Alaska immediately. The local lore contains many stories of desperate newcomers abandoning all their possessions in order to take the next plane south.

"If winter comes, can spring be far behind?"

Winter grudgingly withdrew at the insistence of an impatient spring. We pasty white snow-bound missionaries watched daily as the sun increased its arc above the southern horizon, slowly sharing more of its warmth. Huge snowdrifts that had grown with each storm now began to recede. And then Old Sol moved quickly back to an easterly point of rising, its arc reaching ever more astounding heights. Everyone began to talk of the coming "break-up," when the river would rise and float its ice out to sea. To be a sourdough, one must live through a winter, from freeze-up to break-up, and we had made it nearly all the way.

The pace picked up around the village. Our senior students had sponsored a few money-raisers at school and in the village, which was their practical project. The money would be used to purchase their class rings, ordered from the Montgomery Ward catalog. With this change in the weather a miracle fell from Heaven: everyone became cheerful, old grudges were forgotten, and smiles returned to school and town.

I began looking around our apartment, thinking of what to pack, what to leave. As we two talked about this we agreed we would surely take along some of the sealskin artifacts our new friends had given us, as slippers with beads sewn on, and the little Eskimo dolls made of deerskin. But the fur parkas were left for some needy persons, perhaps other greenhorns even then being prepared for their initiation. I wished them patience and spiritual fortitude, a measure of humility and the ability to laugh at themselves.

And that was our introduction to missionary work, an introduction we had never anticipated as even remotely in our future. It cost us. We flew away with a deficit at the mission office for the foodstuffs and supplies we had to purchase that year. Just a few hundred dollars, but enough that I wondered at the workings of the system. I supposed that we should have looked out for ourselves with less abandon and more attention to the bottom line. Whatever we might conclude about our duty, it was apparent that we could not continue to go into debt at this rate or eventually we'd have to get a good job doing something less spiritual.

I sat silently and reflected upon this, my first missionary year, for the navy had taught me a practical lesson about self-reliance. Early on in my training I had been besieged by the typical onslaught of homesickness and feelings of despair that a recruit undergoes. Then one day, as I trudged across the parade ground to an assignment as a dishwasher, I sensed a deep depression that I could not handle, and just when I thought all was lost, that I was an abandoned soul, a voice came to me from somewhere — now understand it was in my head — "Timmy, if you don't look out for yourself, no one else will." And I answered, "Yes!" That was all. But from that day I became a man, a sailor and a hard nosed realist. But somewhere in the preparation of becoming a missionary I had passively become a dreamer, thinking God would take care of me without any responsibility on my part. was about time to change, to take the tiller and work with the winds and the tide.

There were many good moments to treasure from that year. We took happy memories of new friends with us as we departed that tundra-bound town, and years later we would see a few of them again, a reward that only a Christian can fully appreciate. But I was not at all swayed into changing my vision from doing my service in South America. Colleen agreed. So then, though may seen somewhat unfeeling, as soon as the school year ended, we packed our bags and were out of there.

But there was one highlight remaining. The river ice broke up before sunrise of the very day we flew away. We witnessed the ice flowing out to sea and accepted the welcome of many locals into the Noble Order of Sourdoughs. Since everyone was watching the ice flow out to sea, no one followed us to the airstrip. It was just as well. As in other short-stop services, we would soon be forgotten. The pilot taxied onto the runway, our only avenue of escape, and then made a power takeoff. We surged into the air and away from our first year of service with such speed we felt unreal for a few moments. However, our flight was not made with our previous pilot, for we learned that he had died in a flipover while landing on an icy lake far inland.

We arrived at Selawikki without delay and were pleased to see O'Ryan patiently awaiting the arrival of our connecting flight from Nome. We sat in his taxi and chatted until the plane arrived. This time, boarding instead of debarking, we were safely seated when the pilot revved up the port engines, so there was no prop wash to send us scurrying. As we became airborne, Colleen opened her pocketbook and took out a tube of lipstick, calmly applied a generous smear and smacked it into place. I smiled. She winked at me. She really was a piece of work.

23

Two Steps to South America

Boston looked good in May, and my books weathered the winte
without visible damage. Shrubs and trees were green again, an
crocuses had popped up from the cold earth. Colleen admitte
that she would like nothing better than to see her parents, for he
father had turned seventy. We checked with the missions offic
and were told that we were definitely going to South America, s
would have a few days for a layover in Miami. That would sav
us out-of-pocket expenses for a flight just then. Meanwhile, m
time would be filled with many activities, so there would be n
vacation that summer. First I would visit a few churches, an
when home, we two would busy ourselves with purchases for
long stay in Andezuela. And there was a lot of packing too.

The annual assembly of church delegates met in Yonkers,
typical near-in town north of New York City, but one with
certain charm. And a race track. Each year some tourist-friend
locale was chosen from the cities that had several of our lar
churches. One of the oldest churches was located in Yonker
and the building — their third in two hundred years — w
large enough for such a gathering. Next year the assembly wou

probably be in Detroit, as the year before those who could afford it flew to San Francisco. One of the really big services each year was the commissioning of outgoing missionaries, which was done with the help of any who were home on furlough. Since Colleen would work as a teacher, she was included in the ceremony. Our salary was to be paid naming both of us as wage-earners, and included a supplement for our daughter. Every new child in the family would merit a subsidy. This set a precedent that, it was said, was not intended to spur population growth but seemed to do so. Well, it was the age of the Baby Boomers too. This population explosion became one more fiscal challenge for the missions budget.

There was an anecdote circulating among the married missionaries that one of the board members had said, when this matter of so many births was discussed, "Well, this ought not go on any longer. I propose that we support up to four children, and then it should just be cut off."

I had been advised by the missions executive that my primary task in South America would be to move the seminary project along. Hanbury had become impatient with the lack of information from the field. In spite of having good schools in both the capital city and some villages, and a dozen churches spread around the high country, we were not training national pastors at a professional level, not for ourselves or the country at large. Since there was no Protestant college or seminary in the land, we were ignoring a significant educational opportunity. I too felt the urgency and was pleased — more than that, really — to have this personal encouragement from our executive. After all, it was the first time in a year that anyone outright affirmed me as a valuable person.

Colleen and I began the complicated process of buying supplies for our new work. We also underwent the red tape of obtaining legal papers as alien residents. *Aliens!* That sounded weird. We knew the country would be full of "foreigners" but had failed to think of them as citizens and ourselves as the true foreigners. Perhaps we were conditioned to see this as unique by having been in Alaska, which we thought of as our own country rather than belonging to the Native population. But in Hispanic America we would have no such delusion. We also endured a series of inoculations against typhoid, yellow fever, tuberculosis, tetanus, and anything else anyone could think of that we just might contract. Of course the shots did not provide immunity from all the parasites we would ingest, especially pin worms and amoebas. "You'll develop a missionary stomach, eventually," was advice intended to comfort us.

After all the activity and paperwork, just when we thought one of us might die of a stroke, suddenly, we found ourselves finished with everything. And we had a week left before flying south. The opportunity was too wonderful to ignore, so I made some swift moves and, with a little bit of luck, we were on the next flight to Miami. We would spend ten days at home. Home. It seemed too wonderful to be true, but we were in the air heading south.

You Can't Go Home Again

We arrived at the air terminal in Miami refreshed and ready to do some visiting and driving around, just to see old haunts. An added perk was that the denomination managed a retirement center outside the city, and one large apartment was reserved for special guests, including missionaries. We rented a car at the airport and drove to the center immediately, where we would call family and arrange some visiting. Colleen was thrilled that her parents insisted upon driving to the center right away. Before long they persuaded us to drive back with them and have a look see around the old neighborhood. After that the episode back home became a blur of activities and contacts with old friends

We managed to visit with some, but found that many had moved on. That's the story of our modern life.

We managed to do some lounging under the summer sun, slowly and carefully tanning away two years of northern pastiness. First, we swam at the community pool in Salem Gables and then over at Miami Beach. We were not too far from the McFadden Deauville Hotel, where we guys used to sneak in and use their very large pool. But this time we basked and swam just a few blocks away from the Palms. It was eerie to be so near that strange spot of so many memories.

I made a few contacts with former members from the Palms who had not followed Gaines into his private church. My conversations confirmed what I had supposed, that Gaines split the congregation over the efforts of the presbytery to keep him and the members within their larger ministry. He termed such efforts interference, whipping the faithful into an angry withdrawal from the denomination. Gaines gave the effort a slant that made the presbytery appear to be interfering in a true church's effort to save souls both at home and abroad.

The loyal remnant of that dynamic membership finally had to disband. They returned the property to the presbytery, as the area was no longer a viable location. Some old friends had moved away, to God knows where. I also learned my dear friend and attorney, Will, had died of a heart attack. Today we know more about cholesterol, but then I imagined he died of grief. Well, he really did: grief and shock plus tight arteries.

And then there was a story about Hal. At the point of the split, he took away a few members of Gaines' dissidents, plus a dozen or so adolescents, to form a new group that soon opened a Bible institute. Hal was the director, and his wife the secretary. This initial effort actually survived for two years. But Hal could not hold his rebels together, especially after he and his wife divorced, so nothing remains of that caprice. Hal, no doubt, went

somewhere and resumed his strange behavior patterns among
unsuspecting but pliable targets.

I sat in my car and took in the scene, struck by the waste that
had overtaken the congregation. There were broken promises,
the outright robbery of money intended for God's work, the
betrayal of confidence and of hope, and rancor. And then
managed to grasp the full impact of the thing: a minister who
plunders a viable congregation cannot look upon what he has
done as petty thievery. The guilty party must keep up a frantic
pace in order to outrun a squiggling conscience. But in ruining
others the plunderer ruins himself, no matter how successful he
might appear for the moment. *Wolves!* Erasmus said it well, *Homo
homini lupus est* — Man preys upon his own.

I summarized it by saying to myself that people who do not
trust anyone cannot themselves be trusted. Paranoia is indeed
sickness that leads to death.

My cousins put on a potluck supper in our honor, so that
we could visit with them during our short layover. In a way
we had become heroes back home. It was nice to be honored,
refreshing change after the cool reception we had in Alaska. But
since our families had not heard about that small-town silliness
we remained discreetly silent. It was hard to restrain myself
but having just been back over some of the nastiness and social
upheaval of our times, I preferred to be blithely aloof to strife of
any kind. Indeed, it was good to be with family, to love and be
loved. Surely, that is what Christ had in mind when he taught his
homey lessons.

Another day, Colleen and I stopped at the Inverness Church
only to learn that Pastor Hatfield recently moved to Tampa. He
went there as a missionary pastor in an inner city church that was
losing membership. He was pursuing his belief in social outreach
attempting to relate to minorities in the neighborhood. And
his colleague, Reverend MacNeal, also had moved, the church

secretary added, as he had become an administrator at the state level. It would have been good to spend an hour or so with my former advisors and to hear about their ministries. They too had become feathers in the wind, blown about on the ecclesiastical currents.

– 24 –

FEARFULLY HOPEFUL

The flight to Costa Rica took us up, up and away as efficiently a
the previous one had dropped us into those comfortable days wit
family. We would tuck those memories into some sacred niche
along with all the others, but for the moment we rehearsed ther
in no special order, recalling items of humor and sharing insigh
into our heritage. Really, though our families had no unusuall
distinctive honors, they were wonderful examples for us, bein
joyful and honest, without airs but certainly intent upon bein
honest. That is what Jesus Christ can do for those who find hir
a truth worth living.

Our interest in this world was beginning to shift from longin
for home to willingly accepting an identity as migrants with
purpose. I looked forward to landing in Central America withi
a few hours, which would seem like a jaunt, after the earlier tri
across America and into the wilderness of Alaska. Even with
brief landing in the Cayman Islands the plane arrived in Cos
Rica before the afternoon was spent.

San José charmed me from arrival to departure. Many ne
friends, both from the school administration and student boo

were organized to welcome and assist new students into the Hispanic environment. The enthusiasm at the language school also picked us up and carried us along in those first weeks.

There were many things to learn, quite a few of them not listed in the curriculum. The very first eye-opener was to glance around the student assembly and take in the differences. Most everyone was Caucasian, but beyond that one characteristic, the stereotype broke down into specific combinations. Some were just plain folk. Others were quite suave, well dressed and coifed. The Episcopal priests wore the clerical collar at all times and gathered, some of them with a wife in company, into a small group to smoke during breaks. Quite a few others also were obviously from comfortable backgrounds, sleek and fresh. Some had found each other out quite quickly, those who needed a comfortable milieu with others of like mind. We were, in all, a rather predictable middle-class Protestant enclave from recognizable denominations. The differences were not great, aside from a few really fundamental people. These too behaved very well in that mixed company.

At our very first assembly, the dean had the students stand and state a few basic facts about themselves for the others, including which church or missionary society sponsored them. This took a very long assembly period, for we numbered perhaps seventy, though we were mostly couples. There was a majority of North Americans. We took our turns decently and in order, some as couples, others from the same sending agency as groups, which helped. Quite a few very conservative folk from smaller groups, as Mennonites, were happy to supply a few details about themselves, uniformly ending with either a Bible verse or an exhortation to service. Two women wore linen kerchiefs atop their hair when in the chapel.

Germany was represented by two couples, a Lutheran pair who looked prosperous and self-confident, plus a couple from a pious orientation, Bohemians, we heard. This latter couple did not smoke, nor did the wife wear cosmetics, but they were soon identified as beer drinkers. I found it a little too much that some had to mention this, but I am sure each group was eyeballing the others, so we were all getting an education in an ecumenical setting. Canadians from the United Church of Canada were there having something of a Celtic cragginess about them, plus a few happy-faced couples from the Christian and Missionary Alliance staunch fundamentalists all. Interestingly, these last were all lean and of medium height, one a flaxen-haired beauty and another a red-headed roguish looking fellow. It felt good to have such wide display of young and altruistic persons together and getting along in a common environment.

One man represented himself, and as soon as he stood and began to speak he gave the impression of being a loner. He did not come from any denomination nor earthly sponsoring agency. Rather, we learned, he stood at his time of introduction and proudly declared that *God* was his sending agent, for he was there "on faith." Just he and the Lord, we were to understand. No one made a sound or stir about this audacious statement but there were whispers among various of us afterwards. Our worst suspicions proved true within two weeks, as this fellow was sought out by the city police for passing bad checks. The word was that he had run out of money, as apparently none of his backers in the States had made good on their pledges, and his bank account went into arrears. I suppose a smart-aleck might say that God had reneged, but that is only a passing thought.

After a week of negotiations on the part of the school director, the bank was satisfied and dropped charges. The dean made an appeal to us, as one might expect, at assembly to take up an offering for our poor brother in order to fly him home. We chipped in, and he flew to the north. The rest of us continued in our studies, content to know that we had earthly sending agencies. There were no other unusual or scandalous events reported during the extended semester. Given the perversity of human nature, and that we were largely unsupervised by anyone outside of school hours and away from the gaze of our superiors back home, we students behaved well.

One pious man stated to a group of us during a coffee break that he was very glad to be going to a country where there were few missionaries, for he wanted to work unhampered in gaining souls for Christ. At home, he said, there was a church on every corner, all of them competing for the same few souls. Why, he added, they were falling all over one another, while out in the far reaches of his new work there would be no one to get in his way. He said it in a manner that made me think he hoped he could remain isolated, alone and completely in charge. I suspected that he would also be away from examination by either those better educated or administrators wiser than he. Later I would learn that such persons are not uncommon in missionary work in isolated areas or unpopular regions, and that many a church is planted and then abandoned when the independent missionary either decides to move elsewhere or is forced home for reasons of finance or health.

Away from classes and social occasions within the student body, most of us individually went marketing or ventured into the shops of San José with fear and trembling. We were surely out of our element, knowing that we not only looked like foreigners but fumbled with the language. And no matter how much Spanish one might have studied previously, there was a need to learn the local idioms and accent. All around Hispanic America "Yankee" is not a term of esteem, so we missionaries in training were advised to refer to ourselves as *Estadounidense*s (Unitedstatesers), a formal but also neutral designation. We had to remember that both Mexicans and Canadians are *North* Americans every bit as much as the Unitedstatesers. Our world was expanding daily, demanding an attention to details where we had previously taken our national culture for granted.

Sociologists talk of culture shock when Americans introduce themselves into the many societies outside their accustomed environment. We students experienced a share of that. As we made our mistakes and misinterpreted what was being said, we began to laugh at ourselves. For instance, one young wife asked a shopkeeper for "one pound of urine," but what she wanted to say was "one pound of flour." *Urina* and *harina* sound nearly alike, the *h* being silent. We had to learn to pronounce syllables in the front of our mouths. I learned to be very careful in pricing things before buying them, for some numbers could blend together in a foreigner's ears. One merchant said the price was *unoveinte* (one dollar twenty cents), but I heard *noveinte* (ninety cents). One little vowel unheard, or perhaps elided, could cost thirty cents or thirty dollars more than expected.

Since we lived in a small neighborhood apart from contact with other students, our daughter was very soon out on the street playing with the other children. She was only four years old and quite adaptable, especially after having lived a year with Eskimos. Within days she began introducing us to new words not taught in the classroom. One day she came indoors and announced to us that she wanted a "papelote." I had never heard the word before, but could sense that it had something to do with "big paper." Yes, she said, it was a kite! Charlotte did not know the English word. Some of the children were flying them in a field down the street and our maid had taken her there as a diversion.

This interlude, a fleeting pause in our flight to Andezuela, ended far too soon. Most of us students had developed small circles of special friends and then had to sever the ties. Like many experiences in missionary life, this touch-and-separate moment would become one bead of memory on a long string of isolated experiences.

The day of departure was routine, thank Heaven. As we finished packing, a taxi pulled up at the house as promised. Quickly then we were aboard, with some of our luggage on the roof rack. The driver, contrary to the usual calm pace in Cos-

Rica, hurtled along the two-lane asphalt road as though the Devil were in pursuit. I managed to keep my peace for only a few minutes and then asked the driver if he would please slow down. He glanced at me, smiling, and said, "What's-a-madder Meester, you afraid to die?" I said no, for I was a Christian, but my daughter deserved her chance at growing up. He reduced speed just a little, and we arrived with time to spare.

The flight was made in two stages, providing an overnight in Panama, at the airport hotel. The change from one airline to the other was accomplished without going through customs, but it meant we were not free to visit the city or even take a taxi out to view the famous Panama Canal. The reason, we learned, was because of the political tensions between Panamanians of all stripes and the Canal Authority managed by the U.S.A.

Latin America was in turmoil over what Latinos felt was an unjust and overly prolonged domination of the United States of America in their local affairs, of meddling in their politics and supporting pro-Yankee dictators. The Canal was theirs, they endlessly protested for all to hear, and they were sick of Yankees. They took some satisfaction in putting the *gringos* last in line at the airport. We northerners were made to wait until all Panamanians were allowed through, and then all other Hispanics were accorded their privilege. Eventually, we perplexed Anglo types were given our turn, and shown to the door leading to the airport hotel. We managed to look out our hotel window before the evening was upon us and captured a general idea of the lay of the land. And then we went to bed early, as the morning flight was to leave at eight o'clock.

I was quite irritated by this turn of events, even if I could sympathize with the game our Latino hosts were playing at that agitated moment in their history. I had hoped to take a taxi for an hour or two and show Colleen and Charlotte some of the Canal and the famous locks not far from the airport. And I had my reasons, for my father had gone to Panama at the beginning of the historic digging of the Canal, during Teddy Roosevelt's administration. Dad had married a Swedish-American woman there and their first two children, my brother and sister, were born in Gatún. After seventeen years in Panama the family moved to Miami, where I was born.

It had been my great privilege, while in the navy, to spend a day and a night in Panama, on the Atlantic side, and enjoy a visit with a cousin and her family. We had driven from shore to shore and enjoyed an evening of open air dining and dancing on the Pacific side before returning to the Atlantic side and the dock. By midnight I was back aboard my ship. But in spite of this pedigree, such an innocent thing as showing my family around for perhaps two hours was denied me by the tumultuous change of nationalism and anti-Yankee-ism.

Eureka!

As the vintage C-54 touched down in Monterrey, I sighed in great relief. What had been offered and therefore anticipated three years before had suddenly become a reality. I tried to take in every detail as we taxied toward the terminal. Once there, a group of missionaries and school teachers, standing on the tarmac outside the terminal, began a riotous waving and cheering as we debarked. As we walked toward them, they all spoke at once, some in English, others in Spanish. I recognized some of them from their photos in the missionary personnel booklet. Yes, we were in the right airport. But then I was distracted by the detail of getting our baggage through customs. Other supplies would arrive later by steamer.

The mighty Andes Mountains ran an irregular path down the western side of the Southern Hemisphere, crossing the Equator not far from our situation. In spite of being at such a full tropical latitude, the temperature grew cool at an altitude of ten thousand feet.. Monterrey was nestled in a valley on the skirts of a quiet volcano, though one not entirely asleep. However, it had not shaken the city in years, I learned, but occasionally spewed out some ash. The locals wore woolen jackets or suits most of the time, usually black. Our light cotton clothing, so necessary in Costa Rica and Panama, was not adequate in the capital city of Monterrey. Having been advised of this, we sent a large trunk of woolen clothes ahead and felt anxious to claim our clothing and get dressed for the new surroundings.

Everywhere we looked there was another church, chapel or shrine. And the bells! Ringing bells were so much a part of the culture that even the Protestants grew to like them, expected them as part of their day. This was a country immersed in ancient religious customs. I could not tell exactly what was going on, having just arrived, and did not wish to make judgments. But so many Christian churches were already in place that it made me wonder where we would find our spot to work without bumping into nuns and priests at every turn, on the one hand, and evangelistic churches on the other. But then I remembered that I had chosen education as my profession and that we had our twelve-year school in Monterrey and several other primary schools in outlying areas. There was great need for education subsidized by American dollars, as the economy was not robust.

I quickly discovered, to my satisfaction, that the mission left the matter of choosing textbooks to the local professionals in our schools, and did not forbid them teaching chemistry, biology and history without religious restrictions. Our graduates could proceed on to a college education anywhere without having to unlearn sectarian ideas in order to catch up with the competition.

But, regarding my first impressions, I found the total ambiance so old-fashioned that I felt I had stepped back fifty years. I would learn that Third World countries often were living in yesterday's milieu simply because they did not have the money to buy the latest things off the production line. Northern industries dumped older models of things and such inventory on foreign shores at a profit. And there was a general attitude o old culture because so much was old. The churches were usually ornate in the rococo style and often in need of repair. Priest dressed in the style of ankle-length cassocks and broad-brimmed black hats, while the nuns wore flowing robes with large starched white wimples shielding their faces. And, unfortunately, in the small towns the priest was still in charge, at times inciting the faithful to acts of intolerance against foreign intrusion, especiall Protestants and their evangelistic projects. *Proselytism!* the shouted. Such intolerance toward missionaries had resulted i the actual physical abuse of a few northern Protestants and thei national protégés. The mission board prepared candidates for a least some of this culture shock, so from a distance, by researc and reading, many major mistakes would be avoided.

Things were looking good, feeling good, even if there wer some adjustments looming on the horizon.

That evening, before slipping under the covers, we two kne at bedside and prayed. We thanked God for such a momentou day and promised to try very hard to benefit from the past year o living intimately within a missionary enclave, where piety was o such primary importance as to overpower a healthy perspective

Such a day! We put everything back into Heaven's hands an slept like angels reclining before the peaceful throne of God.

25

Alaska Redux

The initial welcoming and excitement gave way to more practical issues the next morning. There were some hints of my previous orientation far up north as soon as we all gathered for the morning session of the Missionary Affairs Committee. When I first heard the committee's name, I thought out loud that perhaps, to avoid any impropriety, they should have named it the Missionary Concerns Committee. I dared to make this little joke because I thought I was back among my peers, they seemed so much like the men at seminary. And the women were really a sharp group, nicely coifed, dressed to the nines and made up like dames going to tea. God forgive me my tendency to assume that my wry wit should amuse the very religious. I made some crack about "missionary affairs" with the silly question if the "home board" knew about such goings-on. It fell flat. I had no idea of how to get out of this faux pas so just sat there trying to smile. Someone came up with a question, and we all jumped at it. I avoided making eye contact with Colleen.

We were at our first business session, held at the senior missionary's home. Seven of the missionary staff — five of them among the larger group who welcomed us as peers the day before

— convened that second day. As they usually did whenever they came into the city, they had in mind to deal with some fresh issues and then with Colleen and me. Interestingly, in the few hours we had for small talk the day before, nothing was said about business matters. It was all personal and social, with a bit of inner-circle gossip thrown in.

The committee members talked about the work in one town and then another, and made a few financial decisions. Apparently such committee meetings were very serious business, as I could detect some reticence among them to joke among themselves. Rather, they stuck with formal issues. Before long they got to what they had in mind.

It had been determined, we were told, that we would not begin orientation at the high school, this in spite of the intent of the missions director in Boston. Instead, we would be sent to small border town far away, where a young couple worked with some forty children and three local teachers. There were perhaps four thousand inhabitants in the village, which would swell to five thousand when the indigenous folk from the surrounding area came in on marketing days.

Committee members made this move sound like a wonderful chance to live and work in a picturesque rural situation. And they added, it was intended as a time in which to get to know the other couple and see what they were doing as educational missionaries. Along with a small elementary school, a chapel was in operation for the neighborhood, so I could practice preaching. The committee assured me that I would be assigned to the high school later, perhaps, when the missionary in charge left for furlough stateside.

Perhaps Colleen and I should have felt charmed into the assignment and so leapt at it. But it was not what I had trained for and not what I was promised. The offer put me into a bind. It was déjà vu and a bit too-too. Too-too? Yes. Too soon after Alaska and too manipulative. What I basically resented was that I had not undergone all my training in order to spend six months living in a rural setting. There was no apparent reason for sending me and my family to the outlying village that needed a nurse more than two more missionaries to stumble over those already there. That imposed stint would be a considerable piece of a four-year term, which began in Costa Rica. Five months there, another five in a village, moving twice and orienting to different situations; the loss of time began to add up. Why, this smacked more of the old GI practice of "hurry up and wait," one of the frustrating irritants of military life. I could feel my stomach tightening as the conversation went on.

I made an immediate decision and spoke against their arrangements, recounting to my colleagues that I had lived in Cuba for a year while in the navy, majored in Spanish at the university, where my professors were Hispanic, and then worked with Protestant Mexicans over a period of some eight months. It was obvious that we two had just come from five months of study at the language school, where we lived among Costa Ricans in an urban neighborhood. How much more of this culture thing need I learn? And wasn't it better to learn it where I would be engaged in day-to-day activities? Nonetheless the mission staff had made their decision, and there was little more I could say without seeming either rebellious or self important or both. But I had resisted, so we were off to a bad start. Thankfully, before I could say more, Colleen and I were given a time-out while the committee went into a huddle

While apart from the others, I reasoned with Colleen that I might still avoid this assignment. So when we were called back in, I informed my colleagues that it had been "suggested" to me that "if" I could find it possible to "help" establish a pastoral studies seminary in Andezuela, I should make that my priority.

When I voiced this, my companions said it was news to them. Besides, the chairman went on to inform me, they had shelved the idea of pursuing such a project, because another missionary society was planning to add a seminary curriculum to their established Bible institute. In fact, the other group was even then engaged in a building project to expand their campus. So then "We," the chairman said, "are negotiating a collaborative effort and will send our ministerial students there for training."

I was stunned. Were they actually planning to send our young highland students to a far different environment and without churches in which to learn ministry? Why, even to worship on Sundays they would have to attend one or another church of extremely strict and narrow views. I was so nonplused that could not think how I might answer this revelation.

We continued the discussion in general, and I learned what I could about such a shift in plans. But I soon argued from religious slant, that our mission was not of the same conviction nor even compatible with the other mission. I knew something about them, for I had studied at a Bible institute years before that was housed in one of their churches. They were outright fundamentalists about matters of doctrine, even to the point of distrusting anyone from a denomination, since they felt that all denominations housed liberals. They were also dispensationalists while our seminary teachers in Boston scoffed at such simplistic ideas of the history of the human race.

I was working myself into an emotional appeal for reconsideration, as there were a few other cultural points of difference I thought the committee should consider. But at that moment, in an unbidden flash of self-awareness, I saw myself as though I were standing in the corner watching my performance. I had been quite critical of other Christians with whom we would socialize in that rather small nation, and had made my judgment before ever meeting them. So I then said, as diplomatically as could, that of course I wanted to cooperate with other missionaries in the general sense of living and working as harmoniously as possible. By then I knew it would be best to stop talking, so I said that I hoped there would be time to work on the details before signing papers that would bind us to the deal.

I began to understood for the first time some of the difficulties in doing ecumenical work. As things were developing, I could see clearly that even within a denomination there were snags in accommodating ourselves to each other.

During the following discussions I turned to the matter of my succeeding the missionary director of the school in Monterrey, which was a more immediate situation. Within a few months he would begin clearing out his office and packing for a year in the States. Before he left, it would be good to learn enough to ask some specific questions about procedures and even the knotty problems of faculty conflicts and compensation.

The senior missionary said that there was no hurry about such matters, for I would be allowed to travel back to the city one day a week to work at the school. I took this last development to mean I would have no further influence in the matter. But that term "one day a week" meant a day's travel on public transportation over some primitive roads through the high Andes, a punishing and perilous trip, and another day for the return: two days on a bus for one day's work. Something was missing from this discussion, something not being said, and with my experience of being walled out of the decision making in Alaska, I feared the worst. What, I asked myself, had they decided about me before we even met? God help me, a certain anxiety had risen within me, eliciting a slow-burning anger.

At that point in the negotiations we took a quick break, as the chairman had to make a few telephone calls. Colleen and I decided during those few minutes that it would be best to stop arguing and just go along with the assignment. We — which really meant I — could not begin this prime time with disagreements. The truth be told, Colleen was, as I knew from as far back as high school, an easy person to like, calm and cooperative, caring too. I was the one who needed to be more sensitive, less direct.

I agreed that I would make the trip back every week as directed, but stay for two or three days as the house guest of the school director. The chairman called the director of the school and ironed out a schedule. This proposal approved, the committee ended the meeting. Everyone seemed intent upon one task or another and lost no time in driving away.

Some Lessons in Rural Life and Geography

The people of Santa Solitud proved to be tolerant of their Protestant invaders. The little mission school was accepted by most townspeople, who did not mind at all having foreigners do what they considered social work among the poor. And the educational ministry provided employment to a few licensed teachers in a small town economy, a redeeming feature in the minds of many.

In spite of the challenges of living in the high Andes in a rural setting, in daily contact with poverty and a lack of sanitation, and in spite of the morning mists and night chill — in spite of all this, I found the sum of things at least to be interesting most of the time and inspiring in unexpected ways. Serendipity was a new word to me, that had begun to appear in popular print for such occurrences, and it fit what I was experiencing. Struck by the rare beauty of the high Andes plateaus, I beheld a distinct world with its unique charms, and that was a reward no one had mentioned.

There were snow-capped peaks and volcanic craters in the same panorama, strange flora and, of course, the enigmatic llama. The Pan American Highway, only a narrow cobblestone lane at that time, snaked its way among the mountains and over table land, providing breathtaking views of lush valleys and sweeping scenes of treeless mountains. The slopes high up beyond normal agriculture were cultivated by the poorest indigenous folk, and by hand, where one would imagine such farming impossible. And then, descending rapidly via one of the most dangerous cobblestone and dirt tracts in that area of treacherous passages, valley came into view that was in one season full of dust several inches thick and at another impassable because of mud. The "natives" there were from Africa: runaway slaves who had found a sanctuary deep within the Andes! There they recreated the huts of their homeland and developed an agriculture that sustained them in freedom, thanks to a river rushing through the valley. I say freedom, but it must be qualified as the freedom to work hard for survival. They were the poorest of the poor, standing daily along the Pan-American Highway — that miserable rut of dust and mud — hawking their melons and squash to the motorists. Such squalor was overshadowed by skies of deep blue, the clouds amazingly white, a gift of God to everyone. Irony.

Was Furnell thinking of anything this extreme or practical when he talked of contradictions and paradox? I doubt it. At one point in my early missionary experience I wrote him a letter with a few questions about the enigmas and conundrums of evangelical theology and the facts of this harsh world where we attempt to "herald the glad tidings of Jesus, redemption and release." He took the time to answer me, saying that my questions were good but unanswerable. He went on to praise me for serving in a missionary endeavor, saying I put him to shame. I knew that his letter was just a little off track because I was not suffering either deprivation or rejection and surely was not vying for any comparison with him. But I did not know then how much pressure he was experiencing because of his own ministry to those who did not consider themselves needy. The righteously self-satisfied never comprehend their own need. Furnell wrote a book to them, in love, and had grown perplexed at their vitriol and unloveliness. Eventually he fell into the hands of doctors, who tried valiantly, in their way, to ameliorate his angst. But, again, I stray from the subject at hand. It is hard to concentrate upon only one line of thought after so many years have carried me to other places and circumstances. God help me to be patient — patient and wise.

The human scene was not often as inspiring as the scenery, in either town or country. For there existed a great poverty and therefore a social imbalance. One could appreciate those ancient people who still hung on to their pre-Colombian language and dressed in the traditional style of white three-quarter pants (pedal-pushers) and serapes at the shoulders, for men, while women wore skirts down to their ankles. The styles change bit by bit as one travels from province to province and country to country, but there is a similarity that still speaks of an Incan empire. The *campesinos* were obviously in a time warp from the Colonial Era, interesting to tourists and an unsolved social problem to the established society.

I learned that there were a few North American and European missionaries at work among the indigenous peoples, both in the highlands and the jungles. Agricultural improvements were welcomed, as was any form of medical help, especially child care and dentistry. The Andean natives were fairly placid, enured to their status as peons. But the jungle tribes remained fiercely independent, some even dangerous, for they had fought the foreigners for centuries and prevailed, in a way, by retreating into the jungle. The missionary and government agencies down the eastern slopes that fed the Amazon River were at work in situations far more difficult than we citified do-gooders would ever experience. It gave me pause to witness such altruism.

A few years earlier, five young missionary men had been killed by fierce lance-bearing natives. To everyone's amazement, some of the missionary widows dared enter into the territory to live with the tribe and administer medical treatments. Nevertheless, it would require patience before the isolated and alienated pre-Colombian peoples of the land, upland or lowland, would finally become receptive to the benefits of modern ways and allow both missionaries and social workers into their homes. Decades later the natives would form their own modern style communes and improve their way of life. By that time Andezuelans of passionate social convictions would be immersed in the daily life of the country people, and things then improved measurably. Both churches and clinics were built side-by-side, and the amenities of electricity and potable water became available through community volunteer work and collaboration.

I must admit that it was not wasted time to have that exposure to a truly fantastic social and geographically unique setting. I absorbed very much in only a few months, which was augmented by several business trips in the succeeding years. But, as I feared, we had hardly gotten settled in that distant town, hardly unpacked our shipping crates and set up the household, when I was informed of a change in plans. The director of the school in Monterrey decided upon a rapid return to the States because of his wife's health. The "Affairs Committee" decided overnight that I would have to begin an intense orientation back in Monterrey. Therefore, I would spend as much time in Monterrey as possible. This would go on for several weeks while the exiting family cleared up their commitments and obtained the many required papers for departure.

My pregnant wife and our daughter would be isolated in the country, not contributing to the work in a measurable way while depending on the local missionary couple for both daily help and companionship. Eventually, they would have to pitch in and help Colleen pack our barrels and crates for shipment back to the capital. They were simply grand in their hospitality, and sympathetic as well, which was due, in part, because they had undergone a similar treatment a few years earlier.

When the school director and his family vacated the rental, I was informed, *then* I could take over *their* house in the capital. This was pretty well what I suspected might happen. Hurry up and wait.

What clinched my growing pessimism about this fumbled beginning was that I learned that the budget, as prepared annually, did not allow us to rent a house in Monterrey upon arrival. So at last the truth was out. Although Colleen and I were assigned to Monterrey more than a year earlier, the mission had not made provisions to accommodate us there upon arrival. However, the mission owned two homes in the outlying village but was using only one. Had this truth been stated simply and clearly at that first committee meeting, I might have been inclined to work out an amenable compromise rather than haggle with them. I swallowed hard and turned to the tasks at hand.

As for my place in the mission structure within Andezuela, I could have saved myself a lot of agitation, for I had overestimated my importance to missionary work. I was far too stimulated to think myself prepared by the hand of Destiny to do a stellar job at something religious in an urban setting. This is clear to me as hindsight. But this was not all of my own invention, for the emphasis at Chaderton was to go out and excel, to become " young man on his way up." My ambition was sparked, and subliminally entertained visions of fame and influence, even if knew such ideas were not really what the Jesus way encouraged The embarrassing part about this confession is that my conceit had taken root within me because I, in some way, gave it permission God forgive me, and God forgive us all!

But personal vanity aside, my profession was in education where I was not bent upon becoming important or famous bu upon developing the gifts of others. I retained an appreciatio of Socrates and Jesus in my idealism, though I thought of them as inspirations more than examples to recapitulate. No, I wa not supposed to become Jesus but to inculcate his principles i young people. My true task was not to die for my ideals but pass them on, to awaken their power within individuals and, b this process, indirectly in society.

Colleen, whom I had dragged along to a foreign countr and then had to abandon in a backward village, managed h duties with the help of our two co-workers. She kept a hom never complaining, always glad to have me back. Finally, sh returned to Monterrey in adequate time for minimal prenatal care. I mentioned that she was pregnant, and I must blame Costa Rica for that. The country turned out to be a fecund stopover for many missionaries, and we were no exception. Some of the locals told us it was the water. *Don't drink the water!*

Our son, William John — in the old days, John William — named to honor both his grandfather and ancestors, arrived in good health and handsome. In June. The hospital, one that was basically Protestant in origin, and staffed by many missionaries, was clean and efficient. Among the nurses who regularly served part-time, there were a few missionary friends, which I appreciated very much.

I was pleased to see that the nurse who wheeled my son toward me in a baby cart was one of the women from the missionary community. She was so professional, in her white uniform and cap, that I felt I was back in the States. Beaming, she said, "Congratulations, you have a son." I looked down into the little carriage she was pushing along the hallway, and saw my male heir lying there, breathing ever so lightly, and I was awe-struck. Anyone who feels there is no God must not have experienced what I did in that moment. The child was big and healthy, and nude except for a diaper dropped across his midsection. I looked up at the nurse and said, "Well, for heaven's sake Sally, show me his manhood!"

She stared at me in disbelief, as her cheeks turned pink first then went as red as apples. But she complied with my demand, gingerly pulling away the diaper, to allow a view. When I was satisfied that everything appeared in order, I looked back to her and said thanks, she could return the diaper to its place before we got a sprinkling. To myself I said that a circumcision was in order. I also felt good for Colleen, who had wished to present me a boy as her firstborn, although I was elated with our baby girl. I wondered if she would then, at four years, be accepting of her little brother, a competitor for her snug place in the family.

Things turned out much better during the next three years of productive educational work, as I had hoped. I had time to get to know many who were exceptional, some of them having overcome hardships of poverty or health; and in a few cases, racial discrimination. For indigenous people were not always respected just as we in North America have failed this primary Christian precept to consider all persons God's progeny.

We mixed bag of foreigners and the local teachers and pastors developed a mutual trust and esteem during those years, a mutuality that allowed them to teach me things I did not know, while I struggled to understand their culture and what made them who they are. I also had extension work to supervise in various towns and developed a growing appreciation of what village life was like. These people of both city and country had managed to develop both a work ethic and an attitude that made life bearable. Indeed, they enjoyed a robust sense of humor and could be picaresque at times. Most of us missionaries occasionally shared a feeling that we probably would not fare as well in their environment, given our pampered condition.

I also made contact with most of the missionaries in our section of the Andes Mountains. And I became friendly with those who were teaching at the Bible institute on the coast. I wished I could say that it was a seminary, but such developments require years of work building up an acceptable library and faculty. For the interim, those friends in the institute exhibited openness, encouraging my interest in *their* work, now supposedly also *our* work. But it had not become our work, for the idea of collaboration was still a goal.

We had sent a few students to their Bible institute by that time, and I visited them occasionally. Then we sent our first student to the seminary, and another the next year, my last year on that first term. I preached at assembly a few times, in which I followed the advice of Professor Beane: preach your beliefs and not your doubts. Apparently my sermons, based on Bible texts passed muster among the faculty, and I grew comfortable at the school, as they grew accustomed to me.

One Eye on Today, the Other on Tomorrow

The first term of service was coming to an end, and I began to think of what I should do while back in the States. I would be expected to locate somewhere within reach of numerous churches, so that I could do regular itinerary and raise support for our mission. Would we reside within the Northeast or somewhere farther west, as in California? Colleen earlier had asked me how I felt about continuing in Andezuela, and I said that we should give it another spin, perhaps at the seminary on the coast. And the missions executive was still hopeful that I could sway my colleagues into opting for our own institution, perhaps using the high school as our temporary quarters. It would be an obvious goal to do whatever would bring these loose ends together, and it would take a few more years.

I have to admit that, with the indecision and disappointments during our first five years of missionary experience, I was strongly tempted to return to the States and take up pastoring. And I was aware that Colleen was thinking about the education of our children, for the choice of schools in Andezuela was limited. The last year therefore was full of things we had not previously bothered to think about.

A Messenger at the Door

A former colleague from Chaderton days, also working in South America, chose that very moment to drop in for a visit. Drop in, indeed, for he took a layover in his flight to Bolivia. He was returning after a year of graduate studies at Princeton Theological Seminary in New Jersey. He encouraged me to take a year there as a step toward forming our national church. The sudden appearance of this friend seemed an answer to prayer, for he sparked my imagination and also supplied names and addresses I would need. His visit also brought back memories of my counselor, Reverend Hatfield, who had earned a master's degree in Calvin studies. Perhaps I could learn what Calvin taught about church authority as he worked in the Swiss and French Reformation churches during the formative years of Protestantism. For those early Calvinists had developed a system of ecclesiastical authority that served them very well. They established orderly congregations over much of France, creating a functioning synod of more than 2,000 churches.

By the middle of my final year of service in Monterrey I had completed the complex arrangements to study Calvin's methods and theology. I would enjoy the guidance of an advisor versed in Calvin's writings, a published author of Reformation topics. I would not call this turn of events predestination but I had to admit that things were unfolding in an amazing way, so I felt God was in it.

My mind nearly exploded with excitement, for roses were blooming all along my path. However, I did not miss the irony of my rejoicing at a year's study at the seminary after avoiding an earlier move there from Chaderton. Furnell would have termed this ironic. He insisted that God may be found in such bemusing turning of the wheels.

"A cloud the size of a man's hand..."

The other missionaries were pleasantly supportive of this turn of the wheels and most of them said so. Only one companion and that the former director of the high school had anything cautionary to say. He had not only been in the country longer than I but also had contacts with others around the missionary circuit and knew something of the mind-set of the veterans. So when I told him the news, he looked at me for a moment without expressing any reaction, just sat there and took me in. Then he began to smile a wry sort of smile with a certain curl of the lip

He said, "Well, Tim, I am happy for you. But you must be warned: you are going to educate yourself out of a job, 'cause these people down here have never done this before. You know what I mean? The locals don't need it, and we've never done it. And you're going to study at an old-line school with ecumenical ties."

I smiled back and chuckled, but what he said was not funny. Then I said, "You know the field, so I won't argue with you, but I do not agree either. I think I'm setting an example for others, if I can manage to succeed with the plan. We need to encourage our pastors, don't we?"

He smiled again, and since I was already on my way out the door, he shook my hand and wished me well. I said I'd write after a while and let him know how things were shaping up.

Our flight back to the States this time was aboard a Pan Am jet, our first experience with this new convenience. As soon as the mammoth airplane lifted off the tarmac it made an amazing ascent, sinking us back into our cushioned seats. Monterrey quickly disappeared beneath the clouds, and we found ourselves in the stratosphere: all whiteness below, endless blue above. Such a miracle! And smooth. Quiet too. We could chat and read and allow ourselves to be pampered by attentive stewards. I suppose there were barf bags hidden somewhere, but with such high-altitude flying they were not a priority.

We had covered many thousands of miles, living at stops along the way, and yet our world was very small and tightly connected. In us, the Arctic Circle had dipped down to the Equator, and they embraced.

Once back in Miami, our children accepted their places as family members as though they had always belonged. I had mentioned Miami several times without thinking how it might sound to a child. Charlotte surprised me then by saying we were going to "Your-ami." William J. was not quite sure if he also had an "ami" but was happy enough with Stateside ice cream. He recognized every Howard Johnson restaurant we passed, at times insisting we stop.

Within ten days we re-packed our bags and flew north, leaving everyone and everything behind, as was our custom. They were now more deeply embedded in our hearts than ever before, as we zoomed high up into the sky.

Colleen felt justifiably nervous about my Princeton adventure, as she termed it, for we really did not have the money at hand to pay tuition and costs up front. A rather Spartan stipend was provided by our mission agency, and the seminary graciously provided an apartment on campus. I had decided that, if necessary, I would float a loan of perhaps a thousand dollars — small item today but quite large then — to bridge the special costs for that year. After all, I told myself, mission work is a faith endeavor. *Hah! I said to myself. Where did you learn that idea but at The Palms?* And true to the old belief, but to my surprise, faith was rewarded. A check for one thousand dollars arrived in the mail! An accompanying letter informed me that my Uncle Jo Dare left the money as a bequest. He had always been proud of me for choosing the ministry, never failing to address me as Reverend. The surprise was because I had only seen him twice in my life, and I was his wife's nephew, not his. A good man in the right place did a faithful service. Great is his reward in heaven.

26

THE IVIED TOWERS OF ACADEMIA

And further, by these, my son, be admonished: of making many books there is no end; and much study is a weariness of the flesh. Let us hear the conclusion of the whole matter: Fear God, and keep his commandments; for this is the whole duty of man.

Ecclesiastes 12:12, 13
From the time of King Solomon,
ca. 950 B.C.E.

Part One: Another Orientation to Academia

Albert Einstein lived down the street, at the house on the corner, a fact many were eager to mention. Well, the famous physicist *had* lived just down the street, only a hop, skip and a jump from old colonial Nassau Hall. He moved a few years earlier to keep an appointment with God, whom he sometimes mentioned in his writing. Princeton was where the wild-haired old genius spent an interim teaching and comparing notes with others in an assembly of theorists. I walked by the house, hoping to pick up some vibrations or insights. *Nada*. Well, I told myself, at least I may have an opportunity to mention the experience sometime to someone.

Another and more impressive item, in my opinion, was the list of distinguished Presbyterian saints, scholars and martyrs who had burned the midnight oil poring over tomes of knowledge some of them familiar with both sides of the street between university and seminary. Their names remain inscribed in stone or bronze at various places like the Speer Library, Miller Chapel and the Student Center. In this last building there are two bronze plaques commemorating the men and women who died a martyrs in foreign lands. A few were poisoned. Their pioneering work was not only evangelistic but served humanity in practical ways. For they helped introduce various nations to the benefit of international cooperation and cultural interchange, all factor in building one world living in peace.

Life at Princeton looked good, rather like "the best of al possible worlds," to invoke Leibniz. That old philosopher, from back in the age of Voltaire, proposed that since God created the world and its patterns, we were living in the best of circumstances And, given that we have no others, Leibniz would appear to b right. But I shall not become philosophically argumentative just now. For, yes, life was good.

Our little family snuggled into a spacious apartment o campus, with an assigned parking space for our like-new station wagon. We were smack in the middle of an older and monie academic setting. The Old Village Center was careful to preserv its unique shoppes and narrow streets along with abundant tree and a variety of old architecture, some from colonial times.

I found opportunities to speak at nearby churches abou missionary work, and there were Latin-American students i some of my classes. With these new companions I could ch about Protestantism in Latin America and Spain, to my benefi usually learning about the Protestant missionary endeavors their countries. Not a few were well aware of past-Preside

John Mackay's connection to the famous Spaniard Miguel de Unamuno and were, in effect, at seminary because of this Presbyterian thrust into both Spanish and Hispanic lands. These intelligent and motivated students were not hesitant to tell me both the things they liked about missionaries and the things that were not helpful. I took notes, mostly in my heart.

Never before had I been so concentrated upon any task as I was that year of study. It was a surprise then when my advisor, Professor Dewey Edwards, called me in after the first semester midterm tests and warned me that I had to do better in the history of doctrine. He said I was not quite comprehending the gist of things, how Protestant pastors became "Schoolmen" after the Reformation, as they sought through debate to define what the true church was and who belonged to it, as well as what was proper to believe about nearly everything. They were the ones who systematized the Bible to a fault, using it to create doctrines buttressed by Bible verses cited from a wide range of sources. Perhaps, Edwards suggested, I should have a session or two with Harry, another master's student, who was specializing in the subject. Harry was very helpful, and I managed to "make the grade". But I was also jolted into a realization that I was not motivated one bit by all that dry history of doctrine. In fact, it was worse than the introductory course to higher criticism I had detested years earlier. Once more I found myself in a study program learning things no one cares to know. But that is a necessary part of graduate study, so I hunched my back, as did Quasimodo, to the work and got into the swing of things.

Another hurdle presented itself the first semester in a course on world missions theory and practice. My advisor recommended the study as he felt that every missionary should be aware of modern social and economic upheavals and their implications for missionary work. He said this was especially important for work in Third World countries, which were increasingly in sympathy with the advances of Communism. The professor who taught the course was a former missionary to China, before Mao's takeover, and was deeply affected by China's collapse and restructuring as a Marxist country. The professor felt that we Americans had much to learn from modern political history. Indeed, we did. But we were not equally prepared for his way of teaching.

I had trouble embracing what was presented as modern missionary praxis, as many of the ideas sounded antagonistic to my mission's endeavor in Andezuela. In fact, the professor's favorable presentation of socialism was contrary to the popular political ideas of a majority of Americans, if one was to believe the newspapers. And, if it is true that America is basically a conservative nation, it is doubly true of the churches most concerned with evangelism in poor nations. Looking back upon this phenomenon, I think it strange that those who claim most emphatically that they have been freed from the world by Jesus should turn their backs upon the poor and the oppressed, and especially ignore their own former slaves.

The professor termed missions such as mine a holdover from earlier Western European empire days and America's Open Door Policy. He said that we were guilty of paternalism. In effect, he asserted, we kept the local church leaders both ignorant of issues and unempowered regarding the management of their churches. He termed us as Christian imperialists abetting modern capitalism. He was specific in showing how the power remained in the North, funded by dollars and in control of industrial and financial giants.

I desisted from my contrary attitude, much as I had with Oldham back at Chaderton Seminary, mostly for the sake of graduating, but also as a concession to my ignorance in the field. My rationale was that I did not have to be a specialist in everything. But I did do some reading on the Open Door Policy. It was quite a revelation to learn just how involved America was in the world capitalist effort to develop a system of trade with underdeveloped countries, not in order to liberate them from oppression but in order to keep them in the market. The arrangement put third world countries into debt to the industrialized nations much the Appalachian coal miners were tied to the land and in debt to the company store. In either example, the workers existed in thrall to the owners. I did not have time then to pursue the subject but came to understand why Communists were gaining so many followers among Latin Americans, where the United States was termed the "Colossus to the North." The clarion call, "Workers of the world, unite. You have nothing to lose but your chains," was a refreshing invitation to millions upon millions of peasants and indigenous folk, all denied the right to their land's bounty, be it agriculture or mineral rights. At last, in the twentieth century, they had come to recognize the chains that bound them. And this was not due to any national governmental program to give them a better education.

Paternalism! Imperialists! They were hard words to swallow. I had spent five years as a missionary without thoughts of personal gain, mindful only that I was working as a companion to my Eskimo and Latino friends. I had to admit that I actually was a poorly informed foreigner about secular politics in my endeavors and so doubtless I made a few mistakes in judgment. And, granted, we missionaries kept control of the money, but we tried to use it for good purposes. We shared the vision of a merciful Christ, who loves us all. In him there is neither east nor west, slave nor free, Greek nor Jew, male nor female, as Paul asserted. I felt that I was a spiritual disciple of John Mackay as much as any Presbyterian, but I did not say so in class. Although there was much to learn about economic theory, ecclesiology was my specialty.

After the mid-term tests, things began to fall into place, and the final grades that semester were satisfactory to my advisor. But once again, as during my first year at Chaderton, I was made to struggle with concepts that were not popular among my fellow church members, whether laic or professional. Back in California there was a lot of chatter among students about being "Neo-evangelicals" rather than fundamentalists. It sounded good in those days because it meant we were attempting to keep an open mind and to find better ways to define our faith. We really did learn very much about the Bible and its history as well as what contemporary theologians were proposing to keep the faith relevant in a post-Christian world.

The impression had grown within me, and was even stronger under the present circumstance, that being Neo-evangelical was not much different, when the arguments had been made, than being fundamentalists. Both camps were still busy scouring cities and the countryside for converts, which included proselytizing Christians of older denominations, who then would be induced to separate themselves from modernity and "unclean" things such as worldly entertainment. Having done so, they would have the time to learn how to become winners of converts in the old fashioned way. We were all busy establishing new churches that would fill up with enthusiasts who would then go out to help others find their way into the church. And this didn't seem to make any difference in the world around us, because we were not involved in the world, not in politics, social causes or acts of random kindness. No, we were as sectarian as any fundamentalist could be, out there to build a kingdom of competing churches apparently bent upon strangling any form of creativity that might shake the foundations of our secular society. We, of course, took it as evident that the old-fashioned way affirmed God, while the newer ways favored worldliness.

This came to me slowly, bit by bit, and I had no agenda concerning these thoughts, no desire to uproot myself and my family from our familiar ways. In fact, the last thing I needed just then was to be disturbed or uprooted. Why, I had already denied myself and taken up my cross... hadn't I?

The second semester was easier, the material similar to ideas and theologies I had studied earlier. I spent much time cloistered at the Speer Library followed by a whirlwind stretch at my new

Smith Corona Selectric typewriter. Having worked at a typewriter since my teenage years, it was a snap putting my master's paper into acceptable form. I had to get it right the first time or leave campus in May without my cherished degree, and chances were, I would never get back to such a program.

At mid-point in my studies, word came from the mission committee that those in charge of the institute in Barranco had approved me as the first male teacher from our group. I would have a preaching class and do something in church history for beginning ministerial students. This is what I had hoped for, even though I knew it would require some careful management of my opinions and theology. I would think of it as a trial run, a bold attempt at ecumenism on a very basic level. Looking back upon all that, I see that I thought having a graduate degree would certify me as an authority in some way, even among fundamentalists; for I had a high regard for education in general and research in particular and wanted to believe they would respect a bonafide education.

Part Two: Developing a Master's Thesis

The following pages are somewhat technical and detailed, but I feel it is necessary to record what went on.

Edwards suggested I concentrate upon Book Four of John Calvin's *Institutes of the Christian Religion.* I was quite impressed by Calvin's clarity in how the Church is to be organized and what it does and by what authority it functions. For I found Calvin to be a thorough person. Whereas Doctor Martin Luther was a robust person and full of homey illustrations — he used to drink beer with his students and teach them theology at the same time — John Calvin was of a singular intent. He did not even try to explain the mystery of God but was bent upon laying out what God had revealed of himself in Scripture and why he had established a Church among men. And this is what I wanted just then.

These are the opening words of the section I would use for my thesis.

The External Means or Aims by Which God Invites Us into the Society of Christ and Holds us Therein

I. The necessity of the church

... And in order that the preaching of the gospel might flourish, [God] deposited this treasure in the church. He instituted pastors and teachers through whose lips he might teach his own; he furnished them with *authority* [italics mine]; finally, he omitted nothing that might make for holy agreement of faith and for right order. ... Accordingly, our plan of instruction now requires us to discuss the church, its government, orders, and power; then the sacraments; and lastly the civil order. ...

I shall start, then, with the church into whose bosom God is pleased to gather his sons, not only that they may be nourished by her help and ministry as long as they are infants and children, but also that they may be guided by her motherly care until they mature and at last reach the goal of faith. "For what God has joined together, it is not lawful to put asunder", so that, for those to whom he is Father the church may also be Mother (Book IV, Chap. 1).

I noted that Calvin asserts that maturity and faith are linked in a process of years *within the Church and under its order.* That means under instruction of the established teachers and minister Calvin implies that simply having a local assembly of free-minded believers is not enough. In fact, Calvin did not approv of the Anabaptists and other sects, as Brethren and other free communities multiplying within Protestant kingdoms of that time. For Calvin, a believer must mature in faith through the instruction of an educated clergy, and seek to be obedient within the institution. It is even more important to understand Calvin's assertion that since God is our Father, the Church consequently becomes our Mother. This twist needs explanation.

The Church — the capital C implies an incorporation of member churches under its oversight — was described by the analogy of "Mother Church" before the Reformation, so it is not a new idea. Calvin's assertion contains a nuance on the ancient Christian idea that, as Cyprian wrote, "You cannot have God for your father unless you have the church for your Mother."

The older assertion places the Catholic Church in command of both Heaven and Earth. Calvin puts the initiative back upon God's primary activity rather than the work of the priesthood, which is secondary. For clergy, he says, are the *servants* of God's decrees, not *writers* of decrees themselves. *The Church does not stand in the place of God but as the vehicle for God's purposes.* God therefore raises up sons and daughters, and they, recognizing this gracious initiative, submit to the admonitions, teachings and sacraments of the Church as Mother. This is what God intends for our eventual and complete salvation. An entire lifetime can be, and in fact must be spent learning the ways and will of God under the instruction of a recognizable and mothering Church.

With this in mind, the Reformers maintained that the Bible is a measuring stick, a canon, of correct doctrine. For them the New Testament was a repository of Apostolic traditions (or better said, Apostolic-era traditions) that provide a corrective to later accretions and superstitions. In fact, Calvin did not regard the ecumenical creeds of Nicea and beyond as superior to the Bible itself. Calvin felt the historic creeds were authoritative in so far as they could cite Scripture for their various creedal beliefs. That is why Reformation leaders rejected papal declarations and rulings of further revelation, when they obviously did not conform to the biblical standards but added to them. This was Luther's argument when he denied the pope's right to sell indulgences, an argument that sparked the Reformation.

Calvin considered conversion to be a life-long process of growth in faith, achieved while maturing as church members. But with Calvin, this does not mean that the Church saves us nor that we save ourselves. For just as Luther taught, so also Calvin the faithful are *justified by faith apart from works of righteousness* so that Christians live in a sense of God's acceptance even when they have fallen short of perfection. God has cared for us and intends to continue caring for us, but via the Church.

Beginning with these seminal ideas I proceeded to develop my thesis. No modern scholar may ignore the centuries of development between Calvin's time and the modern church. So then, what was I to do with these teachings that had not already been done in recent centuries? My answer was to learn from my mentor and to apply my knowledge to the present. I needed to know, in brief, how others better prepared than I had resolved the later problems. That is the gist of an ancient idea that Sir Isaac Newton expressed, saying, "If I have seen further than [others] it is by standing upon the shoulders of Giants." Of course, I was writing a master's thesis, not a doctoral dissertation, so had no need to be exhaustive in my studies.

Calvin argued that we believe the Church, for instance *because we are fully convinced that we are members of it.* I took this idea to indicate that church members are convinced by the *authenticity* of the Church much more than its *authority*. It mean that believers are won more by example than demand, and that while one might not understand everything that is taught, one may develop a trust in Christ and the Church's teachers.

I write these observations from a period of history in which we have lived in a democratic republic for over two hundred years. Calvin wrote from within a perspective of Roman Catholic domination that had only recently emerged from the Late Medieval Period. In his time, the Protestant Church was still part of the ancient Holy Roman Empire. He and Luther were *Reformers*, not sectarians. Those old-timers had, no doubt, become convinced that they were more rightly the True Church of the Holy Roman Empire than the papal Church based in Rome.

Whatever one's orientation, we Protestants are encouraged to remain within the Church, and *we do so because we are inwardly convinced that we belong to the Church.* That is, we do not run off and establish sects and call them the Church, as though Christ had any such idea in mind. For there is much to be said for belonging to a historic Church, that is, a church with a very long history reaching back to early times and therefore with some calluses and warts on its skin, a Church that identifies with the saints and martyrs tracing all the way back to ancient times. We then have to remember that our Protestant predecessors did not withdraw from the Church of Christ but the Pope arbitrarily declared Protestants to be heretics.

This ancient division within the Church has been slightly mollified by the more recent declaration by Pope John XXIII that Protestants are "separated brethren." And Pope Benedict XVI has stated that we are "incomplete" churches. But this development is not part of my thesis. I am encouraged, nonetheless.

In some way, we ought all to think of ourselves as Catholics or ancient Orthodox, who confess the Apostles' Creed, even if we are not obedient to the pope. I suppose that here I should mention that the Eastern Church, the various area Orthodox Churches, do not acquiesce to the Pope of Rome. For they came to a parting over Rome's insistence upon usurping their historic religion. So, even before Protestantism, there was not an absolute papal power in the Old World, or better said, within Christendom.

Charles J. Duey

The place of authority in the church

Calvin wrote that the first priority of the Christian Religion is the teaching ministry (*magesterium*), and that the Spirit within us woos and convinces us that such instruction is valid. To that end, the Bible is the source of such teaching, and this Bible is made accessible to everyone for both devotion and instruction, *but within the Church*. Love also has its place in this dynamic, for Christ's own ought to feel love for their leaders as well as each other. Perfect love casts out all fear, so that trust and respect for each other lend themselves to maturing as Christians.

Although this Reformer spent much time in Geneva, he was not Swiss but French. He studied law at the university in Orlean and in Paris. He also studied theology but was somewhat restricted by his father's insistence that he stick with law. Wherever he traveled he studied until he began to teach, following his deeply felt "conversion," that induced him to join the Protestants. He esteemed Erasmus, another humanist and widely-read scholar of the century. It is obvious that he was well read in Christian history, showing deep knowledge of the early Fathers.

Calvin's writings were an attempt to be reasonable, to convince his readers and auditors that the Christian Faith is good for us, nutritious to our souls, and the Church is an instrument that enhances civilization. However, and there seems always to be a proviso, it is also a given among scholars that *Calvin was limited by his century and level of education*. He provided a good definition of the Reformed Church and its authority, even if we who know more of history and science may modify his teachings.[4] In fact, Calvin himself provides room for this idea, for he taught the principle of *progressive revelation*, which is found in the process of the centuries within Scriptural records, as is shown in the following paragraph.

The Church may and will adjust to further knowledge and insights, even if this principle causes some further debate among the faithful. Progressive revelation simply means adding to or emending older ideas as a means to better understanding. It does not mean that God changes but that our concepts may change, which in turn give us a clearer idea of the divine Mystery.

In the teaching of Jesus, God was portrayed as a loving Father. That was a change from the older idea of God as the avenger and leader of the army. It became true again in the earlier history of the Church, as theologians addressed knotty issues. This will cause us to look back to previous centuries and see how one saint or another who was right "in context" could not provide all the details of an ever-widening vista. In fact, the very first cause of the Reformation was Luther's refusal to accept the papal approval of indulgences for the forgiveness of sins. These pieces of paper were sold to fund the construction of Saint Peter's Basilica in Rome. Luther did not have in mind forming a new sect or leaving the historic Church, but was eventually made to flee for his life.[5] Imagine that! An Augustinian monk and doctor of the Church protested an abuse of Church-wide proportions and was set up by the regime to look like a sinister minister!

Implications for My Own Situation

I summarized my conclusions after an intensive year of study. It was exhilarating to come into such liberating and orderly ideas, knowing that I was not alone. I had willingly joined the *ecumenical* Church, a Church without borders and beyond nationality. Indeed, were not the old-line and historical Protestant denominations attempting to find a way to a more biblical Faith? But there was a proviso in my studies I could not ignore: I was no longer a Presbyterian, for I had moved into a free church situation, which put me at a disadvantage.

Charles J. Duey

The Protestant Problem of Continuing Division in Search of Purity

My problem would come from trying to practice Reformation principles *within a community that encouraged a sectarian mentality*. A simple definition of sectarian is to say it is not concerned with keeping the unity of the Church but stresses purity as its goal: purity of conduct, purity of doctrine, purity of worship. And wherever a lack of purity is evident, there is cause for division. In effect, we pious and small denominations cannot continue to exist apart from our particular doctrinal slants and sectarian origins. Our refusal to join with anyone is a sign of our insecurity. To give up the particulars of our history would be to give up our reason for existing as separate denominations. *The inclination of sectarians is not to be inclusive but exclusive.* In contrast, ecumenism seeks to open a door — to throw open a window — to collaboration and eventual unity.

With such thinking in mind, I probably should have moved back into the Presbyterian Church, which was seeking to reverse the divisions that had taken place since the Protestant Reformation. But it is not a simple matter to move away and make new commitments and then see-saw back again. I also had commitments that implied loyalty to the sponsoring organization. In effect, I *owed* the denomination. It is a bit like marrying and then divorcing, taking on new relatives and finding them good and lovely, then divorcing and remarrying the first partner and hoping that something like former bliss can once more be achieved. Who pays for what? Who forgives whom? Indeed, I had made my commitments with a clear conscience, and it was up to me to prove useful, first of all, and then to nudge the situation along as opportunity availed. But my old idealism and hopeful day-dreaming were shaken.

A Conundrum

It was a strange thing to have achieved my goal of *defining an authority of the Church that complements the validity of the Bible* but sense some futility about applying this model among my missionary associates and national pastors. And as I reflected upon this, I could see that even in the States our pious leaders were the products of such independent churches and had to handle their supporters with kid gloves. Perhaps everyone was so immersed in the thing, and had been for so long, that no one could evaluate it as I was now doing from afar.

I felt dismayed that at the end of such arduous study done for the improvement of the churches, I was in effect in a bind. It seemed no one was going to win, and everyone was in danger of losing. Even more, over a dozen years from my beginning search for clarity within religion, I was at a stalemate. The evolving world was still offering nonsense, some of it violent and some of it by withdrawal from involvement. That the churches did not either know any better or were too meek to face harsh realities did not help.

My fellow director of the high school was right after all: I was educated beyond the confines of my employment and in danger of losing my job.

There seemed no way back for me nor a clear way forward. I was returning to Andezuela to fill a position I had disapproved of from the beginning. I was going to help establish churches that would simply go out and multiply themselves apart from their surroundings, unaffected by the political upheaval, and many of them preaching the return of Christ any day as the only hope of salvation. There was, in effect, denial and reaction along with a fear of collaboration among missions.

Pageantry again, but Bigger and Better

Commencement was held in the majestic behemoth of a chapel on the university campus. The building was a fine example of Gothic Revival and one of the largest to be found among the academic campuses of the entire world. This impressive structure was not threatened by tremors, as was the chapel at Chaderton, so had been built of stone piled upon stone in the ancient tradition, reaching high into the sky, as though waving to God.

I could only think as I processed along the main aisle that it was ironic to be there. This was only a thought, for my career had moved along beyond repine. I gave thanks to God for my year of study and growth, praying also for the humility to admit I still did not grasp things beyond my limited knowledge. And ironically, what I did not know was my own vulnerability. Others would reveal that to me in due time. Oh yes. The ways of God are mysterious, beyond finding out.

The bi-annual assembly of my denomination was held that year in Ann Arbor, Michigan, and I was told to be there. The Board of Missions had me on the agenda for a report from South America. Reverend Hanbury, still engaged as the director of missions, attached a hand-written note to the copy of the agenda I received, saying how nice it would be to have his personal interview with me during my visit to the assembly. His congratulations upon my successful completion of the degree program was quite flattering.

The meetings went well, and it was pleasant to see various classmates and exchange news plus a little gossip. After I presented my report on Andezuela, and as everyone was picking up loose papers and zipping up their leather note pads or snapping the attaché cases shut, Hanbury pulled me aside to chat. He was very pleased and showed it, his praise spilling out in compliments and affirmation. Obviously, I was doing things right, which had been the impression I had from him since our first interview seven years earlier. In fact, he seemed to think I could do no wrong, and I felt a little uncomfortable with that. I recalled how he said he hoped I could help in Alaska at least a little during my year as principal. He was quite irritated that I was not allowed to assume that post and had some sort of heated exchange with the field supervisor about it. I had learned about this after the fact. When we talked about my educational work, he said it was his hope that I could get the seminary project underway in Andezuela, because, he said, no one was doing anything and not answering letters about the subject. Hanbury hoped I could set things aright. That was a bit heady, but after the Alaska experience it was nice to hear some affirmation.

And then, in this brief chat after the interview, Hanbury said something that amazed me. Beaming, he said, "So now, you have your second master's degree. That is a wonderful achievement: a master of education and a master of theology. I think you will become, finally, our person to help straighten out our educational work in Andezuela. You know, missionaries are an independent lot when it comes to following directives from the home office. But they have no problem leaving it up to us to fund their entire budget, including their salaries. Some of them, especially the men, have been a great pain in the..., um, shall we say 'elbow?'"

I was stunned. I had a bachelor's degree in secondary education and a bachelor's degree in divinity; nothing more until my master's from Princeton, and the ink wasn't dry on that document. So, hesitating just a moment, but careful to define this thing, I said, "Excuse me. I do not have a master's in education."

Hanbury looked stunned, as I had been a moment before. "You haven't?" he said. "I thought I heard you say you did." The thing seemed important to him, as it ought to have. But he was wrong. And then I thought that this executive was flying too fast. For my entire résumé was in his files and had been there for years. He wasn't reading as he ran, apparently.

Just then we were interrupted by one of the office staff, and Hanbury was hustled away without so much as a goodbye. I walked away and was quickly distracted by a friend who wanted to tell me something over a cup of coffee. And that was the end of that, "for all a' that."

The return to Andezuela would be a replay of the first trip five years earlier: a stop to see family in Miami and then an amazingly rapid high altitude flight that would deliver us into the Andes Mountains. Miami, by then easily identified by both children as "My Ami," slipped away as the jet rose to its assigned altitude so high up one could view the outline of Florida's coastline and the bead-chain of islands running south to Key West. I tried to take it all in.

A Postscript B Heavy Stuff

There is a theory in psychology that the memory is a simmering pot filled with bits and pieces of past events, where fears, festivities and minutiae rise to the top and then sink back into the mix. Following this metaphor, dreams are prone to combine various past events into a fresh combination of amazing pictorial creativity. Freud first explained dreams from this analytical insight. The ancients, however, took vivid dreams to be predictions of coming events, omens, or a message from Heaven. We moderns are more inclined to wonder what significance a dream has in relation to our past than to our future. *Now why did that come to mind?* we ask ourselves and begin to examine events of the last few weeks. Nonetheless, the more religious among us still wonder if God is saying something to us as individuals, rather like a warning to be on the alert.

➠

Mother had dressed her little boy in his new knickers and cotton stockings. Finally, she put a nice shirt on him topped with a tiny vest sweater and sent him out the back door. "Now don play in the sand, you hear? Just go back to the shop and show your Daddy how nice you look."

He stood at the door of the garage and peered within. It was empty. No car, no one at the tool bench nor at the scrap pile in the corner. As he looked around he saw a strange creature coming toward him, longer than his hand, nearly black but reddish, like deep rust. It had several skinny legs on each side and two arms in front with sharp things like pliers at the ends, and behind was a long beaded tail. Its hard little eyes were set upon him, apparently, for it approached without hesitation. The boy had never seen such a thing before and stood there in awe of its speed as it advanced. And then, when it was next to his shoe, it turned around, coiled its tail and snapped a stinging surprise right through the stocking. The pain was sharp, and Mommy's boy began to dance around, bawling loudly, while the scorpion skittered back into the shadows.

⪢

I awoke from my nap, sat upright and looked around. I was still aboard the plane, my family seated with me. I sat back and looked at my children in facing seats. *Yes, They're okay*, I thought, *just a dream*. But I mused on the painful lesson. I was a preschooler back then, and that memory was the earliest I retained. The scorpion's stinger had not only snapped into my ankle but also awakened a consciousness of self in a world that hurts its guests. That was when I began building both memories and awareness of danger. After that I could remember many things, and never forgot what a scorpion does if it has the opportunity. I learned, slowly and painfully, that the world is full of many stings.

Why that dream? And why now? And then I remembered that we were flying to the coastal tropics. There would be scorpions, and my children would have to learn about them. With that easy conclusion I closed my eyes and dozed off again.

Only time would prove the revelatory nature of the dream.

27

FACING *MAÑANA*

Barranco, a port city, offered newcomers a variety of distractions but fell short of being a tourist mecca. There was a coliseum fo soccer games, but one would be wise to attend in company o several men for mutual protection. Pickpockets and gangs o ruffians were quite brazen in assaulting individuals in broa daylight. The city housed perhaps a million souls in constan motion, but many of them were looking for work or anything els they could pick up. A visitor would be impressed immediately b the poverty that was never far from sight.

The Old City, in contrast, sustained some of its previou charm from various eras of prosperity across the centuries. Lyin just a few miles upriver and on slightly higher ground, it was th desired locale for the estate hierarchy, who took pride in thei ancient university. In that colonial and genteel environmen there was a modest brick and stucco cathedral facing the plaz which included stately palms along the walkway leading to th great central doors. The first time I saw the sight I was cast bac in time to The Palms Church on the beach. But this church wa still doing its job as it had for centuries, calling the faithful t

Mass and communion with Christ, ringing out its mission for all to hear.

A slightly curved boulevard with restaurants, cinemas and various stylish shops caught the eye as one strolled along on broad sidewalks. Narrow winding streets ran off the main artery tempting the visitor to snoop around for surprises. A genteel charm invaded public life up there, where policemen stood at intersections controlling traffic, and little kiosks and *bodegas* were mixed in along the streets. Colorful hand-crafted *guaguas* (small buses brightly painted) moved slowly along the avenue, neatly passing around the occasional two-wheeled cart pulled by a burro. Each large residence had its solid walls around the property, built basically for privacy but also somewhat for protection. Thorny bushes were planted along the inside perimeter of the yards: rambling roses and bougainvillea, their blossomed branches sometimes reaching over the walls and hanging down to the sidewalks.

The mountains in that area cascade as tumbling giants to the sea, interspersed by luxuriant flat lands near the shore, rich in rice and bananas, and in an earlier era, cacao. Tropical rainstorms are forever washing the fertile mountain soil downriver into the littoral. The lower and tumultuous Port of Barranco therefore is situated upon a shallow delta that pushes out into the salt water, from which fishing fleets bring in their catches of shrimp and fish in great variety and sizes.

Our rental property was located in a suburb on the north side, on a tidal island recently developed and mostly occupied by middle-class merchants and foreigners. It was one story, a three bedroom cement block stucco house painted pink. A brick wall enclosed the property, with the added precaution of broken glass cemented to the top, a deterrent against wandering animals below and petty thieves above. Iron bars were set into every opening of the house, and the only door was of heavy hardwood and double locked.

That house had squatters, we discovered, who were not mentioned when we signed the lease. Hangers-on lived in the attic: small black furry mammals, that tumbled out from the eaves about five o'clock each afternoon, to swoop into the air in search of insects. *Bats!* They would return within two hours, deftly fly up to the eaves, fold their wings, catch the wooden ridge with their claws and crawl to their roosts. There they would squeak for awhile and then grow silent.

I figured there were more than a hundred of them. Being mindful of all the droppings that must have been deposited upon the attic floor, I feared for our health, but no one we consulted seemed alarmed about bat bits. Since they had lived there longer than we, I left them alone. After all, they ate all manner of insects, mosquitoes, roaches, ants, moths, flies, to name a few among the tropical pests that munched our flowers and invaded the canister in the kitchen, some biting us as well.

The bats were not half as offensive as the large rats that lived in the sewer pipes laid along the streets just beneath the surface. Some rats burrowed under the foundation slabs of houses and managed to invade the plumbing. Any number of tales surfaced from time to time about rats or snakes found swimming in toilet bowls. A municipal pest control worker came around irregularly and sprayed a poisonous gas into the rat holes around the foundations of houses, thus creating a further problem rather than solving any.

The Amenities

A bi-lingual elementary and high school, sponsored by the business community plus the United States Information Agency, was a godsend to the foreigners. The school was pleasantly situated in open country less than a mile from the city limit. Students were mostly locals but complemented by children of diplomats and other foreigners. Both Charlotte and William rode the school bus, along with a few other missionary children, and were easily absorbed into the system, as the parents of Spanish speaking children wanted such North Americans as companions. English was the second language, of course, but was spoken as well by Europeans and their children.

There were only a few missionaries in residence on Sunnyside, who sponsored neighborhood churches in other neighborhoods, and most of them with a national pastor in residence. These missionaries pretty well kept to themselves and their church work, having each other over for tea and genteel conversation about differences of doctrine among the missionaries. And, oh, the gossip! I learned that some felt it was not gossip but a helpful communications system, so that they could pray more specifically for others. In this style, Charlotte Marie provided us some choice tidbits about the cocktail parties put on at the slightest provocation by the business and government community. Charlotte often spent overnights with her classmates. I had to brief my daughter why her mother and I were not usually invited to such socials. In part this was a self-imposed exile, because we teachers would not wish to give a "wrong impression" to our students by being seen at cocktail parties. It was a bit tacky of Colleen and me to listen to our daughter so attentively, but entertainment was scarce, and everyone seemed to be open about their vices and tolerant of each other, which we found refreshing. What was reported by those little spies remained privileged information.

Aside from the few Episcopalian missionaries, who ministered to their own and left evangelism to others, there were no liberal or mainline foreign missionaries in all of that wide city and its satellites. Only a few of the most zealous fundamentalists had dared to take up the challenge there since the revolution some seventy years earlier had broken the Catholic grip upon the government. And their no-nonsense doctrine appealed to many of the poor, who had no place in the older society. Some congregations were well established with stern pastors raised up from among their own. And they ruled the Protestant network.

This then was the climate into which our young men were pursuing their ministerial training.

Three couples were assigned to the mission school. The wives taught few courses, limited to English classes, music and domestic skills, as they were not permitted to conduct Bible studies with the students. Colleen was excused from such duties, mainly because the other women already were doing what was available to them, and in part because I needed her help in establishing a mission church.

I enjoyed a wonderful rapport with the faculty. In fact, they were quite open and humorous in relating their own adjustments to missionary life. From there they began to share personal experiences. One couple had our group in stitches as they related how prior to their first term as missionaries, and as newlyweds, they had set out to buy a supply of condoms. Having no idea of how frequently they might need them over four years on the field, and embarrassed about buying such a large supply, they made a quick estimate and put in the order. They had enough for twice that time, so after about six months they became known as the source for other couples who had failed to plan ahead. But after two years the stock was useless, having rotted in the tropical heat. And that was how their little Bradford came to be.

The child served as the faculty's unofficial mascot and enjoyed the notoriety. "Brady," as everyone dubbed him, was cute, with mop of blond hair and freckles on his nose. He also lisped, which added to the picture. This was not an impediment but came from having lost his two upper front teeth plus one below. Everyone loved the tyke, and he had the run of the campus.

Brady and Charlotte played together quite often, usually indoors at one home or another. I heard them one afternoon playing church next to my office at home, so did a little eavesdropping.

"Okay, now, you thith here, and I'll be the pweacha," he said. "You know, I have to tell you about Jesuth. You gotha get thaved if you wanna go to Heaven. Are you thaved?"

Charlotte was a veteran missionary child — we didn't dare say "brat" like they do in the army — and had heard the Good News of salvation many times. She replied, "Oh, yeah! I got saved when I went to kindergarten at the missionary school up in Monterrey a long time ago. The teacher said we were all on our way to Hell if we didn't have Jesus in our heart, so she had us all bow our heads and she prayed for us. And then while we had our eyes closed she asked how many of us got saved, to raise our hands, so I raised mine."

"Didn't you have to go forward, like to the fwont of the room, and kneel down on th' floor?" Brady sounded doubtful about Charlotte's account, so went on, "Thath the way we do it in our churth."

Charlotte said, "Nah. We just sat there with our hands folded and our eyes closed."

"Man! Th' only way to get thaved ith to go forward." Brady sounded quite sure of this procedure.

"Well," Charlotte asked, "did you get saved that way then, going up in front of all those big people in church?"

"Oh, yeah. I walked rigth up fwonth," he said. "Ith eathy. And afterwarth the folkth are tho nithe to you. I been thaved theveral times."

At dinner several days later this subject came up, and I had the opportunity to tell my children that Jesus loves all the children of the world and surely isn't going to let them go to Hell. Then I taught them a children's chorus that was popular back at the Palms:

Jesus loves the little children, all the children of the world.
Red and yellow, black and white, they are precious in his sight.
Jesus loves the little children of the world.

We sang the chorus several times so they could get the melody and words straight, and then we went on with dinner. The next day I heard Charlotte teaching William the correct version, which she insisted he get straight.

> *Jesus loves the little children, all the children of the world,*
> *Red land yellow, black and blue, they are precious in his sight,*
> *Jesus loves the little children of the world.*

"No, Charlotte, it's, *Red and yellow, black and white*," I said.

"Oh no, it's not! It's what I just sang, *red and yellow black and blue.*"

I decided to let well enough alone. Eventually even Charlotte would learn the truth, and in that truth she would be thaved.

When I returned to Andezuela, landing first at Monterrey and making contact with my colleagues from my previous work at the high school, I learned that I was being tagged as a Bultmannian. The label implied that I was a disciple of Rudolf Karl Bultmann (1884-1976), a German professor of theology, who became best known for his no-nonsense denial of the miracles of Christ. He gave them rational revisions for a twentieth century mind-set. Put into theological terms, his approach was to demythologize the New Testament. Some missionaries in Andezuela took the word myth to mean falsehood, so they said Bultmann did not believe the Bible. And to deny miracles performed by God's Son was worse than heresy, it bordered on blasphemy.

Soon after arriving in Barranco I found it necessary to define my position on these ideas to the dean's satisfaction, distancing myself from being a follower of Bultmann. This was not difficult as I did not approve of his frontal attack upon the mysteries of our religion, and what he did was not original, of course. I tried to b as calm as possible in allaying any fears of heresy, informing the dean that I confessed the Apostles' Creed at my ordination and still abided by its tenets. This disclaimer satisfied him, even if it would not later satisfy some members of his missionary society.

I was being squeezed and knew it. And this is what I had warned my missionary colleagues about five years earlier. So, the caldron was simmering. I could not help but wonder at my wisdom in taking on the assignment, for this was the first time in my professional career that I had been directly confronted about my faith and theology, the first time that I was not entirely accepted as an adequate and sincere minister of the Christian Religion. In effect, my denomination also was being questioned about its authority, or at least its wisdom, in ordaining and sustaining me. And all this hubbub came from *hearsay* rather than heresy.

This serious twist in the relationship of the two missions hardly sounded like a collaborative project. It had never been hidden from anyone that in our denomination we had quite a broad spread of opinions about religion on any level, and students were encouraged to read widely from the treasures of literature of all sorts. If anyone felt they could not work within the denomination they were free to disassociate themselves.

There was, however, another reason for the old-timers to wonder about me, as I had made a political mistake — also a professional blunder — before departing Princeton the latter part of May. I had fired off a letter of protest to the editor of a very conservative and independent religious periodical, because he had done a shoddy job of reporting on the new confession under consideration among Presbyterians. A few years earlier, the majority in the Presbyterian churches and institutions had voted to update the denomination's teaching materials, and wished to produce a new confession, a modern one phrased in contemporary English. They came under pressure from the conservatives to keep the centuries-old Westminster Confession, couched in older English and teaching methods. The editor in question had sided with the reactionaries. He felt no need to apologize for his zeal but dove into denominational matters outside his own affiliation. It was easy to see that such a crusade on his part was designed to increase the circulation of the magazine, along with, of course, an interest in "saving the old Faith."

I wrote my letter of protest in haste, admittedly, pointing out that the editor had not interviewed any of the Presbyterian scholars involved in the new statement. That was not surprising, for the matter was none of the editor's business. I would not have bothered to respond to such a predictable bit of tawdry reportage were it not for the fact that my old Chaderton professor, "High Frequency" Oldham, was the editor, while his object of attack was my advisor, Professor Edwards, one of the principals in the project.

My sense of indignation overrode my usual reticence to enter public debate, especially via a letter to an editor. But I felt I had to speak out. I could also have been urged on by having just received my master's from a Presbyterian institution. I wrote very hot letter that was not designed to "turn away wrath," as the Bible advises. Dear old Shakespeare would number me among his mortal fools, I am sure.

I pointed out that the information Oldham published was privileged but deliberately lifted by someone present at an alumni informational meeting, which I had attended. In fact, I had seen someone turn on a tape recorder even after Edwards had asked that no record be made of that informal meeting. The discussion, I added, was not the official position of the committee but review of provisional sections. I told my old ethics professor he had implicated himself in a shoddy affair. Not only that his article was designed to stir up opposition from persons and groups usually looking for such provocation. Why would he want to provoke them to anger? I pointed out that neither he, the editor, nor his magazine were under the Presbyterian aegis. So interfering in that denomination's work-in-process was hardly ethical. Moreover, the committee was not "rewriting" the ancient creed, as that would be both unthinkable and actually laughable. Then I mentioned the obvious, my zinger, that a professor of ethics should be tactful, at the very least, and that I was troubled by his interference. After all, had he not taught us to be ethical? And hadn't he cautioned us not to behave like the fundamentalists of yesteryear, who had embarrassed the majority of conservatives by constantly stirring up doctrinal battles? I mailed the letter in haste, and continued packing for travel.

That summer I was sent on a frenzied tour of supporting churches prior to departing for Andezuela, so I missed the next issue of the review. By the time I had my family settled in our new house in Barranco, the issue of the theological review with my letter and the editor's response had arrived in the mail of a few missionaries. They spread the news around, and I suspect they embellished it as it went. God help them, fundamentalists love a fight over faith and doctrine, always have and shall forever enjoy them.

Oldham, the editor with an agenda, had put a heavily edited version of my letter in his review. He then proceeded in his rebuttal to make me appear a dullard, omitting entirely my challenge to his own smarmy behavior. Of course. Anyone who has taken Debating 101 knows about slanting things in an argument.

Like some of my fundamentalist friends at The Palms, who did not understand the concept of ethics and felt no need to be ethical, this popular orator and scholar — think William Jennings Bryan redivivus — failed to believe enough in his chosen field to abide by its premises. This was his unintended and final lesson to me: Do not trust those who are spoiling for a fight when they can decide the time, place and weapon. Well, then, I asked for it.

The scorpion, after so many years hidden among the debris in the corner of the garage, had come out once again to sting me. Again, I stood there and watched him walk right up to me and flick his stinger into my tender skin. But this time I did not cry. I deserved it, damned fool!

Time picked up its pace, and the story slowly took on a character of its own.

Working with the immediate

Five of our students attended classes at the school: two men in the seminary and one man and two women in the institute. I was to employ these young hopefuls in practical work as my assistants in opening a new church, a "start", somewhere within the sprawling city's growing edge, where nothing was already established. Our team quickly found a growing housing tract on the flat land leading west to the new port. To one side was a recycling plant where old glass was collected for new bottles, and next to it a number of fields where coffee beans and such were dried under the sun, in the old-fashioned way. On the other side was the new highway to the port. There was a very small Catholic mission at the far corner of the area, apparently struggling for survival. I felt there was room and more for an endeavor like ours. We six visionaries began visiting the residents door-to-door. We were well received by nearly everyone, even those who professed to be Catholic.

A fair number of families were already Protestants or were, as they said, "sympathizers." I began the basics of building up a congregation from a nucleus of five families that said they would help us get started. A few others said they would come by occasionally, but felt loyal to their churches nearer to the center of the city. Public transportation being rather unpredictable, staying close to home some Sundays and evenings was tempting.

We rounded up our contacts: a few Pentecostalists, one family from the mission that managed the Bible institute, and a family of Holiness background. I would not discover until much later that one family was from a village high in the Andes. Why they were on the coast remains a mystery. But they had a large family, so our Sunday school began with enough to fill two rooms. On of those children was so full of pep that he climbed under the benches and ran around, so that I lost patience one day and nick-named him *Dinamita* (Dynamite), and it stuck. Colleen was not amused by my sense of humor, but it was too late to undo what I had said. The locals, including the family, considered the sobriquet apropos and adopted it.

I undertook to preach a Gospel message that was faithful to the best I could discern from my education and experience and at the same time be traditional enough that I would not disturb the leaders of other missionary societies. Either I could and would do it right by the old evangelical standards or I would abandon the effort after a time. By then my Spanish was about as good as it was going to get, and I was picking up the local idiom. I preached and taught, mostly preached from my heart. In a simple setting I offered my auditors the silver and gold I myself had discovered in the New Testament and the history of the Christian Faith. They came, they listened and they stayed. Apparently they could capture the essence of a timeless Gospel without needing a lot of the add-ons typically offered in mission churches. Nor did I ever preach prohibitions of any sort, did not waste my time trying to make anyone conform to old "blue laws" of strict Protestantism.

The neighbors in our area were wonderfully tolerant and even curious about us, so they would stand around outside the windows of our rented house and listen to the services, which was a good thing for evangelism. There were no lawns in that district, so standing on the sidewalk outside was even better than sweating in a close room. We sang our best in unison, not even attempting to achieve harmony, sang the happy sounds coupled to a cheerful declaration that Jesus saves sinners. I was convinced that this limited message did not negate any more sophisticated ideas the Church might entertain. It was the basic truth. And I joined to it a healthy measure of the Gospels. This approach gained the approval of many out on the sidewalk. Some came inside and soon joined us. Before long I had a nucleus of neighbors ready to commit to becoming a congregation.

Colleen played the keyboard she had purchased stateside, and I led the singing, swinging my arms in tempo, more or less. We had no illusion about our musical talents, but there was no one better qualified, so we did what had to be done. God blessed our efforts, and that is what made the difference. We also received some help from a university couple who were interested in neighborhood social organization. They were Protestants and familiar with the city and its people, so their attendance was a real boost to the work. By the time they developed their own community work and left us, another university worker joined us as a bonafide teacher and counselor. She married a local man a while later, and they remained solid members during the formative years.

I actually became an evangelist, laying out the basic requirements usually proclaimed for becoming a Christian, just like Billy Graham. I even took a large gulp and desisted from my practice of infant baptism. *Imagine*, I said to myself in those days, *me, an evangelist, and now, me, a Baptist, and finally, me, a re baptizer.* This made me an Anabaptist, technically, a reactionary movement not regarded highly by either John Calvin or Martin Luther. If the angels laugh in Heaven, they surely were chuckling at my zig-zagging run through that playing field.

How had I managed to change so much? Looking back at the situation, I see that I changed one step at a time, and in part because Colleen and I were a minority wishing to fit in for the sake of our common cause, which is what the ecumenical movement seeks to do in various ways. Looking back upon it, that is a rather effective type of prayer. And I compromised, admittedly, because I had a goal that went far beyond the immediate. My hope was for a seminary within my mission's work. I told myself that the work was more important than my personal opinion. Immersion was, after all, an original form of Christian baptism, so I could adapt to the ancient practice. And then I believed, from early Reformation teaching, that many differences among Christians are "adiaphorous," which is Greek and means "not worth arguing about," since no harm is done to core issues. So, as St. Paul had done, who became all things to all men in order to save some, I bent my will to local customs that were indeed Christian in a historic way, some more, some less.

All this took place while I was struggling with my post at the seminary. That endeavor was destined to grow bizarre, building upon itself.

28

HERESY OR HEARSAY?

I stepped into my only major theological morass during a class
discussion of church history. But one mistake can lose a war.
This faux pas confirmed to a few key people that I was not on
their doctrine. I mentioned in class that Jesus had not written
anything himself that has ever been discovered, and what we have
was composed by Matthew, Mark, Luke and John decades later
using a combination of oral tradition and some earlier writings
no longer available. I went on to say that the *Acts of the Apostles*
was composed by Luke, who was not an apostle nor an eyewitness
of Christ but the traveling companion of Paul of Tarsus.

Such ideas were standard stuff in scholarly circles at that
time, but not usually considered among old-time literalists. For
them, God had taken care of the need for an inerrant history of
the church in the *Acts of the Apostles*, and they felt no need to
waste time reading any other history. And if Jesus did not write
anything? Why, he was busy about his Father's work, and his
disciples could recall what he said word for word, every jot and
tittle, for did not Scripture say he would call to mind all that was
necessary?

I went on to say that even Paul was not an original apostle, but a self-proclaimed one. Therefore it was necessary to look back at the ancient documents that make up our New Testament and decide what they meant in that time and place. Simply to quote Scripture as proof of what we think is not correct, basically, and also an inadequate use of Scripture.

"Text in context" was my constant phrase to remind my students to read and teach by considering the various facts known from research and the date of each biblical work. These facts were available to them in both textbooks and annotated Bibles. I hoped to awaken their intellects to the possibilities of a more learned approach to Bible interpretation.

I pointed out that the early chapters of *Acts of the Apostles* are an effort to give an account of the early church, which Luke did not know personally. It is interesting to note that our first Christians had not taken any pains to record their own experiences but left the task to a later generation to rediscover by whatever means they might have at hand.

Luke presents a scenario of the resurrected Jesus telling his disciples to wait for the visitation of the Holy Spirit. Then the Lord ascends into the clouds, leaving his peasant disciples to carry on without his supervision or further instruction. I did not mention that nothing further was needed, as they all expected the Lord to return very soon, a fact I felt anyone could easily see. If they did not, ordinary thinking students would eventually come to me and ask a question or two, if they had grown to respect me and trust my teaching.

These original twelve — make that eleven — disciples, now officially Apostles, became Christ's successors. Leaders of later generations would rely upon this "oral tradition" for their own decisions in determining what was acceptable within the spreading Church, and that history would prove to be rife with disagreement. But one item at a time. As people learn they try to put the pieces together. I was trusting the process.

As we pondered this section of *Acts*, one student turned the discussion to how a human body could possibly rise into the air. As I look back upon that question I wonder if I was being set up, but it seemed an honest discussion at the time. The proper fundamentalist answer to such questions is that Jesus can do anything, for he is the Son of God and a miracle-worker. But I answered that Christ was no longer fleshly, having been transformed into a "spiritual body," which was fitting to his eternal nature. And this was not wild conjecture, after all. Intelligent thinkers, by that time in biblical history, agreed that the spiritual is the true and everlasting, while the physical and temporal are limited, always subject to further change and eventual decay. This is what resurrection means for us: *becoming spiritually awake, which is to participate in a Christ life beyond earthly sensuality.* Paul often used the term God-in-Christ with this same understanding. Paul stressed that we are in him and he is in us.

I also mentioned that on the first Easter Jesus *appeared* to his chosen disciples in a locked room. And, although he was an apparition, Thomas could see Christ's wounds, for even if Jesus was no longer flesh he could *appear* to them, and on that occasion he was there to exhibit his victory over death, so he showed his wounds as a guarantee. After all, Thomas had demanded exactly that. A few days earlier, I went on to say, he ate supper with two of his followers, whom he had joined on their walk back to Emmaus. Neither of them recognized him nor did they report any tell-tale wounds in his hands or forehead while at table. Only when Christ broke the bread did it occur to those two downcast disciples that the man with them at table could be the Lord, whose death they were mourning. Further, Mark writes that Jesus "appeared in another *form* unto two of them." Again, in John's account, Jesus appeared to some of his disciples at the seashore, and "none of his disciples [dared] ask him, Who art thou? knowing that it was the Lord." How did they know? For he did not identify himself nor did he look like their former rabbi

They *knew by some spiritual sensation*, of course, for the Christ of God had undergone a transformation, even as he had done upon the Mount of Transfiguration. I cannot help but think that they *tingled* as he spoke. I surely had vibrated to a heavenly frequency when he spoke to me that day on the road home, though I never saw anything. He was a foretaste of the kingdom that he said was not *in* the world but *within the faithful* by the power of God. Our conversation went on like this for awhile before we moved on into the following historical record that Luke wrote for those third generation Christians.

My method of teaching got back to one of the "power" pastors in town, and in the following weeks this pastor and a senior missionary, who had always sniffed around the Bible institute for mistakes, began to build a case for removing me from the faculty.

Soon enough I began to sense that things were changing around the school. There were more visiting pastors showing up on campus, who attended chapel services and had private conversations with the students. On more than one occasion I was aware that a pastor would occupy the empty classroom next to mine while I was teaching church history. I suspected that some listened to my instruction through the flimsy walls. As the saying goes, "Just because I'm paranoid doesn't mean they aren't out to get me." This sense of snooping inhibited my teaching style. The excitement went out of it, and I found myself wandering, trying to stay out of the fire. God forgive me, I was waffling.

I cannot recall any other time when I felt so completely alone.

At that same time word came to us that President John F. Kennedy had been assassinated. An entire generation of young people in the States and beyond were stupefied by this sudden turn of history. We had begun thinking we were entering a period of political Camelot, the Age of Aquarius. America would go beyond the old prejudices, would shine anew among the nations. We would prove Russian atheistic Communism wrong by showing how superior Democracy is to any form of Totalitarianism. America was still a beacon for the entire world for its dreamers, its poor, its huddled masses. And we would no longer look back to those old prejudices of religion that had caused so many wars, for we had freely elected a Roman Catholic as our president, a first in American history. Tragically, our young and handsome president was gunned down by some misdirected zealot with a sharp-shooter rifle. Then he in turn was gunned down by a maniac. We were in shock. And, as we soon learned, the assassinations were to continue.

The world had gone mad! Richard Nixon and Eugene McCarthy and others of that old dirty, paranoid type were still active, just within the shadows, so there was much to fear.

We were confused, and we were angry. And I was reeling. Viet Nam was raging, so it too was large upon our consciousness. There was an accusation abroad of a Christian crusade in which America was killing communists for Christ, to put it in its bluntest phrasing. The Americas, north and south, were split in their opinions about money and politics.

It was a bad time to be a Democrat in a fundamentalist school in a poor third world nation. A majority of the missionaries could not separate their religion from their belief in America's sacrosanct capitalism. Enlightened capitalism, of course. And sadly, I felt many of my seniors and not a few of my colleagues around the country were not exactly sorry that Kennedy had been violently removed from office. A few had said it outright: God was working things out for good. After all, JFK had failed in his invasion of Cuba, hadn't he? I felt he was *accused* of failing, though he had inherited the plans and preparations from the Eisenhower administration. My associates felt that, had Eisenhower still been in charge, Castro would have been overthrown, and Cuba still have been within the Northern Umbrella. Many of my fellow Americans were embarrassed before the world, and not a few my missionary colleagues were embarrassed too. Yes, it was a very bad time.

But back to the story, for as I said, there is much to tell.

One of the older men from the other mission, a tall and rather handsome man, still of great vigor and self confidence, came around quite often to visit and pry into things. I learned from the faculty that he was the one who had wanted the position I held. *Aha!* There existed a plot no one had mentioned until that moment — so I was suddenly being forewarned a few months after the fact.

Lennart Klewes was a classic fundamentalist Bible preacher and a wild kind of enthusiast for prophecy. Those who knew him best were the most wary of him, for he had a way of doing things in the worst way, making snap decisions, creating divisions among his associates and in general causing people to raise their eyebrows in disbelief or to sigh in despair. Nonetheless he was one of their own, even if he could be so... *what?* In one moment he was a friend and then became a frothing adversary, leaving his associates in a state of confusion. But his older co-workers accepted him as sincere even if disruptive, because he was a pioneer of the Faith. And, they reasoned, wasn't he *ordained?* He had given his working life to Andezuela in some very difficult assignments in rural and very blighted areas. Yes, the man bore scars for his love of Jesus.

Much later I would read *The Poisonwood Bible,* by Barbara Kingsolver, and identify exactly what I had been dealing with in those months. The antics of the missionary in that story, Nathan Price, were not too different from those of Lennart Klewes.

Lennart had been invited to preach at a chapel service during one of his visits, and since I taught homiletics I was especially interested in learning how he would deliver his sermon on that occasion. I alerted my students to this opportunity to be his kind critics, which, I had to explain, did not mean they disapproved of him but were going to analyze his technique. I had earlier stressed such learning tools as analyzing a sermon to learn how to preach in various ways, according to what one wishes to accomplish. Perhaps they would learn how to preach to church members without repeatedly evangelizing them; to inspire them instead of instilling a guilt complex; to encourage rather than punish. That was my hope as a teacher. I therefore attended the service with some expectation that my students might pick up some fresh material. And I was curious.

The speaker wasted no time in greetings or other introductory matters but got to the address, reading from the Olivet Discourse as presented in Matthew's Gospel. He chose the Parable of the Ten Virgins, who took their lamps and went out to meet the bridegroom and bring him on to his wedding party. Five of them were wise and five were foolish. The foolish ones took only their lamps, while the wise took both lamps and extra oil. The end of the parable says that only the five wise virgins got into the wedding feast, because they were prepared for the bridegroom's arrival, running to greet him with lamps and guiding him on his way into town. But the foolish, who were away looking for more oil, arrived later and were shut out of the party. Then the Gospel writer drew this conclusion: "Watch therefore, for ye know neither the day nor the hour wherein the Son of man cometh."

The lesson is obvious, in context: that a disciple must be prepared for an indeterminate wait for the arrival of Jesus. Most trained preachers across the history of Bible commentary would go into this parable to draw out a lesson on prudence or patience.

Lennart chose the parable because he wished to preach about sexual permissiveness. This is what is called taking text out of context, which makes it a pretext. I made a mental note to ask my students if any of them noticed that disjunction.

Also, it has been understood among scholars of biblical Hebrew as well as Greek that the word virgin in either language is used generically for young maidens, that is unmarried young women. In this case as in most biblical readings virginity is not the issue, so we may assume that there were ten young unmarried women in the story, their virtue not important to the parable, only their preparedness in having enough oil for their lamps.

After reading the parable, Lennart began his sermon with great energy, in Spanish, of course. I translate here rather freely in order to give the flow of his message, and leave out some of it for brevity's sake.

He began, "Back in biblical times a woman was praised for her virtue, and to be a virgin was an honored status. In fact the entire family helped her to remain unstained by sex. They knew she could not catch a husband if her reputation was soiled. Every man expected to marry a virgin. But today a man doesn't know what he's getting most of the time, and some men do not care. But I add, sometimes he does know what his girlfriend is, because he has had previous experience with her. I say this to his shame and to hers.

We live in liberal times, and women have come to feel it is their liberty to play it loose. Why, many girls from our Christian homes think nothing of dressing like harlots and painting their lips and cheeks like them too. And when they do they are announcing to the world around them that they are ready to play the game the young men have in mind. But the young men do not always play fair. No, they find out they've gotten a girl in trouble, they take off for the hills.

"Now you young men, you have to take what I am saying just like I say it. The Apostle Paul says that we men are under obligation to lead pure and holy lives. It takes two to sin, you know, so what is good for the goose is good for the gander!" Here our speaker attempted to translate the English phrase literally into Spanish, which left room for confusion, perhaps in two ways, but he moved on.

Lennart kept at it in this vein for awhile, building his case for the looseness of the worldly culture around us and how we are exposed to temptations on a daily basis that can bring us to the brink of Hell. As he warmed to his subject he raised his voice and his arms began to move about, flapping out to the sides without any apparent relation to what he was saying. Then he began stepping out from behind the pulpit and leaning against it or even walking over to the side of the platform and turning back just in time. Such antics did help to keep his audience attentive.

Hardly anyone made a sound. This was his show, and he didn't need anyone saying amen, so he streamed on like an over wound Victrola. Some liked his style, so there was an occasional outbreak of approval, as a clicking of the tongue or a grunt. I heard an occasional groan too. This then was an appeal for "getting under the conviction of sin."

He continued. "Why just the other day I was walking on the streets of Barranco, and here I am a man of God, a sanctified preacher, and I spend time in prayer every day, but I want to tell you, there were some nearly nude women downtown, and I could not ignore them. *Right out in public!* And they were strutting around as if they owned the town! Some of their thin little dresses were so tight that I could see the outlines of their underclothes. They jiggled along shamelessly, swinging their hips and smiling their big red smiles. *Why, it was all I could do to keep from sinning with my eyes!*" He then removed his glasses, and blinking, stared out at his audience, the corners of his mouth pulled down.

I was so caught off guard that a laugh came gurgling up from my gut, and I barely squelched it in my throat. I was stunned and hoped I was doing a good job of maintaining a neutral exterior while choking on my desire to laugh out loud at the clown. God forgive me, but he was bad, really bad. Fortunately, he was not looking at me. In fact, he did not once actually look over at my area of the chapel, which made me think he somehow had me in mind.

Lennart preached on, but his change of spirit and emphasis was suddenly coming from some other source, for he shifted subjects without a blink of the eye. Or perhaps he always got two or three subjects into one sermon, and another one had occurred to him. He moved into praising the Bible as God's literal Word, the only source for truth in a world full of half-truths and lies.

He made his point. "Now, there are some people in positions of leadership who seek to undermine the authority of the Bible. It seems they want to rewrite it to agree with their modern ideas. They would have you believe that it needs interpretation. But what they do is lead young people astray, give you permission to read the Bible as you prefer, to allow liberties that God never intended. I must warn you: Be vigilant. Do not turn from your first love of Jesus, to follow after the vain philosophies of men. And do not turn from your fathers in the faith, your teachers and your pastors, who have shown you the way to true religion and eternal life. For the Bible warns us that many will come teaching falsehoods and vain philosophies, denying the truth and leading the saints into error, *if they can.*

"My dear students, you are preparing to serve the Lord, and Satan knows it, so he's after you. Don't think you can escape the wiles of the Devil without the help of your elders. You need to have a disciplined life and remain within the fellowship of the saints. You need to spend time reading the Bible and praying. *And...* you must avoid the company of worldly-wise types who think they can rewrite the Bible according to what they call a higher education. I tell you, they will pay for their guile, just like those foolish virgins did in the time of Christ.

Remember, when the wedding feast began they were not there, for they hadn't been ready for the Lord's arrival. Why some of them may have been enticed by one or another young man to sneak away to the bushes with them! And later, when they knocked on the door and asked to be let in, the Lord said to them, 'Verily I say unto you, I know you not.'"

That was the end of the sermon, and we were directed to sing a hymn of invitation to accept the Lord's mercy. Afterwards Lennart prayed for the students, ending by inviting all there who wished to make a rededication of their heart to "the faith once for all time delivered to the saints" to do so by coming forward and getting right with God.

Not a word was uttered from the floor. No one stood. The silence grew embarrassing, so Lennart finally said "Amen, so be it."

We filed out silently to our classes. I was glad to have a task at hand, so left him visiting with his companions but was struck by how easily they shifted into a fellowship mode and chatted cheerily up front, before the podium.

Things Happen in Threes, or Four or More

The next day I awoke feeling strange, rather upset, not hungry and thinking that something serious was taking place in my body. By noon I was sick, dizzy at first and then nauseous. Colleen said I had a low temperature, and my eyes didn't look good. That night was awful, painful, disorienting. I tossed and turned, retched at some time after midnight, although I had not eaten since breakfast. I decided to visit the doctor the next day.

In the morning, before I could say anything, Colleen told me with great concern, "Your eyes are yellow."

The doctor confirmed that I had hepatitis and admitted me to the hospital, to the isolation ward, and began the simple treatment they had for such a disease. He said, "It will run its course. This sickness is usually caused by filth; something you ate no doubt. It is not dangerous unless you make it so by ignoring the precautions. You must go to bed, avoid fats, eat sweets, take in liquids, as broths and clear sugar drinks. Do not strain yourself, do not kiss anyone, do not tax your liver in any way: no coffee, no alcohol (no problem), and stay in bed even if you think you have strength. A relapse is one of the worst things that could happen to you right now."

I was given a shot of gamma globulin plus an intravenous feeding, a few days bed rest, and then sent home, where I would continue in isolation. The doctor stopped by and gave me a shot of vitamin B12. The rest was up to me and my body's ability to heal itself.

There is the dizziness that disorients, then the accompanying nausea, the aches from total bed rest and even worse, the predictable sour frame of mind. And the loneliness. Colleen had retreated to Billy's room.

In my despair I wrote some negative poetry, or at least stabbed at writing poetry.

> *Abed and sick, and sick of bed,*
> *and sick of sick,*
> *and sick of soul as well.*
> *What means this curse,*
> *whence comes this hell?*
> *Oh, send a cure*
> *that breaks the spell.*

I titled it *Hepatitis of the Soul.*

As soon as possible, I began to read. My first book was *Catcher in the Rye*, which was fascinating but hardly what I needed just then. Poor Holden, he was running so hard. But it did make me wonder about my own frantic pace and what I might be covering with my endless stream of work and preaching. I read my mind into other places and different thought, as much as my body would endure, from a collection of new books bought while in the States. This included some of the paperbacks circulating among enthusiastic Catholic theologians, works written by Pierre Teilhard de Chardin, a Jesuit priest and renowned paleontologist. I also slipped in some novels missed in the last several years. Most of those books were less challenging, just full of information and different ways of writing. And so I whiled away the days.

A Bold and New Era of Christian Theology

My imagination had been previously fired by the soaring thought the creativity and broad education of Father Teilhard. He was recognized paleontologist, who participated in the discovery o Peking Man and had written various scientific papers on the ide of where humanity was going in its process of evolution. He wa also a professor of chemistry, so that he had the respect of th academic world.

He proposed a new age of mind, called *noosphere*, which implied an envelope of intelligence layered over the bioti envelope. He was making a bold attempt to bring the Christ idea into modern thought as the One who was leading the world int a unified Faith that would agree with scientific findings. Wel this is my definition. He is inspiring, in his way.

His efforts nonetheless were censured by the Catholi guardians of dogma. His views therefore could not be publishe during his lifetime. But they were circulated among scholars i mimeo form. Meanwhile, he lived out his years as a Jesuit i New York City, never renouncing his vows. Teilhard was popula with a great many theologians from both Catholic and Protestar schools of thought. As it turns out, he still is. In fact, he ha regained status among the Catholic Church's scholars as havin proposed the only vision of a unified world that melds biologic and theological themes.

I had a few of his books in my collection, which were discusse among my colleagues in private gatherings at Princeton. Tho books saved my intellectual life at that low time in my spiritu pilgrimage. *The Phenomenon of Man* became recognized as h master work. I must admit that it had a deep effect upon n thought, as I found my first solid, religiously creative treatme of the theory of evolution in his work, and a higher model but still theological understanding of Jesus Christ.

Colleen stayed home with me, going out only when necessary. Others in our circle of friends and associates rose to the moment, running errands, shopping, and helping see the children off to school. Our student pastor took over the worship services. I was pleased but also surprised at how well everything continued without me, so learned at least temporarily how to be at peace and accept the help of others.

After six weeks of bed rest, my skin had taken on its former healthy coloring, though paler, and I was permitted to go out and walk. My diet shifted from broth, oatmeal and such pap to heartier fare. I celebrated by driving into town for an ice cream sundae. That was the test. My stomach, springing to life, thanked me. That evening I had a steamed lobster, with melted butter; a bold assumption of healing. Nothing ill came of it.

The next day I felt even better, so took a walk around the neighborhood, stopping in at the seminary to announce my return to duty. The dean was personally quite happy to see me out and about, but he seemed strangely reserved about my duties. The visit was brief, as he was between tasks, so I returned home.

What I did not know about my duties was that I no longer had any. During my time away from teaching, I would learn later, the faculty had been summoned to a meeting with their missionary leaders, in a hush-hush session. The elders were gathering evidence of my errors in doctrine. Since the faculty knew that some of the older missionaries and pastors were in cahoots to tighten the reins on them while getting rid of me, they especially feared what might happen to them in short order. They gave a positive report of my teaching and denied knowing anything about heresy. The elders then called a plenary session of their missionaries and forced the issue. They concluded that the cooperative teaching agreement was not satisfactory and therefore should be aborted. The faculty had no choice but to agree to the decision, other than to resign en masse, which they would not do. I would not have wanted that.

No one in my mission knew about the decision, or at least no one told me. Given the practice of whispering secrets within the larger religious community, it is amazing the decision had not gotten out. It appeared that the leaders were waiting for my recovery before lowering the boom. So, on the evening of the day I announced I was no longer sick, three men came to visit the president of the other missionary society, the dean of the institute and a faculty member. They had called ahead, so I knew something was going on, and I figured it was not good.

Once inside, the leader informed me that their mission had decided to discontinue the cooperative educational effort. Therefore, I would not be needed any longer. And that was that, no speeches, no thanks, no sympathy. The man was a task-oriented person, and he did what he came to do. My colleagues from the seminary apparently were brought along to serve as witnesses and nothing more, for they sat silently and avoided eye contact.

I was actually weaker after my illness than I suspected, for I hardly reacted to this parody of doing things decently and in order. I sat there and looked at them. Perhaps I gave an impression of being stupid. For I was anticipating some sort of fiery trial or a confrontation, some accusation and an exchange of ideas or an offer for a second chance, perhaps a recantation à la Galileo. Well, that sounds grandiose. But I must have been immobile for a while before I felt the pain. I was stunned, so time became relative to my condition. But I regained my senses soon enough, for the news really was not news, only confirmation. Controlling myself better than I sometimes did, I said in a few words that my ministry had been swept out the doorway without so much as a thank you. And that was all right, because I could not say that my time at the school had been a pleasure. Unable to continue speaking — and indeed there was nothing more to say — showed the trio to the door.

That was the beginning of a very difficult time in which I had to separate my several feelings and reactions in order to know my own mind. I also had to find some way to face both old friends and associates with dignity. No doubt I did not then see myself clearly nor behave well, but with the patience and warmth of Colleen and a few friends — and by the grace of God — I made it through, adjusted and picked up the pieces.

It came to me rather soon in my reevaluation, that although there was an agreement reached between the two missions regarding a cooperative work, no legal contract or even an informal paper had ever been written. None was presented to me nor had my own mission even given me any guarantees. And I had never thought to ask for documentation of any aspect of the cooperative endeavor. For during those crucial negotiations I was in the States, and was informed that my next assignment would be to the seminary. Things seemed to have slipped from one stage of development to another under the assumption that it would all work out. Or would not.

I never signed a contract with my mission or with the other mission, nor had I bothered to ask for any firm assurance of equity or tenure. Interestingly, looking back on that episode, no one ever asked me to sign a creedal statement or undergo a formal examination of my theology before joining the faculty. Things were handled on a day-to-day basis. Under these conditions we should have had, at the very least, some plan of accountability and definition of mutual responsibilities. Well, so much for my theories of ecumenism. It became clear to me that getting various denominations together was far more difficult that I had dreamed.

An Insight

Immediately after that initial shock, when the bearers of bad tidings had rounded the corner on their way back to the campus, I had a revelatory experience: a weight was graciously lifted from my shoulders. The relief was both physical and spiritual. I audibly sighed, and then I laughed at my reaction. This both surprised and pleased me. My desire to be free of the matter apparently lay just under the surface. But I must have been operating on the assumption that I owed them something, or owed my mission something, and finally, surely, I must have feared failure. Perhaps I did not know when to quit.

I asked myself, *Why had I not simply terminated the relationship earlier?*

That question provoked further insight. Why, indeed, had I not risen up in protest and terminated my previous assignments? I did not wish to go to Alaska, really. But I went. Why had I not at least asked for some concessions? Why did I not threaten to return to the States years before, when my assignment was whipped out from beneath my feet upon arrival in Monterrey? Well, the questions came easily at that moment, but I could see that it was not upon me to bear all the blame. Beyond this immediate anger and shame, I truly lacked an understanding of how the church as an organization works, of how passive-aggressive we are and how we mix our spirituality and ego investments. And there was the matter of prayer. We trusted in the Lord and "leaned not on our own understanding," as it is written. In all our ways we sought to look for the invisible hand of God working things out for good. And I suppose God did finally work some good out of that situation. But I now think God would not have been displeased had I exercised some independent judgment in many cases, as I used to, before I became so task oriented.

The unilateral decision to terminate that education partnership confirmed to me that my teaching ministry anywhere in Andezuela had ended. Why, immersing myself in our new church planting was far more interesting and rewarding than anything I had encountered at the seminary. And I had no desire to return to the highland work. If there was such a thing in my future as serving in a seminary anywhere, I knew it was not to be found in Andezuela. And the more I thought of it, the stronger that conviction became.

As for the direction and support of the executive in Boston, to whom I had felt some sort of obligation: it seemed he had misdirected me in both Alaska and Andezuela. He had done me no favors. I then could see that he expected me to go into those situations — though I was never let in on the plan — and he would have some power through me to emend irritants that were of long standing. How then could I have hoped to be welcomed by the experienced missionaries who resented interference from their chief back in Boston?

Whatever might prove to be the final analysis, it was becoming clear to me how completely "no-win" the situation was. I sighed again, and this time it was a spiritual groan that made me wonder about all the prayers for me in the supporting churches in America, all the good intentions and prayer meetings we missionaries had shared across the years, and our mutual efforts to get along, to be supportive of each other. Were we sincere or just doing what dutiful missionaries are expected to do? At such a moment a believer in God entertains questions of *What if?* and *Why?*

I had no need to deny anything any longer. There was an undertow of resentment and anger churning in my gut, and I was being sucked under. I found myself going all the way back to those early visits to jail on Sunday afternoons, and how some of my companions seemed to resent me. And why not? I was set up by Will, the lawyer, as his chosen preacher. Me, the university student on his way to ministry. I stepped into the laymen's project and, if for only a moment, came up with a unique testimony that stole the show. I had been eager and willing but not at all perceptive. Brash? Yes.

The scorpion had snapped its stinger into me a third time. But at least I was free from that struggle, free to look into my own heart and find there some useful idea, some gift as yet not realized, perhaps some happy resolution to this pathetic situation. Indeed, it was as though God were speaking inside me, and I was listening — finally listening rather than rushing in where angels fear to tread. Yes, that was it: I hadn't sat still and listened to God for a long time! How could I when I had become so busy skipping from task to task and place to place that I could not or would not give my mind a rest from religion?

I recalled an exchange between Reinhold Niebuhr and Supreme Court Justice Felix Frankfurter, in which Frankfurter termed himself a believing unbeliever and Niebuhr replied that he regarded himself to be an unbelieving believer. I needed time to heal, for I was not sure who I was just then.

> *Oh wad some power the giftie gie us*
> *To see oursels as others see us!*
> *It wad frae monie a blunder free us,*
> *An' foolish notion.*

Robert Burns, *To a Louse*, Stanza 8; 1786

29

AFFIRMATION

My brain boiled from the heat of my indignation, self-righteousness, and in the end, self-pity. Oh, poor me, the *victim*. Basically, I was sorry for myself for having failed in my ministry, no matter that I might blame someone else. Perhaps it all came about because of ambition, for ambition drives a person mad. And then there were my dreams of doing theology in a professional setting and helping organize a national denomination. I rehearsed the indignity I felt of being considered too green to have valid opinions. And, had I not put my children at risk and whisked my wife away from her career, all of that old stuff? Yes. I was digging deeply into the past.

I now think back upon that episode and am ashamed to recall that I never once thought of Pastor Gallegos, who was rejected not for any fault but for being too refined for the tastes of his flock. He sighed a great sigh and moved on, ever the gentleman. It would have served me well, and soothed my confused psyche, had I more fully grasped at the time what he must have suffered.

Having made my peace with myself and then with God, grace began to work its resurrection power in me. Indeed, the transformation was amazing, revelatory. And the result was what one ought to expect from an existential faith: Jesus lives, and because he lives, we live in his victory and power. Because he rose from the dead, we too rise to newness of life. If he suffered in spite of his best intentions, what ought we who follow him expect? My self-pity dwindled before the living faith that rises from the ashes of failure. This is a miracle of liberation.

As soon as I grasped what was happening I could see that I was hurting myself in place of hurting others. I began to think it odd that I would neither curse nor harm my associates but had no qualms about beating up on myself. Knowing much more about both psychology and spirituality now than then, I can see that I really had a pretty low self-esteem, which I was trying to bolster with great honors won by scholarly accomplishment. I could not see it then, as I covered it over with lofty objectives. Now, seeing it from the perspective of decades later, I smile and say to myself, *Oy li.*

My mind cleared a bit more, and I saw that my wife and children were under their own stress because of my turmoil. Why had I not played the man sooner instead of moping around the house those first days? Colleen was good to me and too valuable to mistreat, and the children too young to comprehend my pouting, so I quit playing the victim. Things went much better after that. In fact, there was a reward I had not expected. I grasped a fresh understanding of paradox, and if I could accept that I was not consistent, then I had to accept contradiction in others. I thought immediately of that paradox named Paul and the paradoxes of Paul. What, after all, did it matter if Paul was at times a raving mystic, if he could at other times charm the soul with his rhapsodic praise of love? The paradoxes of Scripture are only an indication of the complex saints who wrote Scripture.

Last of all, I accepted the paradox of God. Yes, even of God. I had heard God was unfathomable, which I thought of more as a scientific or physical matter. But God the Spirit took on fleshly form, and being in a body, he submitted to death, even death on a cross. Imagine, humans killed God. Is that rational? God is both angry and gracious, leaves us to our own ways because of our rebellion but then intervenes in our affairs for good. Why, I too was a living paradox, a jumble of self-contradiction! And I had imagined myself busy about making sense out of nonsense, as though it were that simple to plumb the depths of Life. My feeble brain could not capture the complexity of the human experiment, much less grasp what God was doing in the Universe.

I had expected someone else to tell me a truth that can only be apprehended by me, and finally only for me, the seeker. I had expected that there were exceptional people out there who would know and act openly and understandably upon a higher truth than anything I had yet discovered. Oh! I was a jumble of self-contradiction and, yes, not a little ego-confusion.

In this mood I thought again about Paul, whom I previously found to be excessively exuberant. That unique Apostle was thought by some to be a madman, but by others only difficult to understand. And small wonder, for he termed himself a fool for Christ, knowing that he was going full face into a contradiction of all that he had learned in philosophy and rhetoric. He turned from the possibility of ever gaining any useful knowledge from the world, turned and left his reason behind, turned and followed his heart. He embraced the paradox: dead in sin yet living in the Spirit, sinful yet a saint, forgiven yet under a great debt, born anew yet forever dying, rejoicing in tears, hoping while in defeat, weak and sick while celebrating his resurrection as though it had already happened. Ah! Who served Christ better than Paul, or with comparable zeal or during personal agony?

Religious faith does not make sense to philosophers, and, really, it doesn't make sense to most of us moderns much of the time. And yet we believe because we cannot help but believe, and so I finally came to my own understanding of what underlies a leap of faith. There is a story in Mark's Gospel that says it well. Jesus counseled a poor father, whose child was apparently epileptic, saying, "If thou canst believe, all things are possible to him that believeth." And the parent cried out, "Lord, I believe. Help thou my unbelief." This feeble plea touched Jesus. He delivered the child to health.

There remains one further confession: I faulted others for building systems or schemes out of proof-texts, as though they could ascend the heights to Heaven itself by way of quoting a bit here and something else there. But I also have cited some of my favorite verses to buttress my own ideas. Indeed, I have done it in this account. I accept it: we all are seeking, groping about, as Paul says, in search of certainty. But what we really need is love. "Thanks be unto God for his undescribable gift."

From Ecstasy to Practicality

One exceptional student in our small church-planting group, Tomás, had many of the gifts needed for ministry, and I began to give him both pastoral instruction and preaching opportunities. He proved to be a loyal friend, given by God. When he learned of my dismissal he had offered to withdraw from the seminary, which I appreciated. But I counseled him to continue studying. For he was truly outside that strange loop of missionary imbroglio and should not become involved. Tomás had invested much in his education and deserved his diploma, which would assure his ordination. For the interim I arranged for our mission to authorize him to preach and do other pastoral duties in our local church as a way to encourage and assure him.

My interest in having Tomás take over went beyond my interest in his professional growth, for I had become convinced that my missionary career was near its end. But, as the Psalmist wrote, Whither would I flee? The answer to that question was even then working itself out, although I was not privy to the details. Apparently I needed some healing and reinforcement before going anywhere

We did not have suburban mail delivery, so picking up the mail in town was one of those things I continued doing. Most mornings, while in the center, I would pause for *café al fresco* at a small coffee shop near the post office. I met two American expatriates there, regulars at the café, and we became an unlikely trio. Both were older men who each decided to remain in Andezuela after their individual contracts expired, and both had many stories to relate. One was Catholic and married to a local woman, the other was Protestant and divorced from his stateside wife. I began to heal as we shared our diverse experiences from day to day. These men were veterans at survival, so they were not delicate in their speech, nor moved much by anything I might tell them. It was humbling to note that my healing was aided by two such men who made no profession of piety. The Protestant was pretty well an agnostic, and the Catholic felt his wife was religious enough for both of them. But, although I experienced some spiritual healing through their friendship, I kept to my decision to repatriate my family to a Stateside environment.

There were also other friends available to me, among them some from the American diplomatic corps, and the director of the U. S. Information Agency. Many were Christians, who in their way were making a contribution to a better world, working to promote peace and cooperation among nations. *Peace and cooperation.* The words haunted me, and I asked myself why it takes so much effort and so long to achieve a little good, but hatred and politics can tear our world apart before our eyes.

During the time of such questioning, a few of my secular friends called on me to help them, which was a pleasant surprise, and restorative too. The director of the American School wanted to take a leave of absence for a year, and the board members wondered if I would be interested in standing in as an interim director. Would I? Good heavens, I was overwhelmed but tried to keep an outward composure. Not much earlier I had read about the popular "worker-priest" movement underway among the Catholic priests in France, which had caught on in North America. The movement was experimental, and various denominations had picked up the idea, at least as far as talking about it. My employment opportunity seemed to fit into that concept, and I felt it was worth trying during that year, for no restrictions were put upon me concerning my spare time. In fact I made it a condition that I would continue to oversee our new church start, even if I was no longer the pastor.

Colleen and I continued under the aegis of our missionary board in Boston, so the matter of our relationship to the mission agency had to be settled. We arranged for a leave of absence, with an agreement that when we decided to return to the States, the mission would repatriate us, which meant they would pay the moving costs. With this legal matter settled, the way was clear to begin a somewhat tenuous experiment. The transition to secular employment went as smoothly as eating whipped cream.

I bought a small car, an Opel Kadet, from a Danish neighbor who was returning to Europe. I also arranged to continue renting our "bat" house from our landlord, and purchased all the furnishings from the mission. It was an irony that we remained only blocks away from the seminary, but we had to live with that. Those few hundred meters could have been kilometers, as we rarely crossed paths with our former colleagues, and that only on the streets, usually near the post office.

In short order we developed a new environment of friends and colleagues, joined the country club and began to enjoy social life with people not related to our church work. I have to admit that it was an invigorating experience that allowed little time for reviewing and rehashing the past. No one cared about my eschatological hermeneutic, my position regarding salvation or anything else religious, which gave me breathing room to make some necessary mental adjustments.

Tomás continued to grow into his new profession. Another encouragement was his discovery of an ideal fIancée in one of the city's churches, a woman who encouraged him in his calling. This would be a bonus in the congregation's development. Two for one, as we say. They were married in her church and moved into the rented house we used as a chapel. It was a meager beginning, but they were happy enough. Third world people do not expect to become rich any time soon. They hope, of course. Yes, they hope and they work and scrimp and make many sacrifices.

An added touch of healing came through one of my secular friends, a neighbor, who directed the downtown English language library for the U. S. Information Agency. Alden and his wife Liz often invited us to go along with them on weekend driving jaunts around the country. Not only did we have mutual playmates for our children but our two cars on isolated roads were better than one. My new friend was an educational psychologist, who proved to be of great help in directing my thoughts into healthy channels. For across the years I had become in my own way quite single-minded, much like my fundamentalist associates. His counsel was just what I needed in recognizing my worth as an educated person who had gifts of value in the secular world. And he encouraged me to be more tolerant by being tolerant and easy-going himself. I have often thought of that. We do not, indeed, cannot save ourselves, for salvation is a collaborative endeavor and ultimately of divine origin. We are all in this together, and either we learn how to make it work in unison, by the grace of God, or we all sink, more or less, into some form of despair.

I believe it was Thoreau who observed that the mass of men lead lives of quiet desperation. If that is true — God help us! — it explains the appeal of going to war. And I cannot help but think of religious squabbling as a coward's escape from confronting an inner vacuum.

30

Anchors Aweigh!

Several colleagues in the Sierra suspected that Colleen and I would not be around much longer. Since our experience of living in New Jersey and visiting the churches of the Northeast had been so rewarding, we were inclined to seek something in Massachusetts. We had made a few discreet inquiries, by letter, as we moved through the school year, and apparently this had not leaked into the wider church stream of insider news. We really wanted to share our anxieties and hopes with a few close friends but knew that the only effective way to keep a secret is to keep it a secret for such news or even a hint of news would become a tidbit to be shared with others, who were sworn to secrecy, of course.

From time to time a few companions would make the trip to the coast, usually for a week at the beach and as an escape from the high altitude. They would stop by our place for an exchange of news and eventually get around to some personal questions. We found it easy to remain mum for we had no idea what might happen next.

Meanwhile, our new way of life was really quite comfortable. We relaxed after-hours at the club, sitting by the side of the pool and sipping lemonade. Well, I did enjoy a beer on occasion.

though Colleen would predictably raise her eyebrows when I placed the order, so I usually managed to avoid eye contact with her when I ordered.

We two attended several of the receptions at the American Consulate in Barranco, especially the evening events, where a United Nations assembly of interesting persons offered lively conversation plus some things worth knowing. But best for my battered ego was having others respect my education and experience. It was ironic that my time at Princeton was held suspect among some missionaries and resented by a few others, but among my new friends it was usually an open sesame to social equality.

I also dabbled in the novel experiment of becoming a part-time minister among the city's varied middle and upper-middle class. The American Church in Barranco had no regular pastor at that time, so I preached there occasionally. That gave me more contacts, and the word got around that I was available for religious services. This led to a few engagements that strengthened the ecumenical community in small ways. I was even called upon to do the funeral of the local beer baron, which would never have happened were I a missionary. He was a North American who had married a local woman. She was Catholic and he Protestant. They had agreed that all girls would be baptized Catholic, and all boys Protestant. They had several daughters, but in spite of the imbalance, he remained Protestant. I buried him with a stately ritual, which his Catholic family found comforting.

An opportunity for ecumenical relations occurred on the way to the cemetery, as the family priest appeared just outside the gates, standing forlornly at the curb. I stepped over and invited him into the procession. We walked along arm-in-arm, and as we processed to the grave-site I asked him to give a blessing at the end of the ritual. He was a real trooper, and fell into place as though it were planned. The daughters of the deceased were ecstatic!

In keeping with the new ecumenical spirit brought on by Pope John XXIII, several of us clergy, including Roman Catholic priests, convened an ecumenical group to discuss current events and the dynamics of such books as those from the Jesuit Teilhard de Chardin. One priest was French and in Barranco as a lecturer at a Catholic seminary. He was from the same area as Teilhard and familiar with the man's work, so led us in a helpful critique of his theology. It was his opinion that Teilhard was really well received among Catholic theologians, who were looking for ways to bridge the gap between dogma and science. Perhaps, he suggested, his theories would become widely accepted, given time. And they have, in ever-widening circles.

None of these activities would satisfy me that I was actually doing anything consistent as a worker priest, however. In fact, I was coming to a self-understanding, that if I worked as an administrator or anything else I would be so taken with it that my part-time religious work would be quite limited. And considering how strongly I felt about giving my family a more stable environment Stateside, it seemed time to take the next step. I sent a second letter of inquiry to the church superintendent in the Boston area. This time I gave up any pretense at indirection, telling him my situation was in a state of crisis, and I was going to have to make some changes very soon.

With only two months remaining in my contract with the American School, and none of our inquiries having raised even a nibble, I was feeling uncomfortable. Worry is a form of prayer, am sure, and I was praying that way a lot, worrying, for I felt like a steer at the stockyards. Worrying paid off, for a letter arrived from a suburban church along the Beltway around Boston, written by a member of their pastoral search committee. This new friend had been at a seminar I gave on methods of teaching the Bible, and we two enjoyed chatting about his church's ministries. Mack really MacDuncan, and I became friends that weekend and had connected again at the summer youth camp in New Hampshire. I forgot about Mack, but he, upon learning that I was looking around for a possible return to the States, apparently felt he had a prime candidate for his church. Would I be interested in an interview for the position of pastor? he asked.

I left the letter on my desk while I prayed over it for a day. Praying meant that I kept it in mind with great anticipation, hoping that this was a lightning bolt from Above. Then, not wishing to appear overly eager, I left it lie there for another day. Meanwhile, I had looked up the church in the denominational yearbook and was pleased with the information. The membership stood at more than three hundred adults and a Sunday school of one hundred and fifty. I knew that the adults would be more than nominally committed to the church, for each church in a small denomination has a scale of desirability among the clergy. One index is the ratio of giving to membership, and this church had a good record, right there in the yearbook. This was an opportunity I could not ignore. As soon as I expressed interest, Mack wrote asking me to call him at his home, and he would cover the charges. I took pains to be punctual in calling.

"Look, Tim," he said, " I've had a glimpse at how you think and teach, but the rest of the search committee hasn't. I told them a few things about you, and they are interested, but some of them are asking if a missionary knows enough about church work to handle a vibrant congregation like this. What say we fly you up here for an interview?"

He paused a moment and then said, "Hello, you still there?" For I was struck dumb. Yes, I was still there, and an interview would be the best way to go. I said it in a calm voice while having a private talk with myself, thinking that any church that would fly a candidate back to Boston from Andezuela had to be doing some things right, were thinking outside the neighborhood. The arrangements were made, the flight taken, the interview held. Sunday morning I preached to a full church, using one of my best sermons from my year of visiting churches while on furlough. I was in good form, and the congregation receptive to my style. Oh, when we want something, really want it, we try to believe in our heart of hearts that it is God's will. It's a lot like marriage.

This time around I checked with the leadership of the church about my rights and responsibilities, insisting that we needed a contract of call and mutual support. There were two lawyers in the congregation, and they provided a model contract for my consideration, following the guidelines of the denomination. I felt it was orderly, decent and fair, even generous. We wrote into the agreement that I would be allowed to pursue a doctoral program part time — one related to ministry — but first I would have to serve the church for at least a year.

Within eight days of my departure from them, a telegram arrived saying that the search committee had recommended me to a business meeting of the church, which accepted my qualifications, and I was therefore called to be their pastor.

I liked that wording, especially "called," for it reminded me of my original calling while in college. And that made me reflect upon my career. I could not think of one thing I had done nor one work I had undertaken where I was actually "called" until then. I was hired, taken on, sent, even commissioned but never called.

If anyone in our mission felt I was abandoning the work then they would have to deal with it. God knows I had. And Colleen had, for she too was committed to our mutual ministry and had worked as many hours as possible while caring for family matters. I, as a dutiful husband, had helped with domestic matters as well. We were a team, sharing the burdens of both family and mission, so the fact that I have used the first person singular in this account does not mean that Colleen was less than a full partner in nearly all of this account. Not at all! My story began when I was a bachelor and continued in my search for definition to my calling. Colleen became my "helpmeet" in the endeavor. It seems right then to fly full in the face of style, at the last, and to shift from I to we, as we were a team all the way. I should include our children too. Therefore, "We" quite often has to be expanded to include the progeny. Oh, were our kids up to their eyeballs in this adventure! I could write a book about their experiences. Of course, they could write their own account, and if one ever does, I pray for mercy.

Home from the High Seas

As a tide ebbs from the shore of an unconquerable land, we began our retreat. First, we sold off nearly all household possessions plus the little car. Then there were the legal arrangements and a few goodbye parties, which we found tremendously encouraging. This time, our shipment of goods for our new home consisted of two steel barrels of precious items, and that included several oil paintings, along with photo albums. I had crated my books in smaller packages and mailed them ahead directly to the church. Colleen and I celebrated our fortieth birthdays during those final months in Andezuela. We had two children and a pocketful of cash from the sell-off. Nothing more was needed, for we were pilgrims, and pilgrims travel light.

The first leg of the flight was to Monterrey, for the "Barranco thing" was not fully resolved among our companions up there, many of them present at our entry eight years earlier; and there were Hispanic friends there to embrace in love a last time. We had the approval of most of our colleagues in the mission for our move, but wondered if a few taciturn comrades privately enjoyed the thought that I deserved my come-uppance, had buckled under, and that I was running back home. Well, no one pleases everyone, and not all are pleased by the same things. Nevertheless, the visit provided a closure of sorts to all of that, so the layover was sweet; bitter-sweet, but well worth it.

Adieu, adieu, mes chers amis. Nous sommes tous enfants du Vent. Farewell, farewell, dear friends. We are all innocents driven by the Wind. This idea becomes even clearer if we recall that the biblical word for the Spirit is breath, in effect, the breath or wind of God, that blows where and when it wills. Again, in nautical terms, we are driven before the wind.

All this piff-paff, the trials and tribulations, suffering and eventually death — even the glories and accolades, the pomp and circumstance — they mean nothing at the end. Life means everything. "And this is life eternal, that they might know thee, the only true God, and Jesus Christ, whom thou has sent."

Amen!

So many moves, so many goodbyes, all the old places and the new, friends left behind but friends waiting at the new location. I quoted to myself that oft-cited verse from Hebrews 11:13, *These all died in faith, not having received the promises, but having seen them afar off, and were persuaded of them, and embraced them and confessed that they were strangers and pilgrims on the earth.* I also recalled my lament early on in my search for a meaningful ministry, how I wished God would just tell me what to do beyond that startling wake-up call. Why, I asked, did I have to cast about so much looking for what I should do? But now the hidden ways of God were taking shape in a manner I could interpret, because I had gained a perspective.

Indeed, I began to grasp a Truth. If I disliked doctrinaire answers to the enigmas of life, then my only alternative was to learn by doing, which is a tortuous path and quite unlike the popular idea of a highway to Heaven. And that made me think of the Divine Nature. Was God possibly learning by doing ... by doing in *us*? Could all of this, simply put, be an experiment that has never before been undertaken? Could God be on a learning curve? And are we created to share the marvel of it?

Coming down to Earth

The plane banked over Boston in a wide circle, entering its landing pattern. We three pressed our noses to the windows, taking in panorama of the metropolis below us, while William John sat back and whimpered, obviously because of pain in his ears. The discomfort would soon pass.

Below, all seemed so orderly and peaceful, the little cars creeping like ants along worn paths. I squeezed Colleen's hand and said, "So, Dear, my answer has come, after all these years. Thanks a thousand times for sticking with me. Remember, 'If winter comes, can spring be far behind?'"

Colleen said nothing in reply, though her slight smile betrayed thoughts all her own. Surely she was thinking that my work would need her partnership and beyond that being a mother of a teenager was going to create challenges aplenty. But I knew she was more than equal to the task, for she had been tried in the fire and came out pure gold. Yes, pure gold, I thought, and thanked the living God.

For my part, I looked forward to settling into the town and going through pastoral routines of baptizing, confirming, marrying, visiting the sick, counseling the burdened and burying the saints. And then I felt a sudden jolt that seemed like a prod from God, for I had forgotten all the worthy causes the church supports, the jungle clinics, orphanages, schools and agricultural projects, as well as social and political issues. It would not be necessary to remind the people that we were to do justice and love mercy, for they were already engaged in such acts.

Seventeen years! I sighed, then sat back and closed my eyes. That is when a voice within whispered quite clearly, *And it's okay if you take up golf.*

The thought was so unexpected that I sat upright, eyes and mouth open. *Golf?* I hesitated, feeling a tinge of resistance, perhaps a self-righteous belief that it was sinful to exercise the body in happy ways. And just as quickly I felt my inner child thinking it might be fun, saying that if I had not tried it I ought not knock it.

Yes! I said out loud. *Yes!*

ENDNOTES

i. Recorded by Lena Horne, 1941; Teddy Wilson and His Orchestra. (The gender had to be switched, of course.)

ii. Annie Dillard, the author of the widely read *Pilgrim at Tinker Creek*, and many other thoughtful books, has written an entire book on this subject of knowing things: *Living by Fiction* (Harper and Row, hard cover, 1982; paperback 1988). On pp. 132-33, she cites the ancient Greek, Arcesilaus, who said we can obtain at best possible knowledge. Dillard then quotes C. S. Pierce, "Let us not pretend to doubt in philosophy what we do not doubt in our hearts." For, she concludes, "we do not really doubt that *some* things can be known and understood - or else we would neither argue nor teach our children." (Used by permission of the author.)

iii. My translation, taken from a compilation by Antonio Serrano, B.D., Th.M.; *Las Mejores Poesías Cristianas Españoles;*1944. There is an English version by Allison Peers that is set to music, found in a few hymnals in America.

iv. Both Calvin and Luther were irritated by the discovery of America and its implications for religion. They downplayed the importance of the fact. Calvin was also irritated by some of the claims of scholars that the age of civilization, as found in ancient Egypt, made it difficult to be literal about the Genesis creation of Eden. He dismissed such claims as lacking piety.

v. Thinking about this, the Reformation lies at the feet of the Pope of Rome and the need for funding a monument. Perhaps it is not too late for the reunion of the riven Church, if only the present pope would admit it was a mistake to have raised money in this fashion.

About the Author

Reverend Duey has traveled widely during both his military years and as a missionary in educational work. He continued in succeeding years to pastor churches in New England. During these final decades of ministry, he visited many nations in Europe, usually in search of his family's history, which includes Huguenots from Flanders. Theological pursuits led him from his native Florida to California and then across the nation, including a year in Chicago. Connecticut finally became his residence during a happy career, first as a pastor and then in service as an interim minister at a few old-town Congregational-U.C.C. churches.

He pursued his theological education wherever he went, spending a year in master's studies at Princeton Theological Seminary. He earned the Doctor of Ministry degree from Andover-Newton Theological Seminary, in Massachusetts.